Historical Fiction Book 2026

Acclaim for Frail Blood

"The compulsive story of a love menaced by the forces of history, set in the luminous streets of Buenos Aires and the shadows where power sinks its bloody claws."

—José Cardona, Regents Professor of Spanish American Literature, Texas A & M University

"Stanton's slow-burn story develops an absorbing romance."

—*KIRKUS REVIEWS*

"This erotic tale will keep readers engrossed through its fateful end, leaving them to wonder if the country's savage history could repeat itself once more."

—Rhonda Dahl Buchanan, translator, *The Devil's Country* by Argentine novelist Perla Suez, winner, 2020 Rómulo Gallegos, Latin America's premier literary prize

"Edward Stanton combines reality and imagination, narrative and lyricism to free the voices of those who died or disappeared during the military regime. Even as *Frail Blood* reveals the depths of human cruelty, a sense of redemption and wonder breathes through its impassioned pages."

—Juan Carlos Galeano, poet, filmmaker and author of *Folktales of the Amazon*

"At an historic juncture when the forces of reaction, violence and oppression are rising in the New World and the Old, *Frail Blood* is an urgent novel for our time."

—Fernando Operé, historian of Argentina, author of *Indian Captivity in Spanish America: Frontier Narratives*

Wide as the Wind

"This novel transports us to an island world both outside time and urgently relevant to us in the 21st century."

—Leatha Kendrick, author of *Almanac of the Invisible*

"*Wide as the Wind* speaks to a fundamental truth: our need to protect the planet's environment."

—John Flenley and Paul Bahn, *The Enigmas of Easter Island*

VIDAS: Deep in Mexico and Spain

"Edward Stanton's youthful heart evokes the cherished moments of discovering, exploring and returning again and again to Mexico and Spain. Unique and stirring memories that evoke the power of friendship, language, legends, foods and wines, ways of life and death, the past, a vibrant present. Through many voices, lyrical prose, a chorus of Spanish *jotas* and *romances*, Mexican *boleros* and *rancheras*, the writer has composed a passionate song that resonates across an ocean, two countries and continents."

—Ana Merino, Winner 2020 Premio Nadal, Spain's premier award for novel

Road of Stars to Santiago

"Edward Stanton recounts his adventures with stylish conviction."

—James Michener (Pulitzer Prize for Literature)

"This book could become a source for understanding our troubled times."

—William Watson, M.I.T.

FRAIL BLOOD

FRAIL BLOOD

Edward Stanton

Waterside Productions
Cardiff, California

Copyright © 2025 by Edward Stanton

All rights reserved. This book or any portion thereof may not be reproduced or used in any manner whatsoever without the express written permission of the publisher except for the use of brief quotations in articles and book reviews.

Printed in the United States of America

First Printing, 2025

ISBN-13: 978-1-962984-49-2 print edition
ISBN-13: 978-1-962984-50-8 e-book edition

Waterside Productions
2055 Oxford Ave
Cardiff, CA 92007
www.waterside.com

Cover design: Jason Parmer, Dapper Agency
Interior design: Jennifer Geist, Pen & Publish

For Dan

Buenos Aires
September 22, 1990

He entered the hotel room with its faded wallpaper, stained mirror and air of tarnished luxury. He undressed and drew a bath. Reclining in the warm water, Robert recalled boarding a plane in Los Angeles last night, the first day of fall, then landing in Buenos Aires twelve hours later, this morning, the second day of spring. He saw again the view from his window seat: the mouth of the Río de la Plata, that river with the sonorous name; the metropolis on the lip of a vast continent where he would meet her; the Pampa rolling toward a curved horizon. Now everything seemed changed, inside-out—the seasons, the cities, his life.

He fell asleep in the bathtub. With a start he awoke from a dream about the divorce: they were saying goodbye to each other on a stormy beach. Observing the bathroom with its cracked, mildewed tiles, Robert remembered he was on the other side of the world with a different woman. Gabriela's purple eyes and night-black hair gleamed through his mind.

He dried himself and walked into the bedroom. When he opened his suitcase, he imagined a cloud of bad memories flew out. Robert stuffed his clothes in the dresser and put on the same pants, socks, shirt and coat.

He dialed Gabriela's number. A man replied, "*Hola*," in a resonant basso that might have issued from a cavern. When Robert asked for her, the voice wanted to know who was calling.

"An American friend."

"I said to call late," she started, almost whispering. Robert did not know if Gabriela had taken the phone from the man or if she was on another line.

He checked his watch. "It's after ten o'clock."

"Still early." She asked him to meet around eleven in a café on Avenida Corrientes.

As Robert peered through the foggy window of his cab, he saw gutters surging. Gabriela's words echoed in his head: "Sometimes I think my heart's full of rain." The colored lights of storefronts, appearing through trees on the sidewalk, shone like a coral reef. Sidewalks swarmed with people walking with umbrellas, chatting, gesturing, reading under the eaves of newsstands and in bookstores, buying tickets at lottery shops, dashing in and out of cinemas, pizza parlors, cafés. Music and aromas of roasted meats drifted through open doors of cafés and restaurants. It was Thursday night, but on Corrientes it felt like a weekend.

Robert stepped onto the curb and walked through rain to the Café Premier. He found an empty table by a window. When Gabriela did not arrive on time, he thought the afternoon with her might have been another dream.

She descended from a taxi at 11:25. She moved with the insouciance of a lady accustomed to having people wait for her. The rain has stopped, Robert noticed, just in time for her arrival. As she glided over the sidewalk, her doe's step made her seem immune to the force of gravity.

Gabriela entered the café, turning customers' heads. With her hair swept back in a knot and her neck exposed, she looked taller and more aloof. She had everything a beautiful woman needed in Buenos Aires: a tailored jacket, a vest, a blouse and silk scarf that stirred slightly as she walked, a long, narrow skirt of suede; bracelets, rings and necklaces of earth-colored stones. She wore her clothing with the ease and grace of a mammal in its fur.

He stood to greet Gabriela. As he hugged her, kissing one cheek, Robert breathed in her scent of crushed spices. Crescents of silver hung from the lobes of her ears. Are those moons waxing or waning, he wondered.

She touched his collar as they took their seats. "Why haven't you changed your clothes? They're still damp." Gabriela leaned backed in her chair and crossed her legs.

"They've brought me good luck."

"What if your luck keeps going?"

"That never happens. I have to change clothes a lot."

Gabriela's lips curled in the dawn of a smile. "Maybe Buenos Aires will bring you better fortune. Why did you come here?"

"You know why."

She laughed, wrinkling her nose.

"When you laugh your nose reminds me of a rabbit's."

"Nobody's ever compared me to a rodent. I'll also have to name you for an animal. What about *Oso*? Or better still *Osito*."

"That works in Spanish but in English it sounds like an Indian's name—Little Bear..."

"What's wrong with that? With those wet curls and clothes and your wide shoulders you could be an Indian brave. Or a grizzly bear."

Robert grinned. "Nobody's ever compared me to a beast."

"We have a proverb in Spanish, '*El hombre y el oso, mientras más feo más hermoso*.' Men and bears, the uglier the better—you know, more masculine." Gabriela's laugh rippled. "You must have had other reasons."

"For what?"

"For coming to Buenos Aires."

"Yes. I just went through a divorce—I had to get out of Los Angeles."

Gabriela raised her black eyebrows in two perfect arches. "Were there children?"

"A house. She got it."

"You probably could have traveled anywhere. Since the war not many tourists have been coming here."

"The country's far away and I know the language." He was going to inquire which war she meant, but a waiter arrived at their table. Like all good *mozos* in Argentina he had given the new customers time to settle. As Gabriela ordered a vermouth and soda, Robert noticed a little mole next to a vein on the tenuous stalk of her neck.

"*Y el señor?*" the waiter asked.

"The same," Robert said. After the divorce he had tried to avoid decisions. The mozo dallied, writing down their simple order, perhaps to revel longer at Gabriela's side.

"What if I'd wanted absinthe or something dangerous?" She spoke in English so the waiter would not understand.

"I would have made it a double."

"You like danger?" she posed in Spanish now that the mozo had left. Her eyes danced over Robert's face.

"So do you, right?"

"Sometimes." Gabriela grazed his hand with hers. "At work I try to keep my patients out of danger."

"You seem too complicated to be a doctor."

"They tell me I'm too young."

"Where did you learn English?"

"Half of Father's family is from England." All at once her eyes darkened to a deeper shade of violet. When Gabriela lowered her long, curved lashes, they formed semicircles above her cheekbones. "We went to British schools in Buenos Aires."

"'We'?"

"My brother and I."

Robert guessed the man on the telephone could have been her brother. "It's just the two of you?"

"And my parents," she responded without looking up. "You have brothers or sisters?"

"No. I'm alone—no siblings, both parents gone."

Gabriela stroked Robert's face with the tapered fingers of one hand. "When did they go?"

"My father died when I was deployed in Vietnam."

"You don't remind me of a soldier."

"It was a long time ago. I'd already been through lots of deaths by then." Robert recalled the plastic garbage bags he had seen on the streets of Buenos Aires that morning, like the black body pouches in Vietnam. "I suppose you've also gotten used to it."

Gabriela did not reply. For a minute they sat in silence. The waiter approached their table with the drinks and a silver dish of nuts.

"*Salud*," he said in her language.

"Cheers," she said in his.

They sipped and did not speak for a while. The bittersweet vermouth tasted good on Robert's tongue.

"I've seen enough of it to know how fragile a life can be," Gabriela told him.

Robert cocked his head. "I like the way you drop a subject and pick it up later. I'd almost forgotten my question."

"Comment not question," Gabriela's voice slipped through the end of his words like water.

"You don't forget anything."

"No."

"Never?"

"*Jamás*," she said with the finality of the Spanish word. Gabriela ran a finger around the lip of her glass, still gazing at Robert. He stared into her eyes, those dark wells, feeling how fast everything was moving now.

To pay the check he fumbled with oversized, multicolored *australes*, a currency destined to die. Their hips brushing, they walked outside. From low clouds a light rain fell. The night had the scent of a wet *maté* gourd.

Gabriela and Robert looked so winsome together that people turned to gape. They passed restaurants where groups and couples feasted at their tables. He felt a throb of hunger in his belly.

They entered a restaurant on Lavalle Street, large as a warehouse. Sides of beef, suckling pigs, lambs, goats, whole chickens roasted on a *parrilla* the size of a soccer goal. Steaks, links of sausage, *morcilla*, tripe, bacon-wrapped pork loins, empanadas and sweating wheels of provolone also sizzled over the wood fire and coals. That imposing grill reigned over the room like a grand piano on a concert stage. Never had Robert seen so much meat cooking in one place.

He and Gabriela took a table in the main room. Too intrigued by each other to study it for long, they skimmed the menu. They ordered two *bifes de chorizo* and a bottle of reserve from Mendoza.

Raindrops fell from Gabriela's hair onto her cheek, making her freckles glisten there. With the fingertips of one hand he touched the moist spots.

"They're like little stars," Robert said. He anointed her forehead, where he sketched a playful sign of the cross. "In the name of the Father... and so on I baptize you Starface."

"As long as it's not *Scarface*," she laughed, wrinkling her nose again. "Or you can call me Gaby like my friends." She pronounced her nickname with open vowels in Spanish. "Just be sure you don't say 'Gab-ee' American-style. Unless you want me to poke out those turquoise eyes of yours."

"Then I wouldn't be able to see those purple eyes of yours. You must have been born at night."

"Why?"

"Your eyes are turned up at the corners like a cat's."

"Not all cats are born at night."

"They should be. What about you?"

"One night twenty years and many, many months ago. You?"

"One night thirty years and many, many months ago." At the same instant both laughed, which made them laugh once more, harder. "What month?"

She smiled but did not answer. The waiter reached the table and opened their bottle with rapid, ritual movements of a corkscrew. He poured the ruby-colored wine into goblets.

"Salud Starface."

"Cheers Osito. I'm glad you came to Buenos Aires." Robert marked the way she pronounced the name of her city, adding a lilt at the end.

He swirled the Malbec in his mouth. It tasted almost sweet after the vermouth and its flavor of bitter herbs.

Gabriela regarded him as she ran the tip of an index finger around the rim of her glass. "You enjoy drinking wine."

"It's like taking in the sun, the air and soil—everything at once. It helps me to know a place."

"Wait till you taste our beef," she said, squeezing his hands. "Our cattle graze on grasses higher than a man or woman, topsoil two meters deep."

"Do you go to the country often?"

As though she had not heard him, Gabriela ignored Robert's words. Does she have a special valve in her ears that opens and closes like a fish's gills, he wondered, depending on whether or not she wants to answer a question?

A minute must have elapsed before she replied. "Father owns an *estancia*, a ranch with wheat, cattle and thoroughbreds." Gabriela lowered her eyes and her cheeks flushed.

During their second glass of wine the waiter served two bifes still cooking in their juices, crackling and popping, hanging over the edges of white platters. The steaks were roasted to a dark, crusty brown. When Robert and Gabriela cut the crimson flesh with their knives, it bled onto their plates, pooling there. They bit into the chewy, wild-tasting meat with its lingering flavor of wood. All the steaks he had ever eaten vanished in Robert's memory.

The fire from the parrilla flickered, warming their faces. Above the clients' conversation they could hear a hissing of meats cooking on the grill. For the first time since the divorce he felt at ease. He ordered another bottle of Malbec.

A scrawny Indian girl approached their table. Mumbling words she must have learned by heart, she offered a handful of red and white roses to Robert: "Kind sir would you like to regale your beautiful lady with a fresh rose?"

Gabriela guessed her American friend would be a soft touch. She asked the girl to go, patting her gently on the arm. The child turned to leave. Robert caught her flowers by the stems and asked for the full bouquet. Some of the roses were as white as their dinner plates, others redder than the steaks' blood.

When the girl handed the bunch to Robert, he pricked a finger, the third on his left hand. "*Lo siento Señor,*" I'm sorry Sir, she said. He passed the flowers to Gabriela and took a handkerchief from his pocket to dab the cut.

Trying to keep his blood from staining the bills, he paid the girl. "*Gracias Señores,*" she murmured and pivoted on her bare, brown feet and white soles. Robert watched her pass the roasting pit, appearing small and frail amid that exuberance of dead meats.

Gabriela sniffed the flowers and set them on their table. She took Robert's hand, raised it to her mouth, removed the handkerchief and sucked the blood on his finger. She checked to see if the bleeding had stopped, waited, licked, stopped, licked until the cut was dry.

Robert rested his hand on Gabriela's. "Gracias *Doctora*. Is that the Argentine method for healing a cut?" She smiled, revealing small white teeth, but she did not reply. With thumb and forefinger he made a circle around her wrist. "See—they touch."

She grasped Robert's hand. "They might reach around my ankle too." He withdrew his hand from hers and extended it beneath the table. "Not now," she laughed.

A minute later the mozo arrived with the check, breaking their reverie. Robert contemplated the grill, the raw and cooked flesh, the cheeses and pastries, the clients gorging themselves. He sensed it was all linked in some way, that obscene abundance of food and the hungry Indian girl, the death around them and his desire for Gabriela. Suddenly he yearned to touch the delicate collarbones protruding from her blouse.

"I'm used to it," she said out of nowhere.

By now Robert had learned to keep in mind his unanswered questions for Gabriela. "*Ella?*" he hazarded, using the customary allusion to death as a woman.

"You're learning." Robert felt as though he had divined her thoughts, she had understood his. "Sometimes I work the night shift in the emergency room," she said. "A lot of people die there." She paused. "Are you afraid of it?"

Following Gabriela, Robert did not reply. He could hold his response for later. She nodded her approval. He paid, they rose from their table and walked toward the entrance. Robert paused to observe the grill's bed of hardwood coals, pulsing like a red-orange heart under the beef, lamb, pork, goats, chickens.

"Put your hand over the grate like this," Gabriela showed him. "You should be able to count to three before it burns. That's the perfect temperature for cooking steaks."

Counting under his breath, Robert tried. After a few seconds he pulled his hand away and held it to her cheek. "How long until it burns here?" Gabriela may or may not have smiled.

When they reached the sidewalk, the headlights of a black Mercedes taxi lanced the driving rain. It sidled to the curb. Like a submarine emerging from the sea, its chassis gushed water.

Her eyes held Robert's, moist and steady. "How did this happen?" Before he could answer, drops of rain or tears rolled down her cheek. She turned towards the cab. "I must go home," Gabriela said as if she were talking to herself.

Robert opened the back door. She slid onto the seat. Leaning into the vehicle, he squatted on the edge of the curb in the rain. With thumb and index of one hand he made a semicircle, clasped her right ankle, squeezed. His fingertips touched.

He looked up at her, expecting a word, at least a smile. Instead she faced forward as though the cab had already departed. Studying her profile, trying to stamp it on his memory, fearing he might not see her again, Robert said, "*Buenas noches Gabriela.*" He closed the heavy door.

She did not wave, turn or make a backward glance while the taxi drove away. That Mercedes lost itself in the darkness of her City of the Most Holy Trinity and Port of Our Lady of the Fair Winds, Ciudad de la Santísima Trinidad y Puerto de Santa María de los Buenos Aires.

2
Hopscotch

The Malbec and dreams of Gabriela made Robert sleep until mid-afternoon. As soon as he awoke, he recalled they had forgotten the roses at the restaurant.

He dressed and rode the elevator downstairs. A clerk at the desk handed him a phone message: "*Plaza de Mayo 5 p.m. Gabriela.*"

Robert had a coffee and croissant in the hotel café. When he walked outside, the streets glistened from the night's rain. A warm breeze caressed his neck and drove him forward. It was the hour when Latin cities come back to life after lunch and the siesta, another morning, a reprieve. For Robert it was the start of his second day in a new country and a fresh season. The color of the light reminded him of honey.

Trees on the avenue already showed green, tender leaves. Women had blossomed too: as they swung their arms in sleeveless blouses, their skirts fluttered like flowers on wind-tossed stems. Men leered, giving them a brazen up-and-down or wheeling to ogle an undulating backside. Nearly everyone seemed to be dressed in smartly tailored clothes.

As he approached a young woman ambling toward him on the sidewalk, her brown curls bouncing on her shoulders, Robert tripped in a pothole.

"*Cuidado hombre!*" Careful man! she called without breaking her stride.

Nobody stopped, helped him to his feet, even looked twice at him. Feeling abashed, he rose and proceeded on his way. Robert trained an eye on the sidewalk and its minefield of craters.

Plastic bags were piled at the curb, spilling garbage onto the street. Once more the body pouches in Vietnam flashed through his mind. When his cab from the airport had carried him along tree-lined boulevards, past sweeping lawns, parks and polo fields, Buenos Aires appeared grandiose in the morning light. Now Robert was in the heart of the city where it was falling apart, and people were dressed to kill.

Clouds rumbled. The honeyed light vanished, the sky turned milky as a pearl. Drizzle moistened his forehead.

At the end of the avenue he saw Plaza de Mayo, where they had met only yesterday. Beyond it he spotted a pink palace that might have housed a weary sultan in a remote, sweltering land. Robert suspected she would be late again.

He had almost given up when Gabriela surprised him from the rear. He spun and the two stood face to face as if they were seeing each other for the first time. Gazing into Robert's blue-green eyes, she tilted her head, her hair cascading over her shoulders. He bent to see Gabriela's eyes more closely; in the gray light they had the color of ripe plums. Black, silky lashes sprouted from their lids.

By now nothing would have shocked them: one more coup by the military, a new civil war, an eclipse of the sun or moon, meteors crashing into earth, angels swooping from the clouds. Both smiled and broke out laughing.

"It looks so different today," he said.

"The *Madres* only meet here once a week. And now it's hardly raining."

As if they were old friends, they began strolling on the avenue. Their shoulders brushing, their hips grazing at times, they passed the large square with the pyramid and palm trees. Like a continent without a name or past, waiting to be explored, streets, parks and plazas opened before them. Now and then Robert and Gabriela stopped to appreciate a flowering tree, a kiosk, a store window, ignoring the drizzle. They spoke in the language of smiles and murmurs.

Soon they found a sidewalk with hopscotch lines painted on the cement. Gabriela removed a serpentine pendant from her neck and tossed it on the wet ground. "Let's play."

She offered him the palm of her left hand. He took it and they jumped—hop, hop, split—one foot, one foot, two. When their shoes landed on the pavement, Robert and Gabriela splashed one another, first by accident, next knowingly, laughing and shouting. They picked up their marker—the pendant and its silver chain—dropped it, losing their balance, picked it up again, stumbled, rose to their feet and broke all the rules to reach the final square, number ten at last.

"*Cielo!*" Heaven! Gabriela rejoiced like a little girl. Holding onto Robert's waist, she asked, "What do you call it in English?"

"'Home' I think. Or 'safe.'"

In a voice like water she said, "Wouldn't feeling safe be heaven?"

Gabriela skipped away. Robert chased her to a secluded park down the block. There they had races—*Last one to the jungle gym is a rotten egg*, played hide-and-seek—*Punto y coma, el que no se escondió se embroma*, like that, in Spanish and English. They mounted swings and pumped their legs, gaining speed, flew out as far as the ropes would go, pointing their feet up, arching their backs to view that other heaven where clouds sailed across the sky. They slowed, leaped off their leather seats and stood side by side on the grass, breathing hard.

Sun emerged from clouds and the rain slackened. Robert knelt to pick a bunch of wildflowers for a garland, rose and tied it to the shining waterfall of Gabriela's hair. The remaining blossoms he placed in her hands. Eyes into eyes they looked at each other.

"Guess what we say when it rains in the sunlight?" she asked.

"What?"

"'A witch is getting married!'"

Gabriela mussed his hair, stuck flowers into his curls and went running down the street. The drizzle had almost ceased.

Robert sprinted after her. When he caught up, a cloud bursted again. He grasped her by the waist. "You're it!"

"*No, tú!*" Gabriela cried, pretending to escape. They tussled on the sidewalk while pedestrians, fleeing the downpour, diverged around them like forks of a river flowing past an island.

The sky cleared. For Robert and Gabriela a new day seemed to dawn. They felt the elation of their meeting, the freshness of this rain-washed air. Other men and women stepped with a brisker pace over the sidewalks and zebra crossings. Mangy dogs perked up their ears and cocked their tails. Boys and girls hopped, dashed, skated or sped home from school on their bicycles. On polo fields horses reared and tried to throw their riders. In the stockyards bulls locked horns. Cows bellowed, stampeding from their pens on the outskirts of Buenos Aires. Colts, fillies and foals bucked, whinnied and streaked across the Pampa.

Gabriela and Robert ran for blocks in the sunlight, then in more rain, seeing who could stay ahead, stopping at times to rest. They collided with pedestrians who carried umbrellas like prodigious black butterflies. Finally Gabriela ducked into a café on the square of Recoleta with a mighty, spreading tree in front of it.

Waiters and clients gaped at the newcomers in the doorway. Soaked, dripping, Robert and Gabriela looked like a god and goddess risen from the ocean, with flowers instead of seaweed on their heads. They walked to a table by the window, leaving a trail of saltwater behind them. Both ordered brandy.

Gabriela turned unexpectedly serious. Almost breathless, she asked, "Are you sure we haven't met before?"

"No. Are you?"

"*Tampoco.*" She paused. Gabriela parted her lips to speak, showing the tip of a pointed tongue. But the words of Carlos Gardel seized her attention, playing on a jukebox in the corner:

> *... Buenos Aires, mi tierra querida,*
> *escucha mi canción*
> *que en ella va mi vida.*

As she turned away from Robert, her hooded eyes clouded. Lightning flashed: through their steaming window they saw the park of Recoleta illuminated for an instant, the giant tree whose shiny leaves shed water in the dusk. Looking outside, listening to the song, for a few moments they sat in silence.

"I love rain," Gabriela said. "Especially at night." She spoke in a voice he had never heard before. It was neither a girl's nor a woman's, muted as though it had crossed miles of fog.

"Your heart's full of rain," Robert repeated her words from yesterday. Gabriela showed the trace of a smile on her lips.

The waiter served their brandies in heated snifters. Contemplating each other, the two drank. The first sips took away the damp chill.

Always alert to others, Gabriela marked the clients around them. Most were couples drinking beer, wine or cocktails and eating *platitos*, appetizers in small trays of sterling silver set on the white tablecloths. Some were still ogling at them, the pair who had brought the sea and a thunderstorm inside.

Gabriela lowered her eyes as if they were burdened by their long lashes. Robert admired her hair, blue-black and lustrous, so much more alive than the dry straw of girls who had dazed his youth with tresses of washed-out wheat. For a moment Diane and the divorce returned to his mind. It happened far away—on the other side of the world, in another age, he thought. For once Robert felt he might forgive the woman who had stolen years of his life. Maybe she forgives me too, he guessed.

Gabriela raised her glass, studied it carefully, twirled it to refract the light. Robert came back from his memories and took her free hand. It was white, smoother than their polished cotton tablecloth; his was tan, its back covered with dark hair. She set her drink on the table and poised her fingers on Robert's wrist. Placing her thumb on the vein underneath, she felt his blood beating there.

Gabriela closed her eyes to concentrate. Her lashes brushed against the ridges of her cheekbones. "You may have high pressure with a pulse like this," she stated in a mockly clinical tone. Robert did not yet know that her rising-and-falling intonation belonged to the Barrio Norte, the most exclusive neighborhood of Buenos Aires.

Gabriela pushed her hair back with two fingers of her left hand, revealing an ear like a spiraled seashell, the silver crescent moon hanging from its lobe. On her neck Robert noticed the vein with the tiny mole next to it.

She surprised him: "What about your mother?"

"What?"

"You only told me when your father died."

"My wife and I buried her three months after we were married."

"You mean your *ex*-wife."

"She was my wife then."

"Now you're divorced and all alone, Osito."

"I don't feel alone." Robert circled her wrist again.

He paid their check with the currency whose galactic denominations he was beginning to understand. As he and Gabriela walked through the door, waiters and customers turned their heads to follow them. When the couple had gone, it seemed a crowd had left, taking the rain and lightning with them.

Robert read a sign above their heads: "*LA BIELA.*" Rhymes with "Gabriela," he thought. As they stood beneath the tree with its dense, waxy foliage, it shielded them from the drizzle.

"I've never seen anything like it," he told her, contemplating the thick trunk, the green canopy above them. "The redwoods in California are taller but not as broad and full."

"It's centuries old, a *gomero*—rubber tree."

Gabriela leaned against him. Robert felt her warm waist, her damp hair on his neck. Sheltered from the rain and darkness beyond the gomero, holding one another, they stood without moving.

She looked up at Robert. With the thumb of her right hand she made a sign on his forehead. He almost asked Gabriela what it meant, but he did not want to disturb the moment. From the tree a chorus of thrushes broke into a unison of hosannas.

Without warning the wind rose, making the gomero's leaves rustle like a restless sea. Lightning struck so close that Robert and Gabriela startled. Thunder rolled, clouds opened. He embraced her. As long as they stayed under this foliage, he imagined, they might be safe.

She worried they would not be safe there or anywhere. Gabriela pulled away from him when a large, sopping bird plunged, banked its sable wings, nearly grazed her hair before gliding away. She shivered and leaned into Robert again. With his head turned, staring at the gomero, he had not seen the dark creature. But he sensed a swift coldness, a pulsation of the air.

They left the cover of their tree. Robert and Gabriela were blinded by the shower until he took her umbrella and opened it.

They walked toward the sidewalk, where a black Mercedes taxi was edging along the curb. He wondered if somehow Gabriela could summon a cab from nowhere when she needed one.

She gazed at him with moist eyes. "I have to work the evening shift at the hospital. Call me late," she told him. Her words from yesterday echoed in Robert's mind.

He opened the taxi's door for Gabriela. Once more she took her seat without looking at him or saying goodbye.

Robert stood in the rain without her umbrella to shield him. She could have offered to share the ride, he thought, suddenly remembering the Indian girl and her flowers again. By the time he found another cab, he was sodden.

He had a sense of repeating the first day as he entered his room, stripped off his wet garments and drew a bath. In the tub he fell asleep. When Robert awoke, he dressed in new clothes and walked downstairs for a late supper in the hotel dining room.

It was after eleven by the time he called Gabriela over his coffee. She answered the phone herself. "I'll meet you at a discotheque called Brujas on the river."

"Will it stay open much longer?"

"You're such an American, Roberto. They close at sunrise."

Walking through the entrance, he saw red neon letters glowing above him: B-R-U-J-A-S. A small sign displayed the schedule: Thursdays through Sundays, midnight to 8 a.m. He was beginning to comprehend why Gabriela had said ten o'clock was still early in Buenos Aires.

He waited nearly an hour before she arrived. He had found a table on a terrace facing the river—a dark, empty space like a calm sea. Both ordered brandies and soda because the characters drink them in a Raymond Chandler novel she had read about Robert's city, Los Angeles, El Pueblo de Nuestra Señora la Reina de Los Ángeles, Town of Our Lady Queen of the Angels.

They danced to the music or without it, talked, drank, ate and lost themselves in each other's eyes. Couples flitted in and out of view like wraiths, back and forth, vaporous clouds of sweat and perfume. As their feet glided over that terrace, the figures of Robert and Gabriela glowed against the blackness of the river. They moved slowly at first, allowed their bodies to absorb the music, then faster until they felt lightheaded from dancing and the drinks.

After the final song she bent to remove her high heels, held them dangling in one hand while they watched the sun rise over the muddy estuary. The storm had ended. Dark birds had returned to the places where they belonged. The Río de la Plata crept invisibly to the sea.

They took a taxi without telling the cabbie where to go. The man cruised, letting other cars pass, checking his rearview mirror for a sign from his clients. The vehicle moved over the gray, early-morning streets of Buenos Aires. As Robert observed them rushing to work or wherever they were going, their faces set grimly behind their steering wheels, he thought those drivers must have dropped from a distant nebula. Just a few days ago I looked like them on the freeways of Los Angeles, he said to himself. Gabriela huddled against him.

"Will you come back to the hotel?" Robert asked.

"No."

"Why?"

"I can't tell you."

She sat up straight and told the cabbie in a clear voice, "Take us to Dragones in Belgrano."

Relieved to have a destination, the driver shifted into high gear and sped through the streets. Gabriela stared out the window. The meter was running up australes by the tens of thousands, but for Robert this money was still an abstraction, and he did not want the trip to end.

They turned slowly onto a quiet street lined with silver acacia trees. "There," she announced in front of a stately three-story home. It had red tile roofs, a monumental wooden entrance, iron-grilled windows, French balconies covered with red and white geraniums.

"A lot of grown children live with their parents in Argentina," Gabriela said. Why did she feel the need to explain, Robert wondered, knowing the same was true in most countries of Latin America?

He started to open the door on his side. "Don't," Gabriela implored. "Please."

"I want to." Robert paid the driver an astronomical fare in worthless australes, banknotes bigger than his handkerchief.

They drew closer to the house in the somber light. As Gabriela walked, she kept her eyes on the ground. With every step her soul seemed to shrink. The ponderous front door, a dark *zaguán*, was carved with images of animals, angels and demons. The brass knocker had the shape of a lion's head.

Gabriela removed a ring of keys from her purse and unlocked the deadbolts—one, two, three—top to bottom. Robert shivered. The cold of early morning stuck to his clothes, still moist from his perspiring on the dance floor.

She pushed the heavy zaguán. It creaked open with a tiredness of years. Without looking at him, regarding the threshold, she said, "Gracias Roberto."

"When I'm with you I'm not afraid of it." A wan smile crossed her lips. "Can I see you later?" he asked.

"I work the two o'clock shift." Gabriela reached into her purse, removed a black fountain pen and wrote on a small card with her left hand. Holding it out to Robert, she said, "Now you have my work phone too. Call before you visit."

He strained to read the letters in the dim light. He managed to decipher the embossed line—DRA. GABRIELA ROCA

DAFIUME above the words "Sanatorio Palermo." Below it was a handwritten telephone number with florid numerals in purple ink.

When Robert leaned forward to embrace her, she recoiled and crossed the threshold. The door groaned then clanked shut behind her.

Robert pulled up the collar of his jacket and stuffed his hands into his front pockets. He began to walk away but turned to look back. Gabriela's house loomed against an ashen sky. A lamp switched on upstairs, casting a square of yellow light onto the ground. Robert felt the allure of Gabriela's unknown life. Through the curtains he perceived an enormous shape like the figurehead on the prow of an ancient warship, whose shadow engulfed the window and the block of light. Her brother, her father, someone else?

Robert strolled through her sumptuous neighborhood. He was not in a hurry. In the cool morning he wanted to know the streets of Buenos Aires, this vast new city where Gabriela lived.

He came out on Avenida del Libertador and took a bus toward downtown. When Robert reached the Hotel Castelar, the fatigue of travel washed over him—the airplane, the change in time zones, this long day and night.

He rode the elevator to the third floor. In the hall he smelled fresh paint. As he approached his room, Robert saw the white door smeared with large letters in red, enclosed by exclamation points: ¡**O J O**! The dripping O's reminded him of two bloodied eye sockets. The J in the middle was so runny that it might have been an S, recalling Gabriela's nickname for him. But it was a J. Robert knew what that word meant.

3

Underworld

He called the desk and told them about the paint. No strangers had entered the hotel, the clerk said. He would send up a bellman to clean the door.

From the far side of sleep Robert imagined rivers of red paint streaming under the threshold, spreading over his room. He woke in early afternoon with fumes in his nostrils and a hangover like a vulture perched on his skull.

When he walked into the hall, he examined the door. He saw the ghosts of three letters and two exclamation points where somebody had tried to scrub off the paint. Robert descended the stairs, wondering if he had somehow missed a day, a night, a season? Everything seemed backwards and upside-down in Buenos Aires.

After eating a snack in the hotel café, he paced along the street. He crossed Avenida 9 de Julio, a boulevard wider than two football fields with its broad median and trees, skyscrapers on both sides. An obelisk of white marble looked like the Washington Monument or a towering sword. Seeing the sun ahead of him, Robert assumed he was heading south, forgetting he was in a new hemisphere. He lost his way.

After circling for an hour, Robert managed to find his hotel. It was still too early to call Gabriela at the hospital. In the vestibule he spotted a sign for Turkish baths.

He read the list of prices and services. A small, bent man nudged his arm and pointed downstairs: "Don't miss the *baños*, friend." Following the stranger's finger with its long, jagged nail, Robert reflected for a few moments. He would have liked to wash away the image of those three letters on the door. He also felt a vague need to cleanse his memories of lawyers and the divorce.

When Robert turned to thank him, the little man had disappeared. He stepped down the wide marble stairs. He paid at a booth ornamented with wrought iron, like the ticket window at an old movie house. As though he were entering a striptease show, the woman behind the counter giggled, eyed Robert with a sort of complicity.

He descended another flight of stairs. A row of dimly lit, open-doored shops lined the wall facing him—a barber, a masseur, a "Café Turco" with liquor bottles displayed beneath a mirror corroded by humidity and time. He was learning that there are few places in Argentina where a bar, café or tavern is not closeby.

Dressed in white, an attendant with a pimpled face took the new client's ticket. He handed Robert two warm towels and led him to a dressing closet. The American hung his clothes on hooks, tied the larger towel around his waist, folded the smaller one on his arm. He noted the Hotel Castelar's blue coat of arms on the plush terry cloth—a rampant lion with a motto, *Ecce Signum*.

He walked down a tiled corridor where he did not see the attendant or another soul. Wooden ceiling fans whirred, boilers chugged like locomotives. Against Robert's feet the floor felt cool. The air became warmer as he drew nearer the baths. He entered a door whose glass was clouded by vapor. When he closed it behind him, the noise of fans and boilers faded.

He was alone in a chamber where steam curled upwards from the floor. The heat caressed Robert's skin. Through the haze he saw a sign with red letters on the tile wall: SILENCIO.

The word painted on the door of his room sprang into his mind. He sat on a wooden chair, leaned back and closed his eyes. The heat enveloped him like an embrace.

"*Bienvenido a Buenos Aires,*" a voice rasped in Robert's left ear.

He startled, opened his eyes, tried to focus and saw a livid face beaming at him with rotted teeth. It was the man who had recommended the baths upstairs, he thought, who was now half-naked, standing on twisted feet covered with fuzzy hair down to their curled, horny toenails. His legs bowed at the knees under a white towel that swallowed the rest of his contorted frame. On his back a protuberance rose like a camel's hump.

Robert drew back from the smiling face. "How do you know I just arrived in Buenos Aires?" His words echoed in the room.

"Anyone can see you're new in my country." The small man placed the index finger of one hand beneath his left eye and pulled down on the lid, as if to say, "I know."

Robert scrutinized that yellow eyeball streaked with veins. It's seen everything, he told himself. Recalling the phrase in Spanish, he replied, "Appearances deceive."

"Yes Roberto, especially in Argentina."

The foreigner sat up in his chair, his head soaring above the dwarf's. "How did you know my name?"

"I know what happens above and below. Come with me. You've never been in the baths before, right?"

"I thought you knew everything."

The Argentine grinned through the gaps of his teeth. "Almost. You'll need a guide at first, maybe at the end too. My name's Virgilio," he said, reaching to help Robert rise from the chair. The visitor was slightly squeamish about touching that gnarled hand. But the man's smile, stretching from one of his pointed ears to the other, disarmed him.

"The end of what?" Robert asked.

Virgilio made an indefinite twirl with one hand. "*Quién sabe?*" He poked the mist where half-naked silhouettes emerged: enveloped in white towels, leaning on canes or crutches, old men trudged along. They evoked marine mammals—walruses or manatees gliding on the sea-bottom. Robert had the impression that he was peering through the glass walls of a giant aquarium. Although he stood only a few yards from those figures, he sensed they could not see him, that he was invisible at Virgilio's side.

"Some of them are blameless," his guide said, "those who did nothing in life, neither good nor evil. The dream of every *argentino*—to do nothing, *il dolce far niente* that we inherited from our Italian forebears." He chortled as if somebody were tickling him. "Do you want to hear my definition of Argentina?"

"I guess so."

"Thirty-five million people waiting for room service!" His laugh ascended through locks of phlegm and mucus. "Come Roberto, let's go on. Like the ancient Romans we have three stages in our baths, each one hotter than the last. We're about to enter the second."

He took Robert's hand. Through the leathery skin of Virgilio's palm the American felt a throbbing pulse. He pondered, Why am I allowing a dwarf to lead me like a small boy? He dropped his hand but followed.

They passed through a glass door to another chamber, hotter and steamier than the first. Robert sweated freely. Virgilio's face and limbs seemed dry. The fur on his skin must absorb the moisture, Robert said to himself.

The Argentine lifted one hand, showing horn-like fingernails in the billowing vapor: "Here you see every kind of sinner." His utterance called forth shadowy bodies from the haze, more aged men who shuffled back and forth, others who sat in chairs, whispered among themselves.

Virgilio proclaimed, "Conspirators, thieves, torturers, executioners—you'll find them all here." Raising his chin to one side, he asked, "See that distraught man over there, standing by himself and gawking at the floor? He was a lover of Malena, the tango singer. There's a song that says 'Malena sings with a voice full of shadows.'"

"I like that. Who's the thin old man with a patch on one eye?"

"Bishop Alberoni. As usual he's surrounded by a bunch of parasites—priests, clerics, monks. In Spanish we have a proverb that says 'In the land of the blind the one-eyed man is king.'" He chuckled. "Want to know something confidential?"

"Why not?"

Virgilio hissed. "Voices say the good bishop funneled gold from the Vatican to the generals during the dictatorship." He paused like a child who has just disclosed a secret, expecting a reward. "Want to know something else?"

"Sure."

"Promise to keep it mum, Roberto?"

"Alright."

"Even if they put you in the fires of the Inquisition?" Robert laughed, beginning to feel fond of the little man. "Sometimes the bishop reserves these baths for his private parties," Virgilio imparted in a hushed voice. "He comes with an entourage of seminarians who could be mistaken for rosy-cheeked cherubs—except they don't have wings."

"If their parties are private how do you know that?"

"Remember I know everything that happens here and up there," Virgilio replied, jerking his head toward the ceiling. Robert regarded the man doubtfully. "Well not quite everything. But in this country even the walls have ears, *m'hijo*. See that decrepit *boludo* on the other side," he indicated, "the one who's staggering, who looks like he's got a stick up his arse?"

"What about him?"

"One of the last surviving ministers of the Perón regime. He doesn't have much time left in the world above."

"They don't seem to know we're here."

"They know alright. But they're used to me and they don't care about you—you're nobody in Argentina." Virgilio placed one of his paws on Robert's arm. "It must be hard to adjust to life in Buenos Aires. It's so different from your city."

"You also know where I'm from?"

"Los Ángeles. Pueblo de Nuestra Señora la Reina de Los Ángeles," Virgilio pronounced the city's full, sacred, musical name. "The only angels here are fallen—with dark oily wings."

"How's that?"

"You'll learn soon enough, *Che*," the dwarf responded with the familiar Argentine word. "Do you miss home?"

"No. It's good to be in a new country," Robert said before recalling the word painted on his door. "I think."

"You're lost, Roberto." Virgilio pressed the foreigner's arm.

"I can't find my bearings—first time I've been in the Southern Hemisphere." Robert surprised himself by confiding in a person he had just met. "I must still be suffering from jet lag."

"It's a topsy-turvy world, isn't it?"

Robert conjured Gabriela in his mind. Yes, he thought.

"Come to see me whenever you feel lonely or confused. When you're not with her, I mean."

"Who?" Robert asked, raising his voice again.

"Gabriela Roca Dafiume."

Robert cried, "How do you know about her?"

The old men turned to glare through the fog, affronted by the voice that had broken their mute torpor. The bishop glowered at Robert, stood to his full height, elevated his right arm and traced an episcopal gesture.

"Let's get out of here," Virgilio whispered. "That blessing could be a curse."

He tried to take his guest's hand again. Robert slapped the man's wrist away. "How do you know about Gabriela?"

Virgilio spun his hand in circles, as if to say, That's a long story. "Come with me."

Robert hesitated. He watched the elderly bathers standing motionless with their eyes trained on him: some had cupped their hands around their ears to better hear his and Virgilio's words. He hung his head and followed his guide into the haze.

Through a glass door they entered another room. Robert saw the outlines of a large, circular hall in swirls of viscous air. His heart was beating quicker from his anger and the heat. On his skin he had a tingling sensation. The towels around his shoulders and midriff were drenched.

In the deepening mist Robert almost stumbled over Virgilio. He grabbed the dwarf's shoulders, trying to avoid the hump on his back. "Tell me how you know!" As he shook that body, it felt strange in his hands—small as a boy's, heavy like a grown man's.

Virgilio had learned to exploit the pity he inspired. "You're hurting me Roberto," he whined, twisting all his features into a woeful mask. He slipped out of the newcomer's hands. "Buenos Aires is a city where everything is known. In fact some things are known before they happen." He paused as though he were reflecting. "We're still reeling from a civil war that lasted longer than yours in America, not to mention our shameful defeat by the British in the Malvinas—what do they call those damned islands in English ... the Falklands?" He did not wait for Robert to confirm. "Then we suffered one economic crisis after another. What I'm trying to tell you is—" He stopped, searching for words. "Knowing about other people is a way of life in Argentina. It's a matter of survival, Che."

"Do you know about the warning painted on my door?"

Virgilio laughed. "That's common knowledge by now," he said, as though to dismiss the subject. He raised a knuckly finger. "After all it happened upstairs in the building where we're sitting. Look around you now—"

"Virgilio," Robert persisted, "why did somebody paint that word on my door?"

"All in good time, m'hijo." The man sighed and shrugged. "We're in the last chamber," he intoned as if Robert had not interrupted him, "the one the Romans called the *calidarium*, where the heat's at the boiling point. Odd things happen inside these walls. People's hearts race so fast that strokes and cardiac arrest are common." He waited a second, turned away then peeked impishly at Robert. "Just joking, *gringo!*" His bellow filled the steamy air.

"By the way," Virgilio continued, "are you planning to write for your newspaper while you're in Argentina?"

"You also know about my work of course," Robert responded, no longer surprised by whatever the dwarf might say. "No. I'm on my first vacation in more than a year."

"It might not be a bad idea," Virgilio advised. He rubbed his knobby chin.

"What—the vacation or writing for my paper?"

"It would put you on the record in Buenos Aires."

"Why would I want that?"

"You might be safer." This word keeps turning up in conversation and your mind, Robert said to himself, recalling Gabriela's definition of heaven. "Also," the man winked, "I could give you some good scoops and sources."

Before Robert could reply, Virgilio was telling him, "Follow me now." With one hand he touched the visitor's arm while he signaled straight ahead with the other.

Robert discerned more old men through the clouds of vapor. They were seated on rows of wooden benches like the steps of an amphitheater. Their heads drooped between their hairless, skinny legs.

"Study those citizens well, Che," Virgilio said, confident he was regaining Robert's trust. "There you see murderers, tyrants and traitors to our country—admirals, generals, colonels, deputies and senators. Some were in jail until the latest amnesty. Believe it or not a few still hold power." Virgilio lowered his voice to add, "Those *hijos de puta* have the deaths and the disappearances of many Argentines on their conscience. Others have no conscience."

"Why are you showing them to me?"

Virgilio made another twirl of his hand. "Someday you'll know why." For the first time he looked utterly serious. With the back of one hand he rubbed his forehead, where the wrinkles looked deep as canyons observed from an airplane. "I wonder if Argentina still has a conscience," the dwarf mused as if he were talking to himself. "Or a soul ... Just consider this advice, my son." He wagged one finger like a schoolmaster scolding his pupils. "Stay away from the politicians and the *milicos*," Don't get entangled with the state or the military. "*No te metás*, Che! They'll tear you to pieces. Same goes for the Church. Though a few good Catholics are on our side."

"Which side?"

Like Gabriela this man ignored Robert's question. Virgilio grabbed the foreigner's arm at the elbow: "One more thing." With bloodshot eyes he scanned Robert's face. "Remember this—don't get mixed up with the Rocas. One of Gabriela's lovers ended up on the bottom of the Río de la Plata."

"What?"

"I'll tell you more when the time's ripe."

It took Robert half a minute or so to gather his thoughts. "It's not so easy for a man and woman to stop—"

"There's still time," Virgilio interposed. "Otherwise the two of you will smash everything in your way. And be smashed yourselves."

Virgilio dropped his new friend's arm, wheeled, doffed an invisible hat, hobbled away. For a moment the outsider believed that he could hear the dwarf weeping in the mist.

Robert's lips and nostrils burned from the heat. Trapped in this stifling room, suddenly he felt his solitude. He walked to the end of the circular hall, opened another glass door and entered a cool, dark tunnel. Finally he emerged from the far side of the baths. Virgilio had disappeared.

Robert followed other bathers who were moving ahead of him like shadows. They reached a wooden bench covered with pads and pillows, where patrons were resting or sleeping on their backs, their faces and torsos covered with large white towels. Shrouded cadavers in a morgue, he told himself. When a waiter from the Café Turco materialized through the thick air, some of those men showed signs of life, groaning, sighing, lifting themselves to place orders. In Argentina there must be table service even after death, he smiled, recalling Virgilio's joke.

Robert reposed on the wooden bench, thinking of Gabriela, everything that had occurred in two days. It seemed mostly like a vision or a dream, but Los Angeles, his work and the divorce— they were even more blurred now, hazier in his mind. Under the whirring fans, in the basement of a hotel in the center of Buenos Aires, City of the Most Holy Trinity and Port of Our Lady of Fair Winds, he fell asleep.

4
Lost Paradise

After the mist and penumbra of the baths, everything looked sharper and more vivid outside, like waking from a dream. Robert stepped onto the sidewalk of Avenida de Mayo. As he emerged from the shadows cast by the hotel, the afternoon sun blinded him for a moment. Maybe I invented Gabriela, he thought, lowering his eyes.

Porteños were sitting at sidewalk tables, reading newspapers or drinking early aperitifs. Others peered into shop windows where rolls of plush fabrics were on display, or they admired summer suits and dresses on mannequins, sinuous bottles of perfume, gold watches and jewelry on trays of red or green velvet. Robert passed delicatessen windows that resembled still-life paintings with their festoons of chorizo, pillars of cheese, balls of mozzarella in milk, jars of olives, barrels of anchovies in brine. He passed butcher shops hung with upside-down capons, hens, turkeys, rabbits, flayed lambs, eviscerated hogs, whole hams, sides of beef, calves' heads—their eyes closed, lips curled, a lemon stuck between their teeth. The sacrificial altars of Buenos Aires, he said to himself, recalling Gabriela and the restaurant.

Robert took a taxi up the Avenida, down the length of Callao to Libertador, the great boulevard that follows the river's curve through green parks and *glorietas*, past embassies, museums and the most palatial homes in Buenos Aires. His driver dropped him at the hospital next to the Hipódromo Argentino de Palermo, where thousands of spectators were cheering their horses to the home stretch in the fourth race of the spring sweepstakes. He paid the driver, his feet hit the pavement and he felt it pulsating from the racetrack.

"Dr. Gabriela Roca Dafiume." The woman at the information desk paged the melodious name on a loudspeaker. Soon Gabriela was walking toward him, wearing a white tunic. Again her raven hair was swept back in a knot. When Robert saw her exposed earlobes, looking smooth as mother-of-pearl with their crescent moons, he had an urge to bite them. Instead he hugged her and kissed her softly on the cheek. They felt the shock: sparks shot and both recoiled, laughing. Robert knew he had not dreamed Gabriela.

"The air must be dry in here," she said. She folded her arms in a pose of mock annoyance. "I thought you were going to call first."

"I forgot. You really are a doctor, aren't you?" He soaked Gabriela in the full smile of his teeth.

"And are you really in Buenos Aires?"

He reached out to touch her arm and both felt the current again. "Yes."

Gabriela tried to smile before checking the nurses, who were ogling them. "Roberto, I'm not supposed to meet friends when I'm on duty." She observed him as she bit her lower lip. "I see you've finally changed your clothes."

He frowned. "I need to talk with you."

She raised the black arcs of her brows. A cloud crossed her enormous eyes which now looked purplish-black in the hospital's light. "First I want to stop by the doctors' station."

They walked down a long, empty hall, made several turns. They passed surgeons in green gowns, doctors and nurses in white tunics, others who milled at a counter, some greeting Gabriela, most talking among themselves. Robert felt like a stranger in this world of people who appeared to be acquainted. How did I end up here, he asked himself, in a hospital on the other side of the world?

"Come. I'd like for you to meet one of my colleagues."

She led him toward a red-haired young woman with a stethoscope around her neck, who exclaimed "*Querida!*" when she saw Gabriela. They kissed on the cheek.

The doctor examined Robert from head to foot, the way a woman eyes a man whom a friend has described to her. "You must be the *norteamericano*," she told him, offering her hand. "Alfonsina Rosas."

"*Mucho gusto.* Robert Wells."

"She's my favorite colleague at the hospital," Gabriela said, taking his arm in a possessive way. "We went to medical school together."

Before the three could talk, an elderly nurse approached them. "I don't have any doctors in emergency," she told Gabriela and Alfonsina, sneaking a glance at the outsider. "None of them wants to work until the feature race is over. Would one of you mind being on duty there, *Doctoras?*"

"I'll do it," Alfonsina answered instantly. "Dr. Roca must attend to her visitor." As she walked away, she glanced over her shoulder and called, "A pleasure to meet you, Roberto."

Gabriela guided him down a white corridor. The curved, silver moons swayed from her ears. Robert brushed her arm with the fingertips of one hand. She stopped. He pulled her toward him gently. In the reflection of their eyes they recognized each other and themselves.

She surveyed the corridor. Seeing nobody, Gabriela pulled Robert into a small storage room, where she rose on tiptoe, extended her arms and placed them about his neck. She sought his mouth and once, twice, slowly they kissed, five, ten times, more. Robert closed his eyes, felt dizzy, tasted her lipstick, her saliva and its trace of salt. As they kissed again, longer, twelve grooms were leading their fillies to the paddock for the sixth race of the sweepstakes at the Hipódromo de Palermo.

Gabriela bit Robert's tongue and drew away from him. As though nothing had occurred, she smoothed her tunic with both hands. She led him down a passageway while Robert dabbed his tongue with his handkerchief. On the white cotton a drop of blood bloomed. Gabriela said nothing.

The two entered the hospital cafeteria. They took seats by the lone window of this sad room with formica tables, linoleum floors and flickering neon lights. Drinking coffee, tea or sodas, a few customers sat in their chairs.

"What would you like?" Gabriela asked.

"Nothing. I want to keep your taste in my mouth."

"And the taste of your blood?" Before he could reply, she said, always alert, "A waiter's spotted us."

"Do they serve alcohol?"

"Of course—we're not in an American hospital. Doctors don't earn much more than minimum wage here but at least we have a cafeteria with table service, wine and beer."

"Have you ever been in the U.S.?"

"I took a summer course in English before starting medical school."

"Where?"

"Stanford. It took months to convince my parents to let me leave the country. They insisted I travel with my brother."

"You didn't tell me you'd been in California."

"We just met, hombre."

"Two days ago. Or years," he said. Gabriela did not smile.

A waiter arrived at their table. Unlike the other mozos Robert had seen in Buenos Aires, this man appeared to be in a hurry. After he took their order and walked away, Gabriela said, "He'll serve us fast so he can listen to the big race in the kitchen. Wait and see."

That was enough to bring Robert back to the world. "Someone painted a warning on my door at the hotel last night."

Gabriela's eyes opened wide. She scanned the room to see if anyone had heard. "What did it say?"

"Three letters in red paint—'*Ojo*'—with exclamation points."

"'Watch out, be careful.'"

"I know what it means, Gabriela."

She dropped her violet gaze to the floor. "Maybe it was a joke," she said, almost whimpered.

"You're the only person I know in Argentina." Robert did not count Virgilio, who came from a different galaxy.

She looked straight into his eyes. "Are you trying to say it's connected to me?" It was a voice he had never heard from Gabriela, harsher and louder, as if someone else were speaking through her. A few customers turned their way.

Robert stared at her, wondering if she could be the same woman who had run through those wet streets with him yesterday, who had eaten, drunk and danced with him last night, who had just kissed him a hundred times, bitten his tongue and made it bleed. With one hand he caressed her wrist—like a stem with five pale flowers, he thought—cold to his touch. He grazed her palm, moist with dew. Both he and Gabriela felt the sparks again. At the same moment all twelve fillies in the starting gate shook their heads and tossed their manes.

She looked up at Robert. "I'm sorry Osito. This all brings back memories," she ended, glancing down once more.

The waiter served their drinks. Robert took a long swig of Quilmes lager. In a demitasse Gabriela swirled her espresso and sipped.

"You don't use sugar?" he asked, hoping to lighten her mood.

"No."

"Isn't the coffee bitter?"

"Yes—not as much as maté though. People in my country like bitter tastes." Noise erupted from the Hipódromo, passing through the cafeteria's open window. "The horses must have broken from the gate," Gabriela said knowingly.

A voice issued from a radio in the kitchen. Gabriela held her cup suspended halfway to her bow-shaped lips, her mouth open, listening attentively as the announcer called the race. The customers around them began to cheer, competing with the roar from the track. Within a few seconds all except Robert and Gabriela had risen from their tables and disappeared.

"What kind of memories?" he asked.

"The war." Their waiter dashed by them to the kitchen. Gabriela looked at Robert with her plum-colored eyes. "See? This is one of the richest purses of the year." She glanced into her cup. "We have a pool going at the doctors' station."

"Good thing I'm not a patient in emergency today."

She laughed. "I know, it's disgraceful—in my country horseracing's more important than medicine." Gabriela reflected. "The Hipódromo's right next door to us. When jockeys are hurt we treat them here."

Robert ran the fingers of one hand through his wavy hair. "I'd like to be an injured jockey when you're on duty."

Gabriela ignored his words. "To know Argentina well you should understand our love for horses." She paused. "Do you recall the Casa Rosada, our presidential palace on the Plaza de Mayo?"

"The old pink building?"

"Yes. It used to be painted with horse's blood."

"No."

"Yes—mixed with whitewash. That's how it got its color."

"You love horses?"

"I ride whenever I go to Father's ranch." She lowered her eyes again. "Today everyone's talking about a thoroughbred who's never lost a race. They call her the 'magic filly'—her name's Mina." Gabriela hesitated. "Do you know what it means?"

"Just a 'mine,' no? As in gold and silver?"

"Yes but in slang it also means a woman, a lover or a prostitute. Haven't you ever listened to tangos?"

"I've never liked them much."

"They're full of *minas*, mostly lost women."

"Everyone seems to be lost in tangos." Robert took another drink of his beer.

"Very un-American, right? Ah Osito, if only you understood how beautiful those songs can be." The cheering from the track mounted, making the walls vibrate as two fillies led the pack down the final stretch.

"They don't make sense to me. It's as though the singers are saying 'Let's make love together, then I'll stab you to death.'"

"That's right—a love that kills. *L'amour fou*," she added in perfect French. "What do you call it in English?"

"Maybe 'mad love.' But that sounds like the lovers are angry."

"How about 'obsessive love'"?

"Better but too clinical." Robert leaned closer. "Do you know a singer named Malena?"

Gabriela looked affronted. "Every Argentine knows her."

Remembering, he quoted Virgilio: "'She sings with a voice full of shadows.'"

"I'm impressed. You don't like tangos and you know that?" A clamor reached them from the racetrack, followed by a rising murmur. "The sixth must be over," Gabriela said, her ears cocked toward the window. Confused voices reached them from the kitchen. She continued as though nothing had interrupted her. "Most tangos sing about a lost paradise." Before Robert could respond, as if she were talking to herself or nobody, she asked, "But aren't all paradises lost?"

She took a last sip of coffee. After moving two fingers around the rim of her cup, Gabriela turned it over. The dregs spilled onto the white saucer, where she swirled them, stopped, swirled again. Searching for a sign there, she became motionless, then shuddered.

"What are you doing?"

"Something my mother taught me." Gabriela covered the saucer with her upside-down demitasse.

"Can I see?"

"No." She pushed her white cup to the far end of the table. At that moment the report of a gun cracked the air. Both Robert and Gabriela startled, and the hospital fell silent.

Within a few seconds the elderly nurse was rushing into the cafeteria. As soon as she saw Gabriela, the woman cried, "Doctora! The radio says Mina shattered her leg before the finish line and they had to put her out of pain."

"Who won the race?" Gabriela asked calmly. Hearing her question, Robert felt a shiver down his back.

"Two fillies in a dead heat," the nurse answered, unbelieving.

"Was one of them mine?" Gabriela insisted.

"Oh Doctora." The woman broke into tears, covering her face with both hands, wheeled and rushed away.

A draft made the room turn colder. The air seemed to quiver around them. Gabriela's body trembled.

She tilted her head and tucked it on her left shoulder. "You'd better leave this hospital now," she said in that other voice of hers. She straightened, stood and walked from the room.

Emerging from the main entrance of the Sanatorio Palermo, Robert looked dazed, as though he had been expelled from Gabriela's life. Smog had darkened the transparent light of afternoon. Clouds filled the sky. He felt as alone in Buenos Aires as when he had arrived.

On the sidewalk he saw people crying, embracing, comforting each other. Robert recalled Gabriela's words about horses in Argentina. Could the country's soul be in them as well as in tangos? If it still has a soul, he thought, recollecting Virgilio's words.

He had to cross Avenida del Libertador to catch a taxi for downtown. He dodged and weaved in and out of vehicles whose breeze blew across his face. Not one of them, not a single automobile, bus, van, truck, motorcycle or scooter slowed or braked for him or the other boludos who were crazy enough to try and ford that unrelenting stream.

When Robert reached the far shore, he looked back and saw the hospital surrounded by trees. Enveloped in a haze of exhaust and smoke, it reminded him of a faraway island. All at once he realized how much separated him from Gabriela.

Robert hailed a cab. Another pedestrian, a man in a double-breasted suit, stepped in front of him and stopped the vehicle in its tracks. The same happened once more, then a third time. Robert was learning that life in Buenos Aires is only slightly more civilized than in the rain forest. Finally he strode resolutely off the curb to commandeer a taxi, exposing himself to a hit-and-run. The black car veered, came to a breaking halt, Robert mounted and slammed the door behind him.

When the cab drove by the Hipódromo Argentino de Palermo, traffic slowed. Cars and people were pouring onto the boulevard from the racetrack. Robert saw a woman sobbing, soaking her tears in a white scarf that fluttered in the breeze.

Without turning his head, as if he were talking to the windshield, the cabbie said, "The race must have been fixed. It had to be."

"Why?" the American asked, still amazed at how horseracing absorbed people in Buenos Aires. Robert remembered Gabriela's words.

"Too many bet on her—Mina was unbeatable. Somebody must have put a lot of money against her, made sure she wouldn't win. There'll never be another horse like her."

"I hear it was a dead heat." Robert pictured the old nurse.

"Almost," the driver said. "The underdog won in a photo finish—filly named *Amour Fou*, 90-to-1 shot, real darkhorse. Somebody cleaned up on her." Gabriela's question rang in Robert's head: "Was one of them mine?"

The taxi crawled through traffic. Talking and consoling each other, gesticulating with their hands, pedestrians on sidewalks were moving faster than the river of cars. The cabbie flipped the dial on his radio, where every station repeated news of the filly's death. It reminded Robert of the day when they killed John F. Kennedy.

5
Río de la Plata

"You have a message, *Señor*." The clerk at the desk handed him a small piece of paper and the key to his room.

Robert read: "*Rev. Segundo Roca Dafiume will meet you in the hotel café 5 p.m.*" Almost a mirror of the message he had received from Gabriela yesterday, he thought, feeling once more that he was living in a dream. He pulled her card from his wallet to confirm her family names: first the father's—Roca, then the mother's—Dafiume. This would to be the brother, Robert presumed. A brother who's a priest, a pastor? He could not imagine it. He checked his watch: 4:25.

Approaching his room, Robert inhaled the coppery smell of blood. He opened the door. At his feet the flayed, severed head of a calf gazed up at him with glassy eyes and two roses—one red, the other white—stuffed into its mouth. The carpet was drenched in blood.

His first reaction was to flee the hotel. Then Robert recalled that he was supposed to meet Gaby's brother in a few minutes. Trying to stifle his rage, he walked back downstairs, where he told the desk clerk what he had found.

"We haven't seen a thing," the man said.

Robert screamed, "How could they bring a calf's head into the hotel without anybody seeing it?"

The clerk did not reply. Instead he asked, "Which room is it, Señor?"

"The one where somebody painted the door last night."

"Oh number 33."

"And how did they get into my room?"

At last the man apologized. He told Robert that he could move to one of the best rooms in the Hotel Castelar, on the top floor, which had a private elevator and a security guard.

"Management will have to pay for the first two nights," Robert stated flatly.

"*Sí Señor*," the clerk assented, handing Robert a set of keys for room 66. "Please return the keys to number 33 when you've moved your luggage. I'll send a bellman with you."

"*Carajo!*" the employee exclaimed when he saw the calf's head and the bloody floor. While the bellman covered the carnage with washcloths, towels and bed sheets, Robert packed his suitcase. No bad memories flew out this time; the present had overtaken his past.

The bellman led the way to the elevator while Robert cursed under his breath.

Number 66, like the old room, was at the end of a hall, facing Avenida de Mayo. The floor plan was similar but twice as big. The furniture looked newer, the wallpaper had not faded, the mirrors were untarnished.

Robert splashed his face to wash the reek of blood from his nostrils. He stripped and lay on the bed. All the death around me, he thought—the horse at the racetrack, the animals in restaurants and butcher shops, the calf's head in my room. With her graceful walk Gabriela floated through his memory. In spite of everything she had stepped into his life. Robert yearned to be with her instead of a priest, her brother, anybody else. Hoping his luck would change, he dressed in more new clothes.

Aromas of coffee and tobacco drove the metallic scent from Robert's nostrils in the hotel café. Again he saw the marble floors and tabletops, enameled mirrors, gilded columns adorned with fleurs-de-lis, gleaming espresso makers, uniformed waiters bearing trays like consecrated vessels. This baroque luxury seemed grotesque after the gory scenery in his room.

Robert studied the crowd from his table. Next to him a pair of balding businessmen was striking a deal with flourishes of their hands, exchanging wads of australes. With their eyes cocked at other clients, whispering to each other, two autumnal matrons took high tea. An aged couple by a window ogled the passersby, leafed through *La Nación*, ate their pastries and sipped their coffee. Most customers appeared nearly as old as the hotel.

A young, clean-shaven priest stepped through the revolving glass doors. He halted to survey the room and his eyes met Robert's.

When he reached the table, he asked, "Señor Wells?"

"Yes."

"Segundo Roca, *a sus órdenes*." The priest extended his hand toward Robert, who rose from his chair.

"No, please sit down," the man said in a high-pitched voice that did not match his large frame. He could not be the one who answered the phone the first night in a resounding basso, Robert knew.

He sat down and regarded the priest. His hair was almost as black as hers. In the man's face he recognized her wide-set, oval eyes, but his irises were gray instead of violet. He had olive-brown skin that made him look like a member of a different family. It was hard to tell if he was older or younger than Gabriela.

"In case you're wondering," the Argentine said, "our parents named me Segundo because I was their second child—two years younger than Gaby." His intuition's as keen as hers, Robert told himself. The priest spoke English almost as perfectly as his sister, also with the trace of a British inflection.

He observed this man and remembered Virgilio's warnings. Now both the Church and the Rocas were wrapped up in one person who was seated at his table; at least the military and the state were not represented here too, he hoped. As he usually did when he was apprehensive, Robert rubbed the cleft of his chin. He could not remove the image of the calf's head from his memory.

A liveried mozo came to their table, wearing a collar that was almost as high, starched and white as Segundo's. Waiters in Argentina are also like celebrants who preside over sacred rites, Robert was learning. The young man carried their orders to the bar.

"I've only known Gabriela for two days," Robert said in a tone as cordial as he could make it. "Can I ask why you've sought me out so urgently?"

"*Pa-cien-cia*," the priest drew out each syllable. He sounded like a curate admonishing one of his flock.

Robert raised his eyebrows. "You didn't show much patience in finding me."

Segundo stroked his face with the palm of one hand, his left. "Any delay might have been unfortunate." As the man spoke, he viewed the other tables in a way that recalled Gabriela—always mindful of the people around her. He and the priest were the only customers who were not speaking loudly or gesturing with their hands.

"Why unfortunate?"

Before Gaby's brother could reply, the mozo was serving a pair of espressos, each with a sterling-silver spoon and wedge of lemon on a saucer, a glass of mineral water on the side. Watching Segundo smile at the waiter with a set of straight white teeth, Robert thought he resembled a clergyman in a movie more than a real man of faith—maybe Montgomery Clift or the young priest in "The Exorcist." If he removed his white collar and black tunic, Robert reflected, Gabriela's brother could pass for a banker or a lawyer as well as a leading man on the screen.

"I'll explain," Segundo said, waiting for the mozo to leave.

He keeps a question in mind and comes back to it later, like Gaby, Robert told himself. And he also takes his coffee black.

In small quick gulps the priest drank his espresso. When he had finished, Segundo slowly turned his demitasse upside down. He dripped the grounds onto his white saucer, where he swirled them, over and over, before concealing them beneath his cup. He did all of this as though it were some kind of daily habit, like smoking a cigarette.

Picturing Gabriela in the cafeteria, Robert was amused. "Does the Church approve of reading coffee grounds?"

"It's a kind of family game. There are too many pagan customs in our country for us to stop them, so we adapt. That's the genius of the Catholic Church." In silence Robert asked himself, Could flayed calves' heads also be a part of some arcane Argentine custom?

Silence grew between the two men. It was like a cloud suspended over their table, a fog composed of all the forces conspiring to keep Gabriela and Robert apart.

"How did you learn that I know your sister?" the American asked, surprised by the irritation in his own voice.

"She told me this morning. It was the first time she's gotten home so late in months." The man pronounced the last words in a low voice, marking the people around them.

Robert wondered if the silhouette in the upstairs window of Gabriela's house, like the prow of an archaic ship, had been Segundo's. "She's an adult," he told the priest.

Segundo faced toward the windows and squirmed in his chair. "I know that," he acknowledged. "It's just that I haven't seen Gaby like this for so long, since—"

"When?"

"The war," the man responded, finally looking at Robert again. "She fell in love with a young student who used to come to the house for her. Dionisio would joke with me because I already aspired to be a priest, or rather my—my family had already arranged for me to study at seminary." Segundo glanced down and seemed to blush.

Robert took a gulp of mineral water. He wished it were a stronger drink. "Why are you telling me this?"

"Because I would not want the same thing to happen."

"What?"

The priest paused. Leaning forward, he declared in a hushed voice, "A fatality."

Virgilio's revelation came back to Robert's memory: "One of Gabriela's lovers ended up on the bottom of the Río de la Plata." He drank more water before asking, "Can you tell me how Dionisio was killed?" Referring to the victim by his first name, as if he had known him in person, Robert knew how much he was enmeshed now.

"I did not speak of a murder, only a death. But you are right," Segundo said in a tone of resignation. "However I cannot tell you how it happened."

"Or you *will* not tell me?"

The priest said nothing.

Robert felt uneasy in his chair. In a way he was anxious to end the conversation, yet he was captivated by this man's story about Gabriela's past.

Segundo waved to the mozo for their bill. "You see my fath—" he stuttered, his lips parting as he struggled to pronounce a syllable trapped in his vocal cords. Robert sensed whatever tortured complex might have led a tall, robust adolescent, as Segundo must have been, to renounce a normal life by taking vows for the priesthood.

"You see my fath—" he said once more, mouthing air. "My family was opposed to the relationship." Segundo's cheeks flushed.

Robert pitied Gabriela's brother, a clergyman who could not say "father," he guessed, who must stammer every time he gives a sermon or says the Lord's Prayer. He peered into Segundo's eyes—almost as large and deep as Gaby's.

"Do you know the story of the minotaur?" the priest inquired.

"Why?"

"You probably remember that the monster devoured his victims in a labyrinth until Ariadne gave her brother a thread to find his way."

"And Theseus killed the minotaur, right?" Robert could not believe that he was sitting in a café with a Catholic priest, Gabriela's brother, listening to a lecture on Greek mythology to the accompaniment of clinking cups and spoons, noisy conversations and steaming espresso machines.

"Señor Wells, this monster will assault anyone who enters his maze. I beg you to forget my sister and to leave Argentina," he ended softly, seeing the waiter approach with their check.

The priest left a pile of australes on the silver tray. For a second the foreigner wished to tell Segundo about the bloody calf's head, the warning painted on his door, about Virgilio's advice. But those facts would only clinch the man's argument for Robert to depart the country.

Gabriela's brother rose from his chair. "Would you accompany me for a short ride?"

"Very short."

Passing through the hotel's doors, the folds of Segundo's black robe billowed as if he would hover in the air. He and the American walked up Avenida de Mayo to the corner, where the priest unlocked the passenger side of a lustrous gray Mercedes sedan, almost the same color as his eyes.

"Please," Segundo offered, opening for Robert. The foreigner settled into the leather seat.

When the priest sat behind the steering wheel, Robert said, "I've never seen a clergyman driving a Mercedes-Benz."

"It's the family car." Segundo started the engine. "I drive it instead of using an official vehicle—it saves money for the diocese."

Robert noticed how Gaby's brother spoke of his "family" when he probably meant his father. This was clearly a man's car, expensive but austere, the kind of vehicle preferred by statesmen, generals and diplomats. Robert tried to pull out the seat belt. It stuck in its track.

"Don't worry," Segundo assured him, "you won't need it. Anyhow we're fatalists in Argentina." He laughed in a shrill tone that grated on the American's ears.

Robert was tempted to ask if the Church also espoused fatalism. But the car accelerated so fast that he had to cling to the seat. Segundo drove as aggressively as any other male in Buenos Aires, where Darwin's laws are proven daily on the streets. He sped up Avenida de Mayo, down Callao to Libertador, past the racetrack, where the crowd had thinned but many people still huddled around the gates. Robert saw more women and men sobbing and drying their eyes with handkerchiefs.

When they came to a stoplight, the priest asked, "Did you hear about the race this afternoon?"

"Yes."

"Many fortunes were made or lost in the sixth. A darkhorse won against great odds."

"I didn't know priests were racing fans too."

"Another pagan custom," Segundo responded with a tinge of humor. "Now that I think of it you're sort of a darkhorse yourself."

"What do you mean?"

"Nothing." The man honked his horn, either to warn a pedestrian or change the subject, Robert guessed. "First of all I should explain to you that I'm a priest but also an Argentine—so I love horseracing and soccer too. I never miss my team's games—River Plate, naturally. Second I'm a priest who is a Roca. My fath—" Again he stalled and failed to release the dreaded syllable, a bird striving futilely to escape a net. The signal turned green, Segundo stamped the throttle and his Mercedes jerked forward, throwing his passenger against the seatback.

"Your father," Robert interposed. He recalled the cavernous voice on the telephone, the large figure he had seen through the curtains of Gabriela's house, who he now surmised had not been Segundo.

The man recovered his voice. "Yes. My family owns a ranch with cattle and racehorses."

"I know."

They passed the Sanatorio Palermo, where she was probably still on duty, Robert estimated. He asked, "Does Gabriela know you're with me?"

"No. There are many things she doesn't know—we're trying to keep her from being hurt. That's why I went to see you at the hotel."

"I thought you said it was for my sake."

"It was for both of you." Robert doubted that Segundo cared about helping an American whom he hardly knew.

"How did you find out I'm staying at the Hotel Castelar?"

The priest did not answer. He headed south toward the Aeroparque Jorge Newbery, the airport for local and national flights. When they reached the river, Segundo hit the brakes and his car lurched to a stop by the jetty, where he turned off the engine.

I'll walk from here, Robert said to himself. As they left the car and stepped onto the embankment, the *malecón*, he felt relieved the trip had ended. An ugly cement wall separated them from the Río de la Plata.

The American and the Argentine contemplated that water, wide as a sea or an endless, muddy lake. For Robert it was unlike any river he had seen, not only because of its size and color: it did not appear to have waves or currents, to flow in any direction. A heavy mist hung over its surface, like a miasma rising from a swamp. Robert still had not seen the Río de la Plata in a storm when the wind blows from the southeast and roils the water like a sea.

"Her *novio*, her boyfriend's corpse is out there," Segundo said. He turned and stared down at Robert. "I don't want you to end up like Dionisio Sarmiento," he declared in the firm, clear voice of a person who had never stuttered. Hearing the victim's full name seemed to make the events more concrete for Robert, almost tangible. That young man had been not only Gaby's lover but a student, a citizen, an inhabitant of Buenos Aires, Argentina.

Segundo looked toward the river. "He had a head of curly, dark brown hair, not quite as long as yours. And blue eyes but without the shade of green in yours."

Small waves lapped almost imperceptibly on the embankment. For a moment they reminded Robert of her voice and her words about the war. He imagined the remains of a corpse—white bones lying on the muddy bottom. "Does Gabriela know he's there?"

"No—it would destroy her. My sister's very fragile." Segundo paused. "Would you like for me to drive you back to the hotel?"

"I'll walk."

"A good idea. You have a lot to think about, Robert." Segundo pointed south with one finger of a manicured hand. "Follow the malecón."

"Why did they kill Dionisio?"

"That's too complicated for a stranger to comprehend, especially a North American," the man replied airily. He offered his right hand to Robert, pronouncing "Goodbye." Segundo's grip was weak, like so many others' in a country where a strong handshake is not considered a requisite of manhood. He hesitated before adding, "Señor Wells, please know that I've spoken today for myself and my family. We have an expression—'*Al buen entendedor, pocas palabras.*'" A word to the wise is enough.

The priest smiled with all his teeth once more. Segundo wheeled, entered his car and bolted through the haze of Buenos Aires.

Robert paced along the boardwalk. The last light of day shone on the water. The image of Dionisio's corpse had stuck like a stain in his mind. He could not have known how many other cadavers lay there, men's and women's, their skeletons rotting in the mud on the bottom of a river that moved slowly, silently, invisibly to the ocean. But Robert knew he would see Gaby again, no matter what Virgilio, Segundo or anyone told him. Their resistance incited him, made him more impatient to be with her, know her more deeply, to learn why the whole world wanted to divide them.

Like a dark bird the evening descended on Buenos Aires. When Robert reached his room, he called Gabriela, expecting to hear a man's voice. Instead she picked up the phone herself, saying "Hola" in a liquid intonation that soothed his ears.

He asked her to dinner at the restaurant on Lavalle Street. She insisted on meeting earlier in the hotel café: "I'm going to be in your neighborhood anyway." Sister and brother in the same place, he thought, the same day. Could she know I've just met Segundo here?

Robert found a seat at the table where he had been with the brother. Gabriela arrived only a few minutes late. When she passed through the revolving door, she brought the spring evening in her walk, stirring the air, drawing looks from clients, waiters and barmen. She had let down her hair and it glistened like a black mane. Her silk dress seemed to fondle each dip and slope of her body. His pulse throbbed.

Forgiving Gabriela for everything, he stood to kiss her: sparks stung their lips, making both of them flinch. Robert breathed in her scent, stronger than whatever was trying to drive them apart.

She scanned his clothes. "Has your luck shifted?"

"I'll let you decide that."

Gabriela ignored his words. "Mine has been good! The staff at the hospital hates me for winning the sweepstakes. I picked up a little extra change, so I'll pay for our drinks."

Robert took her pale hand. They could feel the current between them. "Gaby, why does everyone want to keep me away from you?"

She gazed into his eyes. "What do you mean? Who's 'everyone'"?

"Your brother came to see me this afternoon. In fact he was sitting right where you are now."

She pulled her hand from his. "You met Segundo here?" She spoke in that other voice he had heard at the hospital.

"Yes." Gaping at her, Robert said, "We've known each other for two days and your family's already trying to separate us. That's the only reason your brother came here. Segundo told me that he's speaking for your family."

"He's not the one. It's ..." She halted, and her eyes clouded to a darker shade of violet. Gabriela blushed.

Robert would have liked to tell her about the calf's head, Dionisio and the river, her brother's tale of the minotaur, Virgilio in the baths. He imagined the small man in the steamy rooms, wrapped in a white towel, who might be directly below them in the hotel basement. But he suspected it would be too much for Gabriela now. Segundo's words floated through his mind: "My sister's very fragile." Robert did not wish to frighten her, to risk losing her so soon. He did not know how many other men had also tried to protect her from the suffering that followed her buoyant step like a shadow through the streets of Buenos Aires.

"What else did Segundo tell you?"

"Just that—to forget about you and leave the country."

"Are you going to do that?"

"No."

With a starched napkin draped on one arm, a mozo stood behind a column, watching the couple. He did not dare advance while an electric storm seemed to hang over their table. When somebody pushed the revolving door, the room breathed in the night air and the waiter sensed an opening.

He took their orders for vermouth and sodas. How much has changed since we had the same cocktail on the first night, Robert told himself. But by the next drink he was lost in the wells of Gabriela's eyes. The flayed head, Segundo, her former boyfriend, Virgilio receded from his memory.

She invited her new friend to Escorpión, an expensive restaurant downtown. The image of a red scorpion stood over the entrance. Only later would Robert learn that it was her lethal, watery sign.

After supper Gabriela took him to a tango bar on Balcarce, where she wounded him with songs of love, loss, betrayal and revenge. They drank, talked, listened to the music, danced, ate, drank more, ended up in a taxi again. Day broke over the muddy river.

Robert told their cabbie to cruise along the avenues. The man affected a curved, inch-long nail on the pinkie of his right hand, proud symbol of a life without toil. As he drove through the gray streets of dawn, the man used that finger to scrape his ears. Every once in a while he checked his passengers through the rearview mirror. He must have felt the current that was galvanizing his vehicle.

Robert held her tightly. After she said something in his ear, he told the cabbie to head for the Castelar. By now their longing for one another was like a pain in their ribcages.

When they pulled in front of the hotel, Gabriela glanced up at Robert, her eyes opened wide the way she had looked the first afternoon. "I can't." She paused. "I must go home," she uttered as if she were speaking to someone else.

"Gabriela."

She whispered in his ear, "Paciencia Osito." His head echoed with Gabriela's words, Segundo's, both at once—he did not know whose anymore.

She sat up and told the driver, "Go to Dragones in Belgrano."

A dark Ford Falcon followed them through the acacia-lined streets of the Barrio Norte. Gabriela observed it from the corner of one eye, while Robert merely thought she was distracted. When they reached her home, it seemed oddly familiar and unknown to him, as though he had dreamed it.

He walked her to the unlit zaguán. Once more Gabriela did not look at Robert as they said goodbye. The door, carved with angels and demons entwined, swallowed her.

6
Killing Fields

Giggling again, the woman sold him a ticket. The attendant with a pimpled face handed him a pair of white towels. Robert walked down the corridor, heard the boilers chug and the fans whir. Without seeing another soul, he entered the first room, the second, the third or calidarium. He expected Virgilio to spring suddenly out of the steamy mist.

Robert sat in a wooden chair. He had to strain his eyes to see through clouds of vapor. He could barely discern the old men who were seated on the rows of wooden benches in the center of the circular hall. They stood, approached, stared at him. From their midst he heard what sounded like a chuckle. A peal of laughter followed, louder, jeers, guffaws swelling until the whole room echoed. Those men pointed at Robert, grinned through their toothless gums, slapped their hands on their bowed knees, ripped off their towels, snapped them on the benches and floor. Now they were doing a kind of shuffling dance, coming toward him again, forming a semi-circle, closer until he turned to sprint away, feeling the hot air and smelling their rancid breath behind him. Finally Robert reached the door, yanked it open, dashed down the dark tunnel, looked back to see if they were following. He felt the colder air and knew he was alone in the baths of Buenos Aires and the world.

When a jackhammer blasted a hole in the sidewalk on Avenida de Mayo, Robert awoke with a scream. He did not know where he was—Ong Thanh with rockets battering the base camp, his apartment in Los Angeles with the rush of traffic outside, in the Turkish baths with the old men in pursuit? But he lay on a bed in his room at the Hotel Castelar. It was Sunday morning.

He would have liked to call Gabriela, but it was too early: 10:25. As much as he dreaded the baths now, Robert determined to seek out Virgilio. Maybe he would tell the little man about the calf's head, about Segundo, their conversation in the hotel café and on the riverfront. Perhaps the dwarf already knew? Recalling Virgilio's joke about Argentina, he phoned room service for breakfast.

The same woman in the booth sold him a ticket for the baths, the same man tendered him a towel. Virgilio had departed an hour ago. "Sometimes he goes up for fresh air," the attendant explained.

Robert spun, returned his ticket and left the scene of his nightmare. He did not understand why he felt so dispirited about not seeing Virgilio. After all he had just met the dwarf and could hardly call him a friend. But so far in this new country the small man was the only person in whom Robert could confide; there were too many things he could not tell Gabriela.

He called her from the phone at the front desk. With a sleepy voice she answered, telling him she had to work the afternoon shift. They could meet tonight.

He thought of finding another hotel in the meantime, but he could not face a move. His room on the top floor was safer, Robert believed, also more comfortable than the first.

The sun shone softly on Avenida de Mayo, where he had walked with Gabriela. He was glad to leave the hotel and its memories for a while, to walk on a spring morning through the streets of Buenos Aires, her city.

Colectivos bobbed up and down the avenue with their vivid colors, reds, blues, yellows, greens, their hand-painted scrolls and filigrees. They resembled big toy buses in a voluptuous, carefree country. Not Argentina, this nation that had suffered the bloodiest civil war in South America, a shameful defeat in the Falkland Islands, enough financial crashes to wreck another state for good.

Robert decided to jump onto the first bus, a yellow colectivo that said *LA BOCA* above the windshield. The name reminded him of Gabriela and the taste of her saliva. He was too dazzled by the honey light to see the tall man in a baseball cap who was following the bus in a black Ford Falcon.

The colectivo was so full that Robert had to stand in the rear with other passengers, mostly men. They jerked and bounced along, the brakes squealing at stoplights, his head bumping the roof with every pothole. Through the window he spotted a slice of mud-colored river, pushed his way to the door and descended at the next corner.

Robert found himself in a neighborhood of buildings with walls of sun-bleached, chipping plaster. Children played in the streets, emaciated dogs slept in doorways, men stood and smoked on corners, women sat by windows and on balconies where hopeful flags of laundry rippled. From courtyards he heard snatches of tangos and boleros. On peeling walls graffiti yelled *¡PERÓN VIVE!* and *¡LA MADONA Y MARADONA!* He passed stores with fruits and vegetables displayed in wooden crates on the sidewalks.

Sweat beaded on Robert's forehead. Closer to the river he saw houses of wood and sheet metal built on pylons, painted in colors like M&M's, red, yellow, green, orange. At a corner he came to a *boliche* or tavern with open doors, where aromas of food wafted onto the street.

Hardly glancing up, a man behind the bar said, *"Buen día."* He had a bald head, brown skin and a neck as stout as a bull's. Around his collar he wore a silver cross.

Robert took a seat at the bar. "What smells so good?" he asked. He could hear the sizzling of a pan or grill.

"Empanadas. How many would you like?"

"I'll start with one. And a cold beer."

"Nobody has ever been known to eat one of our empanadas without ordering a second or third, Señor."

The owner took a bottle of Salta lager from a refrigerator and poured a glass. He placed it on the wooden counter in front of the newcomer. When he disappeared into the kitchen, Robert surveyed the room, where he saw tables, chairs and faded calendars of saints on the whitewashed walls. The man returned in a few moments with the meat pie on a plate.

Robert punctured the light brown crust with his fork. The fragrance of spices issued from the holes made by the tines, filling his nostrils. It was too hot to eat. But he could not resist biting into the empanada.

"What do you think, *pues*?" the man inquired with a grin.

"You're right," Robert admitted. The roof of his mouth burned. "Another please."

"Beatriz, *otra*!" this man called to the kitchen. "Later on she'll make empanadas from fresh tuna. We buy the best beef and fish every morning in spite of the inflation. *Qué situación!*" He threw both arms above his shoulders. "The country's going to hell. First the generals screwed us, then the English in the Malvinas, now the politicians—always the politicians. How much longer can we go on like this?"

"I only arrived a few days ago."

"Where are you from?"

"The United States." Robert kept himself from saying "América," knowing Latin Americans do not believe the U.S. should have a monopoly on a word that belongs to the whole Western hemisphere.

"You didn't help us a damn bit in the Malvinas," the owner said—"the 'Falklands' as you call them in English. Actually Argentina isn't all that bad in spite of the generals and politicians. You can still live better here than anywhere. Che, tell me where you could find an empanada like that one?" He pointed to his customer's empty plate. "I'll be right back with the second." Robert was surprised by this assault of national pride in the same man who was decrying his nation a minute before.

The owner returned with the new meat pie. "This is how we make empanadas in my home town of Salta," he said, expanding his chest. "They're famous all over the Republic. Have you been in the north?"

"Hombre, this is only my third day in Argentina." Robert listened to his own words, wondering if it was true—it seemed so much longer, his life changed forever, he thought.

The man observed the foreigner's glass. "Another Salta?"

"Yes. Another empanada too."

"I warned you. Beatriz, *otra!*"

Serving the beer, the man said or asked, "You don't mind if I keep you company with a little wine?" He did not wait for a reply, poured himself a glass of red. "Did you know the per capita consumption of wine is higher in Argentina than anywhere in the world? I'm doing my part to keep us in first place—my patriotic duty." He quaffed the red as though it were a shot of whisky, then refilled his glass.

"*Ya está!*" came a voice from inside.

"*Traéla vos!*" the owner called.

Carrying a steaming empanada on a plate, her face beaded with perspiration, a lady trudged out of the kitchen. Her shoulders were stooped as if she had spent a lifetime cleaning, cooking and serving. She wore a food-spattered apron and a white scarf on her head. The women in the Plaza de Mayo flashed through Robert's mind, who had the names of their lost children, grandchildren, nephews or nieces embroidered on their scarves.

"*Mi mujer,*" the man pronounced in the possessive Hispanic way.

"Mucho gusto, Señor," she said. She set the meat pie before Robert and removed the two empty dishes.

"The *caballero* is from the United States," her husband told her.

"*Los Estados Unidos,*" this woman repeated in a singsong, as though that country were on the moon. She looked up at Robert. "You have a nice thick head of hair, Señor. Are there bald men in the United States?"

Swallowing a bite of his third empanada, he tried to suppress a smile. "*Sí Señora,*" Robert mumbled, "*pero muy pocos,*" just a few. He would not have liked to destroy her illusion. The woman plodded back to her kitchen.

"Did you hear about the *la potra tràgica?*" the owner asked.

Robert reflected for a moment. "The horse they sacrificed at the Hipódromo yesterday?"

"Right—that's what they're calling her now, the tragic filly. I have a customer in the business who told me the generals made a killing."

"They're in racing too?"

"They've got their fat mitts in everything. A bunch of them own *Amour Fou*, the darkhorse who won the sweepstakes."

As the man swilled wine, Robert remembered Gabriela, her words at the hospital. Also when Segundo compared him to a darkhorse—what in hell did he mean by that?

The owner smacked the bottom of his glass on the bar. "Where else have you been in Buenos Aires?"

"Only the Plaza de Mayo, Palermo and a few other places."

"Did you see the Madres and *Abuelas* march on Thursday?"

"Yes."

"My own mother, my wife and sister all went there every week until a few years ago. Then my mother died and my wife"—he pointed to the kitchen—"she's always tired from work. My sister and her husband still go once in a while but it makes them sad."

When the man leaned forward with both elbows on the bar, Robert could tell that he desired to talk more. "Did they lose somebody in the war?"

"Their daughter, my only niece, fifteen years old and a flower of a girl." As if there were people nearby, he scanned the room and spoke in a lower voice: "She was one of the eleven thousand who 'disappeared'—one of the biggest euphemisms ever created. Some say there were as many as thirty thousand. We know who the *podridos* are, the bastards who ordered the killing but we're helpless to do anything. They're still powerful and they've got the politicians by the balls," he said, cupping both hands in the traditional gesture. "That's why President Alfonsín signed the amnesty laws and Menem keeps doling out executive pardons."

Robert felt awkward eating in the presence of the owner's anger, his loss and the fate of those thousands of women, men and children. The memory of Ong Thanh blew back into his mind, his dream in the night, his comrades who had died or disappeared in action. Although he still had two-thirds of an empanada on his plate, Robert put down his knife and fork.

The man understood. "I'm sorry," he said, looking directly into his customer's blue-green eyes. "If you were Argentine I wouldn't have said anything about those years. With foreigners I feel the urge to let them know how terrible it was. When your life is worse than your nightmares, it's hard to forget." The man paused. "Did you fly into Ezeiza Airport?"

"Yes."

"Did you notice the park and picnic grounds on the road to town, with all the eucalyptus trees?"

"Yes." They had reminded Robert of Los Angeles, the tall, pale trees with fragile limbs and flaking bark that he and his friends had climbed as children.

"It was a killing field, *amigo*. At dawn the police would discover burnt-out chassis of cars with incinerated bodies strapped to the seats. That's how they found my niece Victoria one Friday morning. The sons-of-bitches must have soaked her clothes in gasoline—she was burnt so much that . . ." The man looked away for a moment and wiped his eyes. "We had to identify her by the fillings in her teeth." Robert conjured villages strafed with napalm, heads, limbs and torsos blackened like pieces of kindling wood; his own comrades, the dead, the wounded ones, splattered with blood and writhing in pain. But in that war, he sensed, thousands of miles from home, he could not have known what this man felt, much less the girl's parents when they saw her charred body that morning in their own city of Buenos Aires.

"There were killing fields everywhere," the owner started again. His neck had turned red from rage. "Right here in La Boca where the people live, in the Barrio Norte where *they* live."

"Who?" Robert asked. He pictured Gabriela's neighborhood.

"The generals, admirals and politicians who arranged most of the killings. But even their places weren't safe. Have you visited Recoleta?"

Robert recalled the rainy afternoon with Gaby, the café and the spreading tree. "I've been to La Biela."

The man sized up his customer and looked at Robert in a different way. "Another battlefield. Both the generals and the guerrillas knew a bombing at La Biela would attract publicity."

Robert wondered why Gaby, with all her bad memories of the war, would have taken him there. Why did she not tell him? He drank the sour, tepid beer from the bottom of his glass.

"We perfected the drive-by shooting," the owner went on, "the bigger the street the better. You've been on Avenida 9 de Julio, right?"

"Widest boulevard I've ever seen."

"Pues many Argentines fell on its sidewalks, gunned down by death cars—unmarked Ford Falcons, normally green. We always used to tell our friends to walk against the traffic."

"Why?"

"So they would at least know which way the bullet came from." The owner tried to laugh, revealing a mouthful of white teeth. He picked up a dishtowel and wiped an imaginary spot from the bar.

Robert rose from his stool. Removing his wallet, he asked, "*Cuánto le debo?*"

"Thirty thousand of those worthless rags." The deadly number made the two men look at each other in recognition. "I hope I didn't scare you away with my stories. Please return, *compadrito*. Where you staying?"

"Hotel Castelar." The red paint and the calf's head rushed back into Robert's mind.

"That place also has a history. Che, don't be a stranger—you must come back to taste our fish empanadas." Extending his right hand, he introduced himself. "Francisco Quiroga, *pa' servirle*. And don't lose hope. Remember, every night God undoes the mess the Argentines make during the day." Both men laughed.

When Robert walked outside, the golden light had melted into the orange sky of dusk. A gale was kicking up. Over the bar's entrance a sign clanked in the wind—*EL BOLICHE Vinos Cervezas Comidas*. As Robert retraced his steps, he saw laundry on plastic clotheslines, streaming like comets' tails from balconies, snapping in the air. Dust and debris eddied on the sidewalks. On spindly trees the dry leaves shook, crackled and whirled away.

Robert observed the candy-colored houses from the rear this time. Their bright façades hid bleak, ramshackle dwellings. He must have made a wrong turn because he came to El Riachuelo, the rank, polluted river that borders La Boca to the south. He saw abandoned cranes, corroded freighters and the beached carcasses of half-sunken trawlers. The wind was heaving billows on the dark water.

In the twilight he boarded a colectivo. Through the windows he watched lights turning on in bars and cafés. Robert felt the accumulated fatigue of travel, a new city, a night and morning haunted by bad dreams. When he jumped off the bus near his hotel, his eyes teared from the wind.

A dark, legless man spotted him and wheeled across the sidewalk on a skateboard, holding out a cup. On his chest he wore a piece of cardboard with bold words painted in scarlet— *VETERANO DE MALVINAS*. They reminded Robert of the letters on his door at the Castelar.

Searching for change in his pocket, he thought of the maimed veterans of Vietnam who wander the streets of American cities. He could evoke some of their faces, those he used to greet in the morning on his way to work downtown, in the evening on his way home. As he dropped a few coins in the man's tin cup, turning his eyes away from the cutting wind, Robert could also see Diane in his mind, her wheat-colored hair blowing in the storm of his dream the other day. Somehow the memory of her and their city, Los Angeles, Our Lady Queen of the Angels, no longer seemed so bitter.

7
Avenida de Mayo

"**Let's meet somewhere else** tonight," he told her on the phone. "The Castelar's not bringing me luck."

"But I'm going to be in your neighborhood again," Gabriela replied in her voice like water.

"Why?"

"I'll tell you when we meet at the hotel café. I'll be there around eleven."

Robert showered, dressed in a new shirt and pair of pants. After taking the private elevator to the lobby, he felt that he was retracing the same path up and down, over and over.

The café had undergone a metamorphosis. From a stuffy private club for doting matrons and patriarchs in the afternoon and early evening, it had become a stylish late-night domain for young people in suede and leather. Robert observed long-haired porteñas strutting through the revolving doors in flawless makeup and miniskirts, followed by their suntanned escorts with gold chains around their necks.

He chose a table as far as possible from the last one, where he had met brother then sister. Once more she arrived late. Gabriela lived as if time had not been invented, he thought, wondering how she had made it through medical school. When she strode through the door, his heart could have skipped: she moved with her light-footed step through the crowd, holding her head high on the white column of her neck. She wore a long skirt with overlapping layers of blouse, vest and scarf, all in tones of amber and beige. Like the other clients she showed lots of leather—a fitted jacket, tapered gloves, a tawny purse, calfskin pumps. Argentina, country of dead meat and hides.

He kissed Gabriela's cheek. Both felt the current between them. In the café's lights her hair shone like a raven's wing. "It's a different place at night," Robert told her.

"Buenos Aires is like that," she said about the city she loved. "Everything changes in the dark." As she took her seat, the curved moons in Gabriela's earlobes, her beaded bracelets and the snake pendant around her neck all swung with her movement.

"You also change?"

"Especially me. Remember I was born at night." Like a model sitting for a portrait she turned in a three-quarter pose and crossed her legs. With her eyes turned away from Robert she smiled, knowing he was admiring her. Gabriela's allure varied with each nuance of angle or light, he thought as he watched her, and how fast he was sinking into her life.

A mozo was eyeing their table. He stood clear of the electric field between the couple, waiting for an opening. When he spotted it, he approached, took their order and carried it to the bar.

Heaving a sigh, Robert settled in his chair. "Gaby. There's something I need to tell you." If he didn't speak soon, it would be drowned in the sea of her eyes.

"What now?" She shifted in her chair, restless.

"When I went back to my room yesterday I found a flayed calf's head on the floor." She suppressed a cry with the white palm of her hand. "The carpet was soaked in blood."

Gabriela shivered and leaned forward in her chair. "Did you tell Segundo?"

"No. It would have made his case even stronger."

"What case?"

"For me to go away."

She turned paler. "You're not going are you, Osito?"

"No. I told you that."

"This is more and more like the *Proceso*," Gabriela said, using the stale, official word for the longest seven years in Argentina's history.

He was tempted to tell her about Dionisio's body on the river bed. But when her purplish eyes watered, Robert realized it would be too much for her at once. Always too much, he thought. Why am I trying to protect Gabriela like her brother? "Who's doing all of this to us?"

She did not reply. They sat in silence. The waiter served their vermouth and sodas.

When the mozo had gone, Gabriela glanced down at the floor of black-and-white marble squares. "You have to leave this hotel," she said in a faraway voice.

"I didn't even want to meet here tonight."

Gabriela examined the shirt he was wearing for the first time in Buenos Aires. With one of her slender hands she rubbed his chest. A sad smile may have crossed her lips. "You've changed your clothes for better luck." After sipping her drink, she paused for a long time. "The Castelar's close to a clinic where I work at night on weekends. That's why I preferred to meet here." By now Robert was used to her way of coming back to a subject, minutes, hours or days later.

"You work there and also do full shifts at the hospital?"

"That's the life of many doctors in Argentina." She looked into Robert's eyes. "I do volunteer work for the Madres in a clinic right down the street from here."

"On Sunday nights?"

"Sometimes on Saturdays too. Nobody else wants to work on weekends, especially at night." Gabriela took another sip of her vermouth. "Osito, why don't you rent an apartment?"

"I can't afford one. I still owe a fortune to my lawyer and I'm already paying rent in Los Angeles."

"A divorce lawyer?"

"Yes."

"Maybe I can help you."

"Didn't you say doctors barely earn minimum wage?"

"I've just come into more money."

"You mean the horserace?" Gabriela nodded. "Didn't you say it was only a little extra change."

Her eyes turned away again. "Sometime I'll tell you."

"Why not now?"

"Too much is happening."

Robert shrugged his wide shoulders. "Anyhow why would an apartment be any safer than my hotel room? There's a private elevator and a guard on my floor."

"You never told me that."

"They gave me a new room after I found the calf's head."

"Oh. Maybe that would be safer." Gabriela talked slowly, as if she knew something she did not wish to reveal. "It's just—" She stopped, blushing. "It's just that it would be easier—"

"For us to be together," he helped her, feeling a rush of joy in his chest.

"Thank you Osito. If I didn't feel so drawn to you I'd tell you to leave the country." She ran a finger around the lip of her glass, gazing at the floor. "Roberto, when I hear your voice on the phone my heart races. When I see you my tongue feels thick, I can hardly speak at first, my ears hum. I want you to stay with me in Buenos Aires. But I'm afraid for you, for us. I haven't been this scared since the war." Gabriela finally looked up, and Robert thought he could see the fear in the pools of her eyes.

"Maybe I should go to the police," he said.

"No!"

"Why?"

"You can't trust them—we learned that during the war."

"It's over."

"To me it seems like yesterday. Or today."

He desired her quickly with a force he scarcely recognized. Robert imagined loving Gabriela could heal everything that had wounded her, all that stood between them, anything her family or others did to pull them apart. He inclined forward in his chair, breathed in her fragrance of salt and spices. With one hand he grazed the freckles on her cheek. Both felt a shock while the sparks hissed between them. Men and women turned toward Robert and Gabriela.

"Let's leave before we electrocute the clientele," she said with a half-smile.

They walked along Avenida de Mayo, holding each other's hand, their hips and elbows bumping with a life of their own. The air was charged around them. She found one of her favorite parrillas nearby, where they ordered two *tiras de asado*, strips of roasted beef ribs that were unlike any cut Robert had tasted. A liter of Malbec evaporated in their glasses.

When they rose from the table, their heads were spinning from the wine and from being together. Customers gaped at Robert and Gabriela as the couple walked outside. She waited on the curb while he searched for a cab, surprised that another black Mercedes did not approach instantly for her. Against the darkness he peered into a galaxy of lights along the Avenida de Mayo, at the cars streaming by on a Sunday evening. A clever porteño tried to impress his date, a tall woman with platinum hair, by stepping in front of the American to hail a taxi.

Robert felt so elated to be with Gaby that he merely smiled, raised his arm to flag down another cab. He spotted a dark vehicle with a single headlight—the left—coming his way. Instead of slowing as it drew closer, the car accelerated, its driver shifted into a higher gear and veered toward the sidewalk. Robert leapt backwards, landed near Gabriela's feet. They saw the car sweep beyond them and over the curb, hit a metal trash bin that careened into a storefront, make a thud as it struck a young man and woman with its right fender, thrust them into the air and onto the cement. People were already screaming when the vehicle swerved to the left, collided with a kiosk, bounced down the curb. For a second it reminded Robert of a newlyweds' car, dragging a loose bumper on the asphalt as it sped away.

Gabriela grasped him by the shoulders, asked if he was hurt. When he shook his head, she dashed off, moving so fast that one of her small, open-toe shoes dropped on the sidewalk behind her. Robert leapt to his feet, retrieved it and attempted to follow, but he was penned in by a shifting wall of backs, shoulders, elbows. Since he was taller than most of the people in that crush, he could see Gabriela ahead of him, clearing a path as if she had a wedge in front of her, calling "*Médico! Abran paso!*"

Now she was standing inside a circle of pedestrians, speaking in an assertive voice he had not heard before, directing the crowd to stand clear of the victims. "*Socorro, socorro!*" Help! the man was calling while the woman writhed and moaned at his side, bleeding from her face, ribs and legs.

Gabriela commandeered jackets and coats from passersby to keep the pair warm, ripped off her scarf and vest to make a tourniquet above the gash where the woman's leg was spurting blood, monitored their heartbeats, took their pulse on neck and wrist. She had kneeled at their side, barefoot now. She stroked their faces, spoke to them softly, comforted them.

With sirens blaring the police arrived. Gabriela told them, "*Soy médico,*" showed some kind of document. Soon they were also obeying her orders, keeping gawkers away, giving the injured man and woman space and air to breathe. With more sirens and lights flashing, paramedics drove their ambulance onto the sidewalk, consulted Gabriela and placed the victims on stretchers. Before departing they told her the name of the hospital where they would rush the injured pair.

The rest of that night was hunting for Gabriela's missing shoe, proceeding to the *Comisaría* with other witnesses, waiting, giving their reports to an officer. Nobody had recorded the full license plate, but the police had cobbled together a possible number from several people. They had also identified the vehicle as an older black Ford Falcon. When Robert heard the name and model of that car, he shuddered. Quiroga's words at the boliche echoed in his memory.

A slick-haired police captain, smugly aware of his status, told the witnesses that he might or might not be able to locate the driver. When he offered to take Gabriela and Robert home, she answered in a tone beyond appeal: "No!" The officer would notify her if they recovered the Falcon.

By the time she and Robert left the station, it was nearly two o'clock in the morning. Traffic still swirled unforgivingly on Avenida de Mayo. Both felt parched. They stopped in a bar for two glasses of wine apiece. In silence they also shared a bottle of mineral water. Gabriela's hands, arms, blouse and skirt were splotched with blood drying to the color of rust.

She surprised him with her words: "Take me back to the hotel. I need to wash and my house is too far away."

When Robert said, "You really are a doctor," she traced one of her wan smiles. "You were magnificent out there, Gaby. It was a battlefield."

"I know. But the biggest war of my life was to become a doctor. One of them anyway."

"Was your family against it?"

"Mostly my mother. None of the women in her family had careers—all they did was get married, raise children and go to charity balls."

"What about your father?"

Gabriela did not reply, but her expression changed. "I don't think the woman's going to survive. She lost too much blood and her pulse was faint at the end. But the man will make it." To Robert it seemed that she had just determined the victims' fates.

Leaning against each other, they walked back to the Castelar, resembling two invalids. Both could feel the wine in their heads, the shock of the accident, the emptiness inside.

A desk clerk asked for Robert's room number.

"Sixty-six."

The man opened a leather-bound register. "I show only one person checked into that room." He feigned not looking at Gabriela but peeked at her from the corner of one eye.

"This lady is a doctor who just saved two lives on Avenida de Mayo!" Robert stated, lifting his voice. "She needs to wash up."

The clerk scanned Gabriela's blood-spattered clothes. "All guests must be registered, Señor."

Robert shouted, "Did you register the bastards who smeared my door with paint and left the calf's head in my room?" His words alarmed an elderly couple in the lobby, who craned their necks toward the desk.

The clerk glanced meekly at Gabriela before facing his customer again. "I must take down some information from the lady."

The man appeared so chastened that Robert decided to go along. Instead of giving her real name, Gabriela choose a character from a story by Borges, knocked a few years from her age and invented an address on Avenida Cruz del Sur. When she had finished, she confided an untranslatable obscenity in Robert's ear.

"I can't believe this could happen in a city like Buenos Aires in 1990," he told Gabriela on the elevator.

She touched his arm. "You're in a country where divorce was only legalized three years ago. In some ways we're still living in the last century." Then she raised the corners of her mouth with the intimation of a smile. "Osito, you'll have to admit the desk clerk had his reasons."

"For what?"

"For being suspicious. After all we haven't been very good for business at the Hotel Castelar."

Robert laughed. "Thanks for making it 'we.' Did you see the faces of that couple in the lobby?"

"*Pobres.*"

As he turned the key to his room, he asked, "What if the clerk had wanted proof?"

"That would have been going too far with a lady in Argentina. We have thousands of petty bureaucrats like him but at least they view themselves as gentlemen."

"But you were taking a chance, right?"

"I had no choice. If Father learns about this he won't forgive me." Gabriela lowered her head and seemed to stare at something on the threshold of Robert's room.

"Is there really an Avenida Cruz del Sur?" he asked her with his hand on the doorknob. It was hard for an American to imagine a street named for a constellation, the Southern Cross. He had grown up in a neighborhood of Los Angeles where most streets had the names of trees or millionaires.

"Yes but I don't live there."

Robert took Gabriela's arm. "I love the way you go from tragedy to humor. Two hours ago you were treating patients in an emergency, now you're making up a story like a little girl."

"I do it to survive. And by the way I am a little girl." Gabriela squeezed his arm.

As soon as he closed the door behind them, her demeanor changed. "I think that vehicle was trying to hit you, Roberto."

"Why?"

"Did you know that Ford Falcons were killer cars during the war?"

"I've heard that."

"I saw it heading straight toward you. Did you see the driver?"

"It was too dark and the car had tinted windows."

"I couldn't make out his face but I saw the outline of a cap on his head."

"The police said there may be enough information to locate him." She sighed. "Alright," Robert conceded, "forget the police."

Gabriela reflected for a moment. "Oh I forgot—the Madres." She glided to the telephone, dialed a number, explained why she had not been able to work tonight. Then she stepped into the bathroom and closed the door. Robert heard the splashing of water in the tub.

Streetlights filtered through the curtains. Feeling his head whirl, he dropped into a leather armchair and reclined. Robert closed his eyes. A stream of bloody animals, the injured man and woman floated through his mind.

Gabriela emerged from the bathroom, barefoot, wrapped in a bath towel. The waterfall of her hair spilled onto her shoulders and her back. "Osito I'd love to have a bottle of champagne. Could you call room service?"

Recalling Virgilio's joke, Robert asked her, "Do you know how some people define Argentina?"

"I don't want to know."

Robert told her anyway. She did not laugh or smile. Gabriela had been ordering room service all her life; nothing seemed more natural.

While he called downstairs, she took a small bunch of wilted roses from her purse, found a glass on the nightstand and filled it with water from the bathroom sink. She dropped the flowers inside and placed them on the dresser. Robert wondered if they could be remnants of the Indian girl's bouquet. But hadn't they forgotten the roses that first night? He felt too drained to ask Gabriela.

From her purse she also withdrew a vial of perfume. She dabbed her ears, neck, wrists, her bare arms and legs. Next she sat by a window in a second armchair, wider than the first, upholstered in leather too. In a posture from an impressionist painting, leaning her head now to one side, now the other, Gabriela combed the water from her hair.

Robert removed his coat. Being alone in a room with her for the first time, seeing her almost naked in the chair, he felt at once thrilled and unsettled. He did not know what to do with his big hands. From the Avenida de Mayo six stories below, the noise of traffic rushed through the half-open windows. It was Sunday night in Buenos Aires, they were together, and they were waiting for room service.

A teenage boy wheeled in a cart that held a silver tray, two champagne flutes, a bucket with a bottle of black-labeled Alvear Brut packed in ice. Robert was relieved to have something practical to do—peel off the silver foil, untwist the metal ring, cover the top of the bottle with a towel before pulling the cork. It exploded: champagne sprayed the furniture, the floor, the bed where the maid had turned back the sheets and set a piece of chocolate in a turquoise wrapper on a cream-colored pillow.

Robert filled the flutes, handed one to Gabriela and raised his own. Peering into each other's eyes, they clinked the crystal, inhaled the yeasty fragrance and sipped.

They were at the stage when more alcohol can chase drunkenness, even kill it for a while. Robert squeezed next to Gabriela on the big armchair. Without saying it, they knew he was lucky to be there, that the young woman could die in the hospital. It made the moment remorseful and irresistible.

Gabriela traced a circle with one finger around the rim of her glass. Cocking her head to one side, she watched the bubbles rising. "Remember the story about the first champagne? What the monk said when he tasted it?"

"*Santé?*"

"No, silly. 'I'm drinking stars.'"

Robert looked into Gabriela's face. As though he was seeing it for the first time, he noted its heart-like shape. "If the monk had known you," he told her, tilting toward craziness, "he would have thought your freckles were the stars." He rubbed two fingers against the constellation on Gabriela's forehead. Both flinched from the static, spilled champagne on themselves, laughed together. He kissed her cheeks and eyelids, feeling a tingle on his tongue and lips.

Gabriela shivered, squirmed away and extended her arm with an empty flute. "*Plus de champagne, mon frère.*"

Robert refilled their glasses. Entwining their wrists and feeling the initial shock, they drank. He took Gabriela's flute, placed it next to his on the table, then eased her onto the bed. He unwrapped the towel from her upper body, uncovering the galaxies of freckles on her shoulders.

"Are these the hidden constellations?"

"You'll have to find out."

Robert reached for one of the flutes on the night table, who knows which one, took a sip and set it down. He swirled the Alvear in his mouth, leaned over Gabriela and let it pass between his teeth onto her warm tongue. She savored it, rose, unbuttoned his shirt, sucked on the wine-drenched cloth, pulled it off his torso and flung it to the floor. As she undressed him, a pile of garments grew there.

They stretched on their sides. With their feet touching, Gabriela's head nestled in the hollow between Robert's chin and shoulder. "You fit so well," he told her. Again he reached for a glass on the table and dribbled the rest of the sparkling wine on Gabriela's shoulders, in the shaved nests of her armpits, the small valleys above her collarbones, on the aureolas of her breasts, on her flanks and belly, her soft center, down to her thighs, ankles, toes. He sought that trail of dew upwards with his tongue, the wetness warmed by her skin and blending with her taste of grass, salt and honey.

Arching her body, Gabriela threw her head back over the pillow. Her throat made a curve and she glimpsed light from the avenue where it shone on the ceiling. From that moment she did not see Robert, she held something inside even when they began to move together, when she made her music, soft as a cat's purr, when she pressed her fingernails against his spine, they rocked back and forth on the bed, flying above it now, the noise of the city faded, she gasped, he cried out and a flock of doves swooped by their window.

They did not come down until a car crashed below them on the street. Both startled. Gabriela lowered her watery gaze from the ceiling and stared at Robert. "Osito, if you knew how many people die in accidents every weekend in my city." She sighed. "Oh how I hope the young woman made it." She embraced him.

"Shall we phone the hospital?"

She considered before saying, "Not yet." She drew a deep breath. "You know we're so close to the Plaza de Mayo that I can't stop remembering the Madres."

"Why? All I can remember is the accident."

"It was not—" Gabriela stopped, her mouth half-open. Robert was growing accustomed to her habit of waiting, pondering before she finished an utterance. He pulled away from her. On her upper arm he saw the ghost of a vaccination, a little circle with two lines in the center, roughly the shape of a cross. He wanted to possess it and every centimeter of her body.

"Not an accident," Gabriela resumed. "All of this reminds me of the war and him." Robert did not follow at first, guessing she was coming back to a subject they had broached earlier. "Dionisio was the first man I ever loved—I mean besides Father." Gabriela's eyes clouded and her cheeks flushed. "When he disappeared I used all my family's influence to find him. Uncles and friends of the family who are colonels, senators, cardinals, industrialists. They couldn't help me."

Robert recalled her brother and the riverfront, Virgilio's story in the Turkish baths. He placed one hand on her shoulder. "Or maybe they didn't want to help you?"

His question took Gabriela aback: how could a foreigner show such understanding of her people and the war after a mere three days in the country?

"Segundo told me about him," Robert said.

"Oh, I thought so. It's been ten years almost to the day since Dionisio vanished." Robert calculated how long ago he had left Vietnam, where he had lost so many comrades—my own desaparecidos, he called them now. Fifteen years.

"It's been even longer for most of the Madres and Abuelas, the Mothers and Grandmothers," Gabriela continued. "I tried to be faithful too." Robert surmised from her body, so nervously sentient at his side, that she could not have been alone during all those years. His mind was spinning.

She held Robert closely, kissed his neck and rose from the bed. "I'm supposed to work at the hospital this morning." Gabriela removed a paper from her purse. She dialed a number on the telephone.

Facing away from Robert, still naked, she spoke into the receiver with her doctor's voice. As if in slow motion her hand returned the phone to its cradle. She whispered, "The woman died at 3:39 a.m."

Robert felt a twinge of pain in his chest. Probably while we were making love, he thought. He embraced her from behind and said, "Gaby, nobody could have saved her." She turned slowly and wept into the hollow of his chest. Both knew he could have been the one who died.

"I'm not afraid of it when I'm with you," Robert told her.

"I know."

"Are you?"

Gabriela lowered her eyes for an answer. He guided her back to the bed. He covered her with sheets and blankets as a father or mother would tuck a child to sleep. When he lay down at her side, Robert felt her body shaking. At dawn he fell asleep while her eyes were fixed on the wall, wide open, shedding tears.

8
Scarlet Eden

They ordered a late breakfast in the room, *café con leche* served in big white ceramic cups alongside orange juice, croissants, butter and marmalade. Lying on her back and looking at Robert, Gabriela had nearly become herself again. She told him that croissants are called *medialunas* in Argentina, half-moons. He liked this name and set one of them on the starry sky of her forehead. When she laughed, it fell onto the sheets that were now flecked with crumbs, stained with wine and the traces of their love.

Gabriela, food and coffee cleared Robert's hangover: a big, heavy-winged blackbird flew out of his head. The couple rested on their backs with the sunlight from the balcony warming their bodies. She took a few of the withered roses from the night table and laid them on Robert's thighs. Picturing the dead woman, the Indian girl too, he knew his life and Gaby's would not be as full without the danger and cruelty.

They washed themselves in the bidet then showered together. Conjuring the river he had seen from the plane, at the disco on his first night, with her brother yesterday, Robert watched the soap and water running down the drain by Gabriela's pale feet. It would go into the storm sewers and all the way to the Río de la Plata, the river flowing silently, invisibly to the sea.

He sprawled on the rumpled bed alone. The light slanted onto the sheets, still marked where she had lain. While Gabriela completed her rituals in the bathroom, he propped himself on one elbow and observed through the open door. It was the first time she had performed them in Robert's presence, those ceremonies of combs and brushes, powders, creams, oils and perfumes. When they do their toilette, an Argentine poet said, all women are goddesses.

She leaned over to kiss Robert goodbye. Her scent mingled with the aromas on the sheets. He fell into a warm sleep suffused by her lingering fragrance.

When he awoke, sunlight no longer sliced through the windows. Robert recalled the attempted murder on Avenida de Mayo, the wounded man's moans and cries, the bleeding woman, Gabriela on the sidewalk, Gabriela at the police station, Gabriela in bed. A breeze moved from the balcony, making the leaves and petals of the wilted roses quiver where she had placed them on the nightstand. He noticed a red spot and a ring of moisture on her pillow. Loving her's a blood sport, he thought, looking at his finger cut by the rose-thorn, feeling his tongue where she had bit him that day.

He surveyed the room: cups, glasses, pitchers, plates with their leftovers, towels draped on chairs, sheets hanging off the bed, his clothes piled on the floor. Every object, every detail evoked a word, laugh, smile, a caress—fingers, hands or lips grazing a neck, shoulder, thigh, foot. He tried to retain them all in his mind, to hold them like the forms and colors of a chosen painting. But the light had changed and Gabriela was gone.

The sound of the telephone jarred him. "I'm at work and I can't stop thinking about last night," she told him in her rippling voice.

"I'm not at work and I can't stop thinking about last night either."

"And I'm already hungry, Osito. Can we meet for an early lunch?"

"That would be the first time we've done anything early."

"Maybe I'm becoming a *gringa*."

"You have a long way to go, Gaby."

"I meant early for Argentina, one o'clock or so? We could have an *asado*."

"I've never eaten one."

"There's a good parrilla on the corner of Juncal and Uruguay—you could walk from the hotel. But why don't you take the *subterráneo*?"

"What for?"

"Remember what happened last night. You'd be safer underground. Be careful Osito."

For the first time since he had come to Buenos Aires, Robert did not feel tired. He was impatient to be in the city again with the woman who had changed his life in four days. As soon as he stepped onto Avenida de Mayo, Robert sensed something different. The street, the city no longer seemed the same. All was transformed: he had nearly been killed here last night, then he had been inside of her. Keeping Gaby's warning in mind, he stayed close to the storefronts, training an eye on traffic.

Robert approached the restaurant and spotted her descending from a cab. He ran, slipped behind her and seized Gaby by the waist.

She spun with a sigh, "Rober—" He swallowed her last syllable with a forceful kiss on her mouth. The electric charge did not surprise them. Shocks had become a familiar, minor hazard of their world.

"First time you're not late," he said.

"I'm often late but always on time." Gabriela licked her lower lip and smiled, revealing her pointed eyeteeth. The sun sparkled on the snake pendant and silver chain around her neck. "Today's a special occasion—our first asado together."

"I'm starved!" With hunger for meat and salt, sequel to love, Robert's stomach growled.

Gaby poked his belly. "*Vení,*" she told him and walked through the door.

They devoured a whole asado roasted on a wooden fire—tender steak spiced with the house *chimichurri*, followed by beef ribs, sweetbreads, offal, chorizos, blood sausage—rounded off by fresh strawberries, all washed down with a bottle-and-a-half of Malbec.

By the time they ordered coffee, the other clients had gone. The restaurant was so quiet that they could hear Mercedes Sosa singing "*Todo cambia*" on the speaker in a faraway corner: "Everything changes except my love." A day or two ago they might not have paid much attention to it. Now it felt crucial, a new part of their life together.

When the song ended, Gabriela's purple gaze wandered around the room, the ceiling, the windows. Robert remembered how she had closed her eyes or stared upwards in bed while they were making love. She was drifting away from him.

"Gaby," he said softly. "I want to be with you again."

She turned toward Robert. Her heavy-hooded eyes showed a darker shade of violet. "I'm supposed to work this afternoon. Anyhow where could we go? I wouldn't return to the Castelar—we might run into that *tipo* at the desk."

"I know."

"You must move from that hotel, Roberto." She waited a few seconds before asking, "Know what we could do?" Gabriela sounded like a girl plotting mischief.

He was beginning to grasp how quickly, without warning her moods changed. "What?"

"Check into another hotel. When they tell us the price of the room I'll say 'That's too expensive!' They'll have to assume we're married." Gabriela wrinkled her nose, laughing.

She had come back to him. Their conversation reminded him that he was in another country, where an unmarried man and a woman could not merely check into a hotel together. "But we don't have luggage," he said. "Won't it look suspicious?"

"We could take yours."

Robert recollected the bad memories that flew from his suitcase on the first day. "I'd rather not."

Without hesitation she said, "Then we'll go to a *telo*."

"What's that?"

"You'll see." She had a gleam in her plum-colored eyes. Gabriela rose from her chair and walked to a public telephone by the bar. He watched her closely.

After making her call, she told him, "Alfonsina's going to work the rest of my shift this afternoon."

"Did you tell her why?"

"None of your business, *fisgón*." She rubbed her hands. "I'm free."

As their taxi sped along Avenida de Mayo, they lurched against each other in the back seat. They passed the scene of the hit-and-run. Caution tape still marked the spot, where people milled around. Gabriela and Robert said nothing.

The cabbie made several turns, then slowed in front of a windowless building with a small sign in gold script on the facade: *AFRODITA*. He drove them into the garage and dropped them in front of a smoked-glass door.

She told Robert in English, "They can't see us from the street if we enter here."

He loved her air of conspiracy. "Who's going to see us?"

Gabriela did not answer. As they walked through the doorway, fragrances of incense enveloped the lovers. A long corridor with a crimson runner stretched in front of them. Brass sconces illuminated scarlet walls and ceilings. At the end of the corridor they reached a lobby furnished with velvet chairs and divans in various tints of red. Copies of classical paintings in gilded frames adorned the walls: *The Education of Cupid*, *Rape of Europa*, *Le Déjeuner sur l'Herbe*.

"It reminds me of an expensive whorehouse," Robert said.

"It's different," she whispered, cupping her hands and drawing close. "Couples come here when they have nowhere else to go—like us." Her eyelashes fluttered like feathers on the rim of Robert's ear.

A man in a black tuxedo looked up from the reception desk where a lamp lit the pages of a morning edition, splashed with headlines about the sweepstakes. He told Robert he could have a room for one night at 400,000 australes in cash or half-a-million with a credit card. Inflation was running around four hundred percent a month, the clerk explained, so the currency depreciated faster than the banks could bill their customers. He addressed Robert, the male and the payer, ignoring Gabriela except for a sideways glance or two. No man or woman could refrain from eyeing her.

With the blitheness of a foreigner whose wallet is stuffed with large bills, six-thousand-to-the-dollar, Robert paid in cash. I'm a millionaire in a worthless currency, he thought. Peeling off the banknotes with their bearded and mustachioed portraits of Argentine patricians, he recalled playing Monopoly as a child, later gambling with chips in Saigon, Bangkok, Las Vegas. The whole place reminded him of a casino with no windows or clocks, no day or night.

Robert and Gabriela ascended a narrow, winding stairway, carpeted in burgundy. They stopped in front of number 66. Both remembered his room at the Hotel Castelar. The maroon door had a brass knocker in the shape of a feline head—a panther, jaguar or leopard, Robert could not tell which.

Gabriela rubbed the metal figure. "They must have known another cat was coming today."

He turned the key. Like two kids breaking into a forbidden attic, they peeked at one another. Robert pushed the door. They inhaled aromas of incense and perfume, heard the melody of a bolero floating from hidden speakers. On the walls more sconces cast a roseate light around them. A pile rug, the wallpaper, a canopied bed, twin armchairs with their ottomans, a love-seat—all in shades of crimson, ruby, vermilion, cinnabar, coral, salmon pink. In one corner of this room a magenta orchid surged from a ceramic pot.

The vast bed stood like an altar in the middle of a sanctuary, with a damask cover, pillows, bolster and flounces. Four carved wooden columns, covered by twisting vines, flowers and feathers, supported a baldachin with its golden tassels and festoons, the only fabric without a trace of red or pink. As they approached the bed, Gabriela and Robert noticed a square mirror in each corner of the canopy, a garnet cord suspended from the brocaded top.

She was laughing. "This bed's my favorite!"

For a moment Robert had the feeling that she had been here before. He was going to ask, but he was too intrigued to stop their tour. They walked into the bathroom, tiled in cardinal red with a wine-colored sink, toilet, claw-foot bathtub and bidet.

"So this is a telo?" His voice echoed from the walls.

"That's the popular name—also 'love hotels.' Officially they're called 'places of assignation' or 'accommodations with a high turnover rate,'" she said with a smile. "Argentines are brilliant at inventing euphemisms."

"What's the difference between a telo and a hotel?"

"Here you can pay by the hour if you choose. And the best telos guarantee their clients' privacy."

"This must be one of the best."

"Would I take you anywhere else?"

Robert nudged Gabriela's belly. "You seem to know a lot about them."

"All porteños do, silly." She left her lips parted and the small tip of her tongue exposed.

When they took each other's hand, the static made them jump. To the cadence of the bolero playing on the speakers, they danced into the main room, leaving a trail of clothes and shoes behind them. They fell onto the wide bed, where Gabriela arched her neck, stared up at the baldachin and closed her eyes. She made her music again, guttural as a cat's purr, still keeping something inside that Robert might never know. How many other mornings, nights, afternoons would he hear that song in her throat? She bled murmurs, soft sounds, greedy noises, words that spoke themselves, Hold me let me go, Stop don't stop, *Pará no parés, Amame cogeme,* Love me fuck me, Help me hurt me, words in Spanish and English and in her language without words.

In the dark they lay together, half-asleep. When he stirred later, Gabriela opened her eyes. Their color had deepened, he thought, changed like her city at night, like the hotel café and its clients. Slowly she grazed him with her fingers—his chest, back, stomach, thighs—scratched him lightly with her tapered nails, now faster and harder, gouged, hurt him, gnawed on his neck and face, pulled his hair while she hummed in his ears, made new tones, syllables Robert did not understand. He lay on his back, looked up at the mirror on the canopy, saw Gabriela's body crouched over him, her arms tearing at his limbs, her haunches moved down and up, around to the rhythm of the boleros and this song in her mouth. He closed his eyes and curved his back as she had done, threw his head over the pillow, did not resist, allowed her to seize him, do what she wanted to him, and he knew the relief of surrender.

When they fell asleep at last, Robert dreamed they were walking together on a bridge between two lofty mountains, maybe in the Andes or Himalayas. Near the edge they peered down and saw a village nestled in a deep valley. They were holding each other's hands when they began to fall, floating, then soared, gliding to the other side. The dream dissolved in a breeze of tenderness.

When Robert awoke, he saw her sitting up, contemplating the sheets. In that room without windows he did not know if it was morning, afternoon or evening. He felt still the buoyancy of his dream.

Gabriela must have sensed he was watching her. She turned to him. "Why are you risking your life to stay in Argentina?"

After his sleep and the silent dream, words sounded strange to him. "You know why I'm here."

"I'm scared. Hug me, Osito."

Robert held her so tightly that there was no air between them. "Tell me, Gaby."

"If you weren't in jeopardy Segundo wouldn't have asked you to leave."

Picturing the Falcon's single headlight on the Avenida de Mayo, Robert stroked Gabriela's hair, lustrous even in disarray. "Your brother warned me about a minotaur who could destroy me in his maze—that's how he put it. What do you think he was talking about?"

For a minute or longer Gabriela did not speak. Then she said, "Maybe you should follow his advice."

"You want me to go?"

"Only if it would save your life."

"The more they tell me to leave—I'm sorry," he tried to laugh, "the more I need to stay." Robert still fondled her hair. "I am staying."

"Who's *they*?"

His hand fell on the sheet. "A man in the Turkish baths at the Castelar also gave me a warning."

"What's his name?"

"Virgilio."

"Virgilio what?"

"I don't know."

Gabriela raised her voice: "You mean you told somebody about us and you didn't even know his full name?"

"He already knew about us—it's hard to explain."

Gabriela began to weep into Robert, moistening the hair on his chest. She grasped for him. The dark odors of incense and perfume, the boleros, this sensation of rushing time, the danger stirred them. They sank farther, deeper into the sheets, into the love that was carrying them along its river, her river, Río de la Plata, wide as a sea.

9
Recoleta

It seemed odd to emerge into day after being in the dark so long. As they stepped onto the street, a pair of swallows darted over their heads, stirring a small breeze around them. Robert and Gabriela felt the light-headed clarity that comes after making love. His back stung where her fingernails had dug in.

On the sidewalk an old mutt approached them. Robert made the mistake of petting the animal, who wagged its stubby tail and followed him. Soon other dogs trailed behind.

"You're such a pushover," she said, bumping Robert with one of her lissome flanks.

"We should've showered again."

"I like the way we smell."

"So do they."

The canines multiplied—males, bitches, mongrels, curs. They trotted around the lovers, trying to sniff them, forcing them to walk faster. The animals whined, whimpered, barked and yelped, some lagging to sniff and pee on trash cans, fire hydrants, mailboxes or streetlights. Pedestrians gaped and pointed at the man and woman with a train of dogs behind them.

"I know a café ahead of us on the right," Gabriela alerted him.

"We're stopping there."

After slipping through the door, they slammed it to cut off the pack behind them. They found a table by a window, peered out and saw a policeman on a motorcycle who was speeding up and down the street, blowing a whistle as he directed cars and buses, keeping pedestrians off the curb. When drum majorettes and twirlers arrived with a marching band, vehicles had to brake, traffic piled up and drivers honked their horns. Behind the drummers came jugglers, clowns, the thin man, the fat lady, the sword swallower, dancing bears, midgets on unicycles, acrobats doing cartwheels, a woman in spangles on a barebacked horse. Meanwhile helicopters began to beat the air above the pageant, hot-air balloons hovered, small planes with blue and white streamers droned overhead, skywriters smoked mysterious words in the clouds.

"What's the occasion?" Robert asked.

"Us. Anyway Argentines love spectacles—we live for them. Some people say that's all we are—one big show of a country."

Laughing at the circus, a waiter approached their table. Robert and Gabriela ordered empanadas with a salad and beers. Eating and drinking together, they forgot about the parades of dogs and people and drowned in each other's eyes. The meat pies could not match the ones made by Quiroga's wife at the boliche, Robert knew, but all other foods tasted better in Gabriela's company. By the time they capped their meal with two espressos, the procession had faded, the animals had lost the lovers' scent and dispersed in the parks.

Robert and Gabriela walked into the honeyed light of late afternoon in Buenos Aires, sweeter than any city unless you are being tormented by the past. The streets were littered with confetti and trash from the crowd, but most cars and people had retreated for the long, sacred lunch hours. How could anything hurt us on a day like this, Robert asked himself. Holding her hand, feeling the tingle up his arm, he imagined their electric field would protect them from any harm. Gabriela knew they were vulnerable on this or any other day.

"Where is everyone?" he asked.

"Eating or taking a nap."

Robert glanced at his empty wrist. "I must have left my watch in the telo."

"Do you need it?"

"Yes. So I'll know when to meet you."

Gabriela smiled from the corners of her eyes. "I'm nearly always late."

"But on time."

"You're learning faster."

As they strolled, Robert recalled his last weeks in Los Angeles—work, deadlines, lawyers, hearings, appointments—his hours synchronized by the gears of clocks. It seemed like a distant dream, the plot of a movie seen long ago. He did not tell himself that it was also less dangerous than loving this woman in Buenos Aires.

They passed through barrios littered with empty bottles, garbage and cigarette butts, residue of the night. Gabriela and Robert took their time strolling through parks and squares, walking off their meal and nuzzling on benches. Before long the avenues grew broader and the neighborhoods cleaner. Striped awnings covered entrances to salons, boutiques and apartment buildings, some manned by liveried doormen. Expensive cars lined the curbs.

Robert and Gabriela turned a corner and suddenly found themselves in Plaza Recoleta with the great tree. The gomero was just waking from its afternoon siesta, stretching its arms while birds flew in and out of its waxy leaves, chirping, banking, soaring. Gabriela stopped and held Robert, rubbing her warm, night-black hair against his chest.

Beyond their tree they saw the sign for Café Biela. He started to recount his conversation with Quiroga in the boliche, but he stopped himself when he saw Gabriela's face. She was staring at the gomero, rapt, her bow-shaped lips parted. Robert did not want to tarnish that moment with memories of the war—not while the sun sank behind this tree, whose crown was catching the fleeing light, and birds darted through its foliage, singing hosannas.

They crossed the plaza, where they saw a colonial church in front of them: a white facade, a tower on one side, a belfry with a clock on the other. As if to celebrate Robert's and Gabriela's arrival, bells pealed.

"The *Angelus*," she said, "my favorite time."

"End of the day."

"The sweetest hour."

"With a brother who's a priest I assume you're Catholic."

"My parents were married here, the Basilica of Nuestra Señora del Pilar. My brother and I were baptized in one of the chapels and two of my grandparents had funerals in the sanctuary." Gabriela pointed to the thick white wall of a cemetery on the left. "Our family has nuns, monks, priests, bishops and a cardinal buried there—not to mention the others who weren't in the Church. I attended parochial schools until I went to university."

"So I guess one could say you're Catholic."

"That's one of the only things you could say about me with certainty."

"Do you have faith?"

Gazing at the wall, she said, "In you," as if it were a plain fact like the weather or the hour of day. "In my country you don't need to have faith to be Catholic. It's in our blood and our past. Sometimes I believe, sometimes I don't. What about you?"

"No priests or monks or nuns in the family—forget about princes of the Church. It's just as well because I'm not a believer."

"Hmm."

"I attended parochial school in Los Angeles but they expelled me."

Gabriela raised her eyebrows in mock disbelief. "You got in trouble, Osito?"

"I'm still in it, deeper," Robert said and looked into her plum-colored eyes. Seeing the little girl buried there, he asked, "Did you wear a uniform to school?"

"A pleated navy-blue skirt with a starched white blouse. Not exactly my style." With both hands she stroked her cotton skirt and its golden arabesques of fruits, vines and flowers. "Why do you ask?"

"I like picturing you as a schoolgirl. We wore black corduroy pants with white collared shirts."

"So you couldn't change clothes if your luck soured?"

"In those days I didn't need to."

"Come with me," she said, and Robert knew he would always go with her.

Beyond the church Gabriela led him toward a portico with white Greco-Roman columns. An austere sign read REQUIESCAT IN PACE. Below it appeared the hours for visits.

"A cemetery is the last place I want to be with you," Robert said.

"Wait and see."

They walked through an iron gate onto a long, narrow avenue bordered with cypress trees. Like close-built houses on a street, jostled against each other on both sides, monuments rose in many styles: Egyptian, Roman, Greek, Neoclassical, Baroque, Gothic, Romanesque, Rococo, Moorish, Chinese. Shrines, mausoleums, chapels, pagodas, obelisks, pyramids, rotundas, temples, pantheons. In some ways those florid vaults reminded Robert of the scarlet room. Almost everything seemed overdone, excessive in Buenos Aires.

Gabriela peered into his turquoise eyes. "Well what do you think?"

"Very different from our simple Protestant graveyards."

"Which tomb is your favorite?"

"The one where you are," he said, looking up at the spiraled columns of the monument behind her.

"I'm not buried yet," she laughed. "Anyhow you can't come to Buenos Aires without seeing the *Ciudad de los Muertos*. Our City of the Dead. Where else in the world can you find a necropolis in the center of a great city? The most expensive real estate in Argentina belongs to the dead."

Her hand, as she led Robert along this somber avenue, grazed his. They winded down pathways lined with crumbling spires, statues of Madonnas, broken angels, gargoyles. They changed direction over and over in the labyrinth of stone and cypresses. Gabriela showed him the tombs of the most illustrious names in Argentine history: generals, admirals, monsignors, bishops, cardinals, presidents, ministers, ambassadors, writers, artists, scientists, more admirals and generals.

"You talk about them as though they were family."

"Some are. Most of them from Father's side, naturally."

"Why 'naturally'?"

"His family is more prominent than my mother's." As she spoke, Gabriela's eyes darkened. She turned away from Robert. "They'll probably bury me here someday."

Through lengthening shadows they walked in silence. She stopped in front of a monument inscribed *FAMILIA DUARTE*. On the gray marble vault they saw a bouquet of red and white roses. Remembering, Gabriela and Robert looked at each other in recognition.

"Do you know who's buried here?" she asked.

"That's Eva Perón's family name, right?" Robert studied the dates incised on the stone, barely legible in the penumbra: 1919-1952. "I didn't know she died so young."

"Christ's age when he was crucified. General Perón was old enough to be her father." Gabriela scrutinized the tomb. "I'll never forget the day at school when they announced the repatriation of her body."

"When was that?"

"Years after her death."

"How old were you?"

"Fourteen." Gabriela frowned. "Somehow I suspected that it was all fake."

"What kind of hairdo did you have?"

"Why, *tonto*?"

Robert shrugged his wide shoulders. He did not know why, only that he wished to hold that teenager in his arms with the woman she had become, his hands grasped around her waist now, pulling her toward his body, his back pressed against the wrought-iron rail. Gabriela looked up at him, her eyes a deep purple in the falling light. They kissed. The shock singed their tongue and lips, and Robert felt desire leap through his groin.

"Bangs," she said in one of her delayed responses, panting.

"What?"

"I wore my hair in bangs."

"Bang like that kiss."

Before she could smile, if she was going to smile, a whistle blew, startling them. Gabriela let out a gasp. A flashlight shone in their faces. When its beam dropped, they could make out a guard, dressed in black, issuing from the gloom.

"*El cementerio está cerrando*," the man said in a strong bass. "The grounds are about to close. Is that how you show respect for the dead—Evita no less?"

Robert and Gabriela drooped their heads, turned and walked toward the entrance, holding hands. With the flashlight's beam searing their backs, they were banished from that mortal Eden by this exterminating angel. As soon as they stepped outside the cemetery, they heard the clang of an iron portal, the grating of a ponderous key in the lock.

They stood alone with their backs to Nuestra Señora del Pilar. Against the lights of cafés, bars and restaurants, the silhouette of the great tree loomed on the far side of the square. Those places and the gomero appeared to beckon, call them away from that city of death and stone.

Robert and Gabriela crossed the plaza. Standing under the tree, they heard a chorus of birdsong.

She grasped his arm. "See that little tree over there?" She pointed beyond their gomero. "Its roots must touch the big tree's." She looked up and sighed. "Wouldn't it be nice if we could be together like that, calm and safe, entwining our roots?"

"We already do that, Gaby. Maybe not so calm." She did not answer.

Gabriela led him into the La Biela, where they drew stares from clients. Again he thought of Quiroga's words about the killing fields. The place reminded Robert of his hotel café the night before, full of young people, well-dressed, warming up for a long evening. All nights seemed like a weekend in Buenos Aires.

Their table was occupied. They found another by the window. When Robert picked up a menu, he noticed the prices were written in pencil: they had shot up since the first time they were here, only five days ago. He and Gabriela ordered brandies and soda.

Someone had left a rumpled copy of *La Nación* on their table. She picked it up, ignored the articles about the horserace and Mina's death, opened to the classifieds. "You need to find an apartment, Roberto."

"What makes you think I plan to stay in Buenos Aires?"

Gabriela closed the classifieds and peeked at him over the top of the newspaper, her eyes just above the banner on the front page. "Remember I was born at night."

While she skimmed the paper for a second time, Robert scanned the room: marble-topped counter and tables, high mirrors, uniformed waiters and a smart clientele. He found it hard to believe that a place like this café had been the scene of murders. The mozo served their drinks.

Gently Robert pressed down the newspaper in Gabriela's hands, revealing her full face. "Is it true they bombed La Biela during the war?"

She dropped *La Nación* on her glass. "How did you know that?"

"They told me the other day in a boliche."

"Where?"

"La Boca."

"You should stay out of that neighborhood. Anyway there were killings all over Buenos Aires." She tilted in her chair and gazed out the window.

"Doesn't it bother you to be in a spot with so many bad memories?"

"The best place to kill is where people feel happy, when they're off guard. I think porteños are happiest in our bars and cafés. That's why so many misfortunes occurred here—I mean there, in those places."

They didn't murder Dionisio in a bar, Robert mused, picturing the river in his mind. He drank his brandy and soda while Gabriela still looked out the window.

Robert removed the newspaper to uncover her glass. It was full to the brim. "Aren't you thirsty?"

"I just remembered that I'm on shift at the hospital tonight—to return Alfonsina's favor. I wonder what time it is."

Robert held up his bare wrist. "I thought we did away with time."

When they left the café, Gabriela asked a waiter for the hour. Bells tolled from the church. A sable bird flew over her head and faded into the twilight, flushing a flock of doves. Shivering, she lowered her heavy, hooded eyes.

"Let's go to our tree," she said. "I feel safer there."

They walked into the shadow of the spreading gomero. Its birds must have roosted for the evening; the foliage no longer resonated with song. Robert and Gabriela stood there for a minute.

As he had done the first night, five days or a hundred years ago, he walked Gabriela from there to the corner. Again a dark Mercedes taxi pulled to the curb, its headlights impaling the blackness. Once more she entered the car without turning or saying goodbye.

He watched the cab drive into the dark. Surrounded by reveling groups and couples, Robert felt out of place, alone, a foreigner. He searched for a well-lit bar where he would have the company of strangers, where he could order a vermouth, a brandy and soda—anything that would evoke Gabriela, their time together.

He bought the evening papers, walked to the corner and entered the Café de la Paix. Sipping the first drink, Robert perused the classifieds, finding apartments on streets and squares with haunting names: Avenida de los Incas, Calle de la Pena, Calle Piedras, Plaza Miserere. Then he tried to imagine, without success, those names in Los Angeles or another American city: Avenue of the Incas, Street of Sorrow, Street of Stones, Plaza Miserere. He circled ads in every quarter of the city. It was a way of imagining a life with Gaby, far from Avenida de Mayo, the hit-and-run, the hotel, the calf's bloody head.

As he read through the classifieds, Robert could not help seeing the missing-persons notices sponsored by the Mothers and Grandmothers of the Plaza de Mayo. One cited the report from the National Commission on the Disappeared, titled *Nunca Más* or *Never Again*, published with 50,000 pages of depositions. Here he was in Argentina, he thought, sitting in a bar called Café de la Paix no less, a full seven years after the end of this country's civil war, and its consequences were all around him. He scribbled words in the margins of the newsprint, tore off pages as he wrote, stacked them on his table, losing track of time.

By the third brandy and soda Robert had composed an opinion piece of 750 words for the *Los Angeles Times*, datelined Buenos Aires, Tuesday, September 27, 1990. In it he argued that the Proceso, short for Process of National Reorganization—the military junta's stale name for its rule from 1976 to 1983—still festered in people's memory in spite of the time elapsed, the recent amnesty laws and pardons. Many Argentines continued to live in fear, he asserted. They lowered their voices when they spoke of the desaparecidos, a word that kept turning up in conversations, echoing from walls, rooms and buildings everywhere, it seemed. Robert ended the article with a paragraph about an "American traveler" whose life had been endangered for reasons connected to the war. "In order to protect my sources," he wrote, "I cannot disclose his or my informants' names." When the words of a tango by Gardel came over the loudspeakers, he found a title for his piece: "... *No olvides, hermano*," Don't forget, my brother ...

Leaving the café, Robert recalled the Ford Falcon and watched his flanks closely. Instead of walking to the hotel, he took a cab from the same stand where he had dropped Gabriela, close to the gomero tree that made him feel oddly secure.

The night clerk had been chastised by the events of yesterday. When Robert requested a typewriter in the hotel's business center, the man treated him like an admiral of the Argentine Navy—before their defeat in the Falklands Islands, that is. The young man had fallen under Gabriela's spell, admiring this customer who had spent the night with a woman so ravishing, even if he was a gringo. Robert typed his article and sent it by fax to his editor in Los Angeles, Pueblo de Nuestra Señora La Reina de Los Ángeles, Town of Our Lady Queen of the Angels.

10
Inner Garden

"Will you live with me and be my love?" he asked with all the hope in his heart. They were sitting on a bench in the secluded park where they had gone the first day. The traffic of Wednesday afternoon hummed in the distance. Low clouds hung over the city.

For a long time Gabriela did not answer. Her eyes brimmed with tears. When she opened her mouth slightly, he held his breath until she replied. "I want to," she told him, biting her lower lip. For Robert it was as though the bank of clouds had lifted, letting in the sun.

He took one of her hands in his. Her palm was damp with the dew of perspiration. "Gaby. I know it's been hard until now—just getting past the desk at the hotel was like crossing a moat. But look," he said, removing from his coat pocket the folded classifieds he had studied in the crowded solitude of the Café de la Paix.

Taking the newspaper in her hands, she smiled wanly through her tears. Gabriela skimmed the ads he had circled in neighborhoods from here to hell and gone, from the slums and ghettos of Lanús and Matanza to the elegant, unaffordable purlieus of the Barrio Norte.

"Silly Roberto. You don't know Buenos Aires." With her fountain pen she struck most of the marked classifieds in purple ink, underlined a few of her own. "What about an apartment near downtown," she mused, "in a nice quarter, not cheap but not too dear either, on a quiet street but close to a subway stop?" Robert suspected that she feared another hit-and-run.

He answered with another question: "Can such a place exist?"

"Quién sabe?"

Their quest began. They knocked on doors, rang bells, pushed buzzers, interviewed agents, managers, *porteros* and concierges, walked up and down stairways or rode in elevator cages like the ones in old French movies. They went in and out of apartments, wanting them to be theirs already, opening doors, poking their heads inside, wanting each other, dawdling in bedrooms for a stolen kiss, ducking into closets for an urgent caress. They conversed in English so that most of the Argentines could not understand their words, rated each flat for its sexual promise, one to ten—the "hopscotch scale," they called it. They measured beds, touched, tested and bounced on mattresses. Landlords, agents and doormen ogled, many glaring, a few grinning, none taking this couple seriously until they learned that Gabriela was a physician and Robert an American, even offering to cut the rent if they paid in *verdes*, greenbacks.

In between apartments the lovers peeked into store windows, dallied at kiosks to read ads for the latest rentals, made detours in parks to hug and smooch, to tilt up and down on a seesaw, play soccer with a pebble or a paper cup. They deciphered graffiti, laughed and wrote their own, baptized streets and squares with new names, scratched their initials in wet cement, carved their names on benches and tree trunks. They dropped into bars, boliches, cafés and *confiterías*, telling one another whole chunks of their lives over an espresso, a vermouth or beer, uncovering their past and themselves while exploring Buenos Aires, almost forgetting the dangers that menaced them in the city. Robert, that is, whose North American optimism made him feel less vulnerable. Gabriela never forgot. Once in a while she reminded him. Both had lived long enough to know they would have to nurture, to shelter the fragile flame in their hearts, to cup their hands around it and shield it from the world, from the winds, the fierce gusts that could blow it away in a second.

One afternoon they fell in love with a furnished studio apartment on the third floor of a six-story building at number 98, Avenida Independencia. It was too expensive for Robert. But Gabriela wanted it, and she was used to having her way. Before signing the lease, they stopped for a drink in a café in their new neighborhood, where they could make up their minds.

Surrounded in a cloud of the other clients' smoke, Gabriela confided, "I've been meaning to tell you—" She paused. "Osito, I won a big purse in that race." She glanced away.

Robert remembered the hospital, the gun's crack, people sobbing in the streets. Most of all he recalled Gabriela hearing the news about the filly's death. When she looked up now, he sought her eyes. "You were going to tell me about it."

"I was waiting for the right moment. This is it—I can help you."

"Is that all you can tell me?"

Gabriela replied with her half-smile, which could mean anything.

Robert recollected the boliche and Quiroga's words about the horserace. Running one hand through his hair in a gesture of impatience, he said, "Okay, I'll write some more articles for my newspaper to pay my share."

"What do you mean, *more* articles?"

"I faxed an opinion piece to the *Los Angeles Times* last night."

"What?"

He pulled the fax from his coat pocket and proffered it to Gabriela. As she read, her silky lashes formed a semicircle under each eye, trembling when she blinked. Robert leaned over and kissed them—those dark feathers that fluttered on his lips.

She drew away from him. "Am I one of your 'sources'?"

Robert was learning from Gabriela to ignore questions or answer them obliquely. "I may write more articles for the money and to protect us. When that piece appears on the newsstands in a day or two—in Los Angeles and other cities where the *Times* is sold—my presence in Buenos Aires will be on record." Virgilio's advice resounded in Robert's memory.

"That part's good. *Pero tené cuidado,* Osito," she warned. "And I'll pay half the rent. The lease will have to be in my name anyhow since you're a visitor, not a resident of Argentina." Robert squeezed her palpitating hand. That was their way of closing the deal.

On Gabriela's insistence they moved at night to make it harder for someone to follow them. Apartment G was so small that they could scarcely stir without bumping into each other. A double bed occupied the main room, commandeering most of the space for other furniture; solemnly they baptized it as "La Pampa." When they arrived with their suitcases, they could not find a place to put them—unless they removed a lamp or chair, and then what were they supposed to do with the night table if every inch of room was already full?

In her bare feet Gabriela pushed the sparse pieces around, creating new realms in corners of the kitchen, the bathroom, around the bed. Scattering her clothes, books, pictures, candles and perfumes, she filled and enlivened those spots. Robert marveled at the transformation of dreary little rooms into warm nests where they could eat, talk, read, nap, dream or make love. Gabriela had brightened the apartment as if it had new windows and a skylight.

In any one of those places she would surprise him with unpredictable questions. "What are you seeking in your life?" she asked him out of the blue one morning.

"You."

"Besides me, tonto."

"What is there besides you, *boba*?"

"I mean what do you wish to achieve in your life?"

"All I want is to live with you and be your love. And become a better journalist."

"I want to live with you, be your love and become a better doctor someday. And—" Her eyes changed into their darker shade of violet. Gabriela turned away and fell into one of her silences.

Or she would ask him another day without warning, "Who are you Roberto?"

"It's taken me thirty years and many, many months to learn that."

She smiled, remembering their first day. "Pues?"

"I still don't know. I guess I'm someone who fought in a war, lost his parents, worked for a newspaper, married and divorced. Someone who's trying to start a new life in a different country."

"Can anyone start a new life?"

"I said I'm trying." Robert poked her ribcage, making her giggle.

Later Gabriela would pick up the conversation as if she had been pondering it the whole while. "But everyone has an old life."

"Oh that. Mine seems so long ago—another time and continent."

"Mine doesn't. If only it did."

"Maybe it will someday."

"When?"

"I don't know. Nobody does."

"Mmm," she would hum and think about it. Then she would repeat the question on another day.

The old gray building with its wooden shutters stood next to a nursery called Inner Garden—just so, in English. So their new apartment had a name. In fact the main room overlooked a courtyard with an ageless fig tree in the center, whose crown almost reached their window. They could hear its rough leaves chafing in the breeze. A few days after moving in, Robert and Gabriela crossed the street and bought one white and two red geraniums at the nursery. She planted them in separate earthen pots on the tiny wrought-iron balcony, too cramped for the lovers to stand there anyway.

Sunlight reached their apartment for several hours in late morning and early afternoon. During the rest of the day a soft radiance filtered through the patio and the old venetian blinds. It dappled the parquet floor, making this room resemble a forest where anything might occur—a fawn could leap, a nymph dance, a hooved god play his flute.

Robert sent a letter for his landlady in Los Angeles to cancel his lease. He also wrote his editor at the newspaper, giving the new address in Buenos Aires, reminding him of some old favors. And would he please move his few possessions in the apartment to storage? In exchange he would send another free article about Argentina, but he would have to charge for further submissions.

"What will the man think?" Gabriela inquired.

"That I'm crazy."

"He'll be right, won't he? *L'amour est fou,*" she pronounced in her immaculate French. Robert recalled the filly's name who had won the sweepstakes, Quiroga's story again, how it kept coming back. But it was swallowed in the joy of living with Gabriela in Buenos Aires.

"Will this affect your career at the *Times*?" she asked later, as though she had been mulling it over.

"If I returned to L.A. I'd be in line for promotion to Latin American bureau chief."

"You're already my chief—Chief Little Bear." Gabriela challenged him: "Want to see how crazy I can be?"

"Show me, mujer."

"Vení!"

She led Robert to a café, where she picked up the telephone on the counter as if she were in her own house. Three or four customers were seated at tables. While the bartender gaped at her, Gabriela called her supervisor to request an indefinite, unpaid leave from the Sanatorio Palermo. Meanwhile Robert ordered two vermouth and sodas, thinking she must have made a killing on that race.

"Aren't you going to miss your work?" he asked when she dropped the phone on its cradle. Gabriela reminded him of a mischievous girl who has committed a naughty and delicious act.

"I'd rather be with you, Osito. But I'll still help the Madres on weekends. I don't want to lose touch with my profession."

When the bartender disappeared into the kitchen, she dialed her house on the same telephone. As Robert listened, she told her mother that she would be staying with Alfonsina, her colleague at the hospital, who had just broken up with her boyfriend and was afraid to be alone. Gabriela became so immersed in her story that she looked intently into the mouthpiece, arguing that her friend's apartment was in a good neighborhood, that it had a doorman for security, and would she tell "Father"?—pronouncing that word in English. Robert marveled at how easily and naturally Gabriela dissembled, creating a coherent one-act play on the phone as she stood by the counter in the bar.

"My parents love Alfonsina," she said as soon as she had said goodbye to her mother. "She comes from an old family."

"What if they phone you at her apartment?"

"Don't worry, Alfonsina will cover for me."

"Is it true about her breaking up with someone?"

Gabriela pouted with feigned jealousy. "None of your business, nosy." Then she changed her expression instantly, glancing sideways at Robert with a flash in her eyes and a graceful curve of her throat. "Osito, will you buy us a bottle of champagne to celebrate?"

In that apartment in the Barrio Sur the two lovers might have been in another country, on an island or a continent without radio, TV or telephone. At first only the smells, the noises and their courtyard linked them to the world outside their walls: aromas of coffee, *tucos* or tomato sauces, chitterlings and *churrascos* from the neighbors' kitchens; the drone of cars and the chug of colectivos on the avenue, horns and sirens of the night; the windblown fig leaves rubbing like sandpaper against the balcony, maids singing sad milongas as they mopped the stairs, a matron on the second floor who drank café con leche in the morning with both hands around her cup, regarding the new day from her window; the adolescent twins who combed and braided one another's hair each afternoon on the floor above, listening to music or soap operas on the radio. When Robert and Gabriela rose from bed to look outside or breathe fresh air, throwing a sheet on their shoulders, those sisters would spy them, blush and bid them *"Buenas tardes."* He baptized them "our guardian angels," while she belittled them as *"esas chicas."* Gabriela was jealous of any female who attracted Robert's attention, no matter how homely or beautiful she was, young or old.

They loved the odors in their apartment and their building. Not only the changing smells of the surroundings and their love. Not only the woman's scent that diffused the small rooms when Gabriela performed her sacred rituals. No, it was these aromas as well as things themselves: the walls with their abstract moisture stains, the woodwormed pine of their single chest of drawers, the thriving geraniums on their balcony; the geometrical parquet of their living room, where they knew every loose or creaky board; the wooden stairs of the building's entrance with their lovely patina, each step bowed in the center by use and time; the worn, white-and-black tiles of their vestibule. Blended in the whole apartment and in their minds, those objects and fragrances composed an aura that existed nowhere else in Buenos Aires, in South America or the world. When the lovers came home, it enfolded them like a warm embrace.

Radios in their building blared most days. The twins upstairs listened to pop music, rock and folk songs by Atahualpa Yupanqui, Mercedes Sosa and Violeta Parra. The older residents preferred songs that had broken hearts in Evita's time. Robert grew familiar with tangos, milongas, boleros, *cuartetos* from Córdoba, *chacareras* from Santiago del Estero, *vidalitas* from the Andes and the Plata basin.

"Why do they still play so many old songs?" he asked Gabriela one afternoon that would never return.

"We have to live in one past in order to forget the other." At times talking with her was like consulting an oracle.

When the refrain of a new tango reached their apartment that day, Gabriela perked up her ears. She hummed along to Roberto Goyeneche's words: *Decí por Dios qué me has dao, que estoy tan cambiao...*" Tell me by God what you've given me, I'm so changed...

When the song had ended, she told him, "It's not just the past." Throwing her arms around his neck, she lifted herself off the floor, crying, "See how those songs can tell us about the present too?"

That evening the portera stopped Gabriela and Robert in front of her cubbyhole on the ground floor. She was a bashful, unmarried woman in her fifties. She reported that their neighbors were complaining about the noises emanating from apartment G. Saying this, the portera turned away from Robert to his lover, her cheeks growing red like the center of a raw bife. Gabriela gave her a female smile of complicity, disarming the woman so completely that she skulked away in silence.

The couple tried keeping their windows closed. But the weather was turning warm, too hot to shut them, also too hard for them to hold back their cries. Or they merely forgot.

If they loved each other in the evening, the neighbors' lights seemed to flicker on and off. If it was later at night, lamps glowed from the basement to the top floor. In this way Robert and Gabriela came to know and summon the force between them. They liked to believe their passion was contributing to the common good, generating power, light and heat for all twelve families in the building. Once the voltage surged so much that their circuit box blew a fuse, their light bulbs shattered into a thousand pieces on the floor and the particles of glass scintillated like stars. So Gabriela found another secret name for their home: the Inner Galaxy. There she imagined they could hear the transit of stars, the shifting of tides on the river and sea.

If you didn't count their tiny bath and kitchen, the Pampa—their bed, 10+ on the hopscotch scale—filled most of their apartment. There they slept, ate, worked and loved. They did everything and nothing there. They spent more time naked than dressed. Even if they wore a shirt or blouse, they were always barefoot. If they had to go outside, their shoes felt tight, their clothes stiff as armor. When they spotted the matron sipping her coffee by her window, they knew it was morning. When they saw the teenaged twins braiding one another's hair, it must be afternoon. They could have set their clocks by those women if they had a clock, if they had not abandoned schedules and calendars, if time had not been obliterated in that small oasis, their Inner Garden.

"I wonder what happened to my wristwatch," he said one night when they were thinking of going to a late movie.

"They probably confiscated it at the telo."

"There's no Lost and Found there?" he asked, knowing the answer.

"Whatever's lost in a telo is lost forever—like almost everything in my country."

Before speaking, Robert paused to absorb her Argentine fatalism. "Somehow I'd like to imagine a customer picked up my watch and took it to the other end of the world."

"We're already there."

"That it sprouted wings and flew from Buenos Aires to—"

"Uruguay across the river, where they live in the past too. Someday I'll take you there."

"Or over the Andes to Chile, where they're also haunted by memories."

"Will you take me there?"

Robert smiled and delayed his answer for a few hours or days. He knew, she knew they would travel anywhere in the wide world as long as they were together.

Often Gabriela slept during the day. If he awoke at night, Robert would see her lying on her back, her immense eyes open, unblinking.

"What's wrong, Gaby?"

She hugged him, her face pressed against his shoulder. The curtains breathed softly against their windows. "Maybe I can't sleep because I'm like a cat," she said, trying to spare him the truth. "Hold me."

As he wrapped Gabriela in his arms, she felt more frail than ever. "Is there something else?"

She did not reply. She refused to be consoled.

They ventured outdoors solely for necessities. To keep the dogs of Buenos Aires at bay, both washed, scrubbed and doused their bodies with cologne before taking to the streets. Robert rarely changed his clothes, trying to protect his streak of luck since they rented the apartment. Every so often he had a foreboding that it might end. But he was too thrilled, too blinded by his love for Gaby to admit their paradise could not endure.

Prices fluctuated so wildly that each trip to the store was like voyaging to a foreign country and learning a new currency. Every day brought financial panic, record inflation and more charges of corruption against the government. President Carlos Menem continued decreeing executive pardons for generals and admirals of the wartime junta along with some token members of the opposition. New exposés of crimes perpetrated by the military leaders would rob those remorseless men of sleep for nights and years to come.

In order to forget about the situation in her own country, with its steady reminders of the war, Gabriela invented disastrous headlines of her own: the United States, China and the Soviet Union had annihilated themselves with nuclear bombs, for one. Robert countered by telling her that a powerful earthquake had struck California, tidal waves flooded the Pacific coast, his old apartment and his office plunged into the ocean. She surpassed him by conjuring Hitler, who resurfaced in Patagonia while Evita rose from her sarcophagus in Buenos Aires, where the two met, courted, married and committed double suicide in a Götterdämmerung witnessed by 150,000 shouting fans at La Bombonera Stadium. Robert surrendered. His American upbringing had not trained him to portray the world as portentously as Gabriela.

Her dreamed-up apocalypses did not appear to affect the Argentine passion for soccer, the national sport. When TV's and radios screamed from their neighbors' apartments or from the streets, when crowds cheered and cars blasted their horns, the lovers knew that River Plate or their archrival Boca Juniors had scored a goal or won a match.

"What's your favorite team?" Robert asked her during one game.

"River Plate, of course." He was not surprised that Gabriela rooted for the same football club as her brother, like nearly all porteños of their class. She doesn't know her boyfriend died in the river of the same name, he thought.

Snatching time from their world, Robert tried to follow the news in dailies, magazines and periodicals. He sent more columns to the *Times* on life in Buenos Aires. Proofreading those articles, he recognized that each word, line and sentence was infused with Gabriela. Before too long the checks began arriving from Los Angeles, allowing Robert to pay his part of the rent or treat her to a meal at one of their boliches, restaurants or grills.

The two slept when they were tired, made love when they wanted each other, ate when they could drag themselves from bed. If they went out, they would buy loaves of bread from the bakery on the corner, steaks from their local butcher, fresh ravioli, spaghettis and tagliatelle on Avenida Santa Fe, fruit and vegetables from the grocers whose displays resembled still-life paintings on the sidewalks of their barrio. It was all new for Gabriela, who had grown up in a home where maids did the shopping, prepared meals and washed the dishes. Now she was like a girl playing house in a toy kitchen. She overcooked pasta and vegetables, charred toast and meats, ruined sauces with spectacular doses of herbs and spices. So Robert took over the cooking and left the drinks to her: café con leche in the morning, dark espressos, hot teas or matés in the afternoon, beers, wines, champagne or Pisco sours at night.

When they ran errands, Gabriela preferred to take the metro. "It's cheaper," she told him, shaking her sequined change purse. This woman who had won a fortune at the racetrack, who could have paid all the rent, who had never denied herself a whim, was the same person who wanted to save a few measly australes on the subway. Robert said nothing, knowing she had other reasons for choosing to travel underground. When he had his way, they walked or rode the bouncing, gaudy-colored colectivos. One morning she confided that she had never taken a bus until she met him.

While Gabriela was volunteering for the Madres on weekends, Robert consumed the empty hours by reading works she had brought from her father's library. They helped to fill the blank space where she had been. "Books are sacrosanct in our house," she told him. "Father has one of the best private collections in Buenos Aires."

So he pored over the Argentine classics in her absence, tomes bound in Moroccan leather with gold lettering: *Facundo, Martín Fierro, Ficciones,* yellowed issues of *Sur* and other journals. Soon Robert realized that Señor Roca had excluded from his library all works by women and most by the avant-garde, the underground and opposition: Arlt's tales of the criminal and insane, Pizarnik's suicidal verse, Cortázar's syncopated, irreverent prose, Sábato's searing novels and essays. He and Gabriela made up for the missing volumes by hunting for their own tattered copies in the used bookstores along Avenida Corrientes, scanning the magazine *Punto de Vista* for reviews of new releases, buying works by younger authors like Valenzuela, Piglia, Giardinelli, Perlongher. As he devoured their writings, Robert felt like someone who had not only studied their books but dwelled in them, known the characters in person, loved, feared and hated with them.

He spent whole weekends reading and learning and dreaming with those writers. Little by little he came to link some of their volumes with the odor of their paper, or perhaps a fusion of the pages and their subjects. Borges reeked of old libraries, Cortázar exhaled aromas of wet streets, red wine and *Gitanes*, Pizarnik breathed blood and dead flowers, Giardinelli smelled of bourbon and capybara leather.

When Gabriela returned from the clinic, she would find him reading on their Pampa. They looked at each other, feeling as if weeks had gone by, as if they had been separated by an ocean. She dashed to the bed and leaped on him. They kissed and embraced among the books, ravenous for the taste of skin and hair. While they rolled on the sheets, Robert had the impression that he was making love to a library, a people, a nation as well as a woman who lived there. If Gabriela dug her fingernails into his back, making him cry out and bleed, he also felt a small part of her country's pain. Rising later from the Pampa, the couple saw those poor books, their pages ripped or dog-eared on the blood-stained sheets or strewn on the floor with socks, shoes and underwear.

There were moments, as they crossed paths in a doorway, when he worried that her feelings had changed. It was not what she said or did, only something he dreaded or imagined. Then she would sneak up on him from behind, throw her arms around Robert's neck, jump onto his back and squeeze him with her sinewy thighs, whispering, almost like a secret, "Osito, *quiero tu amor.*"

As they loved one another through the nights, the building panted like a living creature. The geraniums climbed over the iron bars of their balcony. The matron hugged a man who did not take his coffee at the window. The moon pulled on the tides of the twins' flowering puberty. The portera swooned, recalling a dance in the Patagonian village of her youth.

Not far away, beyond San Telmo and the port, the owners of El Boliche were finally closing their doors, locking the deadbolts as their customers headed up or down the streets to the candy-colored houses where sailors, fishermen and stevedores lived, dreaming of the World Cup, the national lottery or Gabriela Sabatini, or maybe having nightmares of police roundups, killer cars and drive-by shootings. In the prodigal neighborhoods of Palermo and Recoleta, uniformed guards patrolled the City of the Dead, the church of Nuestra Señora del Pilar tolled its bells, the gomero tree soughed in the breeze. Across the railroad tracks, somewhere in the sprawling slums of plywood, corrugated iron and plastic of Matanza, the flower girl slept on the dirt floor of a shack with her mother, aunts, uncles, brothers, sisters, cousins and emaciated dogs.

City

The earth wheeled around the sun, the weather turned hot, jacarandas opened their violet pannicles. By this time Robert and Gabriela had nearly exhausted their solitary life. Their world had expanded then contracted as though it were a universe or their own hearts, blurring the boundaries between the two. Now they yearned to spread their bliss. After weeks of living barefoot in their Garden, sleeping together by the biblical shade of the fig tree, they began to reclaim Buenos Aires. Gabriela should have known better, but like Robert she was swept out by the riptide of their love.

They bought more newspapers and magazines at their corner kiosk, chatted with their baker, florist and grocer, took coffee, drinks and snacks in local bars, had more lunches and dinners at neighborhood boliches. Gradually they moved beyond their barrio, their beloved Sur, to other quarters of Buenos Aires. They roamed, they mounted garish colectivos, they wandered for miles, following their noses into a sweet-smelling café or pastry shop, into a glowing parrilla for a beefsteak, chop or meat pie. They walked up and down 9 de Julio, the avenue lined with jacaranda trees whose blossoms floated down, covering the sidewalks with a bluish-purple mantle. They removed their shoes and socks to feel on their soles the cool petals against the warm cement, skipping, running, racing over that sea of flowers. The ground sang under their feet. They bought jasmines at *floristerías*, stuck stems behind their ears or in a buttonhole, regaled them to astonished passersby who found redolent nosegays sprouting in their arms.

One of the few spots they did not visit was the Plaza de Mayo, where on their first day they had seen that deluge of flowers in the rain.

"It has so many other memories for me," she said one day near downtown. "From before."

"You know, Gaby you've never told me what those two Mothers whispered to you in the square."

She did not respond nor did Robert press her. He was learning to let her reveal certain things in her own cosmic time. He merely said, "The Madres were our guardian angels." While he spoke, the twins stepped onto their balcony and saluted shyly, as if those words had convoked them. Robert returned their smiles.

Frowning, refusing to acknowledge those neighbors, Gabriela declared, "It's too soon. Maybe we'll go back one of these days."

They also avoided the green Barrio Norte, where her parents lived. "They miss me," she said one afternoon, eyeing the fig tree.

"It was time you left home—you're almost thirty."

"Twenty years and many, many months," she corrected, wrinkling her nose.

November days shimmered with golden light. Buenos Aires appeared as a colossal spectacle for Robert and Gabriela, one they seemed to view sometimes with a single pair of eyes. On corners and in metro stations they watched musicians, dancers, puppeteers and mimes perform. On avenues and streets they saw strikes, protests and parades by labor unions, priests and political parties: the Popular Front, the Communists, the Trotskyites, the Peronist Party of Justice, the anti-Peronist Radicals, the anti-Peronist and anti-anti-Peronist Movement for National Dignity. They combed streets and plazas, fleeing moneychangers who accosted them in search of verdes, skirting lines of irate customers who thronged around ruined banks, watching businessmen punch their calculators to compute the latest plunge of the austral. On sidewalks they leaped over puddles and dodged crater-sized potholes. They saw weeds opening cracks in the streets and paint peeling like snakeskin from walls. They witnessed Buenos Aires collapsing around them, hoping that it would survive so long as they sustained it with their love, so long as it provided the milieu of their enchantment.

Gabriela guided Robert through the city she knew so well. He liked how she walked in her own space with that doe's step, her head high, stirring the breeze. She would stop in a store, insinuating herself into its center and into the hearts of salesmen and shopkeepers, sniffing, touching, inspecting whatever was on display. Food, plants, flowers, pets, books, tapes, jewelry, clothes, perfumes—Gabriela stroked, caressed and fondled them. She bought things as though money were molten metal scorching her purse, ballast to be thrown overboard on a ship. Robert failed to understand why other males were not disturbed by the clicking of her heels on the sidewalk, why their eyes were not dazzled by the radiance of her midnight hair, why their blood did not race when her scarves waved in the wind. If he had not been so absorbed in Gabriela, he would have noticed how merchants, teenagers, men and women sighed when she passed in her cloud of spices.

Odd details endeared her to Robert. Her habit of leaving her mouth slightly open before she asked a question, holding her breath until she spoke. Her knack for keeping a straight face in public as she squeezed him in the most unexpected places. The way she would hold to her chest whatever she had just bought, addressing Robert as though it were a gift. "Oh thank you, Osito, *eres un cielo*." Gabriela.

Late one afternoon she guided him to the Teatro Colón. She showed him the cream-colored friezes, capitals and columns of the city's most beautiful building, worn and stippled by time. Near the entrance a young couple in caftans was completing a chalk-painting that covered the sidewalk. Robert and Gabriela saw the familiar profiles of Perón, Evita, Menem and Maradona in pastel colors on the cement, the images of a racy couple dancing the tango, a *delantero* for the Boca Juniors kicking a goal, a gaucho on a horse galloping across the Pampa—all the myths of Argentina compressed into five yards of sidewalk—figures as evanescent as the closing prices of the stock market, as the morning's rate of exchange. An upturned baseball cap lay on the ground for donations.

"Don't you love it Osito?" Gabriela asked. She hopped up and down, tossing fistfuls of worthless change into the artists' cap.

Soon patrons were arriving for an event in the concert hall. Ladies dressed in the spring fashions of Paris, Barcelona and Milan, accompanied by their escorts in tuxedos or tails, alighted from their BMW's, Mercedes, Rolls Royces and strutted into the portico. When the sky rumbled and raindrops began to fall, those couples popped open their umbrellas and scurried for cover.

Robert and Gabriela laughed, letting the rain soak them, recalling their first and only day in the Plaza de Mayo. The lovers ran over the sidewalk where they had seen the chalk-painting. Just a few ghostly vestiges of color remained as the shower pelted the concrete, erasing the images there, splashed over the curb and into the gutter, flowing down the storm drain to the sewers, the river and sea.

Robert stopped, seized Gabriela's arm and looked into her eyes. "Is your heart still full of rain?"

Those words surprised her: he also knew how to retrieve enigmas from the past. But she did not answer. Instead Gabriela stared at the wet pavement, took Robert's hand in hers and led him down the street.

Although he did not know they were being tracked, the memory of the Ford Falcon lurked somewhere in his mind. She knew but told him nothing. Gabriela did not wish to spoil what could not last forever.

They spent most of their time in the thousand bars, boliches, cafés, confiterías, tearooms and *whiskerías* of Buenos Aires. The best had gleaming marble floors and tables, mirrored walls, gilded chandeliers suspended from high ceilings, lamps shining from the walls day and night, waiters dressed like dignitaries in pressed tuxedos, customers reading large newspapers in leather armchairs. Surrounded by a tempestuous sea, those places were islands of peace and calm. No matter what happened outdoors, in spite of panic, inflation and unrest, Robert and Gabriela could always find a table in a clean, well-lit place for a cup of espresso served with a cool glass of water.

Those spots were a neutral territory of the soul where anyone could take refuge from the war in the streets. There all women were *damas*, every man a *caballero*. The waiters, attired in the uniform of their locale, seemed less surly than their proletarian brothers outside. In those sanctuaries no one had to rush. Why abbreviate the truce by which the laws of battle on the sidewalks were graciously suspended?

Dragging their feet, Robert and Gabriela would depart. Outside they might see an archangel directing traffic—white cap, coat and gloves, a black baton for a flaming sword. They knew once more they had been expelled from a small Eden. She would seize his arm and say, "Let's go back for another," spin and pull him to a new table, where they ordered a second or third coffee, tea or drink and stretched the sorcery a little longer.

"Osito, why don't we try to break our record today?" Gabriela asked one morning in bed. She was sitting and hugging her knees to her chest.

"Which record? We set new ones all the time."

"The day we had two morning coffees at our neighborhood café, followed by a pot of tea, then an *aperitivo* around noon, lunch with a bottle of wine at a parrilla in Barrancas, two more coffees and a liqueur at the bar in Recoleta where we listened to the music..."

"Then supper at the Italian restaurant in Montserrat with two bottles of Malbec, a final coffee and a nightcap..."

"Except they weren't final because afterwards we went to the tango place in San Telmo—"

"Where we ordered two more nightcaps—"

"Before I fainted on the table."

"And I carried you to the taxi stand."

Gabriela reflected. "It might be hard to break our record after all, Osito."

"*Vamos*, mujer," he told her, thinking she must seek those excesses in order to forget.

They haunted La Biela with its giant tree and broad veranda, their first and favorite rendezvous. Café de la Paix, elegant as its namesake in Paris, located in Plaza Recoleta too, where Robert had written his first article datelined Buenos Aires. El Estaño, Premier and La Paz on Corrientes, always full of customers. Gran Iberia and the taverns on Avenida de Mayo, where Spanish exiles drank wine and dreamed about the days of freedom before Franco and their Civil War. Gran Café Tortoni up the street, with its golden skylights and aged barmen, where the wood-paneled walls had the luster of old cognac. Clásica y Moderna on Callao, perhaps the only bookstore and café in the world that never closed. The old Confitería del Molino facing Congress, with its marble tables, gilded columns and fragrant confections. MgGoo's and Detalles in Belgrano, where couples petted each other in the leather booths. Tabac, Ser and the slick sidewalk cafés on Avenida del Libertador. Barila and My Friends on Santa Fe, flanked by boutiques, specialty shops and restaurants. Verona and the dives in La Boca, packed with sailors, fishermen, soccer fans. The tango bars in Balcarce and San Telmo, where they heard unending songs about tragic love, spite and treachery. They frequented those spots and many others whose doors have closed and whose names have been forgotten. They were in Buenos Aires and in all cafés at once, in the Algonquin and Gramercy Tavern, Sloppy Joe's and Harry's Bar, the Elephant and Castle, Pedrocchi and El Gijón, Les Deux Magots and La Closerie des Lilas, those places where life goes on regardless of decay, calamity and death.

When they returned to their Inner Galaxy one early afternoon, Robert kicked off his shoes and reclined on the Pampa. Gabriela began to undress, dropping her blouse, panties and skirt in a small pile at her feet. Her pale body was striped by the sun streaming through the blinds.

"I'm going to see my parents tomorrow," she announced, shivering. As she walked to the bedside, Gabriela shook a sandal from her foot. "To tell them about you. That I'm no longer staying with Alfonsina, that I won't be moving back home."

As Robert listened, conversations with girls in college floated through his memory. But how could he compare Gabriela to the young women in California whose families, friends and lovers had not been kidnapped, tortured and killed, who had not endured civil strife and a dictatorship of 2,818 days? Robert placed his hands on her delicate collarbone. "How will your parents take it?"

She considered for a few seconds. "He'll erupt," she said as if her father alone counted. "His only daughter living with a strange man. A foreigner."

"And on a street named Avenida Independencia no less. Do you want me to go with you?"

Gabriela looked at Robert as though he were a child. "Are you mad? That would make it a thousand times worse."

"Are you afraid, Starface?" he asked, sliding his hands down her sides.

"Father loves me. I've always been his favorite." Gabriela's hooded eyes darkened. Her cheeks flushed, and she turned away.

He thought how little he knew about her family, her friends. He had talked to her brother one time. But Segundo, whose name she rarely mentioned, seemed to have disappeared from her life. Robert had also met her colleague Alfonsina just once. Since taking her leave from the hospital, Gabriela no longer saw that young doctor. For weeks the two lovers had existed in a domain of their own, without relatives or acquaintances, without work except for Robert's occasional articles and her weekends with the Madres. He wondered how long it could last like this, their life without others. Just as sooner or later they had to forgo the minor happiness of bars and cafés, they must relinquish for a while their greater paradise, themselves and the Inner Garden.

The next day Gabriela went out on her own. Robert stayed in bed, on his back, remembering the morning she had left him alone in the hotel. Then too her scent had clung to the sheets, every object had evoked images of her. Meanwhile Gaby's red and white geraniums on the balcony trembled as they pushed their shoots between the branches of the ancient fig.

Robert imagined her descending from a taxi on the street of silver acacias, unlocking the tower of locks and deadbolts, passing through the ponderous zaguán. Would both parents be home? Doesn't her father work during the day? How would Gaby break the news? Would she admit that she had made up the story about sharing Alfonsina's apartment? How would she describe him, Robert Wells, her new boyfriend—a man some ten years older, a divorced American, a journalist on indefinite leave? He had to confess that he didn't sound like much of a prospect for parents with a nubile daughter.

After eating a small breakfast, he couldn't stand the wait. He threw on some clothes and climbed the shaky service stairs to the rooftop. Robert had only been there once, the day he and Gaby had moved in and needed to explore every inch of their new building, like two kids in a treehouse. His head emerged into the honey light.

The flat roofs of Buenos Aires form a separate sphere, a jumble of chimneys, antennas, water tanks, clotheslines, wash basins, perhaps some chairs and chaises for sunbathing. Number 98 Avenida Independencia had all of them and more, including a bursting dovecot and a vacant chicken coop. From six stories high Robert gazed out at the city in the late-morning sun. He bent over the crumbling, low brick wall around the perimeter to observe their street. If Gabriela came home in a cab, he'd be able to see her alight on the curb, but if she approached on foot from a bus stop or metro station, the trees and awnings would veil his view of the sidewalk. In the distance he tried to locate her neighborhood of Belgrano. Somewhere in that sea of parks and polo fields, Robert feared, his fate was being decided by people he did not know. The leafy Barrio Norte appeared remote as an island, cooler and more verdant than this sun-drenched, steaming rooftop.

He gave up after an hour of stifling in the midday heat, listening to the cooing and jostling of doves, the blare of horns, the buzzing of scooters, the hum of traffic below. Robert trudged down the stairs to the Inner Garden. Feeling useless, he stripped off his shirt and threw himself on the bed.

In a while he heard the sound of footsteps, hands fumbling for keys, the turning of locks. When she opened, Robert's heart bounded. He sprang to enfold her in his arms, knowing how deeply, how lastingly she had pierced his life, how she was his life now.

"I told them, I told them," Gabriela repeated as though she had to unburden herself of an oppressive weight. Drops of perspiration had collected above the small bow of her lips.

With one hand Robert brushed her hair, still warm from the sunlight. "What did they say?"

"Mamá went along but Father couldn't hide his rage." Gabriela stepped back from Robert. "He threatened to take me out of his will, to disown me—all kinds of horrible things because I'm the first unmarried woman in our family to live..." Her voice trailed off. Then she leaned on her lover's naked chest and sobbed.

Fondling Gabriela's hair again, he yearned to be outside with her. "Shall we go to La Biela?"

Gabriela had never been know to decline an invitation for a drink or meal in Buenos Aires. She dried her eyes with a handkerchief before answering, faintly, "Can we take the *subte*?"

"Why should we be underground on a brilliant day like this?" It was the last time she would make that request. Like so many Argentines she was a fatalist who did not believe misfortune could be averted for long.

They walked to Recoleta, sticking on the shady side of the streets to escape the torrid sun, staying close to storefronts in order to avoid a runaway car. When she and Robert saw the gomero tree before them, they exchanged glances, half-smiling. It was their favorite place in the world besides the Inner Garden. On this Saturday afternoon the plaza was crowded with people walking dogs, milling around the tree and the park.

They sat in the seats that had become their own, the ones they had occupied on that rainy September afternoon and many other days. When the waiter served their vermouth and sodas,

Gabriela flicked the silver moon on her left ear, making it dance in the sunlight pouring through the windows. Robert still could not tell if that crescent was waxing or waning.

She gazed outside and turned quickly somber. "It's him again."

Robert looked in time to see a tall figure, dressed in dark clothes and a black baseball cap, darting behind the trunk of their gomero. A crease furrowed his forehead: "Who's that?"

"Somebody who's been following us."

"You mean you've seen him before?"

"I think so. He looks like the driver of the killer car."

Robert slammed his glass on the table. Gabriela watched him run for the door, collide with a waiter, jump the front steps to the street and sprint toward their spreading tree. The man had gone. Like a dog who had failed to find an old bone or shoe, Robert moped back to the café.

"Why didn't you tell me?" he asked before he had taken his seat, almost accusing her. His hair was disheveled, his brow beaded with sweat. "Why would anybody follow us?"

Gabriela regarded the clients in the café. Some were watching her and her companion in expectation. Turning toward Robert with deeper shades of purple in her eyes, she whispered, "Why wouldn't they? During the Proceso they tracked me for months. He was on their list."

When Gabriela spoke of that period, she never used names. *They* referred to the government, the admirals and generals. *He* meant her vanished lover. Fourteen years after the war had started, as though that struggle had not ended, she still honored a code of silence and allusion. Robert found it hard to believe that she was the same woman who had lain in bed with him for weeks, now so aloof on the opposite side of a table that could have been an unfordable stream or river.

"That man knows our cafés," Gabriela lamented. "Maybe he knows about the Inner Garden too. I can't tell you why I feel that—but I do. None of our places seems safe anymore."

"You're safe as long as we're together, Gaby."

She sighed, "Oh Roberto, *ojalá*," I wish.

"That reminds me—did those cops ever find the Falcon?"

"The captain kept phoning the hospital to give me updates. When he asked me out for a drink I told him to forget it."

Both felt an urgent need to go outside, do something, anything to stop being passive objects of scrutiny. They left the café and crossed the square to Avenida del Libertador and its remorseless flood of traffic. Exhaust and vapors had dimmed the transparent light of afternoon.

Waiting for a moment to race across the thoroughfare, they held each other's hand. In Los Angeles, Robert mused, someone would have slowed, even stopped to let them pass. It was one of few instances when he had recalled his native city with nostalgia.

For minutes they stood on the curb. Robert searched for Gabriela's eyes, but she did not withdraw her sight from that unforgiving cataract of cars, buses, taxis, trucks, scooters, motorcycles. The two of them appeared small and helpless, unable to escape their pursuer, like a pair of stalked animals trying to cross a turbulent stream.

When they glimpsed an opening, they dashed for their lives. Robert and Gabriela reached the farther shore, breathless, where the College of Law loomed above them on a hillock. The building's sooty columns, pediments and flights of stairs made it resemble a black Parthenon against the dull sky. They walked through a park where statues of patriotic heroes on horseback gestured in vain among the flowering trees.

"Look," Gabriela said, pointing to a large sculpture in a *glorieta*, a little square at the junction of several paths.

They approached the statue of a centaur, its breast pierced with arrows, blood dripping from its wounds. Its human face was frozen in a grimace of agony, its body strained like a quarried prey. While the torrent of vehicles seethed along the avenue, without speaking a word, Robert and Gabriela both ran their hands over the pocked marble of the creature's flank, as though they could somehow soothe its pain.

At last he waved down an empty cab. She told the driver their destination. Sitting in silence, Gaby stared at the rear of the cabbie's seat. When they reached the Inner Garden, they found an envelope under their door, sealed with red wax.

Gabriela's soul shrank. "Father's stationery," she moaned. The envelope had the golden sun, the blue and white bands of the Argentine flag.

Like a fearful girl she looked at him with wide-open eyes. She shuddered. Robert felt a cold quiver in the air.

He shut the door behind them. Gabriela bent slowly to pick up the letter. He saw a halo of perspiration on the armpit of her blouse. "It has my name on it with our street address, even 'Departamento G.' That's his handwriting." She peered up at Robert as if she had done something wrong. "I simply told him we were in the Barrio Sur. At first he thought I was joking—his family has always lived on the Northside."

"And how could he have gotten the envelope under our door?" Robert asked, incensed that their privacy had been breached for the second time in an hour or so. "Unless the portera let your father in the building."

"He would never deliver anything by himself," Gabriela said vaguely. "He has people who do those things for him." Robert noticed that she had forgotten to take off her shoes. As she sat slowly on their bed, he knew something had changed.

She inserted one of her long, tapered nails under the flap and tore it open, leaving her finger inside the envelope. Robert remembered her hands grazing, tickling, scratching his chest, stomach, back, groin, thighs. Taking Gabriela's finger from the envelope, he placed it between his lips, biting her flesh and nail with his front teeth. He could taste the salt of her skin.

"Let me read it, Roberto." She pulled away from him. He poked Gabriela under the arm, pinched her and tried to seize the letter from her hand. Without smiling she spun and hurried to their bathroom. She locked the door behind her.

"What day is it?" she called in a minute or two.

"Friday." Robert recalled the dateline he had seen on a copy of the evening paper, *La Razón*, on a corner kiosk.

Emerging from the bathroom, Gabriela asked, "What time is it?"

"How would I know? Nighttime."

"It's an invitation for us to dine at my parents' house at nine o'clock."

"Tonight? Carajo!" Robert shouted like a good porteño. "Couldn't they have given us more time?"

"I'm going to check the portera's clock."

"Ask her about the letter too. I don't trust her now."

Gabriela showered, dressed and walked downstairs with her wet hair tied in a bun. Robert removed his clothes and collapsed on their bed where she had dropped the letter. For some reason he felt reluctant to touch that expensive stationery, 100 percent milled cotton, monogrammed in decorous calligraphy with the name of *César Roca Steele*.

"It's a few minutes after eight o'clock," Gabriela told him when she returned. "I used the portera's phone to call home and tell them we might be late. Father was not happy." Robert perceived the ghost of a mark where she must have pressed the telephone hard against her ear and jaw.

"We don't have much time," she said. Gabriela ran the fingers of one hand through his wavy brown hair, then traced a line from his forehead to Robert's naked belly. "It's funny," she said, leaving her lips parted. "When I'm clean I want to be dirty again, Osito." He felt the stab of her tongue in his ear.

The room sighed and a beast panted under their bed. Robert and Gabriela fell onto the Pampa where her father's message lay like a miniature flag of Argentina. Within a few minutes that sumptuous envelope and letter had been crumpled, she was loosening her hair in Robert's face, sipping at him with soft murmurs, made the music in her throat, gouged him, drew blood from his spine, rolled, straddled, took him while the electrical system went haywire, power surged on-off on-off, fuses exploded, light bulbs shattered to smithereens, the entire building glowed like a fireworks show on the ninth of July, Argentine Independence Day. In the shade of the primordial fig tree the trio of geraniums spurted.

As Robert and Gabriela rose from their bed, they saw her father's letter on the mattress, shredded to pieces and stained with the first blood of her period. Already late for dinner, they threw on their clothes, bolted downstairs, ran through the main door to the street. As they tried to hail a taxi, they smelled the acrid odor of burning wires.

They mounted another black Mercedes. Through the windows they saw fire engines with red lights flashing, sirens shrieking. Power lines sparked and crackled.

"*Qué despelote!*" What a mess! the cabbie cried. The lovers sneaked glances at one another. She told their driver to take them to Calle Dragones in Belgrano. Robert felt blood oozing from the lacerations on his back.

"Well what did the portera say?" he asked her in English.

"Claims she doesn't know how the letter got under our door," she replied in the same language. "She's going to be furious because of the blackout."

Robert attempted to smile, but he was too nervous. He placed his hand on her thigh. "What kind of welcome should I expect?"

Turning somber, she gazed at the parks along Avenida del Libertador, where they had walked in the afternoon. They spied an old man on the curb, dressed in rags, waiting hopelessly to ford that onrushing stream of cars.

"*Pobre hombre,*" Gabriela said under her breath. When the pedestrian was out of sight, she told Robert, in her usual way of answering almost-forgotten questions: "My parents are very civilized. But they're also possessive—especially Father. I'm his firstborn and only daughter." They had entered her treed, grassy Barrio Norte. "I've never gone so many days without seeing them. The funny thing is, I don't miss them at all," she said with an intimation of regret.

They turned onto the quiet street lined with silver acacias. Their cabbie stopped in front of the three-story mansion. Against the night it stood, lamps in the windows, like a hulking ocean liner with lights in the portholes.

"How long have you lived here?" Robert asked.

"All my life."

"What about your family?"

"*Desde siempre,*" she said in the Spanish phrase, Since forever.

As he paid the fare, Robert felt her leg against his, warm and shaking.

12
Dirty War

Three times Gabriela rapped with the door knocker in the shape of a lion's head. Robert heard the sliding of deadbolts. The zaguán grated open. A young maid greeted them in a black uniform with a white apron and starched collar. When Robert stepped inside, he felt that he had crossed a threshold into Gabriela's past.

Madame Roca was waiting in the vestibule, flickering her eyelids and trilling to her daughter, *"Tanto tiempo querida,"* Such a long time my dear. She spoke with an exaggerated singsong, the intonation of the Northside. This small, slim woman floated toward Gabriela. They embraced and kissed.

Señora Roca welcomed the stranger. *"Bienvenido, soy Cornelia,"* she introduced herself standing on her tiptoes and proffering a rouged cheek for Robert's lips. Before kissing her, he looked into her upturned eyes: they were light blue instead of violet, but he saw Gabriela's there.

Madame looped an unsubstantial white arm in her guest's and guided him toward the living room. Robert felt the physical tie between a man and a woman whose daughter sleeps with him.

A firm tapping sounded on the hardwood floor. Señora Roca exchanged glances with Gabriela. The maid scurried away.

In the doorway a tall figure loomed, dressed in black. Leaning on a silver-topped ebony cane, carved in the form of a feline head, he wore sunglasses so dark that his eyes were invisible. Señor Roca looked around sixty, some ten years older than his wife.

"*Buenas noches*," the man announced. Those four syllables seemed to emerge from the depths of a cave, resonating in the room, making the hairs stand on Robert's arms. Unlike Segundo's high-pitched stutter, Roca's speech matched his immense torso. Was he the one who answered the phone on the first night he called Gabriela, Robert wondered. He did not know that voice was feared by people from the Río de la Plata to Tierra del Fuego, revered by others in high stations across the country.

"Buenas noches, Father," Gabriela said—like that, in both Spanish and English. She spoke in a meek tone that Robert did not recognize.

Roca's posture straightened and his pale countenance brightened. In a tender voice he called his daughter by a name that Robert could not decipher. The man's broad-shouldered, pinstriped suit framed a white shirt and crimson tie. Wearing a sport coat and open collar, Robert sensed his own clothes were too casual in the host's arresting company. His shirt had stuck to his back where the blood had begun to dry.

Gabriela stood on her toes to kiss a cheek of her father's prodigious head. In the black wings of his embrace she almost disappeared.

Madame presented the newcomer to her husband. For a few seconds the man stood motionless, towering above Robert, his wife and daughter. Señor Roca pronounced "Good evening" in English. Toward Gabriela's friend he extended a large, blue-veined hand—his left—while the other supported his weight on the black cane. Although Robert's hands were big, that paw engulfed his own. How can I court a woman whose father dwarfs me, he asked himself, whose speech drowns me, whose grip swallows mine?

"I'm sorry we're late, Father. The traffic was terrible."

"I forgive you. Your sense of time comes from another age." Instead of bending toward Gabriela as he spoke, Señor Roca looked into the air. Robert guessed that he could be blind. "In any case Julia is never punctual," the host said in a softer timbre.

Julia? Robert asked himself.

"That's one of Father's nicknames for me," Gaby clarified in feeble, quavering words. Her face flushed and she turned away. Robert had never seen her so disturbed, so apprehensive, not even when they spotted the man in the baseball cap.

Madame Roca intervened. "Let's make ourselves more comfortable," she said, pointing beyond the vestibule.

They followed her into a vast living room with a high ceiling crossed by monumental wooden beams. Robert contemplated the viceregal splendor: a ponderous bureau and tables of dark mahogany, brocaded sofas and chairs, a concert grand piano, an austere pendulum clock, glass bookcases filled with leather-bound volumes, family portraits of soldiers blazoned with medals, wan ladies who might have been expiring from tuberculosis. Planted with arching palm trees, ceramic urns guarded the room's corners. Ancient Persian carpets rested on the wooden floors. Robert recalled the Inner Garden: what would Gaby's parents think of their cramped, one-room hideaway on Avenida Independencia?

Roca tapped his way to a tall chair that resembled a bishop's throne, whose legs were carved in the form of a lion's paws. The lovers sat together on a sofa facing the host. To their right, between them and her husband, Madame perched on a divan.

The maid took orders for drinks, avoiding the foreigner's eyes. She referred to him as *"el Señorito,"* the young gentleman, while she called Gabriela's father *"el Señor,"* the master of the house. In fact Robert felt diminutive and vaporous in the presence of this man. Compared to Roca and the solidity of his home, family and lineage, his own life seemed ephemeral—like those figures sketched in chalk and rinsed away by the showers in front of Teatro Colón.

"How do you like Buenos Aires?" Señora Roca asked.

"Oh I like it," he said, knowing the city and Gabriela were inseparable for him. He moved his foot and unconsciously bumped her shapely ankle; both flinched as the current shot up their calves. Fortunately the old man's half-blind, he thought, and his wife's not facing us. A breeze fluttered gossamer curtains on the windows.

"My family has been in Buenos Aires for nearly four hundred years," Roca started in Spanish, exaggerating by a century or so and aiming his words at the guest.

Where did that come from? Robert asked himself before countering, "My mother's family fought in the American Revolution," stretching the truth in turn. He was astounded by the abruptness of the father's utterance, by his own instinct to defend himself.

"A mere two centuries ago," Roca said.

Before Robert could reply, the maid entered, carrying drinks on a silver tray. She served white wine to Gabriela and Madame, Scotch on ice to Robert, neat to Señor Roca.

"Cheers," the old man said in English with a British accent, raising his glass.

Madame Roca inquired, "What is your line of work, Roberto—do you mind if I call you that?"

"Not at all, Señora—"

"Mr. Wells is a journalist," Roca interceded, returning to Spanish. His emphasis on the name for Robert's profession made it sound menial. "He is a roving correspondent in Latin America for the *Los Angeles Times*."

"Normally I cover Mexico," Robert said in the same language, surprised that Roca had learned about his work. The man's trying to test my Spanish, he thought. "But I've filed a few stories since I arrived here. Not what you'd call 'roving.'"

"This is your first trip to our country," Roca said.

Robert could not tell if the father was making a statement or asking a question. "Yes." He rubbed the deep cleft in his chin.

"And you have been here eight weeks."

Robert had to count in his head. "Yes," he confirmed, feeling disarmed by this man who appeared to have so much knowledge of his life.

"Your articles are quite good for an outsider."

"You've read them all, Sir?"

"Skimmed. I read a dozen national and international dailies and do not have time to dwell on every story."

"I'm glad to hear that somebody reads those articles."

"You are too modest. By the way it is sporting of you to protect your informants by not mentioning their names. But in Argentina even the walls have eyes and ears." Two of those sources are your own children, Robert responded silently, wondering if Roca knew that also.

"Señor Wells," the host continued, "your first article was datelined September 27th, five days after you landed in Buenos Aires. Did you not feel hesitant to write about a new country after such a short time?"

"If the paper had not liked the article, Señor Roca, it would have been rejected. Most editors prefer their correspondents to be informed outsiders. They don't want their writers to go native—that's why they don't allow them to stay in one place for too long."

"My," Señora Roca managed to interject, "your Spanish is perfect. I would never have suspected you're an American."

"Thank you, Madam."

"Well then I have two questions for you," Roca said in English. I must have passed his language test, Robert hoped. "Señor Wells, do you consider yourself to be an 'informed outsider' after two months in Argentina? And is that long enough to 'go native'?"

The guest did not answer. Roca's repetition of those words made them ring false: had Robert really said that? In order to break the tension he tried to laugh, but the sound stuck in his mouth like a syllable in Segundo's throat. It was as if Roca, like dark matter ingesting a galaxy, had gulped the room's atmosphere, making it hard to talk or breathe. At that instant Robert sensed how a childhood in this house could have paralyzed a boy's speech. He felt a jolt of pity for Gaby's brother and conjectured that it might have impaired her as well.

"Argentina mocks many foreigners," Roca resumed. "Just when they think they know her, they realize that they understand nothing."

"I suppose that's true of most countries."

Gabriela's father made a mountainous shrug. "There is no other country like ours."

To change the subject, Robert said, "Gaby has told me a few things about your work, Señor Roca. But exactly what is your profession?" The question hung awkwardly in the air. Mother and daughter tensed like two people caught in a photograph.

The master of the house took his time to respond. "Mr. Wells, I can excuse this curiosity because you are new here. Let me satisfy your interest by saying this—I protect my nation from her enemies." He enunciated those words as if they were etched in travertine. The trace of a smile may have crossed Roca's lips.

Robert knew he should not pry further, but the man's condescension goaded him. "I don't know what you mean, Sir."

Again the host delayed before speaking. He must have judged that Robert's questions did not merit prompt replies. "It is far too complex for a newcomer to understand," he said finally. "At any rate we would prefer to talk about your profession, Señor Wells—our guest's." Roca tapped his walking stick on the wooden floor. "In your articles about the Proceso you reveal a belief common to many young persons—that all wars are fought out of benighted ignorance."

"I might say that about Vietnam, not World War II or Korea. My father served in both and was proud of it."

Roca drew himself up in his chair, puffed out the wall of his chest and pronounced in Spanish: "My ancestors and my family have fought every war in my country's history, from the first to the last."

"Which was the last?" Robert queried. Too late he recognized that either answer—the so-called Dirty War or the Falkland Islands—would be fraught. Both had disgraced Argentina.

"To which conflict are you referring?" Roca switched back to English. He was making it clear that he knew Robert's language, the same spoken by the British combatants in the Anglo-Argentine war, suggesting all these nuances in a short sentence. On the divan Gabriela and her mother cowered.

Robert bit his tongue so hard that he broke the flesh. He was aware that he should not be arguing with a person who had invited him to his house, with whose daughter he shared a bed and apartment. Yet Roca's animus tempted Robert to spar with him. For her sake, her mother's also, he resisted for the moment. The host's question would have to go unanswered, like some of those he himself posed to Gaby.

Impassive and erect, Señor Roca dominated the room from his wooden throne. Gabriela's mother simply observed, so petite and timid that Robert had almost forgotten her. Gaby appeared to grow smaller at her side.

"Your country has a savage history, *joven*," Roca reopened. "War after war."

"I fought in one of them."

"Vietnam," Roca demurred. "Your enemies were ragtag partisans."

How does he know where I served, Robert wondered. Gory images flared in his memory, his vocal chords quivered. The flayed calf's head also rushed through his mind. Trying to restrain himself, he said, "Sir, I saw many comrades die there."

"I saw many of my compatriots slain by terrorists," Roca rejoined.

"You're referring to the Proceso?" Robert despised the bureaucratic euphemism coined by the junta, but his host had already used it, and he did not wish to nettle Gaby's father with more accurate names for the deadliest time in Argentine history—the repression, the dictatorship, the military regime, the state terrorism.

Again Roca disregarded the question. Perhaps his daughter had learned the habit from him, Robert guessed. He turned to look at Gabriela and saw the affliction on her face. Recollecting her lover's disappearance, he sensed how she could have suffered in her own family, how she and her father must have favored opposite sides in the nation's strife. Robert reached subtly for her free hand. The familiar voltage charged his fingertips, while she strove to conceal the shock.

"Yours was a foreign war and ours was domestic," Señor Roca told Robert, ignoring the women in the room. As if he had timed his statement, the grandfather clock sounded ten strokes.

"Are you referring to the state terror?" Robert asked. Gabriela and her mother startled when they heard his question.

Roca waited before replying. "All wars are filled with terror, joven, no matter how justified. None more so than the civil variety. Especially when the state has to cleanse the country of agitators and malcontents. And if our government was so bad, why did yours support us during those years?"

"Not the whole time."

"Most of the war. I know because I met with American agents during the events." Robert would have liked to hear more, but Roca changed the subject: "And let's not forget that you committed your share of war crimes in Southeast Asia." Gabriela's father spoke as if the guest were responsible in person for all actions by his country.

Robert took a long drink of his Scotch. The single malt was old and costly like everything under this roof. Silence descended on the living room.

"An angel must have passed," Señora Roca noted.

"I don't understand," Robert said.

"It's a saying we have," she explained, fidgeting on the divan. "When there's a lull in the conversation—a silence."

Roca was not thinking of angels. "You massacred hundreds of people at My Lai," he proclaimed as though his wife had not spoken.

"I wasn't there, Sir."

"Many of the victims were unarmed civilians, women and children."

Recalling his conversations with Segundo, with Virgilio and the owner of the boliche, Robert could hold back no longer. "Sir, many of the victims in Argentina's bad years were also unarmed civilians, women and children."

Madame Roca recoiled; she had never seen anyone dispute her husband, much less in their own house. Gabriela shrank from the scene.

Roca remained impassive. "The war years were really not so 'bad' for those who knew what was best for Argentina," he intoned, making quotation marks with his long, bony fingers. Those manicured, chalk-white hands have never worked, Robert told himself, never cleaned, cooked or washed a dish, never planted a tree. "And reports of casualties were exaggerated," Roca ended.

"A writer once joked that reports of his death had been greatly exaggerated." Robert hoped his reference would lighten the conversation, which was becoming more lethal with every exchange.

As if he had heard all of this before, Roca said tiredly, "I have read Mark Twain so you need not make allusions to his work. The Americans bombed cities and massacred whole towns in Vietnam. In contrast the Argentine military made selective strikes on terrorists."

This time Robert did not hesitate. "According to the *Nunca Más* report there are at least 11,000 missing, not to mention those who died in battle, in the streets and concentration camps. Some say the total number of desaparecidos is closer to 30,000. That doesn't sound very selective to me."

When he had spoken, Robert cursed himself for getting drawn into a battle of words. He was not only defending his nation's action in Vietnam—a war that never made sense to him anyhow—but also attacking his hosts' country, Gaby's too, for a war that concluded seven years ago, far from the United States. For a moment he felt outside of his own body, hovering over the living room, watching Roca and himself engaged in combat. It did not matter: nothing he did or failed to do that night could have prevented what was going to happen.

Gabriela's father had reloaded for his next salvo. "Whether it was 11,000 or 30,000, those figures pale compared to the one million soldiers and civilians killed by you and your allies in Vietnam." His syllables rumbled like rounds of artillery, growing louder with the numbers.

Robert did not wish to appease César Roca, but he could not deny those facts. "I've seen the figures. I confess that we've never been held accountable for our crimes in that war. On the other hand, Señor, your country was the first where civil justice prosecuted and condemned a military dictatorship on its own soil."

"If you're referring to the 1985 trials, they were a sham."

"Supper will be served soon," Señora Roca inserted in a nervous falsetto. Her husband turned his colossal head and trained it so intently on his wife that she cringed. Robert suspected the man might have eyesight after all.

Gabriela seemed to wither on the sofa. She was staring into her wineglass—almost full—holding it in her lap, her hands around the stem. Is she the same woman who was rolling in bed with me a few hours ago, Robert asked without speaking, who clawed my back with her fingernails? How he would have liked to place his head on Gaby's lap instead of trading volleys with her father, to feel her softness, knead her thighs. But something was driving his speech, Roca's too, something related to the past, he supposed, to her dead lover, her cruel passion.

Quaffing the rest of his Scotch, Robert prepared to rejoin the fray, unwilling to let Roca bully him to surrender. Before he could begin, a cry rose from the rear of the house, followed by a scuffling noise and two Doberman pinschers pushed through the door, their paws skidding on the hardwood floor. Abruptly Gabriela came back to life, greeted the dogs in Spanish, cooed at them, called them by names that Robert could not decipher. Wagging its docked tail, the smaller of the two leaped on her, licked and slobbered her face while the larger animal headed straight for her lover. Robert braced himself, Gaby's mother cried out for the maid and a resounding man's voice ordered: "Heel!" The Dobermans stopped in their tracks, then cowered to Roca's side.

Peeping her head into the doorway, the maid pleaded, "Forgive me, Señores. The dogs sneaked in the back door. Dinner is ready."

"Lock them in the patio," Roca commanded.

As if nothing had occurred, Madame announced they could adjourn to the dining room. The three Rocas preceded the newcomer into a hall that was barely illuminated, whose walls were hung with etchings of the *Guerra al Malón*, Argentina's Indian wars: beleaguered soldiers holding off hordes of mounted natives armed with lances and *bolas*. In spite of its grandeur there was something ghostly about this home—its dark rooms, creaking doors, restless curtains. Robert lingered behind, watching Gabriela between her parents as they moved shoulder to shoulder. How could I ever walk with them, he asked himself, ever break into this family? The words of Virgilio's warning throbbed in his head.

In the dining room a table fit for twenty people had been set for five. Roca stood at the head. His chair was taller and wider than the rest, imperial like his throne in the other room. Leaving an empty place between them, Señora Roca sat on her husband's left. Gabriela took the chair to her father's right, letting Robert have the seat beyond her, as if to separate the warring males. The guest slipped one hand between his shirt and his sport coat, worried that the blood on his back might stain the chair's plush fabric. The cuts made by Gabriela's fingernails had dried.

"We always set the table for the whole family," Roca pronounced in a more convivial note, as though he had not harried the visitor a minute earlier. "Even when one of us is absent, like my son. Or Eulalia."

"Eulalia?" Robert repeated.

"Another of Father's names," Gabriela murmured in that faint tone, her eyes trained on the beige linen tablecloth. Her cheeks blushed. The teardrop chandelier shed its refracted light on her face, making her skin look smooth as mother-of-pearl. Robert could discern the blue veins at her temples. How he would have liked to touch them, her face, to feel her warmth in this dining room, this house with its oppressive gravity. He searched for Gaby's foot. Their shoes touched and both lovers felt a shiver up their leg.

"Segundo may arrive later," Madame Roca interposed, trying to end the uneasy silence, touching the back of the empty chair at her side. Robert suspected how much she, perhaps her husband too, had suffered from Gabriela's absence during the past weeks. "I hope you have the opportunity to meet our son," the Señora added.

Her husband rasped, coughed and heaved a sigh that sullied the air, enveloping Madame in a tainted cloud. Robert might have revealed that he had met Segundo, but the fumes seemed to stifle his breath. He would not have been surprised if Roca already knew about that meeting in the café of the Hotel Castelar.

"We are very proud of our son," Gabriela's father said. "And of Leonora," he assured, disgorging another name unknown to Robert.

"Father calls me that sometimes," Gabriela explained in faltering speech, as though she needed to defend the man. Her cheeks had turned crimson.

Roca resumed, "I persuaded Segundo to go to seminary—in case you did not know, the heads of some preeminent families in Argentina still place a son in the priesthood." He paused between his sentences, like a man whom nobody dares to interrupt. "He has a brilliant career ahead of him in the Church. And it was I who encouraged Beatriz to study medicine."

The American did not gratify his host by asking about the alias this time, nor did Gabriela proffer still another explanation. He understood that Roca was using those nicknames to torment him: each was a prod in Robert's side, an insult, a reminder of a past, an intimacy between Gaby and her father concealed from him. He felt alone at the table, a foreigner, an outsider banished from whole parts of her life. Exchanging glances with Señora Roca, who also appeared to be excluded from the bond between her husband and daughter, for a moment he felt closer to her. Could Segundo have been banned too, he wondered? And Dionisio, Gaby's lover? Robert did not comprehend how she could be so akin to her father in some ways—shared memories, a secret language—yet so distant in others—their politics, the war...

As the maid served, he scanned the room. Religious paintings filled the walls: saints on wooden panels, Slaughter of the Innocents, the Holy Family. Mahogany cupboards held china and crystal, sterling maté gourds, gaucho knives in tooled sheaths of silver. The house and decoration reeked of provincial style and plundered wealth, like an outpost in a distant colony. Robert could not conceive of being raised in such a home, so different from his family's small bungalow in Los Angeles. How could children have played, grown, dreamed here?

"*Buen provecho,*" Señor Roca pronounced the Hispanic expression to open a meal. "*Bon appétit,*" his wife echoed in French not nearly as good as Gabriela's.

During the first course, vichyssoise, and the second, an asparagus omelette—both accompanied by a Chardonnay from the Tupungato Valley—a fragile peace prevailed. With her head bowed, her eyes fixed on her plate, Gabriela hardly ate or spoke. When she raised her chin to take a sip of wine, Robert imagined he could see the liquid percolating down her translucent throat.

He tried to converse with Señora Roca. But as he talked and listened, the lines of some ancient text on warfare echoed through his head: "The hard and stiff will be broken, the soft and supple will prevail."

During the main course—beef Wellington accompanied by an aged Malbec—Roca broke the truce. He started with a skirmish. "The meat reminds me of those words spoken by the Duke's archenemy—God is always on the side with the bigger battalions."

Robert believed that Roca was wrong about the quote, but he did not wish to contradict the host. Instead he answered with a question. "Didn't Napoleon say that providence favors the army with the last reserves?"

"Therefore we may conclude that the side with both the last reserves and the bigger battalions is sure of victory," Roca boomed with a deep-echoing voice, making the glasses clink on the table. "Wellington and Bonaparte would surely have agreed." As if to sanction its owner's remarks, eleven strokes of the pendulum clock sounded from the house's depths.

They ate in a silence without angels. Robert had not tasted such superb cooking in a long time, yet he could not savor it. Roca's mute hostility and the dead air prevented him from settling into the meal. Anticipating the next fusillade, he sat on the edge of his chair.

After taking up the dishes, the maid served a bottle of sparkling Chandon from Mendoza, cradled in a silver bucket, with four goblets on a tray. Robert glanced toward Gabriela, who had recovered a little of her grace. Without smiling, she returned his look; her eyes had darkened to a shade of maroon. Both she and Robert must have remembered the champagne they had drunk their first night in the hotel, prelude to love. It seemed decades ago.

As the maid stood behind him, Roca removed the foil from the top of the thick green bottle. He began to uncork it like a demolitions expert defusing a mine. For a second Robert considered turning his head in case the Argentine elected to fire the stopper in his direction. Then he laughed to himself, recalling that Roca is half-blind and anyhow he simulates the laws of hospitality.

With a loud pop the cork flew from the bottle and shot by Robert's left ear, almost winging Gabriela too. The maid cried, "Oh!" and pressed both hands on her mouth. The near-miss brought memories flashing into Robert's mind: the hit-and-run on Avenida de Mayo, the man stalking them in Recoleta. He observed Gaby's father with a sudden clarity that made him appear transparent, larger and more menacing.

Except for the fizz of champagne the room was silent again. Handing the foaming bottle to his wife, Roca did not alter his mien or apologize, as if shooting corks at guests was routine in his domain. With tremulous hands the hostess poured the straw-colored wine into the goblets.

All waited for the old man to make a toast. Leaning toward the newcomer, Roca proclaimed, "May you have a safe trip back to the United States."

"I'm not planning to go there soon, Sir. Here's to your family's health. Salud," Robert ended, raising his goblet.

"One never knows what will happen tomorrow," Roca presumed.

As they drank, Robert whispered in Gabriela's ear, "I'm drinking stars." She did not change the somber expression on her face.

Both she and her mother had begun to retreat again, mere spectators of male warfare. Staying clear of the battle zone, excusing herself, the maid returned to the kitchen.

"My family has been in Buenos Aires for close to five centuries," Roca started again. His neck was turning red above his starched white collar. "You are a parvenu who arrived just weeks ago. What kind of stability can you offer a woman?" Without waiting for a reply, supposing he had his combatant on the run, the father pursued: "How long do you expect to stay in that ghetto? I do not want her to go on living in a *pocilga*, a pigsty." He used the terms in both Spanish and English, rubbing them in. Robert noted that this man now referred to Gabriela with a pronoun, not as his daughter or by her given name.

The visitor placed both hands on the table, sat upright and drew a slow, deep breath. He cleared his throat before speaking. "Señor Roca," he said looking directly into the host's sunglasses, "all I have to offer Gabriela is my whole life." For the first time that fateful evening the Argentine did not retaliate. As though the words had struck him, he winced, lowered his shoulders and head and turned away from Robert, who thought the man's body shuddered. After a few seconds Roca straightened his torso and tried to reestablish his aplomb, but his mouth twitched, his face flushed to the color of his neck. Meanwhile the Señora sighed, beaming from the American's declaration.

Robert turned toward his lover and leaned into the field of warmth from her body. Gabriela held her goblet in one hand but had not drunk a sip of the champagne. Napoleon's statement about the last reserves drifted through Robert's head. Taking his own goblet in his left hand, he placed it next to his wineglass—still half-full of Malbec—leaving his fingers in contact with both vessels. He extended his foot and poised it by Gabriela's right shoe, hoping her father's presence had not cut the electric field in her limbs. Meanwhile Roca was shifting his weight in the throne, rallying from his brief repulse, marshaling his forces for a new charge.

Robert moved his free hand under the table toward Gaby's, interlocked his fingers with hers at the moment his foot pressed against her ankle. The energy arced through the circuits of their wrists and legs, sparks hissed, both of them jumped from the twin shock. Gabriela screamed "*Ay!*" as her goblet, his too, the glass—all three—exploded in a hundred pieces, spraying red wine, champagne and shards of crystal over the room.

"*Ay Virgen!*" Señora Roca cried, springing from her chair. She went shouting for the maid, her daughter broke out in tears, the dogs yelped in the patio while Roca bolted upright, rose on his cane and hobbled from the room. Without looking at Robert, Gabriela trailed her father into the deep shadows of the house. Madame lagged behind them.

Sitting by himself in the dining room, Robert surveyed its havoc: rivulets of dark wine crossed the beige linen, carrying pieces of glass that glittered like stars. Those sparkling streams mingled with the champagne, sloshed over the table's edge, flowed across the coral rug, trickled and died in pools on the parquet floor.

The maid gasped when she returned: "Señorito, *que Dios nos ayude*," God help us. The young woman did not avoid Robert's eyes this time; hers were light brown. In them he could see her knowledge of Gabriela's family, her fear of Roca, her sympathy for an outsider. From upstairs they could hear the patriarch's rebukes, pealing like thunder.

The maid stared at the wreckage, heaved "Ay!" and began to sop up the mess with towels and sponges.

Feeling guilty among those ruins, Robert stepped through rubble and walked down the hall, where he halted to examine the etchings of the Indian wars again. Her house is full of ghosts, he said to himself as he continued to the living room.

On the top floor Roca ranted. Robert heard no other voices. Was the old man railing at himself, at his wife, Gabriela, both of them? Hearing their master's yells, the dogs paced, rustled and bayed in the patio. The maid hummed a milonga as she cleared and cleaned the table.

For a moment Robert felt an instinct to flee. What could he do there in the living room, a visitor to Roca's home, while the master reproached his wife, his daughter or himself upstairs?

But how could he leave Gaby alone in this house without angels? He felt his solitude here, in Buenos Aires, in Argentina.

Robert strayed around the living room, inspecting the portraits more closely: thin-lipped, sallow maidens and haughty men-at-arms. Full of memories the antique clock in the corner ticked. Robert perused books in glass cases, identical calfskin sets with Roca's initials engraved in gold lettering on the spines— Greek poetry, drama, philosophy; volumes of Machiavelli, Hobbes, Gracián, Nietzsche—all European, no writers from the New World, not a single woman. The Argentine classics must be in another room, Robert guessed, picturing the works that Gaby had lent him from her father's library. "Books are sacrosanct in our house," she had said one day that seemed years ago. As he observed those volumes that appeared untouched, her words made a hollow echo in Robert's head.

He wanted to handle those books, feel, smell their covers and vellum pages, but the cases were locked. He turned to the music collection in a cabinet by the piano. It contained no tapes or CD's, only vinyl 78s, 45s and 33s, mostly operas—*Orfeo ed Euridice, Aïda, La Forza del Destino, Elektra, Tristan und Isolde*. In the corner a console stood with a turntable on its top, its legs carved in the shape of a sphinx's legs and paws. Robert would have liked to play one of the recordings to drown the dogs' wailing and Roca's abuse. But the cabinet was also under lock and key, impenetrable, like so much in this house, he thought, from the front door to Roca's occupation, this family's past. Anyhow he'd rather listen to the maid, who was singing a tango in the dining room:

> ... *Pero hay cosas, compañero,*
> *que ninguno las comprende ...*

He heard high heels on the stairway, more outbursts from above, sounds from the kitchen. Robert remembered Virgilio's warning about this family.

Madame peeked into the living room, inquiring, "*Se puede?*" as if Robert lived here and she were the guest. The woman had arranged her hair and applied new makeup, but it did not conceal the redness of her eyes or the traces of tears on her lashes. She drew near, sighed and embraced him. You're mixed up with the Rocas now, he told himself, hearing in his head the dwarf's admonition, as mixed up as anyone can be.

The hostess looked up into his eyes. "How can you forgive us? We didn't serve you dessert, coffee and a *copa*."

"That's all right, Señora," Robert said, astonished she had said nothing about the scandal in the dining room. He also sensed relief that the meal had not been prolonged: it would have been agony for all except Roca, who must enjoy tormenting their dinner guests.

Suddenly the Señora buried her head in Robert's chest. To him she felt small and weak like her daughter. She glanced up, her face so close to his that he could see little red clouds in her light blue, washed-out eyes. I'm holding Gabriela twenty years or so in the future, he thought. "*Veinte años no es nada,*" Twenty years is nothing, the tango's lyrics ran through his mind.

The gossamer curtains rippled against the windows. The maid had stopped singing, the dogs' whining had ceased with the storm upstairs. At last the house was quiet.

"Can we meet tomorrow morning, Roberto?" the lady pleaded. "I must talk to you in private. Please."

How could he deny the woman when she was grasping his shirtfront, beseeching, gaping at him with eyes that were Gabriela's too? He nodded his assent. In a way he was thankful to Señora Roca, who had tried to be a peacemaker in the war between her husband and himself. She's sought me out when

I'm alone here in the living room, Robert recognized, in the whole country it seemed, when I most need company in this strange house, while Gaby and her father must have forgotten me.

Madame Roca composed herself, pressing the wrinkles out of her skirt and blouse, patting her hair with her delicate hands. "We can meet early—at 10:30 in the Dome, the new lounge at the Park Hyatt on Cerritos." All at once Robert was back in the world of schedules, clocks and appointments, everything he had wished to leave behind in Los Angeles. "Please make yourself comfortable on the sofa," the woman said.

When he sat there, she sidled up to Robert, precisely where Gabriela had been seated earlier. As though nothing abnormal had occurred that night, Señora Roca made small talk about her friends, the opera season, charity balls and benefits. He tried to follow her speech. But at the same time he was straining to catch any sounds from the second floor, also the melancholy tango the maid was singing from the kitchen again. The pendulum clock in the room tolled midnight. Robert wondered why Gabriela remained upstairs with her father. She might as well be at the top of a mountain, he thought, unreachable. Or the bottom of a river.

Finally they heard the sound of heels on the hardwood stairs. Robert and the lady stood. "Now you won't say anything about our date tomorrow, will you?" Madame whispered in a tone of conspiracy, and Robert could could feel her warm breath in his ear. "You can call me Cornelia." As her daughter entered the room, Mrs. Roca linked her arms around his neck, standing on tiptoe. Gaby did not show surprise.

The woman released Robert and faced her daughter. "Querida I'm so sorry about tonight," she said as if they had not spoken since the detonation at the dinner table. The two women hugged each other. When Robert regarded his lover's face resting on the Señora's shoulder, immobile and pale, it resembled a porcelain mask. With fresh lipstick, mascara and rouge, her hair perfectly in place, Gabriela stared past him at the wall.

Still embracing her mother, she stated, "We must leave. You'll feel better tomorrow, *Mamá.*" Gabriela had become the more mature of the two, the one who was in charge and consoled the other, the helpless, forlorn child in her arms.

Madame approached Robert. "*Hasta mañana,*" she said softly in his ear, giving him a long shake with her weightless hand. Her palm felt moist and icy.

He took Gabriela's arm as they followed her mother toward the vestibule. Passing one of the potted trees in the corner, Señora Roca said, "My those palms must have had a growing spurt." Robert searched Gaby's face, hoping to see a smile of complicity there. She looked straight ahead.

The maid was waiting to open the dark zaguán. She kept her eyes trained on the ground.

"*Adiós queridos,*" Madame said, waving a wet handkerchief and fluttering her eyes toward Robert. Gabriela did not say goodbye.

13
Revolutions

They walked into a cloudburst. They did not have an umbrella nor a spreading tree to shelter them. "Her heart's full of rain," he said in silence, remembering.

They saw a cab parked in the halo of a streetlamp. When Gaby needs a taxi, it preternaturally appears, Robert told himself. Had Madame Roca called it? Through slanting rain the car's headlights blinked.

In the back seat Gabriela leaned the waterfall of her hair against his shoulder. She shivered. The cab drove from that quiet neighborhood onto streets crowded with cars and people. It was Friday night in Buenos Aires.

Gabriela was still trembling when they reached the Inner Garden. Robert felt almost as he did after a firefight in Vietnam, exhausted, dirty, astounded to be alive.

"Tell me," he whispered to her.

"Not now. Please be patient, Roberto."

That's the third time she and her brother have told me that, he thought. "Didn't you say your parents were civilized?"

"I also told you Father was possessive." She began to undress.

"'Possessive'? Shit, Gaby. The only reason I didn't walk out was because of you and your mother."

"Osito, please forgive Father. He and Mamá aren't used to having their children gone."

"That gives him the right to attack and insult me?"

"You got your revenge and made me your accomplice," Gabriela pouted. "Nobody has ever humiliated him like that."

"I tried to be courteous but at a certain point I had to defend myself. It was also a sort of way to defend you, the Madres and the desaparecidos." Robert took Gabriela gently by the shoulders. "How does he know so much about me anyhow? Did you tell him?"

"No." The word came from far away.

"He knew exactly how long I've been in Buenos Aires, when I published my first article, that I served in Vietnam. Carajo!" Robert heard his own voice growing louder.

"He has many contacts," she said. Gabriela turned her head away and exposed the tiny mole on her neck.

Robert asked in a calmer tone, "What kind of contacts?"

As usual she did not answer him directly. "Father simply needed to learn about a foreigner who's sharing an apartment with his daughter."

"Why—is that against the law in Argentina? Are you a minor?"

She squirmed away from Robert and slipped under the sheets of the Pampa. "You don't understand," she said in that frail new speech.

"You're right—I don't understand what in hell your father has against me."

Gabriela curled up on her side. Robert could barely hear her muffled whimpers. After removing his damp clothes, he lay down behind her, pressed into her back, rubbed her flanks to warm her cool skin. He heard a moan that seemed to come from three stories below and deep in the ground.

"Talk to me, Starface," he spoke into the spiral of Gaby's ear, smelling her fragrance of salt and spices. Robert remembered the lyrics of a tango: "*Hablame, rompé el silencio,*" he said to her, Talk to me, break this silence. Gabriela did not speak.

Robert grazed his lips on her silver moon. Gaby's body twitched. Like an animal she made the low, plaintive sound once more. The subject of dinner at her parents' house was going to be another taboo, he guessed—like her lover's death, the bad years, so many things.

From the far side of sleep Robert listened to the rain starting, stopping, returning. He heard Gabriela's soft cries. The ashen light of dawn bathed their apartment. After the sun had risen, he forced himself to leave the bed. The rain had stopped.

He inspected his back in the house's only mirror, hung askew over the tiny bathroom sink. In the tarnished glass he saw zigzags of dried blood where scabs were already forming.

He regarded Gaby before leaving the apartment. Robert noticed that he was holding his breath most of the time so as not to wake her: how much he and others were willing to do for this woman who had her head tucked on her chest, her arms and legs drawn up like a fetus.

The pannicles of jacaranda trees appeared dull and pale on the avenues. After meeting Gabriela's father, the city looked different to Robert—bleaker, more perilous. He opted to take the subterráneo. A clock on the platform read 9:50. Swaying back and forth in the old metro car, he thought about Gaby by herself in apartment G, farther and farther away with each click of the rails. Her pallor, her violet eyes, her wrinkled nose when she laughed. Does she still laugh? He could not recall the last time.

"*Hoy solo?*" Alone today? asked the waiter behind the bar at Café Romeo. Robert smiled, glad to be acknowledged, realizing that he had never been here without her. His acquaintances in Buenos Aires: mozos and bartenders, neighbors and shopkeepers, a small man who dwelled underground in the Turkish baths, a large man who wanted to drive him out of Argentina.

"Sí, hoy solo," Robert told the waiter. Like Gabriela now, he added without words. He started to drop a pair of sugar cubes into his café con leche, but he placed them on the counter instead. Also like her, like Segundo. Robert repeated her words from the afternoon in the hospital cafeteria: "People in my country like bitter tastes." As he sipped the coffee, he saw himself reflected, multiplied over and over in the waters of the bar's stained mirrors, clouded by the bluish smoke of cigarettes and the steam of espresso machines.

He walked down the avenue to the Park Hyatt, a modern tower that could have been in Buenos Aires, Los Angeles or almost any metropolis in the world. The digital clock in the lobby read 10:19. Robert took the elevator run by a uniformed attendant. He rode to the top floor, crossed a rain forest of potted plants and reached the Dome, a revolving glass room far above the city.

The host greeted him in English and led him to a sunken chair by the window. "The lower the seats the more expensive the bar," Gaby had told him once. He surveyed the glass-topped tables, floor-to-ceiling windows, black leather chairs, palm trees in white urns, the young mozos garbed in tuxedos. Robert evoked her favorite bars, cafés and confiterías, so unlike this American-style lounge, with their worn furniture, marble floors and tabletops, wood-paneled walls, aromas of tobacco, coffee and pastries, their aged waiters who speak only Spanish. All those cherished spots in the city that stretched beneath him in the morning sun.

He studied the river's mouth. From that distance the Río de la Plata had the color of a dirty lion's mane. Roca surfaced in Robert's memory, merging with Segundo, then with Gaby when he recognized the monumental shape of Teatro Colón. Farther out he sighted other scenes of their love: the green parks and glorietas of Palermo and Belgrano, Recoleta with its park, church and cemetery, the crown of their giant gomero, then the pink Casa Rosada and the Congress downtown, Plaza de Mayo where the Madres and Abuelas march on Thursdays, where he had met her in that deluge of rain and feathers. He contemplated the gray streets and buildings, the wash basins, water tanks and chimneys on the roofs of their neighborhood, where Gaby was sleeping in the Inner Garden. He could not identify their building, lost among so many others. Beyond the edge of the city and the horizon's curve, Robert distinguished the line of the Pampa, imagining wheat and grasses taller than a woman or a man, swaying in the breeze, rolling toward the Andes and Tierra del Fuego.

The bitter coffee had not cleared his head. He ordered a double espresso, black like the ones preferred by Gabriela and her brother. Robert waited, watching their city below, remembering her, the months they had been together, the time that had become a place, this city, this Buenos Aires.

When Madame Roca arrived, the room had made more than half a turn. He spotted her at the entrance, chatting with the host, now following him toward the tables. Like her daughter she moved with nonchalance, like a woman accustomed to having people wait for her. As she approached, Robert observed the lady's slender figure, attired in a linen jacket with matching vest, a silk blouse, a full-length skirt with arabesques of fruits, flowers and vines, a turquoise collarband around her neck. Her hair was swept back in a knot, making her appear younger, taller and more serene than the night before. She wafted to Robert's table.

"I'm so sorry, *querido*," the woman said, as though he were an old friend. Madame Roca tendered a pallid cheek, which he kissed as he inhaled her fragrance of flowers and spices, barely different from her daughter's. "The traffic in Buenos Aires is worse every day," she sighed.

After the host had helped her to sit, the lady inched her chair toward Robert's. "A vermouth and soda," she ordered without looking at the server, the way she had spoken to her maid last night. Seeing the coffee cup in front of him, she asked Robert if he wanted a drink.

"Whisky and soda," he told the mozo.

"And bring platitos," she added. Robert conjured the first time he had gone to a café with Gaby, La Biela, where they had eaten those snacks on little sterling trays.

Señora Roca seemed to enjoy the panorama of the city below. As she took in the view, Robert noticed a silver spiral swinging, dancing on one of her earlobes, the left. Her clothes, jewelry, hair, perfume—everything reminded him of Gaby but even lighter, airier and more expensive.

Madame realized that Robert was admiring her. She continued gazing out those windows in profile to him, stirring just enough to keep that spiral swaying in a small arc and glinting in the sunlight that streamed through the glass. Then she turned slowly, ever so slowly toward him, blinked, glanced at him for a second, made a flick of her head that propelled her earring into its minute orbit, and said, almost whispered to Robert, breathless, "Ooh what a view!"

"Yes."

As she looked at him in the noonday light, he perceived minute specks and striations in her pale blue eyes. He could also make out the crow's feet forming at their edges. Under the rouge on her cheeks Robert discerned freckles—Gaby's constellations, her galaxies after all.

He ran the fingers of one hand through the brown waves of his hair. "You really do favor your daughter—or the other way around."

Madame smiled. "But in some ways we're opposites. She's a Scorpio and I—"

Before she could say more, the mozo arrived with their drinks and platitos, silver trays of cheeses, olives, nuts and potato chips. He put them on their table and reached for Robert's coffee cup, empty now.

"Don't touch it, please!" Mrs. Roca commanded without looking at the waiter. The man recoiled, said nothing and walked away. "Sometimes I read coffee grounds for fun."

She took Robert's porcelain cup and turned it upside down on the white saucer. Studying them, Señora Roca swirled the dark grounds. Her action felt almost invasive to him, bolder than Gaby's and Segundo's, who had gone through the same ritual but with dregs of their own coffee.

The lady frowned and pouted, making her face appear older. "I can see that you take your espresso without sugar." She pushed away the cup and saucer. Robert had a fleeting notion that all the Rocas were acting out a play for which he was the sole spectator.

Gabriela's mother seized an anchovy-stuffed olive from a tray. She placed it on her tongue and cried, "Ay *qué rica!*" Delicious! She glanced at Robert, gave him a conspiratorial smile, licked her tapered fingers with their immaculate, peach-colored nails. Like a child filching a piece of candy, she snatched a second olive and swallowed it.

Robert could scarcely recall her eating food at the dinner party, where she had been an ethereal bystander. Watching the woman devour those olives made him hungry. He speared one with a toothpick.

Madame sipped vermouth, peeking at Robert over the top of her glass. "*Mm, qué sabroso,*" So tasty. "Oh! We forgot," she said, toasting Robert with her drink. "*Cin-cin!*" Mrs. Roca's words and the clink of their glasses were out of tune with everything that had occurred last night. They were like a signal, a bell startling Robert from a dream.

"Lo siento," I'm sorry, Madame said. She lowered her glass.

Like Gaby and her brother, she knows, he told himself. "You don't have to apologize, Señora. Your daughter never does."

"My husband taught her that. Roberto—do you understand her?"

He wanted to tell her about living with Gaby—the river of changing moods, her silences, the delayed replies. But Robert knew it would take hours. He wondered if the lady might have posed the same question to Dionisio and Gabriela's other suitors.

"Maybe. Do you understand her, Señora?"

Mrs. Roca looked down to examine her white hands, laden with rings. Would she neglect to answer like Gaby? She glanced at Robert and responded with another question: "Do you love her?"

Fully, recklessly, he thought, doubting he could condense his emotions into words of Spanish, English or both. A tenderness, desire, a want in the deepest part of himself. Yearning, surrender, *rapto*, risk—each fell short and off the mark, and together they did not nearly add up. All the love and longing a body can hold, Robert wished to say with both hands on his chest, *en las mismas telas del corazón*, down to the bones and marrow. But he did not tell her. And how would this woman ever understand the rain in her daughter's heart? How would he or anyone?

With wide-open eyes Señora Roca waited for his reaction. Robert merely said, "There are no words," feeling betrayed by language and himself.

After absorbing his reply, she stated, "You and Gaby must not go on living together."

"Why?"

Madame lowered her eyelids. "He's always been jealous of her *novios*." She paused. Robert understood to whom *he* referred.

"His family is old," she went on, "very old with their Anglo-Argentine bloodlines. He would only accept a spouse for his daughter who belonged to that privileged caste—if he accepted one at all." Gabriela's mother stared at Robert with those alert, pale eyes.

"And your family?" he asked.

"Spaniards and Italians who came here in the last century. Parvenus, he calls them, as though his people had been here forever."

"That's what he called me last night."

"I know. You can only imagine how much I've suffered because of that, for years . . ." Mrs. Roca's voice trailed off. "From him, I mean." She took a last sip of vermouth. Her smile hinted that she would like a second drink.

Robert wanted to retain a certain clarity in his head, like the midday sun that brightened the lounge, but he calculated he would need more Scotch to fuel this conversation. He called their waiter and ordered a new round. The room had commenced another rotation.

Robert leaned forward in his chair. "Señora, I don't want to be intrusive, but if your backgrounds were so diverse, why . . . how . . . ?" He allowed her to divine the rest.

"I believed—" Madame began, looking nervous. "Roberto, although it may surprise you, as a young man my husband was very insecure. I was his only *novia*, the first young woman who could make him feel comfortable—even though we were born into such different classes." She fixed her blue gaze on Robert, imploring him to guess her meaning. "He's not as bad a person as you think. He can be very brave and generous. During the Proceso he risked his own life to save soldiers and policemen from the rebels, donated money to families whose sons or fathers died in the war. He supports some of them to this day."

Madame Roca sighed and took a long swallow of her fresh drink. "My husband still depends on me. He doesn't even know how to prepare a simple meal! Ever since the children left home he stays in a hotel when I visit my family in Rosario, because he can't take care of himself or bear to be alone."

"You have a full-time maid, don't you?"

"She goes home at night unless we have guests. And she doesn't count for him." Señora Roca fell silent for a few moments. She drank once more, twice. "Sometimes I don't count either," she added sotto voce, as though she were talking to herself. "Ay, he's so steeped in pain and death ..." Her voice faded. She twirled the ice in her nearly-empty glass. "But tell me about your family."

She drinks faster than her daughter, Robert noticed. He spotted their waiter, caught his eye, pointed at the lady's glass for one more vermouth. "I'm divorced and my parents are dead," he told her. "They were only children like me, so I don't have uncles, aunts, cousins, nieces or nephews."

"How lonely that must be. Any children from the marriage?"

"No."

She did not ask more. It would have been difficult for Mrs. Roca to comprehend: her friends belonged to large clans whose lineage stretched back for generations. Only bohemians and other eccentrics tended to live outside a family in this country of tribal rules and wars.

Gabriela's mother viewed the vast arm of the river that shimmered in the sun. "Oh how I would like to escape from this city! But it's too late, too complicated now. There are so many memories, good and bad ... See the Teatro Colón down there on the avenue?"

"Yes."

"He took me there for many concerts when we were dating ... Years later six young men were slain in reprisal for a guerrilla attack and two of the bodies were thrown on the steps of the Colón, wrapped in Argentine flags. I knew their families." Robert remembered the drawings in colored chalk on the rainy sidewalk. So it was another killing field where Gaby had taken him, another place whose past she had not disclosed to him.

Their waiter brought Madame Roca's third vermouth. After taking a sip, she turned her eyes to the window. "Look out there." Robert observed the glittering, muddy expanse of water. Beyond the Río de la Plata he could detect the coast, a faint, blurred line on the horizon.

"They used to fly their captives out there in helicopters," she started. "Drop them in the middle of the estuary. At first they didn't know the currents would wash those bodies onto the beaches at Punta del Este in Uruguay, where many of our generals and admirals spend summer vacations with their families. Naturally those officers didn't relish seeing corpses float ashore while they were sunning themselves at their resorts. You can imagine the scandal." The lady pointed to the river. "Afterwards they learned to shackle their prisoners with iron weights before throwing them from helicopters. Or slit open their bellies with a knife so they would fill up with water and sink." Madame looked toward the east: "They also made death-flights farther upstream over the Río Paraná." She shifted her eyes in the opposite direction: "Others over the Atlantic."

Robert was moved by this woman's honesty, the change in her tone and voice, so different from last night. He wanted to see how much Gabriela's mother would reveal. "Didn't they dredge the river after the war?"

"By that time most of the corpses had decomposed and couldn't be recovered. There's a place just off the coast from Jorge Newberry Airport—navigation marker 14 where they've found bodies with nothing but shreds of skin on the bones. When he saw them one of the divers said he felt like dying of sadness, like a character in a tango." For a second Robert believed she might be joking. But her eyes glistened with moisture.

In his hands Robert took one of her wrists, as small-boned as her daughter's. "Señora Roca, your son drove me there."

"You've met Segundo?"

"On my third day in Argentina."

With her free hand she took a long drink from her glass and heaved a sigh. "He'd stop at nothing to keep you away from her."

"Your son?"

"No—he wouldn't hurt a fly. *Him*." Madame Roca's wrist was shaking in Robert's hand.

"What can I do?"

"Run away with her," the Señora spurted without hesitation, staring at the river. "Far away, to the other side of the world. So you can rescue Gaby from her father and herself."

Robert released the Señora's hand. "Would she come with me?"

Gabriela's mother turned her eyes toward him. They were wet and full. "You stand for everything her father does not—a break with the past, freedom, a normal life," she emphasized. He told himself that his life with Gaby could be called many things but normal. Yet he dimly grasped the woman's intimation.

"Roberto," Mrs. Roca said, "last night when I heard you say, 'All I have to offer is my whole life,' I felt happy for my daughter—the first time in years. But you'll have to do even more to help her, to save her and heal her wounds. You'll be the doctor, not Gaby."

"What kind of wounds?"

"Señor Wells there are certain things a mother cannot tell about her daughter." Madame eyed the river again. "I once had a love like yours," she said wistfully. Before resuming she waited a few seconds. "I don't know if Gaby would ever leave Buenos Aires. She's very close to her city and her father—he trusts her more than me or her brother." She took a long drink of vermouth. "The two of them have business deals that don't include me, Segundo or anyone else in the family. Were you in Argentina during the spring sweepstakes at Palermo?"

"Yes." Robert felt suddenly closer to Señora Roca. She too was banished from the complicity between Gabriela and her father.

"Well my husband's military friends secretly advised him to bet on a long shot. He shared the tip with Gaby. Before the race somebody tampered with the favorite filly—Mina was her name. That's probably why she broke her ankle near the finish line and the darkhorse won. They had to sacrifice the poor animal right there on the track! I was watching from our family box."

Robert recalled when this woman's son had compared him to a darkhorse. He wanted to ask her about it, but the lady was already rambling on: "Thanks to her winnings Gaby can afford the apartment on Avenida Independencia—not that it's exactly the best neighborhood in Buenos Aires." She set her lips firmly. "How my husband hates the name of that street!"

"I pay part of the rent, Señora."

"It's Cornelia," she insisted. Then she said with a passion he had not heard in her voice: "Oh please take her away!" Gabriela's mother appeared desolate now, the way Robert had seen her at dinner. "Do you know about her boyfriend during the war?" He nodded. "Dionisio was willing to give up his fight against the generals and elope with her to Brazil. Unfortunately that wouldn't have been far enough. Oh Roberto, take her to the end of the world forever!" She studied his turquoise eyes. "You remind me of him."

The lady's words gave him an odd sensation, evoking Segundo's similar comments by the river. He was tempted to ask her for more details.

Madame Roca may have perceived the curiosity in his eyes, because she offered, "You both have—or rather he had—long, curly brown hair and bright blue eyes." She reflected for a moment. "But his eyes did not have green in them like yours." She inhaled a deep breath. "Judging by your words last night and the articles you've written I would say you're also an idealist. Maybe not as innocent as Dionisio, who never saw his thirtieth birthday. You also remind me of that poor boy because you're practically alone in the world."

"What do you mean, Señora?"

"Cornelia, *por favor.*"

"*Perdón.*"

"I forgive you this one last time," she said with resignation. "Anyhow Dionisio had a family but he was ashamed to introduce them to Gaby. They lived in Matanza, one of the *villas miseria,* the slums outside Buenos Aires. His parents could not understand why he was taking classes at the university instead of working a full-time job like everyone else they knew. So in many ways he was alone like you, but for other reasons."

Trying to keep the conversation on Gabriela's old boyfriend, Robert said: "Your daughter seems to think Dionisio might still be alive."

"He's not." Mrs. Roca peeked down at her glass, almost empty. "I'm going to need another one." She quaffed the rest of her dark-red vermouth.

Robert signaled their waiter for two more drinks.

"My husband didn't bother to tell me until a few years after the war," Madame said, "but I sensed it long before that." She removed a lace handkerchief from her purse and dried her tears. She looked straight at Roberto. "Oh I've lived my own dirty war ever since I married him." She paused again. "He's close to many of the generals, admirals and brigadiers. He didn't want our daughter to resent him, to think he was somehow involved in her boyfriend's disappearance."

Robert almost had time to ask her if that was true, but Señora Roca looked away and saluted two older women at another table.

"A porteño's never alone in Buenos Aires," she told him. "I asked you to meet me here because it's a new place—most of my friends frequent private clubs or old-fashioned confiterías. Those ladies are the wives of two former ministers who have business ventures with my husband."

Gabriela's mother lifted her chin subtly in their direction. Robert waited a minute before sneaking a glance, just long enough to know those women were gaping at him. "Some new evidence has turned up against their husbands," Madame said, "who've both been put on trial for crimes committed during the war. In recent months there have been dozens of new charges made against the military and its supporters. My husband's afraid he could be indicted too—that's why he got so furious about the war last night. You shouldn't have provoked him."

"Señora Roca, he provoked me."

"Call me Cornelia! This time I don't forgive you, Señor Wells! But yes, you're right—he's not used to people who don't agree with him. Especially in his own house."

As their waiter served a vermouth and a whisky, Robert knew it would be hard for him to use the lady's given name. It reminded him of a Roman matron, not the woman who had given birth to Gabriela, who had confided in him last night and today. He and Mrs. Roca took long drinks from their glasses.

As a horse glances sideways, she observed her two friends. "Roberto, do you know where people went for privacy during the war?"

"Where?"

"Assignation hotels."

"You mean the telos?"

Señora Roca laughed for the first time in his presence. "Oh you know about them. That's what the younger people call them nowadays. The husbands of those women own one of the most luxurious retreats in Buenos Aires."

"Do you mind if I ask what it's called?"

"Why? Afrodita. It's famous." Robert moved in his seat. "During the war several factions used the assignation hotels for high-level meetings."

"Why?"

"Because the management was known for maintaining absolute discretion on behalf of its clients."

"Couples didn't go there?"

"Oh that never stopped," she said, amused. "After all this is Buenos Aires. But when the generals imposed their morality reform they had the police raid the telos to inspect the owners' licenses and the guests' papers. One of the jokes at the time was that coitus interruptus became a national phenomenon."

Both smiled. Madame tilted her head and looked deeply into Robert's face. The silver spiral danced on her small, shell-shaped earlobe.

"Your eyes are nearly the same color as my collarband," she said. Señora Roca rubbed the turquoise stones around her neck.

The room had almost completed another revolution. Robert decided it was time to pose the question that haunted him, the one he had been holding back. "Could he have prevented that death?"

Gaby's mother did not reply for seconds. "I believe so but I can't be sure," she divulged in a whisper, checking that pair of women before turning back to Robert. She placed both hands on her chest.

Robert leaned forward with his back to the ladies, shifted in the chair to block their view, clasped the woman's hands for a moment. "Thank you for your confidence and for trying to help us," he told her. "You're a very different person when you're alone."

"Sometimes I feel that I'm a *desaparecida* in my own house."

"I'm sorry Señora."

"Alright I give up," she said in a brighter tone. "You'll never call me by my first name."

"Cornelia. Thank you."

"*Finalmente* Roberto! When you refused to be surrender to him last night, when you told him that you'd give up everything for my daughter, I promised myself to aid you and Gaby. You're the first person who's ever stood up to him in our house. Maybe anywhere." Madame squeezed Robert's hands. "Who's survived, I mean. So you must be very cautious—he won't forget." She hesitated before saying, "I can't risk seeing you again in public. Tené cuidado." Gabriela had once told him the same. "Goodbye."

Looking into her watery eyes, Robert held her hands tightly. At that instant he thought he knew Señora Roca, understood her almost as well as her daughter. She rose and walked off, swaying her hips and clicking her high heels.

Robert observed the city and the Río de la Plata one more time, reciting the questions he should have asked her, too late now. What happened upstairs at her house last night? Did she know about the man in the baseball cap? The hit-and-run on the Avenida de Mayo? And should he tell Gaby what her mother had revealed? How could I fail to tell her, he answered his own question.

Guessing that he might not see Mrs. Roca again, he already thought of her with nostalgia, like a friend from the past. For this woman to meet him at the Dome had been an act of grace and valor. More than her daughter she had told Robert her truths. In contrast to other porteños he knew—Gaby herself, Roca, Segundo, Virgilio—she did not speak in riddles.

When he rose to his feet, his head still felt light from the whisky. The two older women gaped at Robert as he passed their table. Like so many people who had been touched by the bad years in Argentina, he was learning to be suspicious of everyone.

14
Pampa

As he left the glass room, Robert recalled that Madame Roca had forgotten to tell him her astrological sign. Will I ever find out, he wondered, and why am I so curious to know—what difference does it make? At least the woman has disclosed Gaby's symbol, deadliest of all.

When an elevator arrived, he was surprised to see it empty, without an attendant this time. It came to a stop on a lower floor. Two stocky men entered, wearing gray suits and low-brimmed hats. One of them had an eyepatch and the other a ponytail. As soon as the doors closed, those men charged: the first butted Robert in the belly, knocking the air out of his lungs while the second seized him from behind. The foreigner gasped for breath, they blindfolded him, tied his hands behind his back and stuffed a handkerchief down his throat. Almost in unison they ordered, "*Silencio Americano.*" It would be the last utterance he would hear from the two men—more a statement than a command, since the only sounds Robert could make were grunts and mumbles through the gag in his mouth.

The elevator stopped on the bottom floor, where they hustled him into the hall. He was dazed and windless, also faintly dizzy from the Scotch. After making two quick turns, they prodded him down the service stairs to the basement, through a doorway to a spatious parking garage. A vehicle waited there, its engine idling. Robert could not see through his blindfold, but he conjured a green or black, unmarked Ford Falcon with tinted windows, the tall man in the baseball cap at the wheel.

They shoved him onto the back seat. Those men sat on either side of their hostage. When the driver sped out of the garage, someone ripped the handkerchief from Robert's mouth. It had all happened too fast for him to catch his breath, much less to mount a defense, make a scene.

The car drove through the noisy streets of Buenos Aires at midday—the long Argentine *mediodía* that extends from noon until 2 o'clock or later, when people finish lunch or start it. Neither the driver nor the two men spoke. Their silence discomfited Robert more than whatever threats they might have made.

To stay alert he invented names for his fellow-passengers in the back seat, based on what he had glimpsed of them: One-Eye and Ponytail. But it wouldn't surprise me if these guys don't even have names, he thought—trained thugs like a thousand henchmen in the movies who might as well be robots.

As the noise of traffic subsided, the car went faster. The roadbed changed from asphalt to concrete. When it turned to gravel, the driver slowed; then to dirt, slower still. Having his eyes covered had already sharpened Robert's hearing. What good will that do, he admitted, feeling the ropes around his wrists, so taut they dug into his flesh. He thought of Gaby's pale, delicate hands, her mothers's too.

The driver braked and turned off the engine. Robert had lost his notions of time and distance. Had the trip taken an hour, two, more, less? One-Eye and Ponytail nudged him out of the car.

The air was cool and moist. From the absence of voices or the hum of traffic, from the sound of wind rustling through leaves, he supposed they must be in the countryside. The two men guided him through a eucalyptus grove, where Robert breathed in the bracing odor from his childhood in California.

He imagined the high trees with their peeling bark, their dry, pointed leaves. How he longed to be there now, in the state and the city whose safety he had taken for granted all those years, Los Angeles, Our Lady Queen of the Angels.

Their feet crunched on layers of brittle leaves. His captors led him through those woods, turned left onto a path, again, a third time. They don't have to bully me here, he knew, in a forest at the world's end. From the pit of his stomach Robert felt nauseous. He also had a strange sensation of lightness, of freedom—from having to make decisions, assume responsibility, take care of her.

The creak of an iron gate surprised him. He shivered. Gabriela and her wet hair drifted through his mind. A kind of impersonal sadness engulfed him, as though this was happening to someone else. From deep in those woods he heard the useless song of a bird, one he had not heard before, one that he could not have heard in Los Angeles, in California or anywhere else.

A door squeaked on its hinges, reminding Robert of the zaguán at Gaby's house. No—*his* house, Roca's. One-Eye and Ponytail conducted him down a long passageway, turned left three more times, crossed a threshold, rammed Robert into a leather armchair and secured him tightly with ropes around his arms. He winced from the pain in the tender sores on his back, traces of Gaby's love. The two men withdrew and closed a door behind them.

He waited. Why should I be surprised if they've abducted me, Robert asked himself. Recalling his conversation with Madame Roca, he remembered: I'm in a country where prisoners rain from helicopters.

After a minute or so he heard the sound of slow footsteps and the tapping of a cane. Breathing hard, someone halted by the chair, untied Robert's arms and released his blindfold. The American's dazzled, blue-green eyes observed a room with heavy furniture, a pendulum clock, a window cloaked by thick curtains, a whitewashed ceiling traversed by dark beams. He looked over his shoulder and saw César Roca Steele standing predictably above him, appearing even taller than the night before. The man was wearing a black suit, a starched white shirt, a crimson tie—the same one? If so it's marked by champagne, Robert tried to humor himself.

Through his sunglasses Gabriela's father stared down at the hostage. "This has been a small display of strength," he said in English with that deep-echoing voice. "I would not think of launching a full attack on an unarmed opponent."

Only kidnap him, Robert said without words, scanning the room. He saw two doors—one at each end, both of them closed. To his right he had the window.

"Escape would be impossible," Roca said drily. "We are kilometers from a town or village."

In that voice Robert heard a sense of tired victory, a fatigue older than the earth.

"Where are we?"

"You shall never know, amigo." It's more terrifying to be called a friend by César Roca than to be reviled by another man, Robert told himself. "All I can say is that we are not on my estancia, as you might be thinking," the man said—"the ranch you have heard about." How would he know that? Robert wondered. "Nobody else in my family has ever been here—not even *her*." Roca did not have to use his daughter's name. It was as if Gabriela were standing there between the foreigner and himself.

As his eyes grew accustomed to the light, Robert saw mirrors on the walls, tables covered by books, manuscripts, globes, compasses. Roca paced around the leather armchair. Unlike the wounded general who had hobbled out of the dining room last night, he strode forcefully, making the wide-planked wooden floor tremble.

He took a seat in a high wooden chair whose legs were carved in the shape of a lion's paws. Robert speculated: a duplicate of the bishop's throne where Roca had been seated at the dinner party? He also pictured the brass knocker on the massive zaguán of the house in Belgrano, the two sphinxes' feet on the console in the living room, the silver-topped cane that the man was holding in his right hand again today. It all made him unsettled and confused.

"Robert, I rather enjoyed our skirmish last evening." Roca sounded like someone talking about a friendly match of chess. "It was good training. A war game, you could call it."

"A dirty war game."

"'All is fair in …'—you know the adage. And do not forget that all wars are dirty."

Are all loves dirty too? Robert asked Gaby's father with his eyes. Is that why you would have allowed your daughter's boyfriend to be murdered?

"Although I have spoken of games," the Argentine continued, "wars are most serious. A wise soldier should enter a battle gravely, with sorrow and compassion—as if he were attending a funeral."

"Lao-tzu?" Robert thought he remembered. Probably disappointed that his prisoner had recognized his source, Roca swallowed. The American pressed, "Have you ever fought in a war yourself, Sir?"

Disregarding the question, his captor parried with another: "Whose funeral would that be?" He waited for a reply that Robert did not proffer. "I confess that I am fascinated by war and its history. Not the facts—dates, generals, troops. They are important at the time but trivial in the end. What attracts me is the flow of battle, the flux, the strategy."

If you'd ever been in battle, Robert told the man in silence, you wouldn't find it so attractive. You're a chickenhawk, he added, the word his father used for warmongers who had never known the horror of combat.

Roca reclined in his chair and stretched his legs. "I suppose you look down on me the way soldiers disdain those who have never served. But you can trust me Robert, I have been exposed to as much danger as any war-scarred veteran. I do not care if you believe me, nor will I bother to give you details." Madame's words about her husband's courage rushed back to Robert's mind.

"Señor Wells, I am very sorry that we could not end our meal at my house *comme il faut*—with dessert, coffee, a copa and a cigar." His wife had said something similar, Robert recalled, without this note of irony. Had she already informed her husband about her meeting at the Park Hyatt, which ended just minutes before the abduction? He could not believe this: her revelations had persuaded Robert that the lady was on their side, his and her daughter's. Maybe Roca simply had me followed from the apartment this morning, he conjectured. An image of Gabriela in bed flashed through his memory.

"In Spanish we have a lovely word," Roca went on, "*sobremesa*—the food, drink, smoking and conversation that follow the main meal. Last night we could have enjoyed it while imbibing cognac from Napoleon's time. But you and your countrymen do not appreciate that type of ritual because you are always in a hurry. Haste is not compatible with what we know as civilization."

Robert detested Roca's habit of identifying him personally with all of America's failings. But he would restrain himself for the time being. Silencio Americano.

"Do not believe everything she told you," the man murmured in a confidential tone. "She has a mental disorder and has been on medication for clinical depression ever since the Proceso."

Robert mulled, Is he talking about his wife or his daughter? "Who?"

Roca paid no attention to the query. Instead he asked, "You do not know Argentina beyond Buenos Aires, *n'est pas*?" The foreigner stayed silent; Gaby's father was already familiar with Robert's movements, so why answer? "Only here on the Pampa can you begin to comprehend our country—the space, the light, the soil deeper than a man's height—even a man of my size." Robert recollected Gabriela's words to the same effect. At least I have an idea of where we are now, he thought with an inward smile, aware that the Pampa was larger than Texas.

Roca rose from his chair, walked to the window and drew the curtains. "Look at that magnificent expanse, joven. Out there we have year-round grasses, teeming herds and flocks, the best cattle and horses on earth, great wealth from meat, hides, wool and grain." Roca softened his voice. "The Pampa is also where one has a sense of solitude, of being far away, at the end of a continent, a hemisphere and the world. But you would not understand," he closed with a weary sigh. The Pampa is also a bed where your daughter and I make love, Robert told Roca in his mind.

Gabriela's father extended his left hand, groped for a moment and gripped a foot-high, ivory-colored sculpture from the table at his side. He held it up for Robert to examine: a skeleton carved of bone, whaletooth or ivory. It resembled a kind of Grim Reaper without a scythe, unlike any other the American had seen.

"This is *San La Muerte*, Saint Death, also known as the Lord of Patience, *Ayucaba* to the Indians or *San* for short—like a nickname for a dear acquaintance." Roca fondled the statue with both hands. "He is our best friend in Argentina, where we are intimate with mortality. Some consider him to be our true patron saint, our only hope." Articulating each syllable slowly, he explained, "*San* has many powers and many forms. This one has been carved from a single human bone, a femur." Roca turned the image round and round in those large, blue-veined hands, training his dark glasses on it. Whose femur? Robert wondered. He felt transfixed by the sculpture, by the Argentine's words and movements.

"Do not listen to the porteños," Roca advised, "who tell you that our country is a European nation, unlike others in the Andes and the altiplano. We have our own Andes, our altiplano and our Indians. Some of them have tattoos of San La Muerte or miniature figurines grafted under the skin of an arm or leg, which they rub in times of need." He glanced down, caressed the smooth bone, then faced his hostage: "Unlike your sterile Protestant sects," he said as if Robert embodied them all, "the Catholic Church knew how to absorb or tolerate these customs of our native peoples." Roca sighed. "But I see you are distracted," he ended with resignation. Her father's not blind, Robert was nearly convinced.

Rising from his chair, the man proposed, "Let us have drinks. But do not worry, young man—I will not serve champagne this afternoon. I would not want to put your life in danger a second time."

"The cork almost hit Gabriela too."

Roca recoiled as though his daughter's name had struck his chest like a stone. Dropping his head, he turned his back to Robert. With both shoulders hunched and shaking, the man remained there so long that the foreigner thought of leaping from his chair and assaulting him from behind. Then images of One-Eye and Ponytail came back to him, along with their driver and who knows how many other heavies in the entourage? Perhaps some ancestral, unconscious taboo also pulsed inside of Robert, thwarted him from assailing a man who had engendered the woman he loved. As Roca stood facing away from him, the American heard or imagined a faint heaving or whimper that might have emanated from the man's body, from another room, from outside?

Without speaking, Roca raised his shoulders, patted down his suit with both hands, walked to a credenza in front of him. There he picked up a pair of tongs, placed ice cubes in one of two tumblers, poured Scotch in both and set them on a silver tray. Finally he turned, approached his captive and extended the tray.

The foreigner hesitated before taking the glass with ice, feeling complicitous and ashamed for not rejecting the man's offer. But he needed the whisky and he was captivated by Roca's countenance: the man's mouth twitched and his face had flushed, just as it had done last night when Robert announced his love for Gabriela.

The host seated himself in the regal chair. He raised his glass, toasting "Cheers," like that, in English, with a faltering voice. Roca tasted his Scotch. "It is not nearly as old as the cognac you missed *chez moi*, but single-malt and old enough." He had recovered most of his composure and his sonorous basso profundo. He smacked his bloodless lips. "Thank God the British gave us their drinking habits as well as their telephones, streetcars, railroads, refrigerators and freezers for our beef. Their Scotch is far superior to the vile *chicha* fermented by our Indians."

Sipping his third whisky of the day, Robert did not reply, intrigued by this man who was Gaby's father. One moment he exalts his country's indigenous peoples, the next he denigrates their ancient drink. First he lords it over me, then he quakes if I mention his daughter's name.

Roca straightened his back. "I know this may sound inconsistent to you, but ours is a nation of contradictions." Robert no longer felt surprised when the man appeared to divine his thoughts. "As I was suggesting," Gabriela's father resumed, "I have brought you here so that you will know our country and our peoples better." Once more Roca grasped the image of San La Muerte. "Without the Pampa and our natives you would not be able to fathom us—our worship of strong, violent men who tamed our great herds of cattle and horses. The *caudillos* who prevented our nation from collapsing into chaos. Centuries of violence have taught us that the only certainty is this," Roca stressed, waving the bone figure in one hand. "I know it is hard to comprehend for an outsider, especially one from the United States. We have a tango that says, '*There are some things, friend, that nobody understands...*'"

In his mind Robert replayed the song hummed by the maid in the dining room after the meal last night. Had Roca heard it too? But the master of the house had retreated upstairs by that time, blustering, screaming at Gabriela, at his wife, both of them, at himself, the walls, who knows?

"You have hardly spoken a word," the man noted. "You must be bored again." No, Robert told himself: terror kills boredom.

Roca returned the statue of La Muerte to the table. "Tell me something, joven. How did you perform that trick with the wine glasses and the champagne goblets? From this combatant to another, it was very slick."

So there's one thing he doesn't know, Robert comforted himself. Assuming Roca's magisterial style, he expounded, "The electrical principle is known as alternating current or AC, which reverses direction at recurring intervals, in contrast to direct current or DC, which flows in a single direction."

"I know how electricity functions. I am asking you what the trick was."

"The human manifestation of electricity requires intense feelings."

Roca scoffed. "Are you telling me those glasses exploded because of some kind of emotion?"

"Yes." The hostage was enjoying his captor's perplexity. He won't acknowledge that another man could find what he ignores in his own daughter, Robert sensed. "In order for energy to flow in both directions," he elucidated, relishing his advantage, "the sentiment must be mutual between the two parties." For the first time since he had entered Roca's bunker, he felt an urge to smile outwardly. But he did not alter the expression on his face.

The man was shifting in his seat. Robert feared he might have gone too far in taunting Roca, perhaps inciting him beyond recall. He conjured Gaby again, alone in the apartment for so many hours, unaware of his meeting with her mother, now this.

"You know, Roberto, you may not believe me but I feel a sympathy of sorts for you. After all you are one of the few men who have enjoyed the bliss of being with her. Naturally you do not know her as I do," Roca qualified. By this time Robert noticed how the man avoided Gabriela's name, the one that others used for her, the one on the lease for their apartment, the one printed on the calling card she had given him that first night.

Lowering his voice, the Argentine queried, "Apropos, how does it feel to live off a woman?" The prisoner marked a change in Roca's tone and did not answer. "Do you remember where it comes from—the money for your rent?" Again Robert withheld a reply. What could "remember" mean? he asked himself. Had Roca told his wife to broach this subject at the Dome? Had the woman even told him that she would meet Robert there?

The man put down his Scotch, placed his hands on the arms of his chair and said placidly, "As you know from your knowledge of military history, a general may have an opportunity to defeat his enemy with a single blow. But sometimes it can be more strategic, more definitive to strike later, when his opponent is at his weakest and his losses will be not only total but humiliating."

How could I be any weaker, Robert wondered. He clenched his teeth. Silencio Americano.

For seconds neither man spoke. Then Roca said, "Do not be deceived by the silence. Angels never pass through here." The antique clock in the room sounded six strokes, as if they came from the house's depths. I know the time now, Robert consoled himself, trying to keep his head straight.

As though he had penetrated the foreigner's musing, Roca pointed at the clock. "Always slow, like our government." Maybe he does know everything, Robert granted, feeling more helpless.

"Before you leave—" the host started, hesitating to see how the stranger might react. Confident that Roca would not turn him loose so easily, Robert tried to suppress the surge of relief in his chest. "I shall tell you a story, joven." The man drew a long breath. "There was a renowned detective who believed that he had solved a series of crimes—the murders of three rabbis—each one committed on the third day of successive months—September 3rd, October 3rd and November 3rd—in spots around Buenos Aires whose positions formed the first three points of a parallelogram." Roca paused. Robert recalled Segundo telling the minotaur's tale. Lecturing must run in their family.

Gaby's father proceeded: "Of course the inspector surmised that a final murder would occur the following month, on December 3rd at the fourth point of the parallelogram, which he determined would be at the precise coordinates of a remote ranch on the Pampa, much like this one. But when he reached that location on the third day of the predicted month, the killer ambushed him, telling him that he, the detective, would be the victim of the last crime, for which the others had merely been a playful prologue. The criminal shot his hostage in cold blood."

Roca waited for a response. Robert remained impassive. "You see, Señor Wells, the inspector presumed that he had found the solution in the Cabala, in the four letters for God, JHVH—the consonants of the word *Jehovah* matching the four points of the parallelogram—because the toponyms of the first three spots began with J,H and V, in that order. You may know that Hebrew does not use letters for vowels, correct?" Robert refused to assent. "The fourth spot did not correspond to the final H," Roca continued, "because it was a site without a name—like here. So the killings actually had nothing to do with Jehovah or Judaic theology. We live in a godless world, Roberto. The murderer simply wanted to entice and kill the detective who had sent him to jail for a previous crime."

Robert could not hold back any longer. "Sir, Jorge Luis Borges told that story once and for all. It would be hard for anyone to match it and it does not require embellishments. I believe his title is '*La muerte y la brújula*,' Death and the Compass."

Roca rose from his chair and turned around as he had done when Robert pronounced Gabriela's name. The American added, "The mistake of Borges's detective was to think too much. He should have known that criminals are motivated by greed and hatred, not religion or geometry."

Without facing his rival, the man said in a voice that had lost its resonance, "Borges happened to be a friend of mine. What is the point of the story?"

Robert did not wish to grant Roca the satisfaction of hearing him say the obvious, like an obedient schoolboy: revenge. Instead he stated, "Al buen entendedor ...," without completing the proverb.

Robert expected another stab from this old man's rapier. Last night had been a battle of more or less equal forces. This afternoon it's a one-sided slaughter, he admitted, except for the time when Roca wilted at the sound of his daughter's name, and now I've caught him regurgitating his sources again. There were females then—Gabriela with her shrunken frame,

Madame Roca with her frantic cries, the maid's doleful tangos. Today there's only Roca and his men—how many?—and me, Robert lamented, no women to temper the bastard this time. He resigned himself to the worst as silence returned to this other house without angels.

Roca allowed Robert to stew for a minute or more. Still looking away from his captive, he said, "Excuse me, Señor Wells. I shall return soon." He opened one of the doors, did not close it behind him.

The old man wants to catch me in flight, Robert guessed, disgrace me before the murder. Knowing an effort to escape would be futile, he stayed put in the leather chair, pondering Roca's physical reaction to "Gabriela," to his daughter's given name last night and today.

Like the bleak plains around him the afternoon seemed to stretch on forever. Robert closed his eyes to think, to concentrate. The clock struck seven. Penumbra spread over the room.

Roca returned when the half-hour tolled, as though he were following a punctilious schedule. "Please forgive the delay, Señor Wells. I was waiting for the right moment." Hearing those words, Robert felt a jolt of alarm. But he calculated, if Roca was going to kill me, why wouldn't he have done it already? "Kindly follow me," Gaby's father requested in that restrained, overpolite intonation.

They walked through spacious rooms before reaching an open terrace. "*Voilà!*" Roca proclaimed. An arresting vista lay before them: miles and miles of Pampa without a bush or tree, flat as a lake, extending to the horizon, where the sky deepened into red and purple clouds. Robert sensed an eerie calm. A burnt-out sun was setting over the continent.

Gabriela's father placed a ponderous arm around the American's shoulder. To Robert it was heavy as the earth. He shuddered, all but amused despite his repulsion: Roca reminded him of a patrician in the movies, proudly showing his future son-in-law the family holdings. The American stepped sideways out of the man's reach.

Roca did not seem to notice. "Do you prefer dawn or dusk?" he asked.

Disarmed by the question, Robert asked himself, For what?

Roca continued as if he were alone. "Endings are more beautiful because they have an accumulated richness—like the colors and shadows of that horizon." A gust of wind blew across the plain, stirring dust that was barely visible, making both men turn their heads and squint their eyes. "And twilight is followed by the night with all its pureness."

Together they observed the darkening sky. When the last threads of light had nearly waned, Roca guided Robert back to the room where San La Muerte stood propped on the table, like a tutelar god of the land, of the house and its owner.

"Forgive me if I have to cover your eyes once more," Gaby's father said. Robert feared this might be the "right moment," the one he had anticipated, when Roca would shoot him as the murderer had killed the detective in the story. "A caballero, a gentleman must respect certain codes," Roca preached. Does a gentleman commit murders and abductions, Robert mused, keeping a sober face.

César Roca blindfolded the prisoner, slowly and almost tenderly, as a father might knot a scarf for his small son. "I am glad that we have come to know each other better, Roberto." He paused before commanding softly: "Stay far away from her." The timbre of those words, their intimacy made the hostage more uneasy than if the man had shouted them.

Roca clapped his hands. Within a few seconds Robert heard his two kidnappers enter the room—at least he assumed it was One-Eye and Ponytail. As they tied his arms and wrists, he breathed in the male smell of gasoline, maybe engine oil as well.

Had they worked on the car while he was inside? The two men balanced Robert under the arms and helped him to his feet, as if they were now his friends and not his abductors.

They led their captive in reverse now, turning three times to the right, then three more, through the eucalyptus grove to the car. A strong wind whirled behind them, blowing from the edge of the world. Robert knew what a man or woman feels when their sentence has been commuted.

The return to Buenos Aires seemed faster. Again the driver and the three passengers made the trip without speaking. The Falcon braked in the same corner of the underground garage where the journey had begun. This time Ponytail and One-Eye did not take the trouble to stick a handkerchief into Robert's mouth. It was too late, he appeared beaten by now, too fatigued to scream or call for help. After escorting him to the elevator, the two men turned, walked down the hall, entered an exit door, slammed it behind them.

Robert removed his blindfold. Feeling unsteady, he pushed a button for the lift. When it arrived, the operator asked, *"Planta principal, Señor?"* Like a man who has been beaten or raped, Robert did not reply. The attendant shrugged and whistled as they ascended the shaft. The foreigner had the impression of being trapped in a metal coffin.

The doors of the elevator opened. Robert Wells passed through the lobby to the hotel's main entrance. As they hurried past him on the streets of Buenos Aires, men and women ignored his stiff bearing and his stunned, wide-open eyes. If those porteños had paid attention, they might have thought he resembled a phantom, or maybe a man who knows the depth of the chasm under his feet.

15
Virgilio

Where should I turn, Robert brooded, feeling his isolation, his solitude. As he stumbled down Avenida de Mayo in the warmth of this December night, there was too much he did not understand. Traffic lights were melting like faces with drooping eyes. The air sighed around him.

From the long day and evening he had layers of sweat and dust on his body, an oily film on his conscience from the hours with Roca. He was eager to wash them away. Robert recalled Gaby in their apartment: she's been alone too much, he knew, but his feet were leading him to the Turkish baths. Virgilio, like Señora Roca, he hoped, had told him truths.

The same veteran of the Falkland war was propelling his skateboard along the sidewalk near the hotel, extending a tin cup for donations. Robert handed him the loose change in his pocket. "*Que Dios le bendiga*," the legless man recited. Although he was not a believer, at this point the American accepted those formulary words as a blessing from beyond.

Once more Robert descended the basement stairs, purchased a ticket, handed it to the pimpled attendant. In the dressing closet he spotted the hotel's seal on his towel of white terry cloth—the rampant lion. Even in the underworld Robert could not forget Roca.

He stepped down the corridor. His dream of the jeering old men drifted through his head. While ceiling fans whirred, boilers chugged like locomotives. The heat and moisture enveloped Robert in their cocoon.

He strained to see through the mist of the first room. He did not spy a soul until Virgilio sprang into view, like a genie leaping from a bottle. Robert felt the comfort of a traveler who has reached a refuge.

"Welcome back," his friend rasped, sidling up to him. The foreigner could smell Virgilio's rancid breath, but it did not repulse him. "I hear you had a hard time, m'hijo," the man said, giving Robert a playful shove on the arm.

"Worse than a nightmare."

Virgilio seemed puzzled. "Are you talking about your dream the other night or what happened on the Pampa?"

"You know about today?"

"I know about today and yesterday, sometimes even tomorrow."

"And my dreams too?"

"Nightmares, Roberto. Didn't I tell you not to get mixed up with the Rocas?"

"I was already mixed up with Gabriela when I met you."

Virgilio's laugh rose through chambers of phlegm. "But you still weren't pussy-whipped, Che!"

Robert seized the man by the shoulders. He was about to slug him when he stopped himself, knowing he didn't have the strength or the will now, looking down at this creature whose head reached no higher than his chest, who was groveling, whose distorted face was beseeching mercy. Robert also knew he must count on the dwarf's knowledge. Despite Virgilio's insult he felt a kind of gratitude to him, an affection he did not quite understand. He dropped both hands to his side.

"Gaby's sweet, isn't she?" Virgilio ventured, knowing Robert's anger had abated. He twirled the end of an imaginary mustache. "Those purple eyes, those long lashes, that purring!"

"*Cállate!*" Robert's command echoed against the perspiring walls.

"And what about those love-wounds on your back?" the man gibed, reaching around the American's waist and poking his scabs with a yellow claw.

Robert flinched from the pain and clutched both of Virgilio's arms. "*Basta ya,* carajo!"

"I'm sorry, amigo." In his memory Robert heard Gaby's father addressing him by that word. "I'm just trying to knock some sense into you," Virgilio said. "They're poison—all the Rocas."

"Even her mother?"

Virgilio freed one of his hands to make indefinite circles in the air. "Not as deadly as her husband but she knows a lot, more than she told you. Like every Argentine she has secrets that she will never divulge."

"How can you be sure of that?" Robert asked, still clasping Virgiilio's other arm.

"Remember, *compañero*—I know things before they happen. Or don't happen. Down here time can flow in all directions."

"Then you can tell me something." Robert released him. "Roca suggested that either his wife or Gabriela has suffered from a mental disorder since the war. Which was he talking about?"

"I'm not a psychiatrist, Roberto. Let's go through the baths," Virgilio urged, confident his friend would follow. Without looking back he turned and headed toward the second room. Robert walked a step behind, his eyes fixed on the hump protruding from the towel on his friend's shoulders. It was crisscrossed by a network of tiny red veins that seemed as complicated as the mess of his life with Gaby, her parents, her brother, all of them.

They passed through the next room without stopping and entered the last, the circular hall, hotter and steamier than the others, more than Robert recalled. A sheen of perspiration shone on the foreigner's skin. Covered with dark, fuzzy hair, Virgilio's limbs and torso appeared almost dry. As he watched the small man walk ahead on his bowed legs, his frame contorted like a question mark, Robert felt a new fondness for him.

He observed the benches, ranged like the steps of an amphitheater where the old men had been sitting the first time, their heads drooping between their legs. He and the Argentine took seats facing the empty space.

Through the rising mist Virgilio pointed at those wooden benches. Robert noticed that the dwarf's curved fingernails had grown remarkably since they had met the last time. "The old sinners are all gone for now," Virgilio said with a smile. "They're lying low like everyone who held power during the war. Have you been reading the newspapers?"

"When I have time."

"You'd better start making the time, Che. After all you're a journalist, right? And it's a matter of self-preservation. I've read some of your articles—not bad for a newcomer," he added, reminding Robert of something Roca had said over dinner. Could it really have been just last night?

Virgilio waved his paws in front of the American's face. "Open your eyes Bobby! There's a national campaign going on, digging up new evidence every day. Old memories have been stirred up all over the country. The *gorilas* and their allies are nervous." When Robert looked at a loss, Virgilio explained, "Oh the gorillas—that's another word we use for the milicos, the *golpistas* who carried out the coup against the legal government—men like César Roca ... Where were we, Che? Right, some of his friends are already under house arrest. His hands are stained with the blood of many Argentines."

Robert rubbed the deep cleft of his chin. "His wife's not certain about his role in the murder of Gabriela's boyfriend. But she thinks Roca could have stopped it."

"*Stopped?* Shit, he may have given the order!" Virgilio hesitated, allowing his words to sink into the foreigner's mind. Robert did not look surprised. "Dionisio, *pobre muchacho*," Virgilio continued in a somber voice. He paused for a moment. "Do you drink coffee, Roberto?"

"I thought you knew everything. And what's that got to do with Gaby's boyfriend?"

"It's what Roca told his army friends to do—give the kid '*Café, mucho café*.' One of the military's codes for getting rid of someone."

Robert remembered Gaby, her brother and Señora Roca reading espresso grounds. "If the old man's so guilty, why hasn't he been brought to trial?" he asked. A furrow creased his forehead.

Virgilio lifted his right hand slowly with the palm down, sighing in a prolonged "eeeeeh" as if to say, How naive you are, boludo! Then he stared into the mist. "Just as Roca took many lives from us, he saved others on his side, sometimes even risked his own survival, *concha de su madre*. A lot of people owe him their lives, money or both. Until now he's had too much power, too many connections in the Church, the state and the military to be prosecuted." Virgilio grinned. "By the way have you heard about Argentina's new space program?"

Robert sensed that he was being set up for one of the small man's jokes. "Alright tell me."

"We're going to stack up all our admirals and generals until they reach the moon." Through locks of mucus the dwarf sent a hoarse laugh into the clouds of steam. Robert smiled only for a second. Virgilio looked suddenly earnest. "You know you're being followed don't you?"

"Yes. Who is he?"

"One of Roca's henchmen, one of those *pesados* who still haven't heard the war ended in 1984. Wouldn't Orwell have liked that?" Virgilio did not wait for a response. "He's also the driver of the car that almost killed you on Avenida de Mayo. The same Falcon that abducted you today."

Images flew into Robert's mind: the silent trip to the Pampa, San La Muerte in Roca's enormous hands, that sunset on the bloody horizon. By this time he would not have been shocked by anything Virgilio said.

"Roberto, tell me more about this afternoon."

"I thought you already knew."

"I wasn't there and I want to hear the details."

When Robert had finished, Virgilio began to whimper, then to cry so hard that his whole, twisted body shook. "Things are moving . . . too quick . . . ," he stammered through sobs. He spoke in a grievous tone, one that the American had not heard before, without the irony that usually spiked Virgilio's words. It was so hot in the third chamber that Robert's pulse raced, his body tingled.

Peering into the haze, the Argentine said, "You need to see a friend of mine. Julio Mazzini's one of the few good people left in this country at war with itself."

"Why him?"

"He also has reasons for fighting Roca—he may even know about some documents that could help incriminate the bastard. But keep this in mind, Che," Virgilio cautioned in a mournful register. "You, Julio and I are like gnats on Roca's arm. He could get rid of us with one slap of his lion's paws."

"Then why are you getting involved?"

"Someday you'll understand. For the time being let's say that Dionisio Sarmiento was close to me—very close. Sure maybe he was too much of an idealist but that was the times." Virgilio coughed in order to keep from bawling a second time. "After torturing Dionisio for hours they drugged him, took him up in a helicopter over the Río de la Plata, shackled his legs and wrists with iron weights and threw him over the side." The dwarf made a falling motion with one of his knobby hands. "Ever since he's been sleeping on the riverbed." Once more he wept.

Robert felt nausea as he listened to that story for a second time. Recalling what Señora Roca had told him, he conjured the glittering expanse of river, the pale line of the Uruguayan coast. He imagined Dionisio plunging through the air, probably thinking of Gaby as he fell and his body struck the water, crushed by the impact, finally sinking to the muddy bottom.

Robert was not certain he could bear this heat much longer. His heart pounded, his temples throbbed, his head spun. But the American realized that he must press Virgilio. Who knows when you'll see him again, he asked himself.

Robert turned to his guide. "Do you know why Gaby's father wanted her boyfriend killed?"

"His excuse was that Dionisio belonged to the Montoneros, the radical Peronists who were fighting the government."

"Was that true?"

"He had friends in that group but Dionisio was merely a young man with ideals, like a lot of students in those days. The same thing happened to many others under the state terror—death by association."

"Maybe Roca had other reasons for wanting Dionisio dead."

Virgilio paused. "Many others. For example, that poor young man didn't belong to the Anglo-Argentine elite, the Jockey Club, the polo and horseracing crowd. Any more than me or you," he added, nudging Robert's chest. "Roca also claimed Dionisio was too old for his daughter but their difference in age was only a few years—he was one of those students who hang around the university for a long time. Even then Gaby liked 'older men.'"

As he uttered these words, Virgilio cowered, raising his elbows to protect himself from another assault. But Robert felt too dejected to move.

"Those were just pretexts," the little man resumed, "the whole business of Dionisio's class, age and politics. There was something else, much deeper." He looked at Robert with compassion in his bloodshot eyes. "The worst you suspect is true of César Roca. I can't tell you more—even I have scruples, especially where women are concerned."

"Tell me what you mean," Robert said in the sternest tone he could muster. To him the man seemed about to reveal something, as if he might show him a lewd photo, something vile and wicked.

But Virgilio merely responded, "I can't, *mi viejo*," using the expression that Argentine men reserve for their male friends, young or old. "All of us have to learn some things for ourselves."

Robert eyed the man for a few moments. He sighed, "Okay. Tell me about Julio Mazzini."

Virgilio rose from the bench and walked into the steam. Soon he came back into sight, then evaporated in the clouds. His voice passed through the mist. "Julio teaches at a high school in San Telmo. But now I realize they're already on Christmas vacation—*la puta!*" he cursed. "You'll have to seek him out at home. I'd rather you didn't because it will put him in danger. *Pero no hay remedio,*" But there's no way around it.

Virgilio reappeared, approached and opened his mouth to continue, exposing his gap-toothed gums. "Julio lives with his family in an old building at the corner of Caseros and Piedras in San Telmo, about two kilometers from here." Robert committed those streets to memory.

Virgilio began to recede into the fog again. "Ask the portero for Julio Mazzini's apartment number," he called over one shoulder as he vanished again. "Say you're a friend of mine." The man's voice turned faint before it grew in volume: "Julio's about sixty years old, has a mop of white hair and a big birthmark on his brow." Coming back into view, the dwarf pointed to a spot above his left eye. "Right here," he said, "about the size of Gaby's nipples."

Before Robert could grasp him, Virgilio slipped away again. The foreigner felt too weak to chase him. He also knew it was mindless to punish the person who had aided him more than any other in Argentina.

A voice emanated from the steam. "You've got to catch Roca off guard." Robert was feeling annoyed by Virgilio's movements, the fading or swelling of his speech, his abrupt departures and arrivals. "Americano!" an order issued from the haze. "Listen! We have a proverb that says, '*El que pega primero pega dos veces,*' The man who hits first hits twice." As he pronounced these words, Virgilio emerged again, making a combination one-two punch, shadow boxing with his gnarled hands.

Robert couldn't help laughing. He rose from the bench and sparred a few seconds with the man.

Virgilio clinched with Robert. "Look, hermano," he said, glancing up and placing a yellow-nailed index finger beneath his right eye, still moist with tears. Robert could feel the warmth of this man's breath.

Virgilio pulled down the lower lid of his eye and displayed a sulfurous orb streaked with veins. There's nothing it hasn't seen, Robert told himself. "*Ojo mucho ojo!*" his friend cautioned, Be careful, very careful! Robert pictured the warning painted on his door at the hotel upstairs. "Roca has murdered people—I mean he's had them killed. He wouldn't think twice about doing away with a newcomer who has no connections in Argentina."

"Then why didn't he do it today?"

Virgilio gave another twirl of his hand. "Quién sabe? I don't want to offend you Roberto, but perhaps Roca doesn't believe you're worth it. He probably thinks you're so scared that you'll leave the country now. Or it could be that he's not ready to make Gaby suffer the loss of a second lover—or maybe even a third or fourth?" Robert showed no reaction to the small man's conjecture. "Most likely the son of a bitch is wary of complications while new inquiries about the bad years are gathering steam. Sorry for the choice of words, Che," Virgilio said with a smile, waving his hands in the vaporous air. "But the old man could have other reasons for waiting. You can be sure of one thing—he's thought it through to the end, all the possibilities and their consequences. Nobody's more astute than César Roca Steele."

"I know."

"Two more things Roberto. One, don't send more articles to your newspaper."

"You're the one who encouraged me to write them in the first place."

"It was a good idea when you arrived in Buenos Aires because it put you on the public record. But if you go on writing about the junta's guilt at this crucial time, Roca and his underlings would have another reason to go after you." Virgilio paused. "Remember—don't wait for him to move again. Hit first."

He feinted another jab, bringing his fist to rest on Robert's moist arm, then opening his palm and pressing. The stranger felt the warmth of Virgilio's rough skin, the beating of his pulse. For a moment he was a little less alone in Buenos Aires.

"What's the second thing?"

"Good memory, Che." The man swung a playful hook at his friend's square chin. "You must take Roca by surprise but you must also stay calm, keep your head clear, Roberto. One of our poets talks about the poisoned root of anger and its honey tip—don't eat it because it can destroy you. It's already consumed your enemy."

"I'll try."

"And come back if you need help, mi viejo." Virgilio squeezed Robert's arm. "If I'm still here, that is." He doffed an invisible hat, turned and walked into the clouds, where his voice called, "*Adiós...*"

As he hurried to a bathroom, Robert worried he might never see the man again. He bent over the toilet bowl and retched a stream of vomit. Its turbid color reminded him of the Río de la Plata.

Walking onto the busy Avenida de Mayo, it seemed many things had changed, that it was a different night and another time of year. Robert stayed far from the curb as he walked, still feeling a little queasy, evoking the runaway Falcon on this avenue, just a few blocks from here. He spotted the dial of a large 24-hour clock: 00:09.

He could not unlock their apartment door from the outside. Gabriela must have thrown the deadbolt, he told himself, waiting. "*Soy yo,*" Robert called. After a minute or so she opened to peek outside. She rubbed her eyes as if she had been asleep. Standing on tiptoe the way her mother had done on the fatal night, she threw both arms about his neck, nuzzled her cheek against his. Robert breathed in her scent mingled with the odors of the Inner Garden. He no longer felt sick. He was home with Gabriela.

When they hugged, her body trembled in her nightgown. She felt so light in Robert's arms that she could float away on her bare feet, he thought, holding her tighter. His heart sped with the love he felt for her.

"Osito, we've never been away from each other so long. Where were you?" Vague shadows clouded Gabriela's face.

"I have a lot to tell you. But I need a drink of water."

"A beer for me."

As they walked to the kitchen, each slipped an arm around the other's waist, their legs and hips bumping, tingling from the current. Gabriela filled a glass of water for him while he opened the refrigerator and pulled out a Quilmes. Robert handed it to her. She poured while he rubbed her thin, pale arms, covered with light down. They returned to the living room, still touching, as if they might be separated without warning.

They sat together on their Pampa. When her fingers grazed his cheek, Robert recalled the touch of Madame Roca's hand.

Where the hell to start, he pondered for a moment. "I talked to your mother this morning."

Gabriela'a hand fell from Robert's face. As though he had betrayed her, she stared in disbelief with her violet eyes. "Where?"

"At the Dome, a new American café downtown."

"What did she tell you?"

"That we should run away together."

Gabriela let out a small cry, spilling some of her glass. "Why?"

Her question astonished him so much that Robert took seconds to respond: "You can't guess?"

She turned away. "You don't know my mother well."

"How could I? What I do know is that she understands us, she's on our side. Everyone else wants to drive us apart."

"It's always easy to defend someone else's parents."

"I don't defend your father, Gaby. Do you?"

She pouted, reclined on a pillow and closed her eyes. Robert realized that sooner or later he would have to tell her more about his conversation with her mother, with Virgilio also, not to mention that her father had abducted him, that he had probably ordered the hit-and-run. But Gaby remained too vulnerable to take in all the disclosures at once. He lay down, knowing he was playing his part in the concert of silence that enveloped her.

They had a fitful night. Each time a blast of foghorns reached them from the port, Gabriela whimpered, moaned and nestled closer. Those sounds resembled the calls of dark, heavy birds floating past their windows.

16
Julio

Around noon he tried to rouse her to say goodbye. Gaby buried herself in the sheets. When Robert passed through their zaguán, the air had turned cool and fog still hung over Buenos Aires. He noticed a strange smell in the air.

After he mounted a cab, the driver said, "The stink's worse down by the port."

"What is it?"

"Nobody knows yet. A big cloud blocked the sun this morning and the air got colder. Reminded me of an eclipse I saw in Buenos Aires years ago."

Robert gazed out his half-open window. The sky had darkened. Amid the diesel fumes from cars and buses he recognized a distinct, pervasive stench.

Standing on the sidewalk at the corner of Caseros and Piedras, Robert looked across the street, wondering if he had come to the right place. A dilapidated five-story apartment building rose against the ashen sky. The smell was stronger now, like the reek of a slaughterhouse.

He stopped to inspect the apartment's mailboxes. Robert did not see the name he wanted. At the foot of the stairway he found the portero's cubicle, where he knocked.

Someone cracked the door. Inhaling the odor of cooked cabbage, Robert perceived the face of a short, bald man who peered out at him. The smell of food made him feel nauseous.

"What do you wish?"

"I'm looking for Julio Mazzini."
"*De parte de quién?*" On whose behalf?
"A friend of Virgilio."
"Virgilio who?"
"Virgilio—the little man."
"Oh *el enano*," the portero smiled, the dwarf. "*Momento.*" For a minute, maybe longer, Robert waited. He heard a muffled voice behind the closed door.

Once more the face appeared. "He's waiting for you on the top floor, apartment D, street side."

The building did not have an elevator. As Robert climbed the worn, wooden stairs, he smelled aromas of pastas and tucos that the neighbors must have been preparing for lunch.

He knocked. A few seconds later he heard a series of locks being turned from inside. "Señor Julio Mazzini?" Robert asked in a sonorous voice when the door had opened. A man with white hair stood in front of him. He had a round, pink birthmark above his left eye.

"*Para servirle, Señor.*"

"I'm a friend of Virgilio's. Robert Wells."

The Argentine extended a cautious hand. "Welcome then. *Pase.*"

Carlos Gardel's song was playing on an old console radio in the small living room:

> *Buenos Aires mi tierra querida,*
> *escuchá mi canción*
> *que con ella va mi vida.*

"One of my favorite tangos," Robert said, recalling when he had heard it that second day with Gaby. It seemed decades, lifetimes ago.

"One of mine too—I can see that we're going to get along. Please take the most comfortable seat." Mazzini pointed to a red armchair, full of ragged pillows, by the open, screenless window. It had a footrest and a slight view of the port, if you sat straight, craned your neck and were as tall as Robert.

Sitting on an old couch, the host said, "Gardel—the musician of memory."

Yes, the American thought.

"Did you see the cloud?" Mazzini asked.

"No but I heard about it. What is it?"

"It formed above the river this morning, floated there for a while then blew onshore, bringing that rotten smell with it." Robert settled into the chair. "You watch," the man said. "The Left will blame the military and the Right will say it's a neo-Communist plot." As if they had known each other for months, Mazzini and his guest laughed together.

"I saw Virgilio last night in the Turkish baths."

The man's brown eyes shone like those of a child. "How is the old boy?"

"Hard to say. I've grown fond of him."

"I know what you mean—it takes a while." Mazzini rose to his feet. "Can I offer you something to drink? How about a beer?"

Robert pictured Gabriela in their apartment. It felt too early for a drink, but he did not wish to reject the man's hospitality. "*Bien.*"

Mazzini lowered the volume of the radio and walked to the kitchen, separated from the living room by a half-drawn curtain stained with cooking oil, wine and tomato sauce. He pulled two Andes lagers from a refrigerator, removed their caps with a bottle opener and carried them to the living room.

"Salud," he said, lifting his beer.

This man's eyes have the brightness of a bird's, Robert told himself. Raising his bottle, sipping, he had the warm feeling of taking the first drink with a new companion. "Have you known Virgilio for long?"

"Many years. He's quite a tipo, isn't he?"

"I've never known anyone like him," Robert admitted.

"Seen everything. He suffered a lot during the war. I'll bet he didn't tell you how he lost most of his teeth." Robert shook his head. "They knocked them out with an iron pipe one morning in a warehouse on the outskirts of Buenos Aires." Mazzini moved his hands vigorously as he spoke.

"Why?"

"Because he was on the wrong side and he dared to speak out against the podridos. They even lashed the hump on his back with a bullwhip. He didn't tell you about that either, right?"

Robert sat up in his chair. "No."

"His wife and his brother were both 'transferred' in the war," Mazzini said, making air quotes with two fingers of each hand.

"What's that?"

"One of the junta's bureaucratic terms for sending people to their deaths."

Robert was starting to feel sick to his stomach again. He placed his beer on the small table by his chair. Sweat beaded his forehead. He had turned pallid.

"Are you alright?" Mazzini asked.

"I've heard so much in the last few days. Sometimes it goes to my stomach." He paused. "Why do you think Virgilio would want to help me?"

"He doesn't put much store in his own life—he'll risk himself for others. He's done it for me."

"But why me? I'm a foreigner he met by chance."

"Señor Wells, nothing happens by chance in Argentina. Virgilio can smell out trouble almost before it happens. He must have seen right away that you're not a mere tourist. You know the language and you've been in the country for some time, no?"

"Only a few months."

"Sometimes that's enough. Where are you from?"

"U.S."

"I wouldn't have guessed. Believe me—Virgilio has his reasons for helping you. Look out there." Mazzini pointed to the only window in the room.

Robert stood and leaned outside. The lowering sky made it look as dark as dusk. An odor of dead meat wafted into the room.

Mazzini rose, walked to the stranger's side and placed an arm around his shoulders. Unlike Roca's it did not feel as heavy as the world to Robert. "Are you better, Che?" He spoke with the intimate pronoun *vos* for family and close friends.

"I'm okay," Robert answered, taking his seat again. Almost untouched, his beer rested sadly on the table.

"Tell me more," Mazzini said.

"I've fallen for a porteña named Gabriela Roca Dafiume."

The man startled, pulling back from Robert's chair. "*Pucha!*"

"You know her?"

"No but I've heard of her and I'm familiar with her father—César Roca Steele, right?"

The American nodded. "You've met him?"

"No," Mazzini laughed. "I don't move in those circles. The Rocas are a prominent family. I know a lot about his activities under the dictatorship—anyone who suffered during that regime dreads his name. Except for his allies. Go on."

Robert told the story of Gabriela, her brother, her parents, the kidnapping, sparing Mazzini most of the details. As he spoke, he still could not believe his abduction had occurred downtown in the broad light of midday, just a few blocks from the Plaza de Mayo and the Mothers, the city's heart. He felt the old terror and rage growing in his chest.

When Robert had finished, Julio sat down in silence, as if he were struggling for words. "That blind bastard," he said finally.

"I'm not so sure he's blind. Anyway Roca told me something I didn't understand. He suggested that his wife or daughter has mental problems."

"I can't help you there—never seen either one of them." Noting the distress on Robert's face, Mazzini looked uneasy. He gulped from his bottle and confessed, "I could use a whisky instead of a beer but I don't have a drop in the house." He waited a second before asking, "Would you like to know more about Roca?"

"*Claro que sí.*"

Robert's host heaved a long, deep breath. "He worked hand-in-glove with the generals, admirals, politicians, bishops and industrialists who backed the junta. Since he didn't have an official post he was untouchable. As he is now—always in the shadows, behind the scenes. Yet I've heard he has an office in the Capitol."

"Virgilio told me about a young man named Dionisio Sarmiento." The name must have brought a stab of memory to Mazzini, who bolted on the couch. "What do you know about him?" Robert inquired.

"He was Virgilio's younger brother—he disappeared the same week as my oldest son, Julio Jr. They were classmates at the university."

Robert was too stunned to reply. Mazzini allowed his guest to recompose himself. "I'm sorry," the foreigner said at last. He recalled the dwarf sobbing, his body shaking in the baths.

"Virgilio's usually quiet about his family," the man said. "Why would he tell you about his brother?"

"Because Dionisio was Gabriela Roca's lover. But Virgilio never revealed that they were brothers."

"Just like him. Carajo, *esto se enreda más*," it's getting more tangled. Mazzini paused. "So if Dionisio was Gabriela Roca's lover she must have known his older brother Virgilio, right?"

"You'd think so. But her mother said Dionisio was so ashamed of his family that he didn't want Gaby to meet them. They lived in one of the villas miseria."

"I can imagine how Señor César Roca Steele would have reacted—his daughter mixed up with a family in the slums."

"He's probably just as horrified that she's living with me."

"You live with her? Pucha, that Virgilio's a smart one to put us in touch. Roca gave the order for my son's torture and death. Maybe he did the same for Dionisio's murder."

"That's what Virgilio believes." Robert looked uncomfortable, not knowing where to put his big hands. "They threw that young man out of a helicopter over the river."

Straining to hold back tears, Mazzini rubbed his eyes and turned to hide his face.

Robert swallowed. "If you and your friends know that Roca's responsible for your son's death—maybe Dionisio's too . . . why hasn't he been accused?"

The host made a long sigh. "Mi viejo," he started, addressing Robert with the same term of affection as Virgilio. "When you ask a question like that it's obvious you're a gringo. This is Argentina, a different planet in another age." As he said these words, air gusted through the window from the port, bearing the stench. "You have plenty of problems in your country but I bet you would never smell that, Che—the odor of decay and death." Mazzini drained his beer. He checked Robert's bottle, full almost to the brim. "I'm going to serve another one. It's not easy for me to talk about these things."

The man raised the volume on the radio and took another Andes from his refrigerator. Standing by the couch, he asked, "Are you ready to hear more, Roberto?"

"I think so."

Mazzini stood there holding the beer, thinking. Then he confided: "Just the feel of this cold bottle in my hand takes me back to the morgue, where I had to go every week to identify my friends and students during the war. I can still see them"—he stopped, flattening the palm of one hand—"stretched out on marble slabs in that freezing room, shrouded in white sheets too short to cover their feet, some of their wounds still bleeding and oozing pus."

Robert had become more restless in the chair. Mazzini looked down into his guest's blue-green eyes, sensing his vast loneliness in Argentina.

Sitting once more, he spoke: "César Roca has so many contacts with the police, the government, the Army, Navy, Air Force, the Church—he's been untouchable. During the war he intervened to save the lives of several milicos, even negotiated with the Montoneros. Carajo, he was one of the only golpistas who dared to meet his enemies in person—without bodyguards. They hated him but had to respect the bastard because they feared him. If they had dared to detain him or harm his person, Roca's men would have pursued their families, had them tortured, killed or disappeared. They knew he had a pair of balls like this," Julio said, cupping his hands in the common gesture.

Mazzini glanced away from Robert and delayed before speaking again. "Forgive me viejo, but I can't do much for you. I have two younger children and a wife who could be in jeopardy if Roca learned I was helping you. Do you have a family?"

"No." Robert stood and strode back and forth on the aged wooden floor. Finally he picked up his bottle, held it for a few seconds and took a long drink. The warm lager tasted bitter.

He faced Mazzini. "But I have Gaby. I'm willing to do whatever I can to get Roca convicted because it may be the only way I can rescue her."

The man rose, approached Robert and gave him a big *abrazo*, Argentine style. "Compañero, what about the girl—does she suspect her father could have been involved in Dionisio's murder?"

"No—at least I don't think so."

"Could you convince her?"

"Maybe." Robert paced again.

"Either way it's going to be hard on her. If she goes along with you she may lose her father, maybe her family's support. If she doesn't—" Robert looked so forlorn that Mazzini hesitated. "You're going to have to take the initiative, Che. Roca's informers know me and I can't expose my wife and children—not after what happened to my oldest son. Neither can Virgilio—he has a sister, a second brother, nieces and nephews. At least you don't have a family they could go after."

"Gabriela and I are being followed."

"Doesn't surprise me, hombre." Mazzini gazed straight into the American's eyes. "Roberto," he warned, "it's going to be dangerous." The man paused so that his words would stick. "Are you ready to hear everything?"

Robert took his seat and braced his back against the cushions. "Yes."

"It's going to turn your stomach."

"It's already turned. Tell me, Julio."

The man took a swig from his bottle. "New corpses have been turning up in Argentina, Uruguay and Chile—countries where the *militares* ruled in the 70s and 80s. All three of them were part of a sinister collaboration, the *Operación Cóndor*. You've heard about it, right?"

"Yes."

"Then you know that most of our continent was in the hands of tyrants during those terrible years. Their regimes conspired to stamp out resistance and they tortured many of their victims. Now in Argentina we're finding skulls perforated with bullet holes, skeletons with missing hands, sackfuls of body parts in plastic bags." Mazzini coughed to restrain his tears, while Robert evoked the black pouches for the dead in Vietnam. "The Madres of the Plaza de Mayo and other groups are growing stronger and more confident. A few priests are even telling what they know."

The stench blew in the open window again. Robert had finally emptied his bottle. Raising it, he said, "I need another beer too."

"Good, I'm glad you're going to join me." Mazzini walked to the kitchen and brought back two more Andes. Again he turned up the volume on the radio, which was playing a sad milonga, in order to cover their voices, Robert guessed.

"The time could be right to press in on Roca," Mazzini whispered just loud enough for his guest to hear. He sat on the couch. "But I want you to realize who you're dealing with—what kind of man he is."

"I think I already know that. But tell me more."

"Let's start with my son's murder. First they picked him off the street in one of the killer cars—right on Avenida del Libertador, one of the busiest in Buenos Aires."

Robert remembered the boulevard and its relentless stream of traffic. "Was the vehicle a Ford Falcon?"

"Right—black, tinted windows and unmarked. So you've heard about those cars?"

"Yes." Robert recalled Quiroga's story in the boliche, also the hit-and-run on Avenida de Mayo, the abduction to the Pampa—although he'd never seen that vehicle. In the back of his mind he also glimpsed a Falcon trailing him around Buenos Aires.

"Then they took my son to an abandoned warehouse near the river. The place was known affectionately as '*la escuelita*,' the little school. Julio Jr. may never have seen their faces because they were wearing *capuchas*—the hoods that would remind an American of the Ku Klux Klan—except here they're normally black instead of white." Mazzini formed a pointed cone with two hands. "First the bastards stripped my son and gave him shocks with the *picana*, a cattle-prod that discharges electricity every three or four seconds." As the man spoke, Robert could not help picturing the explosion of wine glasses in Roca's dining room. "That went on for several days," Mazzini said, "but when Julio Jr. refused to sign a confession they decided to do away with him. Have you ever heard of *empalamiento*?"

"No but I can imagine what it might be." Robert was squirming in his chair and clutching his bottle in both hands.

"They took a thick pole and shoved it into my son's rectum until it lacerated his intestines." Mazzini shuddered. "After removing the pole they opened a hole in a wall of the warehouse—" He hesitated, his eyes watering. "Stuffed him inside and plastered it shut. We'll never know if Julio died of internal bleeding or suffocation." Robert lowered his head. "Now do you understand why I can't put the rest of my family in harm's way?"

The foreigner nodded three times, staring at the floor.

"Do you also understand why I'm willing to take some chances to help you?"

"Claro." Without raising his head, Robert asked, "How did you learn about your son's murder?"

"One of the guards got sick of torturing innocent people and fled the country. When President Alfonsín approved the so-called amnesty laws in the mid-80s the man returned to

Argentina and confessed to me but not in public. He told me that César Roca Steele had a colonel in the Army issue the order for Julio Jr.'s seizure, torment and murder."

Mazzini went on, probably trying to test his new friend, to find out if he had the *bolas* to deal with somebody like Gabriela's father. "There were other kinds of torture. They used instruments and techniques with graphic names like 'the submarine,' 'the telephone,' 'the grill' and 'the daisy.' I know they sound like exotic positions for making love but they were for inflicting pain and killing. A murder like Dionisio's in the river was known as a '*mojadito*,' a little dip." Mazzini allowed the term's callous irony to take effect on Robert. "Some prisoners were placed headfirst into tanks of human waste, where they drowned. No doubt you've heard about the girls and women who were raped, whose breasts were cut off or had the picana stuck into their vagina and rectum. Bodies were doused with diesel fuel then burned with old tires to help cover the stink."

Robert's memories of Vietnam mingled with the story of Quiroga's niece, incinerated in a car. "Where's your bathroom, Julio?"

"In that corner, compañero," Mazzini pointed.

As the American retched behind the door, the man winced. When Robert emerged, his face appeared almost as white as Mazzini's hair. A furrow lined his forehead. He moved slowly, his shoulders stooped.

He stopped and looked at his host. "Can I ask you a question?" Robert's voice faltered.

"Whatever you wish, viejo."

"What did your son do to make them torture him?"

"Nothing. My wife and I raised him to be a good Catholic. He loved his books, went to his classes and stayed out of politics. But the devil never rests, as we say in Spanish. By bad luck he got to know Gabriela's boyfriend, who was active in strikes, demonstrations and protests on campus. I already suspected that Roca could have given the order for my son's death but I never understood the motive. Now I'm thinking—after the bastard had Dionisio killed he would have wanted to get rid of the young man's close friends like my son, so they wouldn't be able to talk later." A puff of wind blew into the apartment, bearing the stench. "They've been gone for a decade now—Julio Jr. disappeared on December 8th, 1980, almost ten years ago to the day, Feast of the Immaculate Conception." Mazzini made the sign of the cross on his chest.

Robert rubbed his jaw. He fixed his eyes, wet with tears, on his host. "What can I do?"

"Come and sit by me. I don't want my voice to carry outside." The ancient couch sank under Robert's weight.

"After all those years of living in terror," the man continued, "having my mail opened and my phone tapped, I'm still wary when I speak about my son's death—even in my own house." He hesitated. "I have a couple of papers," he said under his breath. "They might help someday. Documents that show ties between Gabriela's father and a colonel who gave the direct command for Julio Jr.'s kidnapping. If you could find something else like that—something to connect him to Dionisio's death for example—we might manage to link the two crimes and make an investigation feasible."

Mazzini drew away from Robert and inhaled a long breath. "Things like this are happening throughout the country now. There's even hope that some of the executive pardons of politicians and generals may be overturned. After all, in spite of our flaws Argentina may be the only nation in history where members of a military regime have been convicted by a civilian court."

"You mean the trials in 1985?"

"Yes. That was just the start."

Looking more alert, Robert sat straight on the couch. "Can you give me copies of those papers?"

Mazzini placed a finger to his mouth. "Keep it down, Che—even the walls have ears. Where do you live?"

"Avenida Independencia, number 98, apartment G on the third floor." As he spoke, Robert imagined the Inner Garden with Gaby curled up like a fetus on their bed.

Mazzini paused before speaking, as though he were reciting the address to himself. "During and after the war we learned to memorize facts instead of writing them down, Roberto. Will you be there later this afternoon?"

"Yes."

"I'll get the papers to you, viejo. You can count on me—Independencia 98, third floor, G as in '*grave*'—" he emphasized the word. "If you find more evidence you can take it all to my friend Daniel Bello. He's one of the only attorneys in Argentina who's courageous enough to take on somebody like Roca."

Robert removed a card from his worn leather wallet and wrote the name and phone number that Mazzini gave him. "Sorry Julio, I need to write it down or I'll forget."

"*No te preocupes,* Don't worry about it. Daniel will be more likely to press charges if there's proof of multiple crimes. He's a brilliant lawyer who's already won a few cases against the milicos. Everyone respects him, even the police."

"So you believe there's still not enough evidence to indict Roca?"

"I hope there will be, Che. I've been sitting on the documents for years, afraid of exposing my family, waiting for something else to crop up. Daniel wouldn't be able to proceed without more details—Roca's got one of the best teams of lawyers in Buenos Aires."

"What about the guard who told you Gaby's father was behind your son's death? Could he testify?"

"No. He felt so guilty about witnessing those events that he had to get it off his chest, but I can't reveal his name. He has a family too. He's terrified of retribution from the militares."

Mazzini placed both hands on the American's arm and felt it quavering. "Remember, hermano," he said, gazing into Robert's eyes, "this is not a Hollywood movie—César Roca and his cohorts have real people killed. But he's so smooth and clever that he passes for a righteous citizen. From what I've heard he could charm you while issuing your death sentence. So as soon as you have a plausible case against him, make your move. Strike fast."

Robert recalled Virgilio's advice. He looked at Mazzini. "Thanks, viejo."

For a few moments they sat there in silence. Angels could live here, Robert told himself. He trusted Mazzini as much as anyone he'd met in Buenos Aires.

The Argentine may have felt the same about Robert. He switched off the radio and offered to consecrate their new friendship: "Let's have something to eat together. A nice bowl of hot broth would be good for you—me too."

Robert smiled for the first time since entering the apartment. While Mazzini prepared their meal, he kept his host company. There wasn't enough space for two people by the gas burner, so Robert stood just outside the kitchen. It seemed that he had known this man for years.

Praying for justice, Mazzini blessed the food. He and Robert toasted two glasses of red wine for Virgilio. They shared a pot of beef broth with a loaf of bread at a little table by the stove.

During the sobremesa of coffee and fruit Mazzini again turned on the radio. They listened to tangos while Robert told the rest of his story in the City of the Most Holy Trinity and Port of Our Lady of Fair Winds, Ciudad de la Santísima Trinidad y Puerto de Santa María de los Buenos Aires.

17
The Other Shore

He stopped for a moment on the sidewalk and considered returning to Los Angeles, fleeing the Rocas and all their ghosts. Robert looked up at the windows on the top floor of that decrepit building, whose panes reflected the hazy light of the falling sun. He pictured Julio Mazzini in his apartment, also Virgilio in the baths, feeling a new sense of gratitude and recognition. The two men had already suffered unimaginable losses, yet both were willing to endanger themselves for his sake. At that instant Robert knew he could not leave this country. He was in too far by now, could never leave Gaby behind, so many things undone.

The sky darkened. A stench of rotten meat spread over the city. Robert took a taxi to the Inner Garden. *"Todo cambia"* was playing on the cab's radio.

He opened the door and saw an open suitcase on the unmade bed, packed with Gabriela's clothes. From the bathroom he could hear the sound of running water.

"She's moving out," Robert whispered to himself. He fell backwards onto the Pampa, straddling her suitcase with his legs, cocking one arm over his forehead to fend off more calamities.

Barefoot and wearing a light robe, Gabriela walked into the room. From the bed Robert straightened one arm and held it out to her. Even with her wet hair matted against her cheeks and neck, without makeup, she appeared utterly beautiful.

She took Robert's hand. Her palm felt cold and dewy. "Where have you been? You're trembling, Osito." Without waiting for his answer, she said, "It was so empty here without you." Gabriela kneeled at the bedside and cupped her hands around his. She resembled a young girl about to say her prayers. "I've never seen you so pale," she told him.

Robert's brow creased. "Not as pale as you, Gaby."

She lowered her eyelids. Her lashes made those two dark semicircles above her high-boned cheeks. Gabriela crawled into the bed and laid her damp hair, like a spreading fan, against Robert's neck and shoulders. "Oh keep me warm, Osito."

"Will you let me?"

"I want you to."

"I can't if you're gone."

"Gone?"

"The suitcase."

"We're going together, tonto." In relief the air rushed out of Robert's lungs. "Will you always love me?" Gabriela asked out of the blue. Before he could reply, she was adding, "More than the whole world? And would you do anything for me?"

"Oh Gaby."

"It's almost summer," she said brightly, "and we haven't been to the beach yet. We're going on vacation." All at once he understood her changed mood.

Robert rose on one elbow and looked at Gabriela in disbelief. "Vacation?" That word belonged to a different language, he knew, not the one spoken in the city whose air stank, where Roca loomed, where Virgilio and Mazzini were pressing him to act.

"We need to get away from here, Osito. Haven't you noticed the stench? Our building smells worse than a butcher shop."

"The whole city stinks, Gaby." His friends' counsel echoed in Robert's head: hit first, strike fast. But he remembered the broad, white beaches of southern California where he had spent his youth, where he had been unable to go last summer, mired in work and the divorce. The idea of swimming with Gabriela intrigued him, while a chance to escape Roca sounded like a reprieve. Her plan was perfect and all wrong.

"*Por favorcito,*" she begged.

"How long would we stay?"

"Forever," she responded. "No—quién sabe? Just a few days. Please say yes, Osito."

Robert deliberated. "Only for a day or two," he consented, already feeling at fault for yielding.

"Oh thank you!" For a second she looked almost happy. Gabriela looped her arms around his neck.

Robert inhaled the aromas of her hair and body. He would not have admitted, even to himself, that he was relieved to be going farther away from the City, from the man who haunted it. It may be easier to tell her everything if we're away, he hoped, if we're out of Buenos Aires, the axis of Roca's dominion. Her cloud of salt and spices had already overpowered Julio's and Virgilio's advice.

"Guess where we're going?" her voice sounded brightly. Without waiting for an answer, Gabriela blew the word in his ear: "Uruguay!" More than the name of a country it rang like a gong in Robert's head, summoning Señora Roca's tale of corpses floating ashore at Punta del Este.

"What beach?" he asked, holding his breath.

"Colonia del Sacramento." Robert felt spared. "It's closer than Punta del Este, where everybody goes. Not so crowded." Gabriela gave him a playful bump on the hip, making a few sparks. "Time to get up, lazy. Our boat leaves in less than an hour."

As she finished her sentence, a knock sounded on the door. In alarm the two turned toward each other: they were not used to having guests, solicitors or anyone visit them in their sanctuary. Then Robert recalled that Mazzini had agreed to deliver the documents about his son's death.

"It's for me," he told Gabriela.

"Who?"

"You'll see."

"I'm going to throw on some clothes in the bathroom."

Robert did not recognize his new friend, who appeared in an oversized hat, sunglasses and a raincoat. When the man exposed his face, Robert's eyes lit up. He gave Julio a hug in the doorway. "*Pasa* hombre."

"Your portera isn't very hospitable. She didn't want to let me in." Mazzini cradled a manila envelope in his hands.

"I don't blame her, Che. Not with that disguise."

Both laughed until Gabriela walked into the room, her hair still wet. Robert introduced her to Mazzini. When she heard his name, she gaped at the newcomer like a startled animal. The visitor peered into the plum-colored eyes of the woman whose father had ordered his son's death. Later he would tell Robert that he did not feel hatred toward her. Like him, like many more Argentines, she was also a victim of Roca's violence. He had lost a son, she a lover.

Turning away from Gabriela, Mazzini said, "I can't stay, mi viejo. Take this." That envelope seemed to singe Robert's hands. The visitor embraced him, whispering in his ear, "I made photocopies. You can always rely on me."

"These are originals?"

"Yes."

The manila envelope felt weightier in Robert's hands. "*Hasta pronto compadre.*"

"Adiós Julio."

After putting on his hat, coat and gloves, the man hugged Robert and shook Gabriela's limp hand in farewell.

As soon as Mazzini had gone, she asked, "Why did he disguise himself, wear a raincoat when it's so hot and dry outside?"

"Because of what he was carrying."

"That envelope?"

"Yes."

"What's in it?"

"I'll tell you when there's more time." Both he and Gabriela knew those words echoed hers.

"Did this gentleman have a son who was also named Julio?"

"Yes. You knew he was killed in the war?"

"I heard." She paused. "How did you know?"

"From his father."

"Julio Mazzini was my boyfriend's classmate at the university," she said with the otherworldly expression on her face.

"You mean your ex-boyfriend."

Gabriela did not react to Robert's words. As though she were waking from a dream, she said, "We're going to miss our boat."

"They'd probably hold it up for you, Gaby. Like that time the conductor waited for you to take a seat before the concert."

"You mean at the Colón? He waited for both of us."

"No, I was already seated and you'd gone to the powder room—remember?"

Robert may have detected the dawn of a smile on Gabriela's face. "*Quizá*," his lover conceded. But in a second she had turned absolutely serious. "He was an old family friend of Father's. I don't know any captains at the port."

"I wouldn't be surprised if he did." Gabriela did not reply.

While she finished dressing and dried her hair, Robert placed the manila envelope with some of his clothes in the suitcase. He also would have liked to pack the afternoon he and Gabriela had met in the Plaza de Mayo, but then his knowledge of her father might have slipped inside. He slammed the top, locked it tight, set it on the floor. It crouched there like an animal.

Instead of her usual layers, Gabriela wore a sleeveless blouse, a silk scarf knotted around her neck, a linen skirt that billowed around her ankles. She had also changed her hair. A single black braid now fell over one shoulder, the left, making her look even slimmer, more exposed.

On the streets the odor assaulted them. The air felt cool, more like winter than late spring, one week before the summer solstice. A dark sky lowered over Buenos Aires.

Gabriela and Robert mounted a taxi. Speaking like the woman he had met three months ago, in a clear voice she told the driver where to go: *"El Puerto."* As they approached the harbor, Robert glanced up and saw the Park Hyatt's tower. Its glass dome barely protruded above the mist of an afternoon that would never return.

At the port a blue, white and yellow Argentine flag rippled on a pole. In spite of the blustery air the smell was more pungent by the river, like a miasma of gases over a marsh. The couple bought two tickets for the *aliscafo*, the hydrofoil from Buenos Aires to Colonia del Sacramento.

"We're going to another country," she said, "a place without memories."

Memories are everywhere, he told himself, starting to think like an Argentine. "They also had a dictatorship in Uruguay."

"You don't need to remind me. I only meant that it's a new place for us."

They boarded the sleek boat. Most of the passengers belonged to families: men hauling trunks and crates, women and children carrying bags, boxes and infants.

"We're moving to Uruguay," a teenage boy told Robert between puffs on a cigarette. "Argentina's going to hell." He spoke with the bitterness of a person three times his age. "It even stinks here," he said, spitting over the rail.

While the other passengers mingled on the covered stern, Robert and Gabriela took seats in the open bow. The crew untied the dock lines and the vessel taxied out of the harbor.

With one arm Robert surrounded Gabriela. It feels good to have a breeze in our face, he thought, to leave Buenos Aires behind with that stale air and those somber clouds. He consoled himself by recalling that nobody could follow them in a car.

"Are there ferries from here to Uruguay?" he asked her.

She brushed away the hair that was blowing in her eyes. "Of course."

They watched the sun falling through haze on the horizon, like a smudge on the western sky. It turned slowly orange, deep red and purple, bleeding into dusk. Robert remembered the sunset at Roca's house on the Pampa.

When they passed the breakwater, their craft accelerated and rose on steel struts. The lovers spotted two *camalotes* off the bow, little flowering islands drifting down the Río de la Plata in the twilight, about the size of human bodies. They had floated there from the heart of a continent, from the rainforests of Bolivia, Paraguay and Brazil, down steep falls and gorges, through luxuriant valleys and plains to the estuary.

"Wouldn't it be nice to ride on them," Gabriela said, "each one of us on our own camalote? Lying on our backs, just gazing at the sky."

"I'd rather share one with you."

"We'd sink, *bobo*."

"What happens when they reach the ocean?"

"I don't know," Gabriela replied, frowning.

Stars came out in the deepening sky. Looking back toward Buenos Aires, above their city's glow, the couple saw the four scintillating points of the Southern Cross.

"Remember the Calle Cruz del Sur?" Robert asked.

"Yes—that *antipático* of a desk clerk and our night at your hotel." Reclining on the cushion of her seat, Gabriela spoke as though it were an event from a remote past. To Robert it also seemed years ago.

The pitching of the hydrofoil, the memories of Señora Roca's story, Julio's and Virgilio's too, all made his stomach queasy again. Robert pictured corpses on the mucky river bottom, skeletons where whole bodies had been, iron weights bound to their anklebones. He pulled Gabriela closer.

Soon they discerned lights off the bow. As if they had crossed an ocean to a new world, the Argentine refugees jumped and shouted, *"Tierra!"*

"Those people are starting over," Gabriela said.

Contemplating the shore, he asked silently, Can anyone start over? You're turning as cynical as Gaby, he told himself.

When they entered the harbor of Colonia, a tiny fishing boat bobbed ahead of them. Sea gulls circled it, squawking, diving for refuse in the ship's wake. From the pier a few people waved white handkerchiefs. The air smelled clean and the sky was clear. It felt warmer than Buenos Aires.

Robert and Gabriela let the families disembark first. Laden with their luggage and possessions, those people walked through a turnstile, where tired customs officials received them.

The lovers saw three vintage American taxis parked in a row. They chose a black Plymouth sedan. The old, small-windowed car evoked a film noir from the 40s.

Gabriela peeked at Robert with the air of conspiracy that he relished. "A hotel near the river," she told the cabbie.

"Everything's near the river," he said.

"Then on the river."

They passed through the center of Colonia del Sacramento, a crooked maze of narrow streets and courtyards, aging houses and crumbling churches. The driver stopped in front of a whitewashed building on the riverfront. A sign said "Hotel" with part of the "o" and "t" missing.

There was no bellhop to greet them, to open the door or carry their suitcase. After they registered, the unshaven clerk said, "Third floor, Room C, facing the water." He gave Robert a key of notched iron that must have weighed half a pound.

"This could open the door to a castle," he told Gabriela.

As they walked up the creaking stairway, she said, "Those families must be desperate to leave Argentina. By the way Roberto—there are no castles in Uruguay."

He inserted their key in the skull-shaped hole of the door lock. Room C had peeling paint and tall wooden shutters.

"If my parents knew I was staying in a place like this . . ." Gabriela's voice trailed off.

"At least we're not in Argentina."

The room opened onto a wide balcony with a table and two chairs. Robert and Gabriela stood there in the breeze, inhaling the air, looking at the river and the dim glow of lights from Buenos Aires. It seemed they would never elude it.

"And there's a view," she said.

You should be over there, Robert told himself, pursuing Roca instead of taking a holiday. He also remembered achingly that he would have to inform Gabriela about the kidnapping, his conversations with Virgilio and Mazzini. He could hold off until they were settled here, wait for the right moment, maybe tomorrow, he hoped. Robert did not wish to quash her last impulse of delight.

He found an old-fashioned strongbox in the room, fastened to the floor by thick, rusted screws. While Gabriela stood on the balcony, he unpacked the manila envelope from their suitcase. He folded it carefully, locked it in the safe, kept the key in his pocket.

As they walked together on the promenade, they passed strings of lights that glittered along the river wall. Parrillas glowed under the eaves of restaurants. Tangos and boleros blared on loudspeakers.

If Robert dropped Gabriela's hand for a second, or didn't hold her exactly the way she wanted, she would stop, pout and tilt her head. "*Ya no me quieres, verdad?*" You don't love me anymore, right?

When he started to reply, she stood on her tiptoes and covered his mouth with hers. They stood there in the center of the boardwalk, kissing, feeling the current coursing through their limbs, unaware of pedestrians who veered right or left to avoid them. Robert and Gabriela began to feel hundreds of miles from Buenos Aires.

They found a parrilla with a wood fire. As she strode across the room with her doe's step, the locals turned to watch. The tile floor shimmered under her feet. Those people could recognize a porteña from a block away.

Heavy blades of a ceiling fan beat the warm air. When Robert pulled out a chair for Gabriela, her snake of a braid brushed his cheek. He felt the current again.

They ordered grilled morcillas, a salad, two bleeding bifes accompanied by a bottle of Cabernet from Ribera.

"Uruguay's the only country that can rival us for beef," Gabriela said.

"I'm surprised to hear you admit that."

"Of course they also claim to have invented the tango. They're liars."

Robert laughed. "This meal reminds me of the first time we ate together."

"I still worry about her."

"Me too."

"She was so thin and frail."

Like you, Gaby querida, he thought. The flower girl brought back images of that first day, the night, the Mothers in the Plaza de Mayo in the afternoon. "You know, Starface, you've never told me what the Madres whispered in your ear."

"That was a long time ago. But let me tell you about even longer ago."

During the supper and their nightcap of brandy and soda, Gabriela opened new parts of her childhood for Robert: early boyfriends, funerals in Recoleta, more boyfriends, her first Communion. Their view of the harbor reminded him of the California coast, so he told her about his earliest recollections of Los Angeles: walking on the beach with his father, skipping stones there, an avocado tree in their backyard, his mother's voice calling for supper.

They walked down to the river bank, where trees shrouded them from pedestrians and the town's lights. Small waves lapped the shore. Leaning against each other for support, Gabriela and Robert took off their shoes. They squatted on the beach. Under their feet the sand was wet but warm, still holding the day's heat. They dug in with their toes.

"We're here," she sighed. Wavelets swished over their feet.

She stood, lifted her cotton skirt, glanced at Robert and waded toward the lighted boats in the harbor. He rolled up his pants and followed. Muddy sand oozed between their toes, and their ankles tingled in the cool river. When the water rose above her knees, Gabriela slipped out of her skirt and tossed it back to Robert, calling "*Ahí va!*" Then she threw him her blouse, panties and brassiere. I love her daring, he thought, as well as all the rest.

Feeling absurd as he held those garments above his head, he cried, "What am I supposed to do with them?"

"Whatever you want, tonto." Gabriela loosened her black braid and dove headfirst. Robert did not wish to leave her alone for long. He turned, sloshed through the shallow water to the beach, dropped her clothes on the dark sand, stripped down to his shorts and raced back to the river. He swam hard toward the boats, stopped and looked around, treading water.

Gabriela appeared with a small splash ahead of him. Her hair fanned out over the surface. She flipped over and floated on her back, gazing at blurry stars. As he approached her, Robert tasted the water, less salty than the sea, with a tang of soil. He thought about Dionisio, dead on the bottom of this river. For a moment he imagined Gabriela there too, her limbs swaying with the tide, her hair matted with mud and algae.

Then she had gone again. After a silence of seconds a feeble voice burbled behind him, "*Aquí.*" He wheeled his head and saw her. Hair, water and silt streamed down her heart-like face. "*Socorro!*" Help, she gasped.

Robert stroked fast to her side. With both hands she clutched his shoulders, almost pulling him under. He locked one hand beneath her armpit, balancing with the other. "Now," he told her.

"I needed to dive," she panted, "all the way to the bottom." Catching her breath, she added, "To feel that mud and seaweed against my body." Gabriela coughed up water. She rubbed a mat of slimy tresses on his face. "Oh how I love the river," she told Robert. "Did you know that Scorpio's a watery sign?"

"It's also self-destructive. You wouldn't do anything dangerous would you?"

"Maybe just sting myself with my poison tail."

"By the way what's your mother's sign?"

Gabriela did not hear, because she was laughing and diving again. Her small buttocks breached before she plunged. The curled, white toes of her feet disappeared behind her. Once more Robert felt the silence around him, broken by the sound of his own breathing, waves kissing the shore.

At last she came to the surface close to the beach. He saw Gabriela emerge from the water and reach the river wall, where her body gleamed in the filtered lights.

"Sea and earth mixed together!" she called as Robert joined her on the sand. "That's how the water tastes." Strings of algae threaded the cascade of Gabriela's dripping hair. She and Robert dried themselves with their underclothes.

"Were you really drowning out there?" he asked.

"No, I just hoped you would save me. Guess what we call it in Spanish?"

"Call what?"

"That," she said and pointed to the river. "*Mar dulce*, sweet sea."

"That could be another nickname for you—Sweetsea," he said, biting her left shoulder.

"So long as it's not Sweetpea. Watch out Popeye!" She flicked Robert with the tail of his shirt.

He retaliated with her brassiere. Next they covered themselves and raced back to the hotel, still snapping each other with their garments. As soon as they had closed the door to their room, they threw off their clothes and dove onto the bed. The seaweed in Gabriela's hair sprouted on her neck and shoulders. Her body moved as though she were gliding underwater. She scratched, clawed him, nibbled on his chest, his arms and face. In Robert's hands her cool breasts warmed, blooming in his palms. He tasted the sediment, the grains of sand on her belly, the sudden heat and salt between her legs. As Gabriela purred and moaned, made the strange, gurgling song that he would not forget, Robert sensed that the taste of love and the sea were the same.

18
Death's Angel

Sunlight poured onto their bed from the balcony. At first he was not sure where he was, in what city, continent or country. Breathing in the smell of seaweed, Robert knew she must be near. She was curled at his side, uncovered, facing away from him, asleep. Still moist and intertwined with algae, her hair swirled to the small of her back. He was with Gabriela on the far shore of the Río de la Plata, the river as wide as a sea.

When he looked into the bathroom mirror, his eyes appeared darker, deepened almost to the shade of her plum-colored irises. How could he have thought of leaving her? Robert twisted his frame and saw fresh, bloody cuts zigzagging across his back. Loving her is like battle, he told himself, recalling his war of words with her father on the fateful night, the next day on the Pampa too. As he stood over the toilet, Robert noticed he was red and swollen: grains of sand specked the tip of his glans. He washed himself in the bidet, whose yellowing porcelain must have seen numberlesss nights of love.

While Gabriela slept, Robert removed the manila envelope from the rusty strongbox. He had expected to find papers there, stamped, sealed and notarized, like so many documents of Latin American bureaucracies. Instead he saw a handwritten note and a grainy black-and-white photo, both wrapped in newspaper. Mazzini had failed to warn him that the junta's false decrees usually bore official stamps, while the real orders had none.

Robert examined the note. It was written in Roca's hand, the same florid calligraphy he had seen on the blue, white and yellow envelope addressed to Gaby at their apartment. The page was addressed to a Colonel Adolfo Sedara and signed with her father's initials, "*C.R.S.*" Its short text read "*J.M.S., Fac. de F. y L. Café.*" The final word was enough to make a shiver shoot up Robert's bleeding back. The rest meant nothing to him.

He took the second document in his hands. It was a photograph of César Roca—at least ten years younger than the man Robert knew—entering what looked like a military post that flew the nation's flag. Two general officers, their uniforms laden with medals, badges and epaulettes, flanked Gabriela's father. Robert turned over the picture and saw a printed date: "*6 de diciembre 1980.*" Two days before the death of Julio's son, Robert recognized, during the regime's last, deadly triennium.

He longed at this moment to be in Buenos Aires, where he could act—consult Julio, Virgilio, move against Roca. But he was also relieved to have a day or two to prepare himself, to devise a plan and talk with Gaby while they were off her father's terrain. In the morning light his hands were shaking.

Robert returned the documents to the safe, showered and dressed for the beach. Gaby remained asleep in her bed of seaweed. He walked to a café across the street, where he ordered two coffees and medialunas for delivery to their hotel. Room service, he thought, picturing Virgilio.

When Robert returned, she was sleeping in the same position, curved like a cat on the rumpled sheets. He lay down at her side and fondled her damp hair streaked with algae. Stretching her arms, she groaned, bit a corner of the sheet and turned to face him.

"Breakfast's on the way," he whispered in the little shell of her ear. Robert kneaded the white lobe with a thumb and forefinger.

Slowly she rose from the bed. Gabriela half smiled at him, her eyeteeth glinting. As she walked into the bathroom, he admired her night-black hair, her ivory back and buttocks.

A young waiter delivered their breakfast on a metal tray. Robert offered a tip in australes. The boy frowned and left the room. Even in Uruguay, one of the world's smallest countries, nobody wanted those worthless bills.

Robert carried the tray to the wooden table on their balcony. Gabriela joined him, wearing a sleeveless blouse. She had braided her hair again: a dark, lustrous coil hung over her left shoulder. She must have washed away the seaweed in the shower, Robert mused. With one hand he grazed her arm.

He began to drink his café con leche. Gaby left hers on the table.

"Why didn't you add sugar?" she asked, picking up a cube from the tray.

"Guess I'm becoming more Argentine—learning to like bitter tastes." He remembered Virgilio's revelation about the code word *café* during the war. For Robert "the war" no longer meant Vietnam but Argentina, her war, now his as well.

Gabriela patted herself between the legs. "I'm sore. Not just from you, Roberto. I must have brought some sand home from the river last night."

"Me too." He grimaced, rubbing his crotch.

Gabriela picked up her coffee. "Little grains from the river on you and inside of me." She glanced out at the water, flat and brown in the hazy light. "You know how pearls form around a particle in an oyster shell? What if a pearl grew inside of me?"

Robert laughed. "It would make loving you either more painful or more arousing. Maybe both."

Gabriela may have smiled for a second only. Viewing the estuary, she observed, "The river's so calm."

"But there are currents," he said. He waited to see how she would react. Still facing the water, she closed her sleepy eyes. When she did not respond, Robert added, "They flow toward the beaches at Punta del Este."

She looked at him knowingly. Before she could speak, bells rang from a church. "It's Sunday," she said. Gabriela sounded suddenly alone.

They watched a hydrofoil motoring across the harbor on its way to Buenos Aires, leaving a trail of foam in the muddy water. Robert knew they would have to follow that wake before long.

"He's out there, isn't he?" Gabriela asked. She peered at Robert with the vivid emptiness of her eyes. Then she closed them again, slumped in her chair, bowed her head and clutched her hands as though she dreaded a reply.

"Yes," Robert said.

She kept her eyes shut and did not change her posture for a minute or so. Her body trembled. "What else do you know?"

"Are you ready to hear?"

Gabriela hesitated. She sat up in her chair, opened her eyes and looked at him as if she were begging for him to decide.

"You should know what Julio Mazzini told me, Gaby."

"Yes," she sighed.

Robert took both of her hands in his. Instead of a jolt of electricity he felt a mere tingle. "The documents he brought yesterday could be proof of his son's murder. They might also be related to another crime." He paused before saying it: "Dionisio was killed in one of the death-flights, thrown from a helicopter with weights on his legs."

Gabriela startled, let out a cry and dropped her hands. She turned toward the Río de la Plata. The hydrofoil was moving beyond the harbor, its wake almost invisible.

Robert placed his hands on her bare shoulders. Her silken flesh was cool beneath his own. "Gaby," he said, drew her close and embraced her.

Without altering her expression, she pulled away and surveyed the river. In his mind Robert saw Gabriela's face resting like a mask on her mother's shoulder the other night. Now the boat was a white dot near the horizon.

He bent forward and took one of her hands in his. Neither Robert nor Gaby felt the current this time, as though it had been cut by the remembrance of that death. "I know you can be a strong Starface," he started. "Listen to me. Your mother believes your father could have prevented Dionisio's murder." Robert did not wish to engulf her in too many details at once—all about Virgilio, how Roca had ordered Julio Mazzini Jr.'s death, the hit-and-run, the abduction to the Pampa, everything else.

"It's so strange to hear his name on your lips," she uttered in a rueful tone. "I used to think the two of you belonged to different worlds." After a few seconds she said, softer, "I suspected it but I couldn't discover anything—" Gabriela turned to him. "Not from Father or anyone else in my family. Maybe they knew about it all along."

Robert looked into Gaby's eyes and pressed her hand. "Your mother also told me that he'll do anything to keep us apart. That's why she hopes we'll leave the country."

"We've already left the country."

"We'd have to go farther than Uruguay or even Brazil."

Those words made her blanch. After a few seconds Gabriela pleaded, "Will you take me far away?"

"If you want me to." Robert squeezed her quivering palm.

"Where?"

"To the end of the world."

"We're already there too."

"Not as long as we're so close to that." He pointed toward the river and Buenos Aires. "We'll find a place, Gaby. First I have things to do there."

"What?"

"We'll talk about it at the right time." My words are beginning to sound like yours, he told Gabriela without speaking.

She withdrew her hand and turned toward the river once more. "What else did you learn?"

After her reaction to the news of Dionisio's death, Robert knew it would be too much to disclose more. To change the subject he said, "I feel sorry for your mother. She would also like to leave Buenos Aires."

Gabriela sighed. "She's been saying that for years. She won't do it. She'd never leave him."

Will you, my Gaby? he wondered. Recalling what Roca had told him, he asked, "Has your mother been on medication since the dictatorship?" Gabriela did not answer.

Trying to fill the silence, Robert said, "I forgot to tell you about the man in the baseball cap. A friend of Julio's told me that he's one of your father's army connections."

"What friend?"

It was still too early to tell her more about Virgilio, Robert decided again. He imitated Gabriela by ignoring her question. "I also forgot to ask your mother about the other night—what happened upstairs at your house. Their house I mean," he amended. *His house,* Robert added to himself, hoping Gaby would respond. She said nothing. "Tell me, Starface."

She did not cease contemplating the river. "Oh the things Father told us," she said finally—"the things he screamed at us. When Mamá went downstairs he walked to an armchair with his shoulders bent, sat there swaying back and forth with his bones creaking. He's becoming an old man, I thought." Gabriela hesitated while the squawks of seagulls reached them from the shore. "Then Father wept—only the second time I've seen him cry. You defeated him."

"What was the first time?"

She did not reply. He could have told her how Roca had rebounded by having him kidnapped the next day. Instead he watched her closely. Gabriela was still avoiding his face, just as she did not look at him when they were making love. Almost untouched, her coffee sat on the table by the medialuna, cold by now. Robert remembered Madame Roca, how different she was, how she had studied him with her wide-open eyes, searching.

Gabriela turned to him. "Why did Julio Mazzini give you that manila envelope?"

If he told her the truth, Robert feared she might defend her father and kill their chances for a new life, an escape for good from Buenos Aires, from Argentina, the whole continent. Echoing Gabriela's own words, he said, "I'll tell you later." He placed one hand on her neck. A warm breeze blew across the balcony, stirring the silky ends of her hair that tickled Robert's skin. "Are we going to the beach?" He felt a need to cleanse his body in the sun and water.

Gaby's head dropped on his hand like a flower with a breaking stem. "Oh yes."

He pondered whether to leave the papers in the old safe. While she dressed for the beach, he chose to remove the envelope with the documents. He discarded most of the newspaper wrappings to make it more compact, folded it, placed it carefully in a pocket of his pants.

Robert and Gabriela strolled through the vacant streets and lanes of Colonia del Sacramento. Both had a hitch in their gait. The town's citizens must have been at church or sleeping late on that ominous day. The lovers saw old American cars parked on the cobblestones, hulked like beached whales. A rising breeze carried a smell of the sea.

They passed the cathedral. A bell tolled for Mass, but the sanctuary's carved door was closed. They had the impression they were moving through a ghost town.

"Sometimes I miss the Church," she mused almost to herself.

"I haven't been for years. But I'd go with you."

"No," Gabriela dismissed the idea as though she had already lost interest. "When I was a girl Father used to take me to Mass. My friends were jealous because they had to go to the Rosary with their mothers." Robert nearly said something about Roca. He stopped himself.

The wind rose around them. They walked along a narrow, pocked road to a beach lined with palm trees. Directly in front of them, through the low haze, they saw the dim shore of the Argentine coast.

"We have the beach to ourselves," Robert said, trying to make Gabriela feel better.

"We have the town to ourselves, maybe the country too." She looked out at the river again. "Millions of Uruguayans fled during their dictatorship." It was the first time he had heard Gaby use that term. Thousands were also killed or disappeared, he thought.

They left their towels in the shade of a palm tree and crossed the sand to the water's edge. Brown waves broke at their feet, the wind lashed their faces. Gabriela walked forward, dove in headfirst, swam, flipped and floated on her back, surrounded by whitecaps.

Robert removed his shirt, pants and shoes to follow her. When the saltwater burned his sores, he winced, but in a few seconds it soothed them. He turned and gazed up at the sky, where clouds were sailing toward the open sea. That view, vast and blue, made Robert dizzy.

He checked for Gabriela: bobbing up and down with the swells, her eyes closed, she was being carried down the coast by the current. He lay on his back and floated behind her. They resembled the camalotes they had seen on the Río de la Plata yesterday.

The tide bore them to a tongue of sand that stretched into the river. Gabriela's head ran aground. "Oh," she cried as if she had awakened from sleep. With both hands she rubbed her eyes. She rose to her feet and walked back along the spit to the beach, where her body appeared whiter than the sand.

Robert swam to the deep water again. When he looked back, he descried Gabriela, a lone figure in the shade of palm trees. He had never seen her from such a distance. She might be a woman you've never met, he told himself, who didn't make love with you a few hours ago, who has nothing to do with your life. Feeling the tender wounds on his back and between his legs, Robert knew that nobody could have more to do with his life than Gaby.

He stroked through the white-capped waves to shore. With the wind behind him he picked up his clothes and walked across their beach. Gabriela was lying on her back. Her sunglasses concealed her eyes, so Robert could not tell if she was awake. He lay down at her side. Remembering last night, he caressed her warm stomach still beaded with water.

Robert began to fall asleep in the warm sun. Above the whistle of wind and the lapping of waves, he imagined far-off howls and cries of shipwrecked sailors. An immense sable bird glided toward the beach and hovered there. The shadow of its great wings darkened the sand. The air seemed to turn colder.

Then Gabriela was leaning over him, shaking him by the shoulders. "Roberto!" she shouted and pointed beyond the trees.

He looked up, his eyes dazzled by the midday sun. As he adjusted to the light, he made out a black Ford Falcon, cruising along the beach road.

"It's unmarked!" Gabriela screamed. "Tinted glass—just like the one on Avenida de Mayo."

The Falcon made a U-turn. There were no other vehicles on the road, not a pedestrian in sight. As the car cruised by, its hood and chrome glittering in the sun, Robert and Gabriela could see its driver leaning out the window, scanning the beach through dark glasses, a baseball cap on his head.

He stood and she grasped his arm: "What shall we do?"

"He can't get lost in a crowd this time." Strike now, Robert told himself, recalling Virgilio and Julio.

She embraced him. "Oh careful Osito," she implored as he moved toward the road. The sand burned Robert's shoeless soles. I'm walking on live coals, he thought, like an Indian fakir. To keep his feet from scalding, he shuffled faster over the beach.

He came to the edge of the strand, where he crouched behind a palm tree at the roadside, hidden from the driver's view. The large fronds made their dry, rustling sound in the breeze. When Robert peeked around the rough bark of the trunk, he saw the Falcon make another turn, then come back toward their beach. The driver held the steering wheel with his left hand while he leaned toward the window of the passenger's seat, surveying the coast through the palms. He appeared secure and protected while Robert felt almost naked, exposed, barefoot, wearing only his damp swim trunks.

The Falcon approached in low gear, moving no faster than five miles an hour or so. Robert concealed his head behind the tree. Virgilio's words raced through his mind: "Hit first." Calculating the vehicle's speed and distance from the sound of its engine, he waited. Just as the driver passed, slower now, Robert whirled around the palm tree, sprinted for a few seconds, caught up with the car, yanked open the passenger door and leaped inside. He saw a semiautomatic rifle lying across the dashboard.

With a sweep of his right hand Robert pulled the keys from the ignition and struck the driver in the mouth. He saw two moles above the man's lips, vanishing behind his own fist. The engine coughed, the vehicle veered right, lurched to a halt. The rifle fell to the floor and Robert's head bumped the dashboard. Recovering from the blow to his mouth, the driver pulled a knife from a sheath on his belt and the cap fell from his head, revealing a bald pate. Robert pulled back, looking into a pair of frightened hazel eyes, a face oozing sweat. As the man thrust toward him, that weapon glinted in the sun. The blade slashed Robert's naked thigh and his blood spurted onto the seat.

He grabbed his opponent's wrist, tore away the knife, raised it to strike when the door on the driver's side sprang open, the man fell backwards, rolled out of the car and onto the asphalt. The American coiled to spring and follow when his enemy turned, rose on one elbow, pulled a pistol from a holster on his belt and fired. The sharp report made Robert start, dive under the steering wheel as a bullet smacked the windshield, making a spiderweb on the glass, spraying shards on the hood and front seat. He lifted his head, saw the tall figure dash across the road and turn to shoot a round that ricocheted off the Falcon's left-front fender. Approaching from the beach, Gabriela plunged to the ground and another bullet whistled by the car. Robert raised his head and saw the man rush into a thicket of trees and bushes beyond the road.

Gabriela ran to the driver's side. When she saw the blood on her lover's left thigh, she called "Osito!" With her frail arms she hugged him. Quickly she became a doctor again, applying pressure to the wound with both hands, removing the top of her bathing suit to make a tourniquet, tying it around Robert's groin, finding a stick on the ground to use as a windlass, twisting tighter until the bleeding appeared to stop. In the noon sunlight the Río de la Plata shimmered.

As she helped him lean back on the passenger's seat, Robert muttered, "Clothes ..." His skin had turned paler than Gaby's. The heat buzzed in his head.

Gabriela was away for a long time—hours, it seemed to him. He could feel the pricking from pieces of glass on the seat, the pulse of his wound, the pain in his gashed leg. He inhaled the coppery smell of his blood.

As soon as Gaby returned, he took his pants from her trembling hands to check for the manila envelope, found it and told her, "Keys on floor." She spotted and seized them, brushed the shards from her seat with Robert's shirt, shook it off and wore it to cover her torso. Gabriela started the engine and drove toward town, watching the road through a sheet of tears and broken glass.

They arrived at the only hospital in Colonia del Sacramento. Two attendants laid Robert on a gurney. In the fluorescent light Gabriela studied his lacerations.

The rest of that day was telling the nurses how he had been knifed in the leg, hearing their lilting Uruguayan speech, waiting for a local doctor, trying to answer his questions. Robert felt the sting of a needle in his thigh. It and the cuts and bruises on his arms, legs and trunk burned. He insisted that Gaby bury his pants under the sheets.

In the night he raved with fever from an infection in the wound. He tossed, clutching his pants with the envelope in one of its pockets. Gabriela could not decipher all of Robert's words, but she heard him repeat "Avenida de Mayo" over and over. Washing and dressing the lesion, taking his pulse, checking his blood pressure, she took over as his doctor, tenacious and vigilant, staying awake at his side.

The next morning a nurse gave her a set of scrubs that fit her willowy frame. Gabriela also found time to call the police and report the crime. The local physicians and the nurses on duty stood in awe of the doctor from the grand metropolis, Buenos Aires, who had stolen their patient and gave him such devoted care.

19
Camalotes

She attended **Robert** without sleep until the second afternoon, when his fever began to fall. She left his room only long enough to seek the local police, bring them to her patient, fill out papers, show them the bullet-riddled Ford in the staff's parking garage. Poised by Robert's bed, she directed doctors, nurses and orderlies as if she were chief surgeon of the little hospital in Colonia del Sacramento.

"I'm going to make you well again," she whispered in his ear with her voice like water.

"I like your bedside manner. But not as much as your inside-bed manner." When he pronounced those words, Gabriela knew that Robert was out of danger.

On the third day Gabriela removed the stitches from his thigh. She helped him learn to walk with crutches. Soon Robert was tottering up and down the corridors.

Late the following afternoon she signed papers for his release and paid for the services in cash. She and Robert walked slowly to the Comisaría; by now he was more agile on his crutches. Like a part of his anatomy the manila envelope bulged from his pocket.

A sergeant with a thick mustache was smoking a cigarette behind the counter. He resembled somebody who had just awakened from a nap. The police inspectors had found no evidence about the driver of the Ford Falcon, he told them. Like so many men he could not help stealing glances at Gabriela.

"Whose name was the car registered in?" Robert asked.

"No registration," the man said in a cancerous voice. "We did find one thing in the trunk." While a ceiling fan pushed hot air around the room, the sergeant waited for Robert to react.

"Well what did you find?" Gabriela inquired first.

The policeman enjoyed withholding information from this beautiful porteña and the crippled American. Finally he said, "More than ten kilos of Semtex."

"What's that?" Robert asked. He had already lost three days in the hospital and here he was, wasting more time with a laggard cop in Uruguay.

After another pause the man replied, "A plastic explosive."

Robert looked at Gabriela. She shrugged her narrow shoulders. Turning to the sergeant, he asked, "What about the rifle?"

The man heaved a sigh as he turned and walked to a table with an old Underwood on its grimy top. Puffing on his cigarette, he pulled a police report from the typewriter's carriage. He perused it like a person who can hardly read.

"They also found a .30-caliber semiautomatic Eibar rifle," he said haltingly. "Standard issue to the Argentine infantry."

"Have you tracked it?" Gabriela quizzed.

"That takes time and the Argentines are slow."

"And I suppose the Uruguayans are fast?"

"*Más o menos, Señorita.*"

Robert asked, "Did you trace the bullets from the pistol?"

The policeman sighed again before skimming the document in his hands. "There's no mention of a pistol here."

"We need a copy of your report."

"Normally we don't release it to the public."

"I'm not the public!" Robert shouted. "I'm the one they stabbed with a knife and tried to shoot!"

Gabriela intervened. "My friend has just been released from three days in the hospital."

"Give me a copy of that report," Robert told the man.

The policeman inhaled the cigarette. "There's a small administrative fee for making a copy."

"Make it," Robert said.

The sergeant took a final pull on his cigarette, threw it to the floor, rubbed it out with the heel of his boot. He made a photocopy and dropped it on the counter without saying a word.

After the delay at the police station Robert and Gabriela almost missed the night-sailing of the hydrofoil. He limped aboard on crutches while she dragged their suitcase. Most passengers were seated in the sheltered stern, but the two lovers chose the open bow again. The aliscafo taxied out of Colonia's harbor.

"We must go back," Gaby declared as though she had been dreading it for a long time. She contemplated a sky with the four stars of the Southern Cross. It appeared fainter with a full moon in the east, whose silver light drenched her hair, face and dress. While the craft motored toward Argentina, she seemed to shrink at Robert's side, no longer the confident physician who had supervised his recovery. That burst of zeal had left her tense and hollow. He held her tightly.

"We'll never get away from him," she said in that thin voice of hers.

"Your father or the man in the baseball cap?"

"Both. Who else but Father would hire someone to follow us?"

Robert felt gratified to hear those words: maybe she had wakened at last from her dream? He told her about his abduction in a low voice so that other passengers could not hear. Watching the constellation to the south, her lips open, Gabriela listened entranced, as if those stars were somehow related to Robert's story.

When he had finished, he asked her, "Now do you see why your mother wants us to escape?"

Without looking at him, dabbing her eyes with her sleeve, Gaby moaned, "Yes. I'm not sure. I think so." She studied the horizon ahead of them, where the lights of Buenos Aires glimmered through a milky haze of humidity and heat. "I was born here—there I mean. I have ties ... I've lived there all my life."

"You lived through a civil war and a dictatorship, had one boyfriend murdered, another almost killed—me. We're in danger and you want to stay?"

"Your accident was in Uruguay."

"Just across the river, Gaby! 'Accident!' Carajo!" Robert exclaimed in good Argentine style. "Just like the hit-and-run was an accident."

"I don't know if I could live away from—everything."

A flowering camalote, caught in the boat's lights, crossed the bow on the moonlit waves. "Those little islands spend their lives in the sweet water of streams and rivers," Gabriela observed, watching it float away, straining to hold back her tears. "Until they reach the ocean. They're not accustomed to saltwater—it must kill their roots."

"Perhaps they can survive in freshwater and the sea. Like salmon."

"I've never seen camalotes beyond the mouth of the river. Maybe that's their life—to be born upstream, to grow in sweet water and die in the ocean."

Robert did not know how to respond. He merely viewed the gleaming waves, sensed that the Río de la Plata was also their love: the wild cataracts and rushing waters at its sources, the meandering streams, the winding rivers that spread and merge in the sea.

The aliscafo plied the open stretch of estuary. Waves slapped its hull, the craft pitched forward, water splashed over its gunnels. The two or three passengers at their side fled to the stern, leaving Robert and Gabriela alone in the windblown, unprotected bow.

As if she were trying to see the riverbed, she bent over the port side and stared down. For a second he feared she might leap. Robert held her closer. We're approaching her city and now she's restless as the wind and waves, he thought. Their wet clothes clung together from the spray.

The metropolis rose before them. Like a shroud a long black cloud hung over the illuminated high-rises. The air was rank, heavy and moist, colder than on the Uruguayan side. Sniffing the breeze, they inhaled that stench, worse than before; breathing it was almost like ingesting smoke and sewage. So much had occurred in Colonia del Sacramento, yet Buenos Aires was still the same, the old reeking city of César Roca.

In a taxi from the wharf Gabriela reclined on Robert's damp shoulder, shivering. They drove by a cream-colored palace where a cordon of policemen circled a milling crowd.

"Podridos," the driver said under his breath, "*cobardes.*"

Robert could not tell if the man meant the police or the crowd. "Who?"

"Those bastards around the Italian embassy. They're leaving the country like rats on a sinking ship."

Robert sighted a pair of women who were scaling a wrought-iron fence that enclosed the building. "Why?" he asked. Gabriela looked embarrassed by his question.

The driver turned around so quickly that Robert feared the man would lose control of his car. "Señor, wouldn't you rather live in Italy?" Finally the cabbie looked forward again. Surmising that Robert was an outsider, he said, "If an Argentine citizen proves he has Italian ancestors he can return to the mother country with his whole family and new passports. The same goes for Spain. Argentina never was a mother—she's a stepmother, a puta, a whore, an ugly beautiful fucking whore. Please pardon the words, Señorita," he said with a flick of his head toward Gaby.

When the cab reached Avenida Independencia, she lifted her dark lashes and peered at Robert through a mist of tears. He did not know if she was weeping for herself, for him too, her broken family, her Buenos Aires or the entire nation. He paid the driver, who was still cursing, "Cobardes, podridos ..."

"Should we move from our apartment?" he asked Gabriela as they stood on the sidewalk.

"No matter where we go he'll find us. Please Osito, I need to be in our Pampa."

Leaning on her arm, Robert staggered up the stairs. She unlocked the door. A blue, white and yellow envelope was lying across the threshold. They recognized Roca's ornate calligraphy; nobody else wrote like that anymore. Robert also noticed the letter was addressed with an initial for his lover's first name: "*Srta. G. Roca Dafiume.*"

Gabriela gazed at Robert with wide-open eyes. All at once she looked more like Madame Roca, older by years. He saw new tears swell over her pupils and irises, spill down her cheeks. With a thud she dropped their suitcase on the floor and bent to retrieve the envelope. She handled it as though she were defusing a mine.

"Tell him 'No' if it's another invitation," Robert said with a flat smile, trying to cheer her. Gabriela's expression did not change.

Moving stiffly, she sat on the edge of the Pampa, inserted a fingernail beneath the flap of the envelope and tore it open. Robert leaned on his crutches, remembering how much he had wanted Gaby when her father's first letter arrived. With his left thigh still pulsing and his body aching, his clothes clammy from the boat, he did not desire her. He noticed that she had forgotten to kick the shoes from her feet.

"What does it say?"

Reading or re-reading the letter to herself, Gabriela was silent. Without their usual array of rings, her hands appeared smaller, whiter than the sheet of expensive stationery. Robert stood there, waiting for her reply. In the dead air the curtains did not move.

"'Welcome back to our city, Eulalia,'" she began reading in a forsaken tone. That name from the fatal night of the dinner echoed in Robert's memory. "'Please tell Mr. Wells that I expect him in my office on Friday afternoon at five o'clock. *A las cinco en punto de la tarde.* Father.'" Gabriela turned to Robert. "Like that, in Spanish and English." She reflected for a moment. "What day is this?"

"They wounded me on Sunday—three days ago. So this must be Wednesday. Is there a date on the letter?"

Gabriela lowered her hooded eyes. "December 19th." She hesitated. "That must be today. So Father had this note delivered in person. He expects you in his office the day after tomorrow." She dropped the letter to the ground, placed both hands on her face and broke out in tears.

Robert threw his crutches on the floor and trudged to the bed. He sat next to Gaby, put one arm around her shoulder. Roca wants to meet on December 21st, he calculated—the winter solstice at home, summer here. Everything's backwards, he told himself, spring came and is nearly gone. How could Robert have known it would be the last season of his content?

Gabriela's body shook as she wept. Her hair and clothes, like Robert's, were still wet from the boat. To him the room and the bed seemed like a small island surrounded by a rising, storm-lashed sea. Or he and Gaby were two camalotes being swept down the Río de la Plata.

She grabbed Robert's wrist and nestled at his side. He hardly felt the static in her touch. As though she were talking to herself, Gabriela said, "Maybe he never learned we were away."

Robert looked at her in disbelief. How could she concede one moment that her father was pursuing them, that he had sent the killer car to Uruguay, then refuse to admit that he knew their movements? Had she not just read the words "Welcome back to our city" in Roca's letter? Gaby was shifting back and forth between acceptance and denial, he thought, like a person in mourning.

"Guess what I would like to do?" For that instant she sounded almost hopeful.

"What?"

She placed the index finger of one hand in the cleft of Robert's chin. "Cut open my breast with a knife, put you inside and sew it shut so you'd be safe there. That way you'd never leave and you'd be inside me always."

Gaby's words were so unexpected, so passionate and forlorn that Robert did not know how to respond. Feeling a throb of pain in his bad leg, he wondered if she, not her mother, might be the one who suffered from a disorder, who had been on medication since the war. In all their time together he had never seen her fill a prescription or take a pill.

Gabriela lowered her moist eyes. Pressing on his shirtfront, she made her low animal cry that came from deep inside or far away.

Robert caressed her damp hair, kissed her head, ears, cheeks, neck, her frail clavicle. "Gaby." He drank the tears from her eyes.

"I need to be in the water again." She sighed and pulled away from him.

"Tell me about his office," he said, hoping to keep her rooted there on the bed.

At first he thought she had not heard, but Gabriela answered, "It's across the street from the Confitería del Molino." They both recalled the old café where they had gone together: its marble tables, gilded columns, aged servers in tuxedos, aromas of pastry and espresso. "Father has a suite in the basement of the Capitol building."

"I have to search his papers." Gabriela looked up at him, dazed. "Julio Mazzini says I must find some information."

"For what?"

"To protect us from your father. It's the only way, Gaby." He estimated it was too early to reveal Mazzini's plan to have Roca indicted for multiple crimes.

"Don't tell me you're going to break into the National Congress."

"No—your father's house." Gabriela cringed and covered her ears, as if to deaden the noise of breaking glass. "Does he have an office or study?"

She buried her head in Robert's shoulder again. "Yes. Why?"

"That's probably where I should look. I'll have to go when the house is empty. Will you help me?"

She did not reply at once. Robert could feel Gabriela's warm breath on his collar. "I think so," she murmured.

"Would you rather search that room yourself?"

"I could never do that." She spoke in the feeble voice she often used when speaking of her father.

"I understand, Gaby. Will he be at the Capitol tomorrow?"

"He's there almost every day during the week."

"Can you arrange to meet your mother for breakfast in a café around nine o'clock—to be sure nobody's at home?" Robert felt strange, plotting to burgle the house where his lover had lived nearly all her life.

"Maybe."

"What time does the maid normally arrive?"

"It used to be around eleven. Nothing's normal anymore."

"Is there a chance your brother will be there?"

"He's never home. Oh I'm afraid."

"Don't worry, Gaby. Does your father have the house guarded?"

"Not as far as I know. But remember the dogs—watch out for them."

"Will you give me your keys?"

Gabriela paused. "Yes."

"Let's go call your mother."

They walked to their neighborhood café. Every minute or so he stopped to rest on his crutches. Robert moved deliberately but stayed ahead of Gaby, who shadowed him like a wraith. Now she appeared to be the wounded one. Sadness oozed behind her, over the sidewalk and street, spreading like a dismal tide.

He ordered two nightcaps at the bar while she phoned her parents on the house telephone. When Gabriela joined him, she took a long drink of her brandy. "I'm going to meet Mamá tomorrow morning at 9:30 in the Dome."

Robert managed to stumble home without the crutches. Like a knight jousting with two lances, he held them in front of himself, one in each arm, with Gaby at his side. His thigh itched where the knife-slash had begun to scar.

She went straight to their bathroom and closed the door. Robert heard water running in the basin while a woman's voice reached him from the balcony, humming a milonga. He hobbled to the bathroom.

Gabriela was already lying in the tub. Her head was back, her eyes closed, her nipples protruding like two dark buds, her mound swaying like seaweed as water plunged from the spigot. Robert sat on the floor of that small room, his legs almost touching the edge of the basin, where her clothes hung.

Although he had seen them a hundred times, he gazed at the four lions' paws supporting the brass tub. He could not escape from Roca in their own bathroom.

Out of nowhere she said, "He's not blind." Gabriela did not open her eyes, enclosed by their night-black, silky lashes.

Robert understood. Yet he asked, "Who?" He did not want Gaby to know her father was ceaselessly on his mind.

She ignored his question. "He can see with one eye. The left."

The proverb floated into Robert's mind, the one Virgilio had cited in the Turkish baths: In the land of the blind the one-eyed man is king. He imagined Roca sitting erect on his viceregal throne—at his mansion in Belgrano, his ranch or that house on the Pampa—his head as immobile as Gabriela's in the clawfoot basin now. He pictured one of the old man's eyes leering at them behind his opaque sunglasses. Robert's anger burst: "He's a cyclops." As soon as those words issued from his mouth, he regretted them, hanging his head.

Like a corpse stirring, Gabriela lifted her head and glared at him. "Remember, he's still my father."

Robert asked in a shrill voice, "When are *you* going to stop being blind? That father ordered Julio Mazzini Jr.'s murder, maybe Dionisio's too. He also must have sent the man to run me over in Buenos Aires first, then to kill me in Colonia. Don't you see, Gaby?"

It was as though he had thrown a rock through a window, and they were staring at the starlike hole in the glass. She peered at Robert with moist, darkened eyes, moving her bow-shaped lips without uttering a word. He conjured her brother, Segundo, the way he stammered when he tried to pronounce his father's name. He felt rage for all that Roca had done to thwart his children, his wife, the whole family.

Robert leaned toward the tub, held out his hand and grazed Gaby's mouth. Like a small bird's wings her lips fluttered, barely opening and closing. Then she licked Robert's hand, glided her pointed tongue over his knuckles, gnawed the hair on his joints, slid one two three of his fingers into her warm, wet mouth, pulled him toward her. He fell onto his knees and started tearing off his clothes with one hand while she sucked on the other. Robert rolled over the edge of the basin, his body stinging from its wounds, cuts and bruises. He fell into the water on top of her. Gabriela's tears and saliva scalded his own.

In the long hours of that night, lost among so many nights, they knew the final, secret places of each other's body, the salty, bitter roots. The taste of their tears, their blood and saliva was the same as the sea or their love. Gabriela gouged his scabs and sores, made him bleed, she bled, moaned, cried. She pulled Robert's hair, spat in his face, bit his neck, arms and legs. She made the haunting music that he would not hear again. Even now she held back something deep inside her. As they fell asleep, Robert sensed for the first time that she was loving and hurting someone else too.

20
Labyrinths

When he awoke, Gabriela was lying on her back, staring at the ceiling. Quiet had descended upon their neighborhood, as though the city outside had disappeared like 30,000 Argentines. Robert glanced through the window. The matron was drinking café con leche on her balcony, swaying her head to a silent melody. It must be morning.

"I heard it again," Gabriela said with a voice that came from far away or nowhere.

"What?"

"The earth. Turning, spilling darkness."

"You never told me about it."

"It creaks and it can hardly move."

Gabriela rose from the Pampa. She walked slowly to the bathroom, where she used the toilet, showered and washed the dried blood from her skin. Lying in bed, Robert listened to her movements.

Gabriela returned with a white towel wrapped around her body. From the night stand she picked up her purse and removed a key ring. When she handed it to him, Robert's fingers grazed her dewy palm.

"Watch out for the Dobermans," she said. Her eyes looked weary, the sockets darker, faintly bruised. "Use the side door—the two oval keys on the chain."

"Where's your father's study?"

"On the top floor, facing the street."

"Carajo," Robert mumbled, thinking of the stairs he would have to climb.

He showered while Gabriela moved around the apartment like a sleepwalker in her bare feet. After dressing, he practiced taking steps without crutches. If he carried them to Roca's house, he knew, they would make him too conspicuous. Robert stuck a small canvas shopping bag in the right-front pocket of his pants. Against his left thigh, the wounded one, he felt the manila envelope. He did not want to be separated from it.

Gaby helped him down those stairs they loved and knew, plank by plank. When they passed through the main doorway, the cool air surprised them, as if they were back in early spring. The vast cloud still hung in the sky. The odor had grown stronger.

He hailed a taxi for Gabriela. When another black Mercedes sedan arrived, Robert recalled the first time he had put her in a cab. Just as on that evening by the spreading gomero, she did not turn or say goodbye. Robert pictured the driver of the Ford Falcon as her taxi moved down the street: he had fought, struck and smelled the skin of that stranger, who in an odd way seemed almost as close to him as Gabriela in her distant moods.

He limped to a hardware store on Entre Ríos. A clock behind the counter read 9:06. He purchased a crowbar and a pair of rubber gloves, which the cashier placed in a double plastic bag. For a second Robert believed it was a regular Saturday in Los Angeles, when he often ran errands and did chores, instead of a precarious Thursday in Buenos Aires. Walking down Avenida Callao, keeping an eye on the surging traffic, to his own astonishment he yearned for a life of innocuous routines—everything he had been fleeing for years at home, all that had eluded him for months in Argentina. A rumble rose from his stomach. Robert realized he had not eaten dinner last night or had breakfast this morning.

As he entered a taxi, he thought of Gaby. Would she have reached the Hyatt by now? He mused about joining her and Señora Roca at the Dome, spending time with the women of the family, watching their city revolve below—how much better than trying to break into her father's house on a bad leg while the dogs howled, where the cyclops might appear. Alright Roberto, he told himself, *Ten calma*. He was already talking to himself in Spanish more than his own language.

The cab dropped him a few blocks from Roca's house. As he scanned the streets, trying to spot anyone who might be following him, the smell assailed his nostrils. He smiled: the opulent quarters of the North were just as fetid as every other barrio in Buenos Aires. He paced with caution in order to avoid a limp. When he reached Calle Dragones, Robert remembered the first time he had seen the mansion with roofs of red tile, the monumental zaguán, the French balconies, the large silhouette looming behind the curtains of an iron-grilled window on the top floor. In a flash of hindsight he sensed that figure must have been Roca's. For Robert the house had resembled a stronghold that concealed Gabriela's unfamiliar world. He had learned about her life, at once too much and too little. Would anyone ever understand her?

He feigned looking casual while walking to the side of Roca's mansion. As far as Robert could tell, he was the only pedestrian on this street. Through an iron gate he spied a stone wall crested with jagged shards of green glass, thick as Coke bottles, shaded by a flowering linden tree whose crown strove for the light.

When he opened the spiked gate, the dogs began to bark. He could hear their toenails scuffing the pavement. Under his breath he swore at them. If they get out, he worried, how will I escape them with my bum thigh?

Robert removed the gloves from his sack. He slipped them onto his perspiring hands, turned one of the oval keys in the main lock and the other in the deadbolts. He inhaled the luscious odor of the linden blossoms, a perfume veiling the filth that dwells inside this house, he thought. Creaking like an old ship, the door opened. At the threshold he stopped to take a deep breath. Every home has its own scent, an Argentine poet said.

She grew up here, Robert reflected as he walked into the kitchen, through the dining and living rooms with their memories of the dinner, down the hall to a stairwell. How long ago, he attempted to count in his head: only six days? They might as well be years—so much has happened, changed since that night. In the patio the Dobermans whined.

Robert struggled to climb the stairs. On the top floor he stopped to catch his breath. Cold sweat dripped from his armpits. Beyond the landing he found a study paneled in mahogany, carpeted with antique rugs, where the stench pervaded the dead air more than downstairs. A plush curtain screened the only window, filtering a feeble light. Mirrors and bookshelves lined the dark walls. Next to a metal filing cabinet he discerned a pair of crossed swords mounted against a full-size flag of Argentina. A penumbra seemed to have settled here decades ago.

He stepped to the large desk by the window, covered by globes, compasses, a wooden chess set, more books, papers stacked in piles. Robert recalled the house on the Pampa. A slab of green marble with letters of inlaid brass—CÉSAR ROCA STEELE—stood in the center by a desk lamp. He imagined the O in the middle of the man's name as a solitary eye gaping at him. Robert also remembered the O's dripping red paint on the door of his room at the hotel. Observing the Argentine flag on the wall, for a moment he thought the round, flaming sun in the center could have been another eye. This whole room was ogling him.

The dogs barked again. Robert's thighs tensed, his throat tightened. He was alone, listening to his own breath, his pulse, his thudding heart. I'll never get away from the one-eyed bastard, he mouthed. Segundo's warning flitted through his memory: "Señor Wells, this monster will destroy anyone who enters his maze."

He parted the small window's curtain, glanced up and down the street. An older lady was strolling on the sidewalk, holding a shopping bag in one hand, moving away. How glorious everyday living suddenly appeared to Robert as he thumbed through stacks of Roca's papers on the desk, opened the heavy drawers and checked inside. With rubber gloves on his hands, the canvas bag with the crowbar slung over his shoulder, supporting his weight against the furniture, he could not work fast.

He found bills, policies, receipts, warranties, letters. In the second-floor study of this house on Calle Dragones in Belgrano, all of César Roca's work, his machinations, his crimes had come to this—documents that must be similar to those of any citizen of the Argentine Republic. Robert jammed a bunch of papers in his sack, hoping they might contain some valuable detail or other.

He moved to the filing cabinet. Finding it locked, he inserted the flat end of his crowbar and pried it open. The snap of metal made the dogs yelp in the patio. Robert searched the hanging files, straining his eyes in the poor light: they had colored tags in the usual order, from *Acciones, Automóviles, Bancos* through *Médicos, Seguros, Testamentos*. At this point he felt vaguely culpable, imagining his own outrage if somebody rifled through the papers in his house, in the Los Angeles apartment where he no longer lived.

Robert was too intrigued by Gabriela's father to cease now. After abusing his wife and children in his day-to-day life, he thought, how would the old man treat them in his will? He opened the file marked Testamentos, where he found a document signed by Roca and a team of lawyers, adorned in good Argentine fashion with stamps, insignia and wax seals, as though it were the national Constitution, dated 21 September 1989. He fingered through the pages until he came to the distribution of property: "César Roca Steele bequeaths 20% of his estate to his surviving widow, Señora Cornelia Dafiume de Roca," he read in Spanish; "70% to his surviving daughter, Gabriela Roca Dafiume, including the house on Calle Dragones; 10% to his surviving son, Segundo Roca Dafiume, who will be nourished in the bosom of the Holy Roman Catholic and Apostolic Church." Those figures astounded Robert, but he did not have time to dwell on them. The dogs were whimpering below, he was suffocating in this room, his bad leg hurt, he wanted to leave. After returning the will to its folder, he tried to close the steel drawer: it stuck on its tracks where he had bent the metal with the crowbar. Roca hasn't disinherited Gaby after all, he was thinking, at least not for now.

He ran his eyes over the titles on the wooden bookshelves, all hardcovers but not the sort of luxurious, gilded leather works he had seen in the living room last week. Moving closer, he saw that they were mostly by Argentine writers, with a single shelf for other Latin Americans, none of them women. A full wall was devoted to Jorge Luis Borges—bound sets of journals like *Sur* and *El Hogar*, first editions, reprints, biographies and criticism. The one-eyed king must have a predilection for the blind poet, Robert mused. He skimmed those works, reading their dedications. One was penned by the author himself to *"mi querido amigo César."* Robert checked for comments in the margins and the flyleafs, where some handwritten sheets had been folded and inserted. Inside a copy of Borges's *Laberintos* he lingered over a document titled "End-User Certificate," issued by the Argentine Ministry of Defense, in English, stating that César Roca Steele "is entitled to purchase products from Nitro A.S., subsidiary of VCHZ Synthesia." Robert crammed it and a few other papers in his pocket. He examined other volumes but found only newspaper clippings of literary reviews, invitations to lectures and book signings, vernissages and exhibits at art galleries.

Tottering down the stairs, Robert hoped he had found something useful, remembering Julio Mazzini and his small son. Then he pictured Gabriela at the Dome, gazing at the river and imbibing vermouths while her mother rambled. Would Señora Roca tell her daughter the truths she had disclosed to him?

He passed through somber rooms. From the mansion's depths the pendulum clock tolled ten-thirty, reminding Robert of the dinner party and the house on the Pampa. He exited the side door while the dogs barked and howled. Cursing them for a second time, the intruder closed the locks, peeked through the front gate to see if anyone was passing, waited, checked once again before stepping onto the street. He turned to look behind him. One day that house will be hers, he whispered to the air.

His sore thigh forced Robert to favor the good leg. After so much walking, climbing up and down stairs, he missed the crutches. At the corner of Juramento he saw a colectivo pulling to a stop. He decided to board it, no matter where it was headed. Robert struggled up the stairs, paid, rode for half an hour or so until the bus reached the end of its route somewhere in Palermo. He clambered down and spotted a trash bin surrounded by bushes in a park. He surveyed the area for cars or pedestrians. He saw nobody. After stuffing all the documents in his pockets, Robert dumped the sack, gloves and crowbar in the metal can. He felt an impulse to set it on fire, but he stopped himself.

He wandered for a minute, mounted another bus and descended on Avenida 9 de Julio, where he took a cab to San Telmo. Before proceeding to Mazzini's apartment, he found a stationery store. There he photocopied the documents he judged might be most helpful to his new friend—the police report from Uruguay, the end-user certificate and a few more.

A young boy opened the door, grinned and greeted Robert, "Buen día Señor." He had brown skin and a sheet of black hair that almost concealed his eyes.

Julio Mazzini dashed to the entrance and placed himself between his son and the visitor. He dug a handful of coins from his pocket, told the child to fetch a morning paper at the corner kiosk: "Take your time, m'hijo."

Robert recalled when Virgilio had called him that. When the boy had left, he asked his host, "Why didn't you introduce me to your son?"

"I'm going to be honest with you." Mazzini clasped his guest by the shoulders. "I'm a little superstitious. Most Argentines are like that—whether we're on the Right or Left, whether we're religious or not—we believe in luck." He hesitated. "You'll have to admit that yours hasn't been too good in Buenos Aires."

I'd take Gaby with all the bad luck in the world, Robert reacted in silence.

"Have a seat, compadre."

Out of breath from climbing the stairs, Robert collapsed on the armchair by the window, reclined, looked at his friend and inhaled deeply.

Mazzini stayed on his feet. "We don't have much time. Let's finish before my son returns."

"It won't take long, Julio. Remember I told you somebody was following Gaby and me?"

"Yes."

"Well he tried to kill me on Sunday in Colonia del Sacramento. He knifed me in the leg and they had to sew it up with twenty stitches."

"Carajo!" Mazzini swore and paced the small room, clutching his belly. "You know I'm feeling a stone in my gut for the first time since the dictatorship. And what in hell were you doing in Uruguay?"

"Gaby wanted to go to the beach, get out of Buenos Aires for a while. She begged me. Now I realize it was a mistake. But maybe not—we have more evidence." Sweat streamed on Robert's brow. "Roca's thug got away but the police found ten kilos of Semtex in the trunk of his car—a killer Falcon."

"Do you have proof?"

"There's the police report and these," Robert said. He emptied all of his pockets except one, where he kept the manila envelope. A rain of scraps and documents showered onto the wooden floor.

Julio knelt and rummaged through the papers. "Where did you get these?"

"I searched Roca's house this morning."

Julio glanced up at the visitor. "Jesus Christ you've got a pair of *huevos*." Returning to the documents, he mused, "Most of these are probably useless." He looked disappointed until he cried, "La puta!" Mazzini waved the end-user certificate in his hand. "Where was this?"

"Folded in the flyleaf of a book by Borges."

"At least the bastard has taste in literature. You're taking your chances, Che." Julio held the sheet in front of him and perused it. "This might help us. It suggests the milicos authorized Roca to purchase products from a company that manufactures explosives—Nitro, owned by a conglomerate called Synthesia." Julio was talking so hurriedly that he had to pause for breath. "We don't have an invoice for an actual purchase or delivery but if this document can be connected to the Semtex in the car, we may have new facts for a case against our friend."

"What's the connection between that company and Semtex?"

"Nitro is the manufacturer. Semtex was the junta's favorite explosive during the bad years. It's also as illegal as can be—plastic, light and odorless so it can slip through metal detectors. That's why terrorists like it so much, in Northern Ireland, the Middle East and a lot of other places." Julio thought for a second. "Roca might claim he needed it at his ranch on the Pampa, to blast an old bridge, install a culvert, a sewer pipe or something else. How many kilos did you say they found in the trunk of the Falcon?"

"Ten."

"Shit, enough to blow up the Teatro Colón."

Robert rubbed his wavy, dark-brown hair. "Why do you think Roca was careless enough to keep the certificate in his study—even if it was buried in a book?"

"Quién sabe, Who knows? The document's legal by itself. Hundreds of them are issued to governments all over the world. Roca probably kept it for the record in case he wanted to buy more explosives someday. The certificate's undated. What's illegal is the product that might have been delivered in the end—the Semtex, whose name doesn't appear on this document of course. Roca's too wily for that."

"There was also an Eibar rifle in the Falcon, standard issue to Argentine infantry."

"And another possible link to Roca." Julio glanced at his friend with a half-smile.

Robert removed the manila envelope from his pocket, creased and worn. "Tell me about the documents you gave me."

Julio recognized his son's steps approaching in the hall. "*Un momento,*" he said, hurrying to the door.

As he opened, the man took more coins from his pocket. "Hijo, buy some *caramelos* and then go see a movie." The child smiled from ear to ear and looked past his father to Robert, who winked at him from the chair. Julio's son grinned once more, turned, his black hair flopping on his head, and he skipped down the stairs.

The Argentine walked to Robert's side. Julio reached down and gave him a pat on the shoulder. "Hermano, I never allow him to go to the movies alone but we need time to talk."

"Yes. Can you tell me more about the documents?"

Julio extended both hands, in which the American deposited the manila envelope. His host extracted the sheet of paper with yellowing edges. "We can prove this note is Roca's because we have samples of his handwriting."

Robert recalled the letter from yesterday. "I have another in the apartment."

"This florid style would stand out anywhere. The document might implicate the people who killed my son," Julio murmured, almost as if he were talking to himself now. "It's addressed to Colonel Adolfo Sedara, who's in a jail cell in Patagonia for the murder or disappearance of seven citizens during the dictatorship."

"What do those initials mean?"

"'J.M.S.' stands for my son's full name, Julio Mazzini Sunseri. He was a student at the College of Philosophy and Letters at the University of Buenos Aires—that's what '*Fac. de F. y L.*' means, *Facultad de Filosofía y Letras.* As for '*Café*'—"

"I know," Robert interrupted, "Virgilio told me. I'm sorry, mi viejo." He saw the pain in his friend's brown eyes that were brimming with tears. He lurched from his chair, stumbled to Julio's side and placed a big paw on his shoulder.

"I feel that stone in my belly again, Roberto. I need to go on talking in order to keep from crying. '*Café*'—that was the most deadly word in almost three thousand long days of dictatorship in Argentina."

The two men stood gazing into each other's eyes. Robert squeezed Julio's arm. "I'm sorry for bringing back those memories. We're going to get rid of that *podrido* so he won't be able to touch your family or anyone else."

"*Compadre*, you're sounding more and more like an Argentine. When you talk like that the weight in my gut goes away for a few seconds."

Julio pulled the photograph from the manila envelope. Pointing to the huge figure in civilian clothes, flanked by two military men, he said, "Roca. The officer to the left is Sedara and the one to the right is General Francisco Aguirre, another assassin who was convicted in the same trial. His lawyers are appealing the decision because the evidence against him is weaker." Julio pointed to the picture again. "This shot was taken by an underground photographer in front of Army Staff Headquarters in Buenos Aires—by a man who risked his life with a miniature Pentax that he could hide in a shirt pocket. He disappeared one week later but he had already passed the film to a friend."

Robert turned the photo and pointed to the date stamped on the back: *6 de diciembre 1980*. Still trying to hold back tears, his host said, "Precisely two days before Julio Jr. was kidnapped by a killer car on Avenida del Libertador. Both the picture and the note tie César Roca to my son's murder. But without more evidence there might not be enough to nail him."

"The guard who saw the torture and killing can't testify, right?"

"I swore that I'd protect him and his family. If we break our promises we become no better than the *gorilas* and their allies."

"And the end-user certificate?" Robert bent down to take the document from the floor.

"Nitro and the parent company Synthesia are Czech firms. Their names have come up in the trials of several colonels and generals." Julio touched Robert's chest. "That may connect Roca to your attempted murder in Uruguay because of the Semtex in the car. It could also lead to an indictment for importing an illegal explosive. But of course it has nothing to do with Dionisio or the other victims of the milicos."

"Weren't they both cases of attempted murder—one successful and one not?" When he realized what he had said, Robert smiled at himself. "Sorry, Julio, I'm not thinking straight. I meant to say that one was a murder and the other an attempted murder."

"Don't worry, mi viejo, I get it. The point is that the two crimes are not connected unless we can link them to Roca." He drew a breath before resuming. "You should also understand that in Argentina some murders are more important than others. Lawyers like my friend Daniel Bello have too much work right now—new evidence is turning up every week. They can't take on all inquiries at once." Again Julio waited a second to catch his breath. "They need to focus on accusations that involve multiple killings, abductions and disappearances. In other words cases with a good chance for success in court. If you could find out more about Roca's part in Dionisio Sarmiento's death we might be lucky and get a conviction. If not the bastard will continue to be scot-free."

Robert appeared lonelier than the day he arrived in Argentina. "I need your help for that, Julio. Can I count on it?"

"I'm tempted to say 'No.' But I listen to you and I relent." He paused. "Daniel Bello's the lawyer who prosecuted Colonel Sedara and General Aguirre. If you bring Roca to trial you can tell Daniel that I'll testify."

"Are you sure?"

Julio delayed before replying. "Yes."

"Thanks, hermano." Robert soaked his friend in the gratitude of his blue-green eyes. "Let's not give up at this point. We've almost got the son-of-a-bitch."

"You're sounding like a real porteño but too optimistic."

"I am one now."

"Not yet, Che. We're never optimistic."

"Don't make me give up, Julio. Where's Daniel Bello's office?"

"Just a few blocks from here on Avenida Patricios. I'll walk there as soon as you leave and tell him your story. That way he won't be surprised when you appear. Don't call him on the phone—it might be tapped. Go there in person. The office is at number 1840."

Robert wrote down the address before pulling the photocopies from his pocket. "Keep these in case we should lose the originals," he said. "You have duplicates of the papers you gave me, right?"

"Yes." Julio was walking in a tight circle. "But let me think, Roberto. Events are moving so quickly that we might forget something, maybe a detail—or make a wrong decision. And Che, I must talk to the girl before we go any deeper."

Robert seemed puzzled. "Gaby?"

"Yes. It would help if I could ask her some questions before her father's been accused." Julio swallowed, looking straight down into Robert's eyes. "You know, viejo, next time you might not get away with a mere knife-wound. You're dealing with a man—men—who're as used to killing as they are to breathing." Julio hesitated. "What if anything happened to you? I also need to hear Gabriela's version."

Robert glanced down, then upward at his friend, seeking reassurance in Julio's moist eyes. "Treat her gently, compadre."

"*Tranquilo* Roberto. By the way I can understand why you'd risk your life for her—*qué mina!*" Julio twirled one hand loosely as if it had been scorched by Gabriela's flame. "She's one of those women who make the stones sigh, as our tangos say." Robert laughed for the first time in days, feeling an instant urge to be with Gaby.

"One more thing, Che. Just from the few words I exchanged with her, I sensed she may be like thousands of Argentines who lived through the bad times. Specially those who were in their formative years like Gabriela."

"What do you mean?"

"My impression was that she can be evasive when it comes to telling what she knows. It was a habit we adopted to make it through those times. The worst part is that it's survived long after the militares, like a bad habit or the memory of a nightmare. Maybe you've had the same sense—that she withholds things?"

Robert did not, could not answer. Already in his mind he was replaying the holes in many conversations with Gaby.

When Julio perceived that the American would not respond, he said, "Tell her that I'll stop by around 3:30 this afternoon. I'll be wearing a different disguise." He hoped these words would amuse his guest.

No trace of a smile showed on Robert's lips. "You need to know something else," he said in a tone that made his host stand upright as a tree.

"What?"

"Roca wants me to meet him tomorrow afternoon in the Capitol." As he spoke, Robert's voice faltered.

"La puta! Are you going to do it?"

"Somehow I'd like to confront him. He brings out the worst in me." At that moment Robert felt his hunger, recalling he had not eaten for hours.

"I know what you mean. If I ever got ahold of the *podrido* alone I'd choke him with these hands, Christ help me."

Robert took in the force of Julio's anger. "This meeting will be in a public place, not a house somewhere on the Pampa."

"*Menos mal.* But the Congreso Nacional belongs to men with power like Roca and his friends. It's a labyrinth—not necessarily 'public,' hombre. And you'll be there on the Friday afternoon before Christmas when most politicians and millions of Argentines will already be on vacation."

Robert drew a deep breath. "What exactly does he do? I still don't know."

"You might say he's a kind of broker, a liaison between business, the government and the armed forces. In the States you might call Roca a lobbyist but it's much more than that. Industrialists, politicians and top brass go to him for favors, not the other way around."

Robert remembered Virgilio's warning about the state and military in Argentina: "They'll tear you to pieces." He asked Julio, "Do you think I should keep the appointment?"

"Pucha." His host stalled for words. "It would be safer not to go but something might come out of the meeting that would help our case against Roca. Daniel Bello knows some honest policemen who could protect a potential witness—you—by patrolling the building."

Recalling Gaby's distrust, Robert asked, "Are there any honest police in Buenos Aires?"

Julio laughed. "A few, compadre. Now I'm the one who's sounding optimistic. What time's your appointment?"

"Five o'clock."

"Call me as soon as you leave the Congreso. If I don't hear from you by 6:30 I'll see if Daniel can prepare a temporary warrant for Roca's detention—one of those based on reasonable suspicion. Maybe the police could serve it on the old man in the Capitolio."

"On what grounds?"

"Conspiracy to kill Julio Mazzini Jr. and probably Dionisio Sarmiento too, importing illegal explosives, kidnapping Señor Robert Wells and attempting to kill him. We still might not have enough evidence to convict Roca but at least we could open an investigation and get his mitts off you for a while. Also give the bastard a scare until we can collect more evidence."

"Then I'll keep the appointment," Robert said in a resonant tone.

"Are you sure, mi viejo?"

"I'm going."

"*Bravo.*" Julio placed both hands on his friend's shoulders. "*Cuidado* Roberto. *Mucho, pero mucho cuidado.*"

21
Matanza

When he stepped from the cab, he saw her seated on the sidewalk in front of their apartment. Robert reached to touch her hair and nearly lost his balance on his tired, game leg.

"I was afraid to enter the Inner Garden alone," she said, almost whispering.

"How long have you been here?"

She did not answer. Gabriela's skin appeared sallow in the gray light. For a moment Robert imagined he could see the blood flowing through the veins on her neck.

He held out his hand, she took it, he helped Gabriela to her feet. She did not stride through the zaguán with her usual doe's step. Robert recalled the night on Avenida de Mayo when both of them had also looked like invalids after the hit-and-run.

As soon as they crossed the threshold, she told him, "I have to take another shower."

Robert furrowed his forehead. "Can't you tell me about the breakfast with your mother first? Don't you want to know what happened to me?"

"Yes Osito." Gabriela glanced at the floor. "Mother told me that we should escape from Buenos Aires."

"Did you tell her about our trip?"

"She knew."

"About the killer car?"

"Yes." She spoke as if nothing mattered.

Robert took her by the shoulders: "Gaby!" She did not lift her eyes. "I found something in your father's study."

Gabriela leaned against him. "What?"

"A certificate for the purchase of explosives." Robert felt her warm breath through his shirt. "I know you don't wish to hear but I have to tell you—it could tie your father to the death car in Uruguay. There may be enough evidence to open an investigation." Gabriela's body twitched.

"Into what?" she asked with her voice muffled on his shirt-front.

"The murders of Julio Mazzini Jr. and Dionisio Sarmiento." Gabriela recoiled. "Not to mention the abduction and attempted murder of Robert Wells."

Tears pooled in her purple-black eyes. She held back a sob, biting it down with her lips and a quiver along her jaw. He held her. "Your father had me kidnapped from the Dome after I met your mother there. His men took me to a house somewhere on the Pampa."

"Why?"

"Just to give me a shock and to make sure I leave you."

"You won't will you?"

"You know that, Gaby. And Mazzini has documents that could implicate your father in his son's death. He thinks Julio Jr. was killed so that he wouldn't be able to talk about your boyfriend's murder." The last words fell from Robert's mouth before he could catch them. She did not correct him: Dionisio had become so much a part of their lives that he might as well have survived the war.

Robert sat on the Pampa. Between the unmade sheets he saw Roca's letter. "By the way," he started, taking the envelope in his hands. "Your father addressed this to *Srta. G. Roca Dafiume*— like that, with an initial for your given name. Last time he did the same. What's this thing he has about 'Gabriela'? He never uses it. When I pronounced your name after dinner he shrank in his chair and his face turned red. At the house on the Pampa his reaction was even stronger—seemed to fall apart."

She took a half-minute or more to answer. "I can't tell you."

"Why?"

"Because ... I don't know."

"He never refers to you as his daughter—just 'she,' 'her' or one of those other names like Julia, Leonora, Eu—"

"Eulalia."

"Where in hell did they come from? For him you're either a false name or a pronoun."

"They're not false. I need to take another shower!" Gabriela cried, rushing to the bathroom. Like thin stalks of bamboo her ankles vanished behind the door. Soon Robert heard water cascading from the shower head.

His stomach growled with hunger. For a moment he thought of going to the kitchen, but he wanted to stay close to her. While she showered, he skimmed the other papers he had burgled in Roca's office, those that Julio had already surveyed and rejected. He rifled through receipts for books, paintings and wines, an award granted by the Buenos Aires Chamber of Commerce, notes written in the rhetorical style of the Argentine bourgeoisie. Robert opened Gaby's suitcase and hid all the documents beneath her clothes, still unpacked from their trip to Uruguay.

When she came out of the bathroom, barefoot and naked, she looked even more pallid. Her breasts were a pair of wan rosebuds. "Will you come with me?" Gabriela asked, slipping on a linen skirt he had not seen before.

"Where?"

"You'll have to trust me, Osito. Like the time I took you to Afrodita."

"That reminds me—did you know our telo belongs to some of your father's friends?"

"Who?"

"A couple of the junta's ex-ministers, your mother told me. Their wives happened to be at the Dome when I was there."

"Nothing happens by chance in Buenos Aires." Robert reheard Julio's statement to the same effect. "Did they see you?" she asked.

"Yes. Why?"

Gabriela did not reply. Instead she implored, "Please come with me Roberto! We have to leave, do something. We're just waiting here for them to come and kill you."

In spite of her forebodings Robert felt relieved, as though Gaby was emerging farther from her daze. He had tired of being the one who spoke up, who acted, took initiatives. Maybe he should be doing something else to strengthen his case against Roca, he thought, right now—he didn't know exactly what.

He took her gently by the shoulders. "I'll go anywhere with you, Gaby." As he spoke, Robert remembered Julio and their appointment. "Mazzini's going to be here around 3:30. He'd like to talk to you for a few minutes."

"Me?" Gabriela mused without expecting a response. She made up the bed and dressed in a plain sleeveless blouse that was also new for Robert. Except for the half-moon on her left earlobe she wore no jewelry. Why does she use one earring only, he wondered again. Did she lose the other? He might ask her, but by now nearly anything might evoke unwanted memories of her father, Dionisio, the war.

He walked slowly toward their bathroom. As he passed his lover, Robert lingered for a second to caress her hair, braided once more on the left side. He sensed a vague absence, a sort of hole in the air, like the missing half-moon on her ear. Gaby's skin no longer generated sparks or exuded her fragrance of ground spices.

In the shower he washed away the morning's anxiety and sweat. He pulled his white shirt and dark pants from the closet. Robert recalled that he had not worn them since the night with Gaby's parents. That event divided all his experience in Buenos Aires—before Roca, after Roca. *Before* was gone forever, a lost Eden, while *after* was a putrid tide, spreading, flooding, drowning the city and the nation, he thought. I should burn these clothes, Robert said under his breath, tossing them on the floor and choosing a sport coat, khaki pants and a linen shirt, hoping his luck would turn for the first time since that portentous night.

A few minutes later they heard a knock on the door. Gabriela retreated to the bathroom, the apartment's single private space, asking Robert to answer. When he recognized Julio Mazzini on the threshold, wearing a gray, curly wig and a different pair of sunglasses, he managed to grin.

Robert gave his Argentine friend a bear's hug. "I'll bet you scared the wits out of the portera with that fright-wig, Julio."

"Actually the *vieja* was nicer today."

"Should we tell her not to admit strangers?" Robert asked, serious now.

"It wouldn't be a bad idea the ways things are going. And I won't be coming back here." Julio checked the front door. Unlike his own and many more in Buenos Aires it did not have locks from floor to top. He let out a sigh. "Che, be sure to throw the dead bolt when you're inside."

"Will it keep them from getting in?"

"No. But they'd have to wake up the whole building to break down your door."

Gabriela walked into the room. Extending a frail hand, she peered at the visitor with her moist eyes. Julio stared at her without speaking.

"I'll go to the kitchen for a snack," Robert announced to break the mortal silence. "The two of you can talk here." Before leaving the room, he faced Julio. "Viejo, I'm sorry we can't offer you a more comfortable place. You and Gaby will have to sit on the bed."

The Argentines spoke to each other from opposite sides of the Pampa. Docile as a child, with tears on the verge of spilling from her enormous eyes, Gabriela related most of what Julio wanted to know. They had lived through some of the same years in Buenos Aires and knew several teachers, professors and students in common, many of whom were gone, victims of the war and time, beginning with Dionisio and Julio Jr. But the two were separated by all the differences between their families, their neighborhoods, their pasts.

Whenever she cited her father, Gabriela dropped her violet gaze, lowered her voice, her cheeks flushed and she barely replied to the visitor's questions. Julio did not insist, did not press her. He had begun to feel intrigued by this woman's life, her manner, her presence. If he had stayed much longer, he would have been caught in the sticky web of her world, like every other man who had known her for long. Later he told Robert that he had the stone in his belly while sitting on the same bed as César Roca's daughter.

He stood, thanking Gabriela for her time. Robert returned from the kitchen. "Would you like a beer, compadre?"

"I'm sorry but I can't stay." The two men hugged with slaps on the shoulder. "About your appointment tomorrow afternoon," Julio said, glancing sideways at Gabriela. She understood and walked into the kitchen.

"Tell me," Robert said.

Julio turned his back to the kitchen and spoke in a low voice: "You'll be in his territory."

"Is there any place that's not his territory?"

"Not in Argentina. But the Congreso's the center of his power. Don't forget to call me as soon as you get out of there. And some good news—Daniel Bello has secured two officers to stake out the building."

"Menos mal," Robert said in words that could have been a porteño's.

He and Julio gave one another a final embrace. When she heard the guest preparing to leave, Gabriela returned to say goodbye before sitting on the bed. How different the two lovers appeared as the man observed them from the threshold: Robert stood straight, looking intently into his friend's eyes, while she sat with her head drooping, her black braid tumbling across her shoulder.

A few minutes later the couple was walking down the stairs into the dim light of another afternoon that would never return. Robert had decided to bring his crutches. They had become old companions.

Clouds covered Buenos Aires like a thick pall. The air felt warmer than yesterday, making the smell more pungent.

As they walked toward a bus stop, Gabriela said, "Julio reminds me of his son—the one who attended university with my boyfriend."

"You mean your 'former boyfriend.'"

"You also forgot to say 'former' today, Osito—before I got into the shower, remember?"

"I was talking about the past."

"So was I. Anyway the past is also the present now. I was just going to say that you can trust Julio Mazzini."

"I know." Robert could not resist asking, "Do I remind you of him?"

"Julio?"

"Dionisio."

"Your eyes and hair," she said without hesitation.

Feeling her old lover's presence again, Robert rubbed his chin before asking, "Did you ever meet any of his brothers?"

"How did you know he had brothers?"

"I've met one of them."

"What's his name?"

"Virgilio. I mentioned him once before. Did you know him?"

"No."

"There's also a sister. Ever meet her?"

"No."

"What about the parents?"

Gaby did not reply. Robert said to himself, She can't absorb, all at once, so many questions about her past, her life.

On Avenida de Mayo they took a colectivo that chugged for miles across town. They passed old slaughterhouses with broken windows, sagging roofs and a reek of decay that merged with the odor of the city. Robert pictured the calf's head at his hotel, the steaks and *parrilladas* that he and Gaby had consumed in this nation of meat, cattle, blood and hides. Puzzling over where she was taking him, he followed her off the bus at the Mataderos station.

They had to wait alone in the heat to board a train for the outskirts. Robert used the time to tell Gabriela more about his abduction to the Pampa, along with other details that he had held back until now. She listened to his story without comment, her eyes hardly open, as if those things had occurred to someone in another age and country.

Tired, sullen passengers sat around them on the train, men and women on their way home from work, reclining on their seatbacks or hanging their heads between their legs. Apartment buildings passed in rows through the carriages's dusty windows, declining into shabby one-story houses, then makeshift shacks of corrugated iron, plywood, tin and plastic. Robert observed those villas miseria, the slums that surround the cities of Gabriela's sad, suffering continent, recollecting that Dionisio had grown up in a place like these. Those flimsy dwellings made the ghettos of South and East Los Angeles seem opulent.

When they stepped onto the street outside the Matanza station, they saw a black Ford Falcon at the intersection, stopped at a red light.

"Is that him?" Gabriela asked with a tremor in her voice, grasping Robert's forearm. Her hand was shaking.

Fright snaked up his back. "I can't see the driver through those tinted windows," he told her. "That car was supposed to be confiscated by the police in Colonia." When the signal changed to green, the vehicle accelerated, turned at the next corner and disappeared from view. Robert smiled to himself, thinking there must be hundreds of cars like that one in Buenos Aires and its sprawl.

Gabriela clasped his forearm to help him walk, or was it from fear? After crossing a vacant lot of weeds and rubbish, they reached a dirt square encircled by tin-roofed hovels, most of them painted in bright colors—red, green, yellow. There were gaps between them, like holes from pulled teeth. In the warm breeze shirts and blouses fluttered on clotheslines.

"Welcome to Rezago," she told him. "The other Buenos Aires, the other Argentina."

"I thought we were in Matanza."

"We are but this barrio is called Rezago."

"Did Dionisio live here?" Gabriela continued walking and did not speak. "Why did we come?"

"You'll see."

She led him to the center of a plaza where it descended into a large pit. From its depths a stink of rotten flesh and garbage rose. Robert heard a faint noise from below.

"The rats gnawing," she said. "When I came to Rezago a few years ago this hole wasn't here. Gradually the earth started to sink and then one day it collapsed. The city has tried to fill it but every time it caves in. Now people use it as a garbage dump. It belongs to the rats."

She pulled Robert toward the ring of dwellings around that square. The stench from the pit stuck in their nostrils, blended with the city's smell. Chasing a skeletal dog, a girl sprinted from a shack. She stopped to smile at them before pursuing the animal again.

Robert asked, "Does she remind you of anyone?"

"That was so long ago."

"Three months." Or a century, he thought.

They followed a dusty path between those hovels. A few had brave, tiny gardens in front, planted with red and white geraniums, bordered by shards of glass. Wearing sandals made from tire-treads, three boys passed, ogling the strangers as though they were visitors from space.

The couple came to a small house where women, men and some children were waiting in a crooked queue. A curved chimney protruded from the roof like the hump on a cripple's back. How could Robert not think of Virgilio?

The newcomers walked to the end of the line as the others gawked at them. Gabriela recognized several women. One greeted her.

"Why are we waiting here?" Robert asked.

"To see Nemesia." When she mentioned that name, other people turned their way.

Two older ladies murmured something that Robert could not decipher. "What did they say?" he asked Gabriela.

"That Nemesia's a powerful woman who can see into the cracks of the world. Some of her enemies wake up in the morning with their eyes crossed and their tongue twisted like a medialuna."

"Who is she?"

Before his lover could reply, a hot blast of air raised a whirlwind of dust. With both hands Gabriela shielded her face until it passed. A film had already coated her hair, brow and cheeks, making her eyes look maroon against her powdery skin.

They had reached the front of the queue that zigzagged to the house. Sweat beaded on their temples, flies buzzed around their ears. The sound of a bell issued from inside and it was Gabriela's turn.

With a tremulous hand she opened the door. An odor of age and fumes invaded their nostrils. There were no windows. Darkness seemed to have grown there for years.

In the center an old woman with white hair was seated at a table. A kerosene lamp shed a sallow light around her. Blowing warm air in their faces, an electric fan buzzed like a horsefly.

"Buenas tardes, hija," Nemesia addressed Gaby in a throaty voice.

"I want to introduce you to my friend. His name is Roberto."

Without responding or raising her eyes, the woman motioned for them to sit down in chairs of rattan. Gabriela took the seat on the woman's left, Robert on her other side. As he grew accustomed to the shadows, he spotted a deck of playing cards between Nemesia and the lamp, illuminated by that sickly glow.

The woman had a wide, dark face, little eyes and skin weathered like a turtle's. She wore a black dress and a mourning band on one arm. When she picked up an old maté gourd, she made a sucking noise as she drank from her *bombilla*, the silver tube that served as a straw. Without paying attention to Robert, she chatted with Gabriela. He noticed the woman's maté-darkened teeth.

While Nemesia shuffled the cards, over and over, cut the deck and shuffled again, Gabriela observed raptly. Meanwhile Robert scanned the room. He saw wood-planked walls specked with stains of dead mosquitoes, hung with fading prints and calendars; a butane stove on the far side under a makeshift altar with a photograph of Evita, adorned by aluminum foil; a print of the Virgin of Luján, the country's patron saint; mirrors tarnished by moisture. He set his eyes on a rusted can of cooking oil, stuffed with dried flowers, with a smiling peasant girl painted on the label. She was carrying a basket of olives on her head—"*Ricoltore, Aceite de Calidad.*" In one hand she held a canister of oil with the same brand on its front, which in turn had a smaller picture of her holding a second container, which enclosed a third and so on. For a moment Robert fancied he was seeing Gabriela on that label: she also seemed to be shrinking away from him, getting smaller and smaller, almost disappearing in the penumbra.

"*Ahora,*" Nemesia pronounced. She arranged those cards, worn smooth around their corners, spotted with grease. It was a Spanish deck with suits of *copas* or cups; swords; gold coins; *palos* or clubs. She dealt them in three piles on the table. Then the woman lifted herself by the elbows and waddled to the stove beneath the altar, filled her maté gourd with hot water and returned to her chair. Gabriela still had her eyes fixed on the deck. Robert had never seen her so enthralled.

Nemesia turned over the top card of the pile on her left, uncovering a three of copas. She eyed Gabriela: "That's you, *Corazón,*" my Heart.

Robert regarded the woman's fingernails, rough and yellowed like an old horse's hooves. Yearning to be outside, he was beginning to feel confined, uneasy. The slum, the stench of the city, even the plaza with the rats' hole might have been better than this room, like a cave with fetid air.

Nemesia turned over the first card on the opposite pile. A jack of swords looked blankly up at them. "A young man, a lover or spouse," she announced in her grating voice. She slurped from her maté gourd.

With a flourish of her hands the woman started to lift the top card from the middle pile. Nemesia waited a few seconds, creating an air of suspense, leaned closer to the kerosene lamp and her shadow grew on the wall. Finally she extracted the card and slapped it on the table. It was a blond, bearded king of palos. "A powerful man," she intoned, "one who can either aid or prevent you from achieving happiness, *m'hija*." She sucked more of her drink. "Three out of four suits have turned up," she went on, spinning a web with her words that spread across the room. "Only the oros, the gold coins are missing. That means you won't be wealthy in the near future, *querida*." Robert recalled the spring sweepstakes and the terms of César Roca's will.

Gabriela scrutinized those three upturned cards on the table. "I don't like this reading," she said with stricken eyes.

Robert felt suffocated by the spell the old woman had woven in the room. He shook his arms as if he could break it—like a thick net, a spider's web, he thought. Beneath the table Robert reached for Gabriela's wrist.

She snatched her arm away as though his hand had scorched her, while the half-moon swung crazily from her ear. "Don't you know it's bad luck to touch a person who's playing cards?" Those words cut deeper into Robert than any she had ever spoken.

"She's right," Nemesia echoed, acknowledging the stranger at last. Her small, dark eyes, buried in folds of leathery skin, trained their glance on him. Next she turned to Gabriela as if Robert were no longer there. "Remember the old saying about luck in cards and love. *El amor es más importante que los naipes.*"

"But love's in the cards!" Gabriela said in a shrill tone. "Love and everything else."

"You'll have to come back," Nemesia said with finality. She swept the cards into a pack, swilled her maté. The electric fan buzzed in the corner.

Gabriela set some bills on the table. She faced Robert and said, "I'm short of cash. Can you help me with 20,000 australes?"

Fumbling for his wallet, he felt duped, as if the two women had caught him in a snare. Before he could withdraw the bills, Nemesia placed a cold hand on his arm and leaned close, whispering, "*Matá al rey de palos, hijo.*" Those words singed Robert's ear.

As he and Gabriela walked outside, people gaped at them. The line now stretched longer than a soccer field. "Why the crowd?" Robert asked.

"Her power grows at night." She paused for a second. "What did Nemesia tell you?" As though she were ashamed of her question, Gaby bowed her head.

He answered, "Kill the king of clubs." How could that old woman know, Robert asked himself.

"Would you do that?"

He thought of Vietnam, the few enemy soldiers he had shot, his lasting remorse, his desire never to kill again. "I don't know."

Robert and Gabriela walked through the maze of pathways in Rezago. Night had almost fallen. In the hovels' tiny plastic windows, pierced with holes, they saw the glow of kerosene lamps. They skirted the square with the black pit, where a noxious reek assailed their nostrils and a grinding sound rasped on their ears.

They crossed the vacant lot. Ahead they glimpsed moving shapes around a bonfire. Those figures turned their way: teenage boys and girls with spiked hair dyed yellow, green and orange, silver rings dangling from their ears, eyelids, noses, lips, navels. Robert heard them repeat "*el cojo,*" the cripple, and guessed they were making fun of him on the crutches.

The lovers reached Avenida General Paz, the boundary between the city and the province of Buenos Aires. Gabriela clutched his arm. Speeding cars did not slow to let them pass. Robert summoned the day when they had tried to cross the boulevard of Libertador like animals in flight. This time he imagined they might be fording one of the last rivers of their life together.

As the night deepened, they rode the train then the bus to town. Morose, fatigued men and women sat around them, exhausted by the workday or dreading the late shift. Robert and Gabriela observed the commuters' nodding heads and swaying shoulders. He was hungry but he said nothing. He knew she would not want to eat. Since they had returned from Colonia del Sacramento, her appetite had faded.

As he inserted his key in their door, Robert worried they might discover a third letter from Roca. But the Inner Garden seemed the same as they had left it.

Gabriela slumped on the bed. He dropped his crutches and went to the kitchen, where he nibbled on some bread and cheese, washed down by a glass of Malbec. He could not finish them. His bad leg throbbed.

Robert lay at Gabriela's side. With both arms he held her tightly. The bed quivered from her sobs, the trembling of her limbs. She cried herself to sleep. In her dreams or nightmares she moaned for hours.

Robert awoke in a room swarming with crows. When he saw Gaby propped on her elbow, gazing at him, he knew it had been a dream. Something had happened to her in the night. It was as though a sediment of sorrow at the bottom of her life, stirred by her love for Robert and her new knowledge of the war, had risen to the surface. It exuded from her pores, altering her appearance: her sleepy eyes and hair had lost some of their radiance, her skin had nearly spent its bloom. As he watched the ghost of Gabriela beside him, Robert strove to repress his tears.

"I heard it again," she said in her faraway voice.

"The earth?"

"A hiss. From the edge of the world." Her eyes peered at the wall. "Osito, did you ever think—no matter how much we cry we never run out of tears?"

"No, Gaby." He wished to tell her about the room full of crows, but it would have been dull compared to her dream and those words. Nor did Robert mention the change in her looks.

He glanced out their window at the dim, turbulent dawn. On the sill a fly had given up its struggle for the light. The city's smell filled their room. Both knew it was Friday. Closing his eyes and leaning back, Robert pictured Roca, larger than the figurehead on the prow of an ancient ship. He tried to concentrate and gather strength for the day ahead.

Gabriela lay on her back. For hours they rested in silence. Both were fulfilling the final roles assigned to them on that day in Buenos Aires.

They heard the wind rise. On the balcony the twins were combing each other's hair and singing, so it must be early afternoon. Robert pressed his body against Gaby's. Lifting the braid that covered her left ear, he kissed it.

"Please don't leave," Gabriela whispered in a voice that sounded like a small girl's. "I'm afraid to be here by myself."

"Will you come with me? You could wait across the street from the Capitol at Confitería del Molino."

"No."

"Why don't you meet your mother again?" Gabriela groaned, shaking her head. "Or wait for me in another one of our cafés, farther from the Capitolio?" She did not answer. Finally Robert remembered her friend at the hospital—what was her name?—the doctor who was supposed to be Gaby's roommate. It rose to his memory: "Alfonsina—would you like to visit her?" Again she did not speak. He had nothing else to offer. Once more he fathomed how alone they were in Buenos Aires and the world.

With the tip of a finger Robert traced the whorls of Gabriela's ear. Then he touched the sharp edge of her silver pendant hanging from the lobe. When he tapped it with a thumb and finger, he saw that it was a waning moon.

"I'll come straight back to you," he said. Gabriela stared at the ceiling. "He wouldn't try to hurt me in the National Congress building, right?" She did not reply.

Robert twirled her silver moon again. It shone in the pale light from their window, casting faint reflections on the walls, windows and ceiling.

"I'm afraid of it," Gabriela said.

Robert recalled the unanswered question from their first date in Buenos Aires. "I know."

"There's no way out of this," she said on the other side of grief. "It's as though it already happened." He raised one hand to caress and comfort Gabriela, but she turned away. He stroked nothing but the air between them.

Robert rose to his feet. After so many hours in bed, his thigh felt a little stronger. While he dressed, he observed Gaby, who was curled on her side in the bed. He would have liked to crawl back into the Pampa with her. But he sensed it would not have stemmed the rush of time and events.

In the gray light Robert bent over Gabriela. Tears glistened on her lashes and cheeks. Kissing her face, he tasted the salt on her skin.

"Goodbye Gaby."

She was silent. At that instant Robert knew that nobody could ever soothe the unreachable pain in Gabriela's bones.

22

Twilight

Wishing he could stay home, he walked down the stairs. He cradled both crutches beneath one arm. He no longer needed them, but Robert felt more secure holding them in reserve, guessing that his bum leg would tire. Also he was going to meet Gaby's father, who would likely be surrounded by his armed entourage. I may need something in self-defense, he thought, picturing himself wielding crutches against the combined firepower of César Roca Steele, his henchmen and the Argentine military.

Foul air whipped across his face when he opened the zaguán. The sky was low and gray. Most of the jacaranda blossoms had fallen or withered on their branches. Before he had reached the corner, Robert already missed her presence.

He asked a pedestrian for the time. Taken aback at first, keeping his distance, the man responded, "Ten-to-four." Still a few minutes to see the dwarf before confronting Gaby's father, Robert estimated. He hailed a taxi.

As he approached the Hotel Castelar, he saw the crippled beggar wheeling himself along the sidewalk, extending his battered cup to passersby. Robert offered him a few coins. The man turned away, scowled and muttered, "*Mala pata.*" Somehow that victim of war must have sensed the bad luck enveloping the stranger like a cloud, or perhaps he simply refused to accept alms from a man with crutches. A beggar with honor, Robert almost smiled to himself, holding out those useless coins in his palm.

One at a time he took the marble stairs to the baths. He did not buy a ticket at the window. The pimple-faced attendant was sweeping the floor.

"I'm here to see Virgilio. Do you know if he's inside?"

"He's inside alright, Che—inside a coffin six feet under. They shot him point-blank a couple of nights ago in La Boca."

Robert felt as though he'd had the wind knocked out of his chest. "I just saw him on Saturday!" he spat out.

"It only takes a second to kill a man." The employee paused before adding, "*En boca cerrada no entran moscas*," If you keep your trap shut, flies can't get in. He held out a hand for the client's ticket.

Robert stood still for a few seconds, staggered, yelled "Carajo!" and pushed by the attendant, who tried to stop the American with his broom. The man called "*Alto! Alto!*" while he chased Robert, who lurched forward with the crutches on his shoulder, tears burning his eyes, past the bar and shops, into the dressing closet, searching for his friend in the steam, down the tiled corridor, through the first chamber, into the deepening mist of the second room with its circular hall where elderly clients sat on wooden benches, immobile as marble statues. They looked up when the intruder screamed "Virgilio! Virgilio!" The attendant had nearly caught up with him, ordering "*Fuera hijo de puta!*" but Robert was already moving out the glass door that led to a cool, dark tunnel. He finally issued from the far side of the baths, climbed the stairway that appeared steeper now. Knowing that Virgilio had died, that his guide was no longer there beneath the city, he felt more isolated than ever. He stumbled onto the sidewalk.

Robert moved like a man in mourning. With one of his crutches he waived down a taxi. When they passed a supermarket where police cars were flashing red lights, the driver said, "People are hungry—last night they started looting markets." Robert eyed the meter ringing up australes by the thousands. He knew his savings would not last, even with Gaby's assistance. Everything seemed to be coming to an end in Argentina. He wept silently for Virgilio.

Grumbling about "*la situación*," the cabbie stopped in front of Congreso. He pointed to the building that resembles a sooty replica of the Roman Capitolium. "There you have the podridos who're to blame!" he blurted. "*Políticos de mierda*," Fucking politicians.

Robert stepped onto the sidewalk and saw the Confitería del Molino across the street, where he had gone many times with Gaby. In the shadow of the monumental Congress the old café reminded him of a dollhouse.

Before approaching the edifice, Robert tightened the knot of his tie. He had not worn one for weeks. Externals counted for Gabriela's father, he understood, but why attempt to please a man who wants to kill you? Then Robert recalled Virgilio's death and felt the ache in his belly. It must have been Roca, he thought in anger, wishing he had carried a weapon today.

He ascended the colossal stairs of the Capitol, like a mountainside for a man with a game leg. A warm wind blew around him. Robert was perspiring and his armpits were damp from the heat.

At the main entrance a phalanx of guards with white gloves and carbines stopped him. When he cited César Roca Steele, the ranking officer checked a list where he must have found Robert's name. "*Pase Señor!*" the man called, snapped to attention, saluted.

The American passed a metal detector and entered between doors of massive bronze. He limped down a marble hall where the temperature plummeted as if he were in a temple or a mausoleum. The place summoned back the City of the Dead, Gabriela, the graves and the guard who had expulsed them.

Larger-than-life portraits glared down at him in the gallery circling the rotunda, stern generals and patriarchs bedecked with laurels like the pale ancestors on the walls of Roca's house, except there was not a single woman here. Noting that the paintings tilted outward from the top, he imagined they were about to fall on him.

Why did the Congreso look so empty? Julio Mazzini's prediction floated through Robert's mind: by now many of his compatriots would be on vacation. Perhaps they've closed early today, Robert speculated, the last workday before Christmas? He had been in the country long enough to know that Argentines are virtuosos in the art of stretching holidays.

It was too late to turn around, to flee, go back home to Gaby. "It's as though it already happened," Robert repeated her words. He felt utterly alone in that sepulchral pile.

He hobbled down a broad flight of stairs to the basement, where Roca's office was supposed to be. When he passed ground level, the air grew colder still, as if he had descended into a cavern. Robert advanced along a corridor whose walls exuded moisture from the floor to the embossed ceiling.

For a second he thought he heard music. It disappeared, Robert went on, heard it again, louder. He followed that sound through a tall, open door to his left. He walked by empty rooms, offices, vestibules, lounges, passageways that might go on forever.

The music guided Robert to a vast, five-walled chamber with speakers rumbling from all sides. He recognized the violins' unbearable sweetness toward the final bars of *Tristan und Isolde*. A single lamp in the rear lit an expanse of wooden desk, raised on a platform that dominated the room. Behind it sat César Roca, attired in a black tuxedo, gazing at the coffered ceiling through opaque sunglasses. He was keeping time to the music with his cane in one hand, waving it like a conductor's baton. With the final crescendo of the *Liebestod* he rose to his feet, lifted and spread his arms like wings, hovered for a moment while the orchestra swelled to its delirious ecstasy, then swept them down as it died away with a longing melody in the strings.

In his basso profundo the Argentine announced, "I have been expecting you." He sighed, sat in his carved wooden chair and checked his watch. "You are punctual this time, Señor Wells." He can read the hands of a wristwatch in a dimly lit room, Robert noted, so how could Roca be blind?

While Gabriela's father engaged in formalities, the American recalled that this man had ordered the deaths of many Argentines, not to mention his own. Robert's wounded thigh pulsed from running through the Turkish baths and walking these marble stairs and floors. He did not wait for permission to take a leather chair below the platform. Across the polished wooden plane of the desk that stood between them, he looked up at the older man.

"We are almost even now," Roca observed. "You have two crutches while I need only this," he said, holding up his cane with its carved lion's head. He doesn't bother to ask why you're carrying crutches. He knows, Robert told himself.

Gabriela's father straightened himself to speak, expanding the wall of his chest and his white dress shirt. "Did you have trouble breaking into my house?"

Robert scrutinized Roca and remained mute. The man's dark glasses reflected the lamp on his desk. There were no other lights in the large, windowless room. The visitor scanned his surroundings: Greek and Roman busts, statues of patricians, gods, goddesses in niches and on shelves. Rows of signed photographs hung on the walls—Juan Perón and Evita; Generals Videla, Viola and Galtieri, Admirals Massera and Lambruschini,

Brigadiers Agosti and Krassnoff; bishops, cardinals and other princes of the Church. In the center, directly above Roca, hung the great black head of a bull with wide-spreading horns.

"A prize stud from my ranch on the Pampa," the man proclaimed, tracking the foreigner's eyes. Robert pictured Gaby nestled in their own Pampa, safe and warm. Silence fell between the two men, signifying one thing: her.

Roca's voice erupted, "I would rather see her dead than living with a common burglar."

Robert could not suppress a laugh. "Is that worse than being a kidnapper and a murderer?" he challenged. "I thought the one you wanted dead was me."

"You will be soon," Roca responded with a drop of acid on each word. He allowed that utterance to sink into Robert's mind before saying, "By the way whatever you stole from my study will be worthless. What did you find there?"

If the missing documents were unimportant, Robert reasoned, Roca would not have posed the question. He decided to reveal just enough to make his opponent anxious. "End-user certificate," he said, enunciating each syllable in English, slowly.

Roca shifted his weight in the chair. His mouth moved without emitting sound, like his son Segundo seeking words. He turned, shoved the chair several feet to his left and unlocked a steel cabinet, from which he pulled a color photograph. He handed it across the table to the American, who examined the figure of a bloody cadaver on a sidewalk, whose eyes were beaten and bloodied into a gory hole. Although the victim lay on his back, he was twisted enough to one side so that Robert distinguished the telltale hump and the body shaped like a question mark. At the bottom of the picture he saw a line of text: "*Virgilio Sarmiento / Buenos Aires / 13 de diciembre de 1990.*" Reading that name and the date, jolts shook Robert's frame. Images and memories spurted into his mind—the small man weeping as he told the story of Gaby's boyfriend, who was Virgilio's own brother; the young man's death, his corpse on the river bottom.

Studying the photo, Robert registered the date, precisely the same as the attempted murder in Colonia del Sacramento. Roca must have ordered both him and Virgilio to be killed on December 13th. The old bastard likes to impose a gruesome symmetry on his world, Robert said to himself.

"Give it back to me," the man directed with a flat intonation, as though he were talking to a servant.

What if I said "No," Robert wondered, what if I ran out of here with the photo? But he remembered his bad leg, his crutches, the maze of rooms and corridors, the long flights of stairs, the armed soldiers at the entrance. And how could he know if the photograph implicated Roca at all? Feeling outmaneuvered already, Robert returned the picture to an enormous, outspread, blue-veined hand.

Gabriela's father crumpled it, grabbed a gold cigarette lighter from the top of his desk, pushed the starter and lit the photo's edge. It flared in his hand. Robert wept inside for Virgilio, for the dwarf's family—the sister, the older brother, the nephews and nieces whom Julio had mentioned.

Roca watched a corner of the picture burn in his hand before dropping it in a metal trash bin. He extinguished the lamp. Except for that flickering photo the cavernous room resided in shadows.

Gaby's father made an effort to laugh. Startling the visitor, that sound heaved from the man's throat without gladdening his face, as far as Robert could discern in the near-dark. "Ugo shot the hunchback three times between the eyes. Point-blank."

"Ugo?"

"The same gentleman you met at the beach in Colonia del Sacramento about ten hours later. He is outside at this moment, waiting to hear from me, prepared to charge the building at my command." Roca held up a walkie-talkie, pressed a button. The small gray box spit out static. "*Atento!*" he called into the speaker.

A male voice responded, "*A sus órdenes Jefe!*"

"*Cambio y corto,*" Gabriela's father ended. Robert portrayed Ugo outside the Capitolio with the black baseball cap on his bald head, cuts and bruises around his mouth.

The fire burned in the dust can, underlighting and distorting Roca's countenance. "So Señor Wells, neither Dionisio nor his hunchbacked brother managed to escape justice."

Gabriela's father turned his chair again, extracted some documents from the cabinet, rumpled them, stood and hurled them onto that pyre. "More *desgraciados*, more poor devils like the dwarf." Cursing Roca in his mind, Robert conjured names on those documents—perhaps Dionisio and Julio Jr., Quiroga's niece, so many others. They were disappearing for a second time now, dying another death in this private conflagration.

As the firelight wavered across Roca's face, Robert perceived the inconsolable misery there, a sadness larger than the world. He felt a brief compassion for Gaby's father: she's right, he acknowledged, this is an old man. But if he had been Julio or anyone else whose son, daughter, sister, brother, aunt, uncle, cousin, niece, nephew, husband, wife, father, mother or friend had been a victim, Robert knew, he would have felt only wrath from the unending loss.

In the dust bin the fire sputtered. César Roca sank into his chair. The American could scarcely make out the man's imperious silhouette in the waning glow. As though he had made a mighty exertion, thrown live bodies into the flames, Roca panted. Robert observed the open drawers of his filing cabinet, pondering how many other fates could be interred there.

The Argentine's head revolved toward him. "The smoke of life. You have seen the last traces of twelve Argentines, burned to ashes." The fire in the trash bin quenched itself. Both men were engulfed in darkness.

Slowly Robert's eyes grew accustomed to the shadows, began to see the outline of Gaby's father again. "*Asesino,*" he accused the man in a calm, resonant voice.

Roca held out both of his palms. "These hands are clean—they have never touched those victims. I am responsible but not guilty."

"You had her lover killed," Robert switched to English.

"That word is very unpleasant."

"*'Killed?'*"

"The other."

"*Lover,*" the stranger repeated, louder. "*Amante,*" he threw in the Spanish too. Roca wrenched his features. In a pointed tone Robert asked, "Is that word as unpleasant as the boy's death to his family? To your daughter?"

"You are incapable of comprehending," Roca pronounced, still short of breath. He changed to Spanish: "We have a proverb—'An old man sitting can see more than a young man standing.'" He paused. "Many Argentines believed our country was being threatened by the guerrillas and other parasites. We tried to rescue the nation. People suffered on both sides."

"Like Gaby."

Roca winced when he heard his daughter's nickname on the foreigner's tongue. He lowered his head and did not speak for a minute or longer. "If she had known the truth," he started in a muted voice, "she would have suffered more. *Toute vérité n'est pas bonne à dire.*" Robert could not capture all of Roca's meaning, but he said nothing. "I can see that your French is weak, Mr. Wells. The truth could be compared to light—both can be blinding," Gabriela's father expounded. "Half-truths cast a twilight that softens everything. Or they bring peace, the night," Roca's words dwindled. "I thought she would forget Sarmiento. But she did not—otherwise she would have ceased in her attempts to exorcize his memory."

Once more Robert failed to understand, but he did not tender the man an opportunity to explain. The silence became thick and airless.

Roca's speech emerged from the penumbra. "All the places where she has taken you, Americano, all those parks, boliches, cafés, confiterías and restaurants—they are the very same haunts she once frequented with him." Robert's mind reeled, and he longed to scream to the top of the high ceiling.

Roca waited, enjoying his rival's dismay before recommencing: "Let us start with the cafés and tearooms. La Biela, Café de la Paix, Premier, Clásica y Moderna, the Confitería del Molino across the street from us. Would you like to hear more?" Robert did not answer. "Then there are the discotheques like Brujas, later an assignation hotel like Afrodita. Oh—I almost forgot!—the Plaza de Mayo on the first day. Much later the cemetery in La Recoleta. And just last week that fleabag across the river in Colonia, that parrilla and the beach."

Each one of those names pierced Robert's memory. In order to know all those places Roca would have had to track Gaby and me from the beginning, he calculated, from the day we met to the first dates, right through our trip to Uruguay. And how had he learned where she had gone with Dionisio, unless he had them followed too? Or had she informed her father? It's what he intends, Robert divined—make me doubt her, draw her away from me. As if Roca knew everything about Gaby and himself, the American felt ashamed and exposed.

He also sensed the bile seething through his body. "You had her first lover killed. Your daughter loves me now."

The man cringed before making one of his mountainous shrugs. "Ergo I shall have you killed. The logic is implacable."

For a moment Robert did not reply. Then he said, "That's what the detective thought about those murders on the Pampa in the story you lifted from Borges."

"You are a good student, Robert. But have you forgotten the detective's fate?"

Again the visitor did not answer. Those few seconds allowed him to reflect, to realize how strange it was for him to be in the basement of the Argentine National Congress at the center of Buenos Aires, sitting across from Gabriela's father, who wanted him dead.

"Our story will have a different ending," Robert said.

Roca articulated slowly, "You will be amazed at how similar it will be, almost identical. All paths lead to defeat. Nothing is ever enough for anyone."

Gaby's father paused and drew a deep breath before resuming. "A man is the slave of his heart," he uttered in a wistful tone, unlike any other Robert had heard from him. "I love Julia with an ardor that you could not fathom." In the listener's mind that name echoed the night of the fatal supper. "I cherish her as I cherish Argentina," Roca proceeded. "For me she *is* our country. During the civil war and later I have never allowed my adversaries to hurt this nation." His speech swelled. "Neither shall I allow them to harm her. And already you have learned about her and Sarmiento—both you and Julio Mazzini. Senior, that is."

The American felt sick to his stomach, fearing for his friend and the boy who had smiled at him yesterday. How could Roca know about Julio, unless he'd spied on him too? Then Robert recalled how Gabriela changed whenever she spoke of her father, also her insomnia, her moans in bed, her scratching and biting, her unwillingness to look into his eyes when they were making love.

"I used to read her books at bedtime," Roca said softly, as though his account demanded intimacy. "I chose them in English so that she could learn the language of my mother's family." He sighed, "She was such a beautiful little girl." From those words and their timbre, reminding Robert of confessionals from his childhood, he suspected Roca might be telling his own truth.

"Later we read novels together, mostly the French and Russians," the man went on, staring into the shadows. "I sent her to the best schools, then urged her to study medicine so that she could have a career, so that people would not think she was trapped at home." Gabriela's father let out a mirthless laugh tinged by regret. "We had our secret. In the meantime her mother was taking lovers. Unlike all my friends, unlike most Argentine men of my class I have not kept a mistress. I have always been faithful to her."

Robert did not know if the man was referring to Gabriela or his wife. He felt queasy and lightheaded. The pentagonal room seemed to whirl around him. I haven't eaten since last night, Robert recalled, but if I had food in my stomach I would have vomited by now.

"I was so close to her," Roca continued in a gentle voice, as if he were musing to himself, "much more than her mother. I was the one who told her about a young girl's body, the one in whom she confided when she had her first *regla*—she was eleven years old. I bought her pills to relieve her cramps, pads to soak up her precious blood of a new woman. By that time it was impossible to forbear . . ." His speech trailed off again. "Nothing matters so long as I can be with Leonora."

Roca's words and the other name for his daughter made Robert gag, nearly retch on the marble floor. He wanted to leap from his chair, run out of that chamber, seek the daylight, but how could he run or leap with a bum leg? He also admitted to himself that he was transfixed by Roca's words; each could have been a spike nailing him to his seat. Aching to be with her, Robert remembered Gaby curled on their bed. How could he ever console her?

"She grew up during the military rule and the Falklands War," Roca spoke into the gloom. "Like everyone else she learned to survive through caution, silence and partial truths. She never had a suitor until the war had almost ended. Dionisio Sarmiento belonged to the Montoneros, the strongest guerrilla organization in Argentina—a threat to order in our country and the whole continent. He came from a despicable family of troublemakers, slum-dwellers who had a history of inciting labor disputes. Even if he had not known her, we would have had him disappeared."

That ugliest of verbs shook Robert out of his trance: this was the man who had tried to have him murdered more than once. "'Matá al rey de palos,'" he told himself, picturing Nemesia. But he sat without stirring, a passive witness to the revelations. In some ways he felt like an accomplice, for Roca was divulging what Gabriela herself had never dared to tell him, if it was in fact real. At that moment he yearned to embrace her, caress, comfort her.

"Then you arrived, Señor Wells. These are black times too and Argentina is being torn apart again. Old wounds are festering. Your end will be the same as the one suffered by the Sarmiento brothers—the first during the Proceso and the second last week."

"I love your daughter and she loves me."

Roca swallowed before replying, "I was the first to love her."

Robert heard the man's labored breathing, a groping around his desk. The lamp went on with a click. For an instant he was blinded, feeling naked in the abrupt light.

"Why do you avoid your daughter's given name?" Robert asked with sudden conviction.

A cloud of agony crossed Roca's visage, making it look ageless as the earth. He reached to extinguish the desk lamp again. In the dying glow Robert saw the man's head droop to his chest.

The two waited in darkness. When the American's eyes had adjusted again, he noted that Roca had not moved. "Why don't you ever pronounce your daughter's name?" Robert repeated in a more sonorous tone.

The man's shoulders slumped and his hands dropped below his knees. "Gabriela!" Robert called, "Gabriela! Gaby! Gaby!" Roca flinched as those names struck him like blows to his torso. He cowered, quailed, sank deeper in the chair until Robert believed the man would collapse to the floor. Then he perceived the muffled moan or whimper he had heard or imagined that day on the Pampa, but it grew louder, distinct, convulsing Roca's frame in sobs, then receding, rising again, now becoming fainter, nearly inaudible.

The two men sat in a silence punctured by Roca's heaving breath. Slowly he straightened his shoulders, raised his arms and rose from the chair. When he had reached his full height, Gabriela's father gazed down at the foreigner. "You are nada, nothing, *gringo de mierda*," his voice reverberated while his chest shuddered between words. Robert could discern the twitch in the man's mouth, the redness that suffused his face and neck above his bow tie and turndown collar.

He could have retaliated by calling Roca a podrido, a rotten bastard and hijo de puta, concha de su madre, along with other vivid expressions he had heard in Buenos Aires. He also could have named him a *pinche cabrón, hijo de la chingada,* a motherfucker and other offerings he had learned while growing up in Los Angeles. By doing so he would have been speaking for Dionisio and Virgilio Sarmiento, for Julio Mazzini and his older son, for thousands of the dead, the desaparecidos, all the victims of César Roca Steele and his cohorts.

Instead Robert reminded himself that this man was Gaby's father, who for some reason fell apart when he heard his daughter's name. And Virgilio had warned about the poison of anger and its honey tip. Marking each of his words, he stated: "Your son, your daughter and your wife are afraid of you. As a father and a husband you've failed. Your career is a failure as well—you lost the war and you're going to die in jail."

The man wheezed and grimaced as though he were trying to suppress a pain. He labored to recover his poise. He switched on the lamp again and tore off his glasses, exposing one eye that was shut while his other, the left, was a bluish-white orb, streaked with red veins, staring straight at his rival.

Roca reached into his desk drawer, pulled out a .38-caliber Luger and aimed it at Robert's head. "Where are your reserves this time, where are your battalions, *maricón*? Mine are here!" he shouted in his thundering bass, as if he had regained most of his vigor. Roca clenched the two-way radio and pushed a button, making it whine and hiss for a second time. "*Mande Señor!*" a voice squawked on the other end. Roca yelled into the speaker, "*Alerta!*"

He fixed Robert in his one good eye. "Stand." The tall man cocked the pistol, seized his cane and slipped the walkie-talkie into the breast pocket of his coat.

With a taste like gall in his mouth, the American took a few seconds to find his feet. Gaby's father kept his revolver trained on the visitor's face. From Robert's angle the old man's head now blocked the stuffed bull's snout on the wall, making the wide, arching horns appear to protrude from Roca's ears.

"*Cornudo!* Cuckold!" he called against his own wishes, cursing the man like a good porteño.

"*Adelante,*" Roca ordered as though he had not heard the insult, the most grievous that one male can level at another in Argentina. Carrying his crutches in one arm, Robert turned clumsily and limped toward the exit. He could hear the man's steps and the clatter of his cane on the polished floor, picture the black weapon pointed at the nape of his neck. He did not feel so much alarmed as nauseous, repelled by Roca's disclosures. Let the man fire, Robert wished, so I won't have to ask her if those admissions are true.

They had almost reached the door of the pentagonal room. Over his shoulder Robert could now detect Roca's thick breathing, the tap of his cane. He did not want to look back, to see the barrel of that gun again, the minotaur with his flaring horns, the cyclops with his blank eye. Then he remembered Virgilio's last words of advice.

Robert wheeled to his right, dropped one crutch and swung the other in a half-arc that struck Roca in the head from the blind side, knocked him over as the Luger fired with a dull report, a bullet skimmed Robert's coat and hit the doorjamb with a thud. The man's cane flew into the air, he sagged, lurched, fell backwards, his head smacked the floor. He lay staring at the ceiling with the white eye open, the other still shut. Blood streamed from his skull and pooled on the marble.

Robert withdrew the walkie-talkie from Roca's pocket. Reassured that it was muted, he set it on the floor and stumbled to the desk, where he rifled through papers in the drawers, searched the filing cabinet, hoping to discover more photographs. He found several documents—warrants, bills, receipts—and stuck them in the pockets of his jacket. Next Robert found the pistol by Roca's body on the floor, where the man lay like a beached orca, all black and white, belly up, gasping for air.

When he clutched the weapon, he saw a silencer attached to its barrel. Robert concealed the revolver under his belt. He gathered his crutches, held them in his arms and walked from the five-walled room. He had to favor his weak leg as he made his way through the labyrinth.

Robert approached the Capitol's bronze doors, smoothing his clothes. He saw where the bullet had scorched the lapel of his coat. He treaded forward and nodded to the guards, giving a wide berth to the metal detector on the entry side.

Hot wind blew the city's stench into Robert's face. He limped down the stairs to the sidewalk and hailed a taxi. Before opening the black door, he looked around in search of Roca's man Ugo: where was he? And the two cops who were supposed to be patrolling the building?

The driver was an old cabbie who knew how to respect a client's mood. After saying "Buenas tardes," he did not direct a word to his passenger. Robert was grateful for silence. It only lasted until he told the man to stop for a minute at the downtown Telefónica, where he phoned Julio Mazzini. He informed his friend that he had departed the Congreso, that he had left Roca unconscious on the floor there, that he would be home in an hour or so.

Robert asked the driver to take him to the malecón. They cruised for miles until they reached a deserted spot at the river's edge, overgrown with weeds. He had the cabbie wait there, scanned the shore, leapt the concrete wall and hurled the pistol into an eddy of the Río de la Plata. He imagined it plunging to the bottom where Dionisio's corpse rested.

For the first time since leaving the Capitolio, Robert did not feel the surge in his chest. Without the burden of a revolver his mind seemed to clear. Why in hell have I come all the way to the river to dispose of that weapon, he wondered—I'm not the one who fired the Luger, right? He laughed at himself, murmuring under his breath: Roca's gun is lying on the riverbed, unusable and lost forever.

23
Blood and Water

The light of Buenos Aires changed as often as Gabriela's eyes, her sulks and moods. By the time Robert reached their apartment, the sun streaked a red, murky sky. He staggered up the stairs. Three times he rapped on the door. When Robert removed his key and turned the lock, the door would not give. Gaby must have thrown the dead bolt from inside, he thought—afraid to be alone.

He knocked harder on the door. He called her name. Robert shook the brass knob, beat on the wood. Perspiration beaded his face. When he dropped his crutches and flung himself forward, the dead bolt came partly off its screws. He thrust with one shoulder then the other, the hinges popped, wood splintered at the frame, the door fell beyond the threshold.

Inside the air felt stifling. Against the window he saw the curtains hanging motionless. The Pampa was unmade and empty. The bathroom door had been shut. He tottered forward, fearing it might also be bolted from the inside. It was unlocked.

He opened, stepped through steam and saw her in the overflowing tub, her head back, her lips parted, her eyes opened wide, staring at the ceiling. "Gaby!" he shouted. He inhaled a coppery odor that brought flashes of his knife-wound and the calf's head. Picturing Roca's inert body, he grasped the door frame as though a gust of wind were about to blow the room away. He drew closer and noticed scarlet clouds in the water, trailing from her wrists and ankles, four wounds like the Southern Cross. Gabriela's skin had a bluish-gray cast. Her hands rested at her side with their palms upturned, as if to plead for something he could not give her.

Robert fell to his knees on the tile floor. He touched Gabriela's face, white and cool, reached for her wrist through the lukewarm water. He thought he could sense her pulse, faint where blood seeped from the cut. Or did he only imagine it? His heart pounded so strongly against his ribs that he could not tell if he was feeling that or her pulse. "Gaby don't go away from me, Gabriela," Robert entreated in Spanish and English. He rubbed her limp hands, tried to embrace her with both arms while bathwater splashed over the basin. The apartment, the building seemed to be collapsing, the walls caving in around him. A rush of blood roared in his ears.

Robert reached over the side of the basin, placed both hands on her chest, one on top of the other, pushed down and eased up as they had taught him in school. He counted to a hundred compressions. Then he vaulted into the tub, sending waves of water over the sides, straddled her and placed his lips on Gaby's, exhaling into her cold mouth, beseeching her to take his breath, his life. Robert repeated the cycle, two, three, four times, attempting to keep track of the numbers in his head. He made a long howl before he threw himself on Gaby's breast, swallowing bathwater, choking, spitting.

He rose, slipped, hoisted himself over the edge of the tub and hobbled from the bathroom, by the Pampa, through the doorway to the hall. With their bad memories of police break-ins, the neighbors were sticking their heads from their apartments like tortoises from their shells. They gawked at the stricken American who was leaving a wake of water behind him.

Robert banged on the door of the twins' apartment, "*Ángeles guardianes, socorro!*" he cried as though he were screaming over endless distances. When they opened, he was saying, "I have to make a call, *urgente, por piedad*," he implored and brushed by the two girls. He spotted the telephone, dialed for an ambulance before dropping the handset on the floor. Robert teetered into the hall where more residents gaped at him.

At the threshold of the Inner Garden he saw his crutches, flat and useless on the floor. Gabriela and Roberto, he thought—two dead lovers. He limped over the shattered door, approached the bathroom, afraid to go in again, to see her body in the blood-cloudy water, her eyes gazing upwards. Robert forced himself to enter, looked and saw it floating by her leg: the little curved moon with a rust-red stain on its silver edge, cutting the surface like a tiny fin. He knelt, saw dark billows in the water against the white porcelain, against her pallid skin, her body bleeding to death and he could not save her. He stretched out his arm, touched her wrist to probe her pulse, next on the vein of her neck. Gasps escaped Robert's chest.

He stared into her dulled pupils until they seemed to pulsate. With thumb and forefinger of one hand he tried to lower her hooded lids. They would not close, they looked through Robert, beyond him. His body shook with weeping.

When the paramedics arrived, they found him kneeling over the tub with the lion's feet, his head hanging over hers, their foreheads touching.

It did not take long for the machinery of death to sunder him from Gabriela. After pronouncing her dead, those men were able to shut her eyelids. With a mobile phone they summoned the police. Apartment G was soon congested with people bumping each other in their black boots, with their holstered pistols and their scratchy radios. Robert felt he was losing Gaby to these strangers, these intruders who were appropriating her body, her being and his own. In his shock and desolation he noted random things like the ball of dust in a corner, the dirt on a policeman's shoes—they're soiling, defiling the Inner Garden, he told himself. He paced the kitchen, the only room the outsiders had not invaded, grasped his head in both hands, struck it on the wall. His body shivered in his sopping clothes.

More and more equipment cluttered their galaxy—caution tape, lamps, a stretcher, cameras, a winding sheet. Later Robert would recall the oppressive air, flashbulbs, questions.

Were you married to her?

No.

But you lived together?

Yes.

Was it suicide?

I think so.

How do you know it wasn't a murder?

The front door was locked from the inside with a dead bolt.

Can you prove that you were not here when the young lady expired?

No. Yes.

He started to say he had been at the Capitol, but he stopped himself. Robert remembered Roca's statement: "I would rather see her dead than living with you." Could her father have sent someone to kill Gaby, he conjectured wildly—Ugo, the man in the baseball cap, another lackey? But how could they have thrown the bolt from the inside, unless they fled through the patio? And if Roca loved her so much, would he have Gaby murdered to spite me, Robert asked himself, if he was going to kill me anyway, I'm going mad.

Pay attention Sir. Where were you?

Downtown.

Do you have a lawyer?

Yes.

What's his name?

Daniel Bello.

Carajo. Is there another way to get in and out of the apartment?

No. Yes.

Robert pointed to the balcony. Two detectives examined it, the fig tree, the three-story fall to the cement patio. That plunge would kill a person, one told his colleague, ignoring Robert. The upper branches of the tree were too thin to support the weight of an adult anyhow, the other remarked, as though this fact was more important than a woman's death, his love, her life. A pair of withered geraniums drooped over the balcony.

They carried her away in a shroud. The police said they would notify the señorita's parents—that's what they called her with the old-fashioned formality of bureaucrats, glaring at the foreign male who had the nerve to live with an unmarried Argentine woman.

"Do not touch her possessions," an officer warned him. "They belong to the family." Confiscating Robert's passport, the chief detective commanded him to leave the apartment at once, to remain in Buenos Aires until an autopsy was completed.

You mean you're expelling me from my own apartment?

This apartment is not yours and it's the scene of a crime. The lease is in the lady's name. If you don't shut your fucking trap we'll take you to jail.

I need some time here.

He walked to the bathroom and closed the door behind him. The tile floor was crisscrossed by muddy footprints where the inspectors and photographers had done their work. They had emptied the claw-foot basin. The water and Gabriela's blood had washed down the drain, into the sewers and the Río de la Plata, her river, now Robert's too, flowing to the sea. Again he fell to his knees, closed his eyes, dropped his head to the floor and wept.

Robert changed and left his sodden pants, underwear and socks in a corner by the Pampa. He kept his jacket with the singed lapel. He packed again, this time for a trip to nowhere. While the cops smoked on the balcony, he managed to remove

Roca's papers from Gaby's suitcase and stuff them into his own, along with the documents he had rifled from the old man's filing cabinet in Congress. Seeing her garments on hooks and hangers, on the bed, he wondered, What will happen to them, all her things? Robert surveyed the room, trying to observe and retain them in his mind, one by one: her willowy skirts and blouses, her books, pictures, her fragrant candles, perfumes, the beaded bracelets, her snake pendant. The sight of each was a knife-blade in his chest. He wished to keep something as a memento or a talisman, but by now the police were hovering as though he were a trespasser.

Burdened with memories, like a refugee, carrying a suitcase and a few plastic bags, he walked to the curb. Robert rode a bus over meaningless streets through Boedo and Parque Patricios to Nueva Pompeya, one of the few neighborhoods in Buenos Aires they had not explored together, where he would not encounter sights that would haunt him. He found a cheap hotel that allowed him to register without a passport, that did not require an ID if a client paid in cash, where he could use an invented name. All night he lay on his back like Gaby in the iron bathtub, like Roca on the marble floor, his own eyes opened wide and spilling tears, expecting his life to end along with theirs. Maybe her disappearance had erased the lines between sleep and waking, being alive or dead, he raved. Would he ever dream again, ever awake?

In the morning he moved several blocks to another hotel, fearful that Roca would pursue—if the man had not died. He read the papers and found neither Gabriela nor her father in the death notices. He would have liked to call Señora Roca to ask about the funeral, but he could not have spoken to her without breaking down in anguish. If her husband's living, Robert was sure, if he's survived the fall and blow to his head, he'll do everything to keep me away from his daughter, even in her death. And if Roca's not alive, how could I attend the interment of a woman whose father I killed? She's no longer mine, he conceded. Was she ever, could she ever have escaped her father, their secrets?

By late afternoon he had gathered enough composure to visit Daniel Bello's office. The lawyer was a brown-skinned man of middle age from Tucumán. He wore a blue shirt with an open collar and rolled-up sleeves. As if they had known each other for years, he embraced Robert, offering condolences for Gabriela's death.

"How did you know?"

"It's part of my job to learn these things."

Daniel was already familiar with facts reported by Julio Mazzini and mutual friends in the resistance. The attorney informed Robert that Roca had been admitted to the Hospital Británico, one of the finest in Buenos Aires, where he had regained consciousness at intervals.

"We issued a warrant for his arrest."

"When?"

"Soon after you called Julio on the phone yesterday. The police found him on the floor of his office at the Capitolio. There was a bullet lodged in the doorframe, caliber matched a .38 registered to Roca. They couldn't find the weapon—what happened to it?"

Robert forced words through his grief-frozen lips: "Bottom of the river. I threw it there."

"Why?"

"I don't know, needed to do it. Look," he said, showing Daniel his coat where the bullet had scorched his lapel.

"Pucha! Close. Take it off, Che—more proof."

"What about the pistol?"

"If necessary you can tell us where to drag the river."

As Robert removed his jacket, the man informed him about the warrant for Roca's arrest. "It cites the possession of illegal explosives as well as complicity in the abduction, torture and deaths of Virgilio Sarmiento, his brother Dionisio and Julio Mazzini Jr., not to mention the kidnapping and attempted murder of Robert Wells—we have your garment now in addition to your testimony." Daniel pressed the American's arm. "Thank you for helping us, Roberto."

"Did Julio tell you he'd testify if we bring Roca to trial?"

"Yes. He's a brave one." Daniel paused before adding, "Roca's lawyers will make countercharges but for now most of the evidence favors us."

The Argentine glanced down at the floor then up at Robert. "I'd like to accompany you to the Comisaría now—before they think you've tried to leave the country."

Robert remained impassive, as if Daniel were speaking about someone else. "First I want to show you these." He handed over the papers he had received from Julio and those he had burgled in Roca's office.

Skimming them, the lawyer said, "Largely unrelated" with the confidence of a man who has examined thousands of similar documents. He dropped most of them on the floor. "But not these," he pointed to some pieces he had separated on his desk: Roca's coded order for Julio Mazzini Jr.'s death, the two photos from the war years, the end-user certificate and a few more.

After making photocopies, Daniel drove Robert to the central police station. An officer and a detective took the American's deposition, while a sergeant typed it on an Underwood only slightly newer than the relic at the Comisaría in Uruguay. Daniel insisted on being present in his role as Robert's lawyer. At every turn he aided his new client, upholding his rights; restrained the police from overstepping their duty, prevented them from squandering time. When they had finished, the two officials warned Robert not to leave the country.

"Mierda," Bullshit, Daniel told him as they walked to his car. "If I were you I'd flee Argentina to avoid a reprisal from one of Roca's heavies."

"The detectives confiscated my passport."

"They can't keep it for long. And I wouldn't return to Buenos Aires until the hearing."

"How long will that take?"

"Weeks, maybe months . . ." Daniel's voice trailed off and he shrugged his shoulders, implying that it could be longer. He waited for Robert's reaction. There was none. "By the way," he proceeded, "I've got a pair of loyal policeman to guard you for a couple of days in Buenos Aires. You'll stay for the funeral, right?"

"Yes. Not that I'll be invited."

The attorney nodded. "I'll secure your passport in a day or two."

"Thank you, compadre."

Following the charges in the warrant, César Roca Steele was placed under house arrest in the hospital. A pair of deputies, handpicked by Daniel Bello, guarded his room around the clock. Soon Roca's minion Ugo had been detained, who turned out to be a retired captain from an infantry brigade. When Robert learned about the two men's fate from the attorney, he informed Daniel that he did not need bodyguards to protect him, he would rather be alone. He did not tell the lawyer that he would just as soon be found and killed by one of Roca's men.

He felt some consolation after the arrests, as much as anyone could feel who was living in a turbid nightmare of tears and sorrow. The dusk spread bloody clouds in the sky and in his waking dreams.

On Sunday morning he read Gaby's obituary, a black-bordered square that covered a full column in *La Nación*. The text did not mention suicide or other cause of death. Her powerful relatives must have concealed the truth that would prevent her burial in consecrated ground. "Gabriela Roca Dafiume is survived by her loving father, mother and brother," the notice stated, ending with a long list of illustrious relatives whose names were studded with titles from the state, the armed forces, the Church, from industry, academies, universities. The funeral would be held at eleven o'clock on Monday, the morning of Christmas Eve in the Basílica de Nuestra Señora del Pilar in Recoleta, next to the necropolis where she would be interred with her ancestors in the heart of Buenos Aires. Robert remembered the afternoon when he and Gaby had visited the shrine and cemetery, when they had evoked their childhoods, when she had told him that she would be buried there someday, when they had been expelled by the guard or an exterminating angel. He sobbed through the day and night.

24
City of the Dead

From afar he watched the solemn ceremony officiated by a bishop. Robert stood in the cool shade of their gomero tree. He heard tolling of bells as the pallbearers carried a gilded sarcophagus from the church to the graveyard. Among them he recognized the tall figure of Gaby's brother, Segundo Roca, flanked by more prelates and acolytes, by colonels, generals, admirals and brigadiers engulfed in starched uniforms replete with medals, ribbons and epaulettes, as well as men and women dressed in mourning. Attired in black lace with a mantilla covering her head, the Señora was bent over the casket. She wept. Robert did not see César Roca's towering frame at her side nor anywhere in the cortege. Yet he thought that somehow Gabriela had returned to her father. Tears coursed down his cheeks and burned.

As he viewed the procession, people swarmed around La Biela on the far side of the square, drinking, laughing, gesturing. It was the hour of aperitifs before lunch in Buenos Aires, the inexorable custom that endures death, war and decay. Bankers, businessmen, politicians, elegant women streamed in and out of cafés, occupied tables on the sidewalks.

Mourners filed through the cemetery's iron gate and disappeared in the City of the Dead. Robert chose to remain under the spreading tree. That morning there was no breeze in the foliage, not a bird in the branches, no chorus of hosannas. Dark clouds and the stench persisted, made worse by the growing heat. It impregnated the air, the woodwork of houses, the deepest recesses of drawers and cellars. There was nowhere to evade it.

Meanwhile César Roca languished in the Hospital Británico. He was a predator who could not thrive without prey, whether it was his daughter, her lovers, a son, a wife or his country. Soon nothing was left of him but a carcass like a pale mummy or the hide of a dead bull.

People said the angel of death had swooped into the hospital on icy wings and carried the man's shrunken soul away. Some believed the city's odor abated afterwards, others claimed it grew more fetid, a few said it had not changed. When Robert learned the news of the man's end, his grief was too raw to be assuaged by a sense of justice or requital.

Madame Roca and her son ordered a gravestone to be erected for her husband on the family plot in Recoleta. At its side they set a wreath of purple roses for Gabriela's tomb. In the Plaza de Mayo, about twenty blocks away, the Madres released a flock of doves in her memory. A bunch of red and white carnations lay under the palm tree where the lovers had met in the rain. For months, maybe years a fresh bouquet would appear each Thursday afternoon. Robert was too distraught to return to the place where he and Gabriela had been born into their new life together. He passed somber mornings and afternoons, everlasting, sleepless nights.

During the days between Christmas and New Year's, on December 29, 1990, when many Argentines were on vacation or fleeing the country, President Carlos Saúl Menem issued Executive Order 2741. The decree pardoned the main leaders of the military junta and a few token members of the opposition. The mothers of the dead and desaparecidos wailed, rending their clothes, filled the air with shrieks.

Drawn to the spots where he had gone with Gabriela, places that used to be theirs, Robert roamed the streets, parks and neighborhoods of Buenos Aires. He walked along Avenida 9 de Julio in the harsh air. Haze blurred the skyscrapers against a muggy, lowering sky. Where was the honeyed light that used to enfold Gabriela in its embrace? He saw the jacaranda trees with their seared foliage. Where were the blossoms that once floated to the ground, flooding those streets like a bluish-purple sea? Boulevards and avenues were pocked with holes, lights were dim, the city stank.

Robert returned to the sidewalk where he and Gaby had played hopscotch. He observed their swings in the park, the leather seats in the still air. He searched for trees, posts and benches where they had carved their names, whose letters had already begun to fade like graffiti from a distant era. Wandering by the bars, cafés and confiterías where they had gone together, Robert found the doors closed, chairs turned upside down and chained to the marble tables. He walked through empty streets, abandoned by people who had gone into exile, by others who had escaped the summer and smell. He was in her city, his too, Buenos Aires, Ciudad de la Santísima Trinidad y Puerto de Santa María, City of the Most Holy Trinity and Port of Our Lady of Fair Winds.

From the leaden sky a centuries-old drizzle began to fall. He watched stylish couples dashing over the chalk-paintings on the sidewalk in front of Teatro Colón, scurrying through the doors like ghosts on board a phantom ship. Walls of buildings wept moisture that expired on the steaming asphalt of streets and alleys. Drizzle turned to rain, rain to a deluge. The world felt as though it were covered in water, drifting, oozing to its end. One more time Robert walked to the Río de la Plata, swollen and wide as an ocean, dull and gray as a sheet of ashes, now moving faster to the sea. The rain stopped. He knew Gabriela was truly dead.

He saw the stray dogs and cats of Buenos Aires, heard their howls in the night. Robert passed beggars on the street, offering them his final, worthless australes. He heard songs from open doors, songs about a love so elusive that nobody will ever grasp it, a love far away and lost forever, so strong that nothing will heal its pain, not even new loves or death.

Born in Colorado and raised in California, Edward Stanton has lived in Argentina, Uruguay, Mexico and Spain as well as the United States. He's the author of fourteen books, some of them translated and published in Spanish, Arabic and Chinese. *Road of Stars to Santiago*, the story of his 500-mile walk on the ancient pilgrimage route to Compostela, was called one of the best books on the subject by the *New York Times*. Stanton's environmental novel *Wide as the Wind,* the first to treat the tragic history of Easter Island, won the Next Generation Indie Book Award for Young Adult Fiction and three other international prizes. *VIDAS: Deep in Mexico and Spain* received the Grand Prize (Bronze) for Best Travel Writing in the 15th Annual Solas Awards. While teaching at colleges and universities in the Americas and Europe, Stanton has also published short stories, poems, translations and essays. The Fulbright Commission, the National Endowment for the Humanities and the Spanish Ministry of Culture have supported his work with grants and fellowships. His students and colleagues recently published *"This Spanish Thing": Essays in Honor of Edward F. Stanton*.

Made in the USA
Middletown, DE
27 April 2025

74757604R00209